BRANDYWINE
Brides

A BLACKWOOD LEGACY ANTHOLOGY

TABLE OF CONTENTS

A TRAITOR'S HEART

By

TERRI BRISBIN

1721

FINLAN BLACKWOOD HAS SURVIVED FIGHTING on the losing side of the Jacobite Rising, but finds himself transported to Pennsylvania in the Colonies to serve out his sentence for treason. Five years and he'll be free to seek out his family in the south and to regain his life. But when the widow Elizabeth Graham find herself at the mercy of an unscrupulous nobleman, Finn must decide if he should follow his family or follow his traitorous heart.

DEDICATION &

ACKNOWLEDGEMENTS

TO GAIL LINK WHO STARTED us on our journey when she began our 'Writers-Who-Lunch' gatherings – thanks Gail for your ideas and support!

Thanks to the other authors in this collection for their unflagging enthusiasm and help as we made our way through the process of creating, writing and producing our Blackwood family's stories. You were all such an inspiration to me. And thanks especially for dragging me – kicking and screaming – across the Pond, so to speak, and to the American side of history…

PROLOGUE

Philadelphia, Pennsylvania
July, 1716

FIN SHIELDED HIS EYES AGAINST the midday, midsummer sun and stared out over the gathered crowd. Some there, he noticed, stared back at him, openly inspecting and evaluating him much like a piece of horseflesh or beast of burden.

Which, in truth, he now was.

He shuffled along the raised platform, until the line of men before and after him stopped. They were called forward one at a time and each man called out his name and occupation. When the man in charge pointed at him, Fin took a step forward as he fought the urge to run and the need for sustenance. His knees shook when he moved too quickly and his voice quivered like a wee bairn when he could speak.

"Finlan Blackwood," he said. The words came out as a squeak so he swallowed hard against the dryness of his mouth and spoke louder this time. "Finlan Blackwood."

"What skills have you?" the man asked. "Were you trained for an occupation, boy?"

'Twas a hard thing, to concentrate on what the man said, with all the people staring and the sun beating down on him. He'd never gone this long eating and drinking so little. Even the months in the prison before his transportation had not been as terrible as the journey on this ship across the Atlantic Ocean to this hot, humid place.

"Skills, boy?" the man yelled a bit louder and pushed at his shoulder with a wooden cudgel.

"My da is. . . . was a blacksmith," he answered, sorrow and exhaustion filling his voice and tightening his throat. "He trained me." His father and the rest of his family were dead or gone now. The only kith or kin he had were scattered along the coastal colonies, transported for their crime of treason against the English Crown and sold, as he would be, into indenture.

"A blacksmith!" the man called out. "A man. . . –" he began. "A boy with skills and much potential to the right buyer!" The seller poked and prodded him again, but he met with flaccid skin and little muscle.

The man's words blurred as the next five years of his life were offered into bonded servitude. No matter the glowing words or points the man made, no one seemed interested. Then, when the man lowered the price, the cost of his transportation to the Colony plus the ship owner's fees, a tall man stepped forward. The man's garb and tall hat marked him a Quaker. A few minutes of quiet discussion led to Fin being directed down the steps and to a table. Sooner than he would have thought possible, he went from convict and traitor to bought-and-paid-for servant. An "X" marked the place on the contract where he had to sign his agreement to the terms.

Five years of good and hard work.

Food and a place to sleep.

His owner would set the rules.

Property now and no longer his own man.

His long-empty stomach clenched in bitter disagreement, but Fin forced his hand to mark the document. As a traitor and convict, Fin expected disrespect and loathing and was surprised to see something different in the Quaker's gaze.

"Come thou now," the man said quietly.

Before they took a step, Fin looked back at those yet remaining on the platform. Those men were the only links back to his homeland and his lost family. Some were distant cousins or neighbors who'd been caught up in the Jacobite uprising's fever. Some were prisoners with whom he'd shared a cell or, more lately, the hold of a ship.

"Have thou belongings to claim, Finlan?" the man asked.

Pain pierced him as surely as a dagger through his heart. The only thing he'd had was lost to him now. His mother had pressed her luckenbooth brooch into his hand as he'd left to follow his father into the fighting. The gemstones on it had saved his life several times but were gone now. Even the gnarled and bent metal had purchased some morsels of food in prison.

"Nay," he said, shaking his head. "I have only the clothes on my back."

The heavy hand on his shoulder spoke of a man used to the hard labor of working metal and yet his light touch gave Fin some succor.

"Thou hast thy life and thy soul and thy mind," the man said. "Many have begun a new life with less."

"A new life?" Fin had only thought on the deprivation and loss of the last year and not beyond it.

"Aye, Finlan Blackwood. Thou hast a new life, an open road before thee to makest what thou will of it. Most men never have this chance."

He stood a little taller then, for he had not considered this an opportunity. The others had spoken of the harshness ahead of them and not once had he thought of the possibilities. Five years was a long time, but if he worked hard for this man who seemed a fair one, he would earn his freedom. If he learned the trade his father had pointed him to, he would have a way to make a living. Then, he could seek out those kin he knew lived farther south, in the Carolinas and try to establish a life and family there. Just then, his life did not seem as filled with loss as it had been minutes ago.

"What do I call ye, sir?" he asked.

"Neither lord nor sir, nor any term that sets one above another," the man said. "Those in *Fellowship* use our given names to address others. My name is Richard Montgomery. So, thou may call me Richard or Friend Richard or simply Friend."

Fin held out his hand and took a firm grasp of the Quaker's larger one.

"Richard," Fin said, shaking his hand. "Friend."

"Come, let us see to getting thee some sustenance and then I can finish my errands here in town."

Fin's stomach grumbled loudly at just the mention of food. His ma had said he ate for three men. His ma. . . . there would be time enough to mourn and grieve, but not now. Now, he had just been given a gift by this man. Questions flooded his thoughts then and he asked them as they walked away from the harbor.

"Where will I live?" he asked.

"Thou will live with me and mine," Richard replied. "My smithy is at the edge of the town, to the south." Richard pointed to the left and off in the distance. "And I offer my services out into Chester County, as well, where my farm lies," he added. "That is where thou will work whilst thou learn the craft better."

Fin followed the man and climbed into the wagon Friend Richard indicated was his when they reached it by the public house. They rode in silence through the busy town to its edge.

Five years.

In five years, his debt would be paid and Fin would be his own man, free to come and go as he pleased.

In five years, he would seek out his kin and make his life with them.

Five years.

CHAPTER ONE

Cooper's Farm, Chester County
July 1721

TAKING HER EASE IN THE shadows created by the front porch, Elizabeth stood in silence and stared across the fields at the dust rising from the road to the east. The clouds above her and the humidity that thickened the air around her promised that the dust would soon be weighted down with moisture. Dust to mud with one afternoon shower was usual for this time of the year in this corner of southern Pennsylvania.

The sound of a cart's wooden wheels was familiar as they approached. The blacksmith was making his rounds of the farms along the Brandywine River, repairing the farming implements and preparing the metal scythes and plow blades for the coming harvest. As soon as the cart turned onto the lane leading to the house, Elizabeth realized it was not Friend Richard but his man, Finlan Blackwood. He nodded as he slowed the cart before her.

"Mistress Graham, how do ye fare this fine day?" he asked. A trace of the Highland accent yet flavored his voice even these five years since his arrival. Elizabeth tugged the handkerchief free from the wristband of her sleeve and mopped her brow.

"Is that what you call it, Mr. Blackwood?" she asked, smiling. Thunder rumbled above them, making one of her points.

"Just so, Mistress," he said, laughing.

Even a God-fearing widow like herself could not help but notice the deepness of his laugh and the broadness of his shoulders. Or the way his voice had deepened as he reached maturity. He'd grown up well these last five years since his arrival here. Aye, he'd grown up well.

"Is there something on my jacket?" Mr. Blackwood asked, brushing his hand over his shoulder as he spoke. He'd caught her staring. So much for the God-fearing and respectable widow demeanor for which she'd striven.

If truth be told, she had enjoyed the physical side of her marriage to Jonah and missed the closeness of it. Still, gawping at the blacksmith would not bring Jonah back or accomplish anything of what yet stood undone in her day. Such as finding a way to pay this man for repairs he would perform on the plows on her farm.

"Nay," she answered, glancing into the distance to cover her perusal. "I was just looking for Nathaniel in the southern field."

The blacksmith turned to look in that direction and the width of those wide, muscled shoulders now blocked her view of anything else. Aye, he had grown up well.

"His leg still bothering him then?" Now, he removed the wide-brimmed hat from his head and raked his fingers through his auburn hair. Standing taller, he tossed his hat in the wagon and took a step away from her. "Would you like me to bring him back in the wagon?"

"There's no need," she said. "The cart is there."

He faced her then, the full force of those forest green eyes on hers, and nodded. 'Twas time to bring her shame to light. No matter how much she'd rather not reveal the terrible state of the farm's situation and her potential loss, Elizabeth was pragmatic enough to know she had run out of time, excuses and money.

"Mr. Blackwood, would you like a cool drink of water? I just brought up a pitcher from the springhouse." She forced a smile on her face and reached for the door. The house was not much more comfortable in temperature, but being out of the sun might bring some relief. And, she would speak easier if he was sitting and not towering over her as he did now.

"With gratitude, Mistress Graham."

She lifted the latch and pushed the door open. Blessed by its position on the hillside, the house caught the best breezes as they moved through the vale toward the Brandywine River. His heavy boot steps followed her inside and, after he'd passed her, she motioned to the kitchen. Leaving the door open, she walked to the table near the window and reached for the stone pitcher and cups there.

"Here, let me," he said, reaching past her to lift the heavy vessel. He managed to stand at her back and reach the pitcher without touching her, his long, strong arms easily lifting the water.

She'd not heard his approach but she was grateful for his help. Elizabeth brought the cups and he filled each one before placing the pitcher on the table. They sat across the well-worn table and Elizabeth took a sip before speaking again.

"I am afraid you have come all this way for nothing, Finlan." There, that was a good way to begin.

"Do yer implements no' need sharping for the harvest?" he asked. Though his fingers still encircled the cup, he did not partake of the water.

Elizabeth pulled her dignity and wits tighter around her and smiled at him, bravely putting on an expression she hoped showed a calm she did not feel. This would be but the first of many such encounters and admissions, so she steeled herself against the shame and fear before meeting his gaze.

"I cannot pay for your services, Finlan. I'm afraid there is not enough coin or crop to cover the cost of them."

Elizabeth had looked down at his hands as she finished admitting her situation and watched as they clutched the cup tightly. Now, she attempted to raise her eyes once more, knowing she must accept the pity she would see, first from him and then from others, once her circumstances were known among her neighbors and friends.

A clear gaze, neither pitying nor judging, met hers. A flash of something else shone there, but Elizabeth could not decipher its meaning. She searched his expression for his opinion and found only an openness she did not expect.

"I ken, Mistress Graham."

The quiet words pierced her. How? How did he know the truth?

"Worry no' on the cost for now. Without the right tools, ye cannot clear yer fields. I could not, in good conscience, allow a friend to face that if I could help them."

In one of their conversations over the last several months, Finlan Blackwood had revealed that he'd kept to his own faith in spite of living with Richard Montgomery, a faithful Friend. With his words, though, he'd shown that some of their practices had, indeed, rubbed off on him during his years here.

Still. . . . his words were very much like a Friend *in Community* would utter. When he reached out and touched her hand with his, she understood that the action was not.

"Mistress Graham, is there no one to whom ye can turn in this distress? A relative or one of yer late husband's family? A friend?" Then, before she could reply, he pulled his hand back and shook his head. "Forgive me for my intrusion into a private matter," he said as he stood.

"You knew?" she asked. A quick and slight nod gave her his answer. If he knew, then who else did? Elizabeth stood as well, gathering the cups and taking them to the sink. "Does everyone know?"

"'Tis no secret from yer neighbors and others."

The shopkeepers who'd allowed her to purchase on credit. The other workmen who waited still for payment. Her neighbors who noticed the fewer and fewer fieldworkers and more uncultivated fields than fields ready for seed. His quiet admissions shredded her pride.

"So, then, I think you will find that the Camerons have need of your services now," she said. She walked through the cabin to the front door, not able to look at him. "I am sorry you came out this way for nothing."

"Elizabeth," he said softly, standing before her as she fought the tears of failure.

Elizabeth? The fact that he'd used her given name finally struck her and forced her to lift her head. Now, those green eyes looked at her in compassion. Something else glowed there but she could not identify it.

"I will tend to the farm plows and blades. We will speak of payment when ye are able to."

When she wanted to argue, he shook his head and crossed those strong arms over his chest. For an insane moment, she wished he would wrap his arms around her and hold her close until her fears eased. Before she could say another word, he nodded at her.

"My thanks for the water. I will see to things," he said.

He walked through the open door without another word or glance. Within a few moments, she heard the sound of his wagon making its way around the house and up the road to the barn near the southern fields.

Only then, as he was almost out of sight, did she give in to the growing despair and fear. Elizabeth walked to the table, sat down once more. Leaning her head down, she covered her face with her hands and let the tears flow.

Only when the sounds of a song being sung drifted through the open door did she lift her head. The faint Scottish lilt in the voice of the singer made her smile.

Finlan Blackwood could carry a tune.

The blacksmith's apprentice, now nearing the end of his indenture, had begun his time here as a frightened, half-starved young man who'd barely survived being transported from Scotland. Richard Montgomery had tended to the young man's body and soul, taught him the skills of a blacksmith and made him welcome in the Community of Friends. Though Friend Montgomery had invited him to stay on as a free man, soon Finlan would leave to reunite with his long-lost kin in the Carolinas.

Elizabeth stood and wiped her eyes. The irony of their situations was not lost on her. Finlan's life here had begun in fear and shame but now he faced a promising future. Her own life had begun on a promise of a good life and now she faced ruin and shame. Her farm was mortgaged and she owed creditors more than its value. In trying to hide her situation, she'd fooled no one, according to Finlan's words.

Well, if her neighbors knew how bad it was, then she had nothing else to hide. She would begin in earnest to find a buyer, a legitimate buyer, and begin to pay back her debt before all was lost.

From the letter she'd received from another neighbor, Henry Lancaster, she was closer to losing all than she'd hoped.

CHAPTER TWO

FIN LIFTED HIS HAT AND raked his fingers through his hair, trying to ease the dampness from the temperature. Though he'd lived here now for almost five years, his body had not adjusted to the heat of this area. In Scotland, in the western Highlands where he'd grown up, 'twas never as hot as this. Cool breezes moved the air, even in summer, and kept it much more temperate than here in Pennsylvania.

Gazing down the dirt path toward the house, Fin wondered if she was still crying.

Oh, he'd heard the desolate, soft sounds of it behind him as he climbed back into his wagon. It tore at his heart to hear a woman like Elizabeth Graham, a strong, good woman, so torn apart by the hardship and loss she faced.

He understood loss. He'd survived losing everyone and everything he once had. The one thing that kept him alive and moving was the hope that he would regain the kin he'd been separated from those five long years ago. Elizabeth had no such hope and the sound of that filled her sobs.

Shuffling footsteps in the dirt alerted him to Nathaniel's presence and Fin turned to find a look of pity on the man's face. As Fin had told the widow, most around here knew the truth of her circumstances and even this man, first a slave but now indentured and working toward his freedom as Fin himself was, realized the problems facing Elizabeth Cooper Graham. Since her husband's passing, the many burdens of running this farm had been hers and hers alone.

And keeping a farm this size without family to help was a challenge that even a strong woman like her would not find possible. Putting his hat back on his head, he nodded at Nathaniel and turned back to his work.

A man in his own circumstances could offer her nothing. He was counting the days and weeks until he would be finished here and could move south and seek out those who'd been transported with him. He'd gotten word from travelers who passed through Philadelphia that most of his cousins now lived near Charleston in the Carolinas and while another one was even closer near Richmond in the Virginia colony. A few letters had even made their way into his grateful hands.

Even understanding that he held no standing to think on matters affecting her, the matter plagued him through the rest of the day as he toiled to prepare the plows as he'd promised.

Another problem was more pressing and he considered the explanation he would offer to his employer when Fin returned to the city in two days. What would Friend Richard's reaction to him performing this work for no payment be?

When the bell rang signaling the two working men that supper was ready, Fin was no closer to a solution to his problem or hers. He and Nathaniel washed before going to the house and soon they sat across the table from the widow as she served a plain but filling stew with freshly-baked bread.

Only then did Fin realize that the girl who helped her in the kitchen was gone. His questioning glances must have alerted her to his notice of such things. For as supper continued, a tension sat between them in spite of the good food. Unwilling to address that particular absence, he, instead, knew he needed to say something to put her at ease now.

He'd sat at her table countless times over the last five years since he'd begun apprenticing to Friend Richard. Too many conversations to count that began first when her father and her husband yet lived and more since those sad and unexpected deaths. Now, he remembered the topic that seemed to cheer her the most.

Scotland. The Highlands. His family.

He'd carefully skirted anything that touched on the treason that had brought him across the sea. But Fin could make her smile and sometimes laugh over the antics and follies of his cousins and others he'd grown up with in his village.

"Have I told you the story about the coo that got into my Auntie Margaret's laundry?" he asked after drinking the water in his cup. "The puir wee thing."

"Puir wee thing? Truly, Finlan?" she asked in reply. "From your descriptions of the size and hairiness of your Highland cows, I cannot imagine one of them being referred to as a 'puir wee thing'."

"'Tis true, they are large and hairy creatures, but they are of mild dispositions, Mistress Graham. The puir creature got out of the field and thought my auntie's shirts and whatnots were quite tasty." Fin shifted in the chair and nodded. "But my aunt found out that, hard to rile or not, coos are hard to move when they have found something good to eat."

Her soft laughter caused something in his gut to tighten. His blood heated and his face burned. It was difficult to take in a breath. For a moment, he thought the air outside had gotten hotter than it had been a short time ago. Then Fin knew the truth of it, demonstrated by his own body's reaction. It shocked him. Her happiness mattered to him. *She* mattered to him.

Nathaniel said something and Elizabeth smiled at his words, but Fin was not able to hear them. The room seemed brighter when she turned to him and nodded. Her gaze filled with mirth and her mouth curved into an enticing smile. 'Twas as though he saw and heard Elizabeth for the first time. Not as the good widow of Jonah Graham or the dutiful daughter of Elias Cooper. Nay, for the first time in his memory, Fin saw the woman there.

Elizabeth Cooper Graham.

With hair the color of new wheat mixed with honey. Her eyes the swirling brown of the Highland stream that ran near his village in Scotland. A woman who laughed at his stories and had never treated him as anything but a welcomed guest.

"Are you well, Finlan?"

Fin blinked several times to clear his head of such fanciful thoughts. He nodded.

"I am, Mistress Graham."

Standing, he carried his plate and cup to the bucket on the table near the door. He returned to collect the rest. Mistress Graham stood as well and shook her head.

"I will see to those," she said, reaching for the bucket. "You have given a full measure of work on my behalf this day." Fin lifted the bucket away from her and shook his own head then.

"Nay, Mistress," he said. "I can see to this while ye see to the rest."

In truth, he needed to place some distance between them now that this revelation came upon him. Washing the dishes outside near the well would be a good first step. Her eyes took on a serious look and then she smiled. . . again.

"Very well, Finlan. I will not argue with such a generous offer of help. Nathaniel, have you finished outside?"

"Aye, mistress," the man replied. "I will see to the last chores now."

Fin let the man walk out ahead of him and then carried the dishes and cups to the well. Tossing the bucket down the well, he tugged off his jacket and rolled up his sleeves before turning the crank to bring the bucket back to him. Pouring the water over the used dishes, he looked around and knew he'd forgotten the soap to clean them. Fin decided to fill the bucket before returning to the house for the missing soap. Caught up in his task and his thoughts, he did not hear her approach until she stood just before him.

The moonlight behind her and the soft light of the lantern hanging by the door bathed her in tones of silver and gold. His mam had told him stories of fae queens who frequented the deep forest glades in the mountains around their villages. Faery creatures of unworldly beauty who could capture a man with one glance of their eyes or with a whispered word spoken in their unearthly voices.

Right now, staring at Elizabeth, he suspected his mam knew more than he'd ever thought she did. Worse, the vulnerability he saw in the depths of her eyes called to a part of him he could not have foreseen.

"You forgot this," Elizabeth said softly, stepping closer and holding out her hand as she glanced at his.

A bare forearm.

Of all the things in this world that could tempt her, she'd never known her weakness would be the muscular forearm of a tall, Scots blacksmith washing her dishes. He held out his hand toward hers and his eyes moved from her face to what she held there.

"Soap. Aye, I need that."

The words were uttered softly, but it was his deep voice that sent chills through her. Was it her desperate situation that now made her weak? That made her notice things like the way the auburn hair on his arms matched that on his head? Or how the muscles in his back had tensed as he'd turned the crank on the well? In her weakest moments, why was her attention being turned from the crucial decisions she must make to this. . . man? Their fingers barely touched as he took the small jar of soap from her, enough contact that she noticed it.

Pulling in a breath, she dropped her hand and watched as he turned to the chore of washing the cups and plates. There were a number of tasks undone that she should see to. There was mending to be done. There were accounts to review, once more, looking for ways to save money and avoid complete ruin and worse.

Yet, she enjoyed watching him perform this simple ritual. Taking the linen cloth from under her belt, she walked to his side and began drying as he finished washing each plate and cup. The companionable silence reminded her of many nights when she would sit at the table sewing while Jonah saw to his tasks.

"Do you know of anyone looking to acquire more land?"

The words slipped out of her mouth, unexpected and yet welcomed, because she really did need to speak to someone about the choices facing her. Somehow, it was easier to talk about it with this man who was more a stranger than kith or kin. He would be leaving soon, so at least she knew he would not be around to watch the coming failure or disgrace that she could no longer avoid.

"I know you have been doing your work all over the county and the next one over. I thought, mayhap, you have heard of someone interested or in need of more fields for planting?"

Thankfully, he did not pause in his task and he did not look at her, for Elizabeth was certain she would fall into crying again. And 'twas past the time when tears would help in any manner. Now, she must act.

"Ye would sell yer father's lands?" he asked, now placing the last cup in her waiting hands. He still did not turn toward her or meet her gaze. She took a deep breath and let it out.

"Aye, if I must. . . . nay, I no longer have the luxury of choice in this. I must sell." Elizabeth faced him now. "Or I will end up in debtors' prison."

Strangely, the admission did not pain her as much as she'd thought it would. Had she finally accepted her failure then? Lifting her head and leveling her shoulders, she nodded in confirmation before he voiced the question on his face. "Aye, 'tis that bad."

He let out a small breath, an exhalation that ended in a soft sound, and nodded at her. "I have no' heard of such an interest, but I will listen for it." His calm manner of speaking helped her hold on to her control. "I will ask Friend Richard if he kens of anyone in need of lands, if ye would permit it."

Richard Montgomery, she knew, was well-connected in three counties and the city of Philadelphia. A member of the Society of Friends and an established business owner in the city for more than a decade, he would be a valuable asset in finding a buyer—if she'd not run out of time to do so. More importantly, the man was discreet and honorable, as demonstrated by the way in which he treated the less fortunate people. Like the way he'd treated Finlan upon his arrival here in the colony.

"Aye. I thank you for your kind offer," she said.

"Kind offer, my arse!" He'd uttered the words under his breath but she'd heard them and could not help the chuckle at the shocking epithet. "I beg yer pardon, Mistress Graham," he said, nodding in deference. "'Tis expected where I come from that friends will help friends in their time of need."

"Is that what we are, Finlan? Friends?" she asked. She'd never thought on it until just now. She needed a friend more than she ever had before and appreciated this young Scot with his direct approach and kind manner.

"I would hope ye count me a friend. Even though I can do nothing more for yer plight than to ask Richard for help in finding a buyer."

Regret tinged his words and the sound of that warmed her heart in a way she had not felt in a long time. His offer, limited as it was because of the conditions of his indenture, was still more than anyone else had offered in these last dark months. Would others have helped her if she'd approached them? Mayhap, but 'twas too late to change the past.

"It may be too late for your efforts." He startled at her admission. "The debt collectors are circling already, so I may have to accept the only offer I have received."

Elizabeth tried not to let her true feelings about the offer show on her face then. It was not an honorable one at all. Instead, the proposition would take control of her farm out of her hands and make her nothing more than a whore. Her father had denied Henry Lancaster's suit several times and the man had not taken the refusal well. Now, he saw a way to lay claim to everything he believed he should have received through a marriage to her and in the most insulting way possible.

And he'd made it clear he considered her part of the bargain. Henry was willing to pay more for her complete capitulation and shame, for he had offered considerably more than would be needed to cover her debts if she agreed to share his bed and live in disgrace as his mistress.

She swallowed against the disgust that filled her at such a thought and glanced at Finlan. There was nothing to be gained by self-pity this night, so she reached out to collect the dishes and cups. Elizabeth would wait until all choices were taken from her hands.

"Here, let me take those," he said, breaking into her reverie.

He efficiently placed the towel in the bucket and then gathered the rest into it to carry it all back into the kitchen. She walked to the house, opening the door and letting him enter first. Without a word, he put the dishes and cups in their places and hung the towel over the side of the bucket to dry.

A smile teased her mouth then, for he had been a visitor so many times in the last five years that he knew where those things should be. And he did it, without hesitation or without waiting to be told so. Had Fin Blackwood become so accustomed to being a servant that he served without realizing it or was it simply his nature?

"Where will you go?" She'd never asked him before. 'Twould have been a breach of etiquette and good manners, but now that he had called her "friend", Elizabeth decided to appease her curiosity about him. "Your indenture is almost finished. Will you go to your kin in the south?"

He walked to the door before answering her question and, for a moment, Elizabeth thought he might not speak. But, he nodded his head as he reached for the latch.

"Aye. I complete my service for Richard in three weeks and will leave as soon as I finish my other commitments." At her frown, he continued, "Richard has allowed me to accept small tasks when my work for him is done. I have several small jobs in the city to complete after I am... free to leave."

She smiled then and offered her thanks once more for his help. He bade her a good night quietly with a slight nod of his head. As she watched him, Fin tugged his sleeves back down over his arms, buttoned the cuffs and picked up the coat he'd left at the well. Elizabeth realized an important thing as his figure disappeared along the path to the barn.

Over the next weeks they would both face profound changes to their lives and situations. Finlan Blackwood would finally be free, his own man, and would set off to find all those lost to him years ago. However, she would face the loss of everything that was ever important to those she'd loved and lost already.

CHAPTER THREE

'TWAS A MAN'S ANGRY VOICE that drew his attention first. Fin was working inside the barn this morn, out of the summer rain that had accompanied the sunrise. He had not slept well or much, thinking on the widow's problems rather than his own plans. Rising at dawn, he got right to his tasks and continued to consider the dilemma before him—how to help her.

At first, Fin thought he'd been mistaken and heard something else. Not a man's voice at all. The second and third times alarmed him, for the anger and volume increased with each utterance. Putting down his tools, he wiped his hands on the thick canvas apron he wore and set off down the path to the house. Softer, plaintive tones interspersed with the male ones as Fin reached the back of the house and followed a walkway around to the front.

Five years had taught him much about humility and pride, but the sight before him made him forget all of it. With a step forward, he interfered where he had no place to do so. Two long, quick strides brought him to Mistress Graham's side where he reached out to block the man's blow before it could fall upon her. When he saw the man's grip on her wrist and the tears on her face, 'twas all he could do not to strike him down where the blackguard stood.

"Mistress Graham," he began as he took another step toward this scoundrel. The man released his hold and stepped back, a coward after all. "I thought I heard the bell for the morning meal."

The man might be hard and cruel, but he apparently was not a half-wit, for he crossed his arms over his chest and shook his head at Fin and the widow.

"Know your place," he ordered harshly.

Fin recognized the man now. Henry Lancaster was the son of one of the wealthy landowners to the west of Philadelphia and a man who was used to taking what he wanted. If and when someone objected, Henry's father would pay the cost to ease whatever damage his son had wrought. That Henry had some interest here did not bode well for the widow. Tempted to lower his gaze as he should, as an indentured man would, Fin remained where he was, shielding Elizabeth.

"Mister Blackwood is my guest, Mister Lancaster," Elizabeth said softly as she stepped around Fin and smoothed her hands down her dress. "That is his place."

"Call him guest or not, I will not ignore this insult," Lancaster snarled, nodding at both of them. "However, I will speak to your master and see to it he takes action while he still owns you. Just see if I do not."

He began to turn away, adjusting the hat he wore. Lancaster turned and faced them once more.

"You have five days, Elizabeth. Agree to my terms or you will find yourself prosecuted for your debts." Glancing from Elizabeth back to Fin, Lancaster shook his head and an evil smile curved his lips into a cruel expression. "Four days, now that I think on the matter. To show you that you have *no one* who can help you but me."

Though Lancaster's words were meant to insult him, Fin cursed himself silently for making matters worse for her. For now the man meant to punish the woman who clearly defied his wishes. Fin knew, without asking, what this bargain included. Regardless of the wording of its clauses and sentences and no matter the meaning of it, these terms would include the woman herself in bondage of another kind to this man.

He heard her gasp and could not bear to meet her eyes now that he'd caused her terrible situation to worsen even more. They watched in silence as Lancaster mounted his horse and rode away toward the Brandywine River and the road to Philadelphia.

She turned away without saying a thing to him and Fin feared that she held him responsible, and rightly so, for Lancaster's additional cruelty. Fin knew that to see the anger or disappointment in her gaze would tear him to pieces. Especially now that he understood the grave danger she faced. The loss of her family's lands was a terrible thing, in and of itself. But to know that Lancaster planned to use her as part of this bargain sickened him.

And there was nothing, not a single thing, Fin could do about it.

The powerlessness to which he'd grown accustomed made him sick now. For five years, he had tamped down his pride and his temper, in order to survive what he'd lived through. And, in spite of being sold to a good man, he had, indeed, been sold like a piece of furniture or a beast of burden. In those early days, Fin had watched as others had failed to accommodate themselves to their new circumstances. In the prison, on the ship and here on land, those who did not accept their statuses and who fought their situations were punished and even died fighting it.

Fin had made the decision early, to acquiesce as he could, to avoid taking stands or speaking too much. To blend into the background of this new life until he could reclaim at least a part of his own. Certainly, 'twas easier for him since Richard treated him less like a slave and more like a valued guest. He tried to stand as a father would to a son on the verge of manhood, guiding his spirit and his honor and teaching him both a skill to earn a living and ways to live uprightly among his neighbors.

Most indentured servants were not as fortunate as he had been. Somehow, though, the powerlessness in this moment while he watched her suffer pushed his temper now and Fin wanted to strike out, in frustration and anger. But when he noticed the expression of misery on Elizabeth's face as she walked past him, any rage of indignance fading away.

"Mistress Graham," he said as she walked to the front door of the house. "I would. . . I would. . . ." She paused there with her hand on the latch, but did not face him.

"Truly, Mister Blackwood, 'tis not for you to worry over." Then she did lift her head and look at him. He wished she had not. "The food will be ready soon. I will ring the bell."

Fin did not argue or protest. He walked up the path to the barn, determination building with every step he took away from her. There must be something he could do to help her. Clearly, her circumstances were much worse than he knew. So the first thing he must do was find out the extent of her indebtedness.

Oh, he did not have enough funds to repay whatever she owed, but there must be something he could do. By the time she rang the bell, he had made the decision to step in and find a way to help her. Now, all he needed was her cooperation and some luck in finding a way.

They shared a silent morning meal with Nathaniel before everyone returned to their own chores and tasks. Fin spoke at length with

Nathaniel, who knew more about Mistress Graham's troubles than she probably guessed. Several hours later, after completing his work on her farm, Fin left, not traveling on to the next place on his schedule but going back to the city to speak to Richard.

❦

Elizabeth stumbled numbly through the rest of that day and the next, thereby wasting two of the precious four she had left before her complete ruination struck. Henry's demands had not changed though now the price of saving her would be more costly. He'd threatened to buy up all her debt so she would have no choice but him and she'd trembled at those words. He'd seen it and, from the glint in his eyes, he enjoyed having someone at his mercy.

No matter that she'd not meant to bring Fin Blackwood into this mess. But his appearance there at her side had, she would admit only to herself, been appreciated in more than one way.

Though now she feared that Henry would seek retribution against the man and jeopardize the freedom he'd worked so hard to achieve. If Henry did, in fact, lodge a complaint against him with the man who held his indenture, it would make trouble for the man who only tried to protect her.

All because of her woes.

She walked from the kitchen window, where she stood staring out at the fields, over to the hearth and pushed the heavy pot closer to the flames. Fetching some of the tea she preferred, Elizabeth dropped a few leaves of the last of her supply into the steaming water to brew. When it was ready, she used the cloth of her apron to lift the heated pot and pour the fragrant tea into her cup. With her hands wrapped around it, she inhaled the tea's aroma and tried to make peace with the decision she'd made.

Henry's fumbling attempts at seduction had proven to her that she could never accept *that* role in his life. Even the thought of his touch made her want to retch. And that reaction did not address the immorality of his offer—one that would damn her if she accepted, even to save her beloved father's lands.

Her choice, the only one her honor would countenance, was to sell off the lands for much, much less than their value and attempt to pay off the debts she owed. Of course, this meant relying on the good nature of those to whom she owed, for even then she might not have enough to pay them in full. If they would not accept her payment and allow her time to earn more to pay the rest, she would end up in debtors' prison or as an indentured servant, as Fin was now.

That realization shocked her, for Henry could then buy her indenture and she would have no rights to refuse him anything. He would own her body and her life and honor be damned! The cup slipped from her grasp and hit the floor, spilling the tea and clanging loudly in the silence. She grabbed up a towel and crouched down to dab up the liquid from the wooden floor where it had spread.

Be practical, my girl.

She caught herself before turning to find him, for she could hear her father's voice just as though he was with her now. The most honorable man she'd ever known had a firmly-held belief that living in the world forced one's focus to that which made it possible to survive. Even things otherwise not considered acceptable. Even, if she remembered her father's lessons well enough, Henry's proposition would ruin her.

She stood as she glanced, once more, around this room where so many wonderful memories had been made. Elizabeth allowed herself to grieve for the last time before accepting her fate. She could no longer afford to hold to her lofty principles if she wanted to stay out of debtors' prison and survive at all. The soft knock at the door startled her, but the person standing there surprised her even more.

"Mister Blackwood," she whispered as she opened the door a scant few inches.

"Mistress Graham." His voice was low as he nodded and removed his hat. "I would speak with ye, if ye would allow it." His hair, usually neatly tucked into a queue or tied back, hung loose around his face, giving him an almost unkempt appearance.

What could have brought him so far in the dark of night? Even if he had been on another farm in the county, only an urgent matter would force such a visit at such a time as this.

"Are you well, Mister Blackwood? Are Friend Richard and his family well?" Elizabeth looked around for her shawl. "A moment, pray you," she said, leaving the door ajar as she retrieved it.

Tossing the shawl around her shoulders and gathering it in front of her, she then tugged the door open wide for him to enter. He held his hat in his hands, shifting it around as though nervous. He stood back as she closed the door and faced him.

"Let me get you some water," she said, walking past him. "You must be thirsty."

He stopped her with a soft touch of his hand on hers. "Nay, Elizabeth. I have no need of refreshment right now."

Had he noticed he called her by her given name? He'd done that once before.

"May I offer you a place to sit?" she asked.

"Nay, I will not be here long. I have something to say, an offer of a sort, and then I will take my leave to give ye time to consider it."

Her thoughts scattered then, for she was unable to even think what he would say. An offer? Elizabeth waited for him to begin.

"I have told ye that I will be heading south to live with some of my kin when my indenture is completed. Some of those. . . who were transported with me. . . ," he stumbled over those words, shame clear in his voice. "Some of them live in the Carolinas and I will go there."

"I know this," she said.

"There would be a place for ye there, if ye would wish to make a new life."

Of anything he could have said, this was never a possibility. She blinked several times trying to fathom the whole meaning of this.

"I confess," she uttered as she walked to the kitchen and sat in a chair there. "I do not understand."

"If ye do no' mind living with others like me," he said, "my cousins said there is a place and men worthy of a woman like ye there."

"Others like you, sir?"

"Former convicts." He whispered the last word, shame imbuing what he said now. "Rebels and traitors to the king."

"Mister Blackwood, whether 'tis the time of night or the unexpectedness of this call, I find myself confused over your words."

He watched her as he walked over and sat in a chair next to her at the table. Their positions reminded her of an earlier encounter. . . when he'd reached out and touched her hand in comfort. This time, he placed his hat there and stared off for a moment or two, his own discomfort clear to her this time.

"I would no' insult ye with an offer of my own," he said. His gaze now fell on his hands as though the message he brought her sat in them. Then he looked at the floor, the table and then the window. Bless him, but his subject was not easy for him to speak about. "But when my cousin, Margaret, Dougal's wife, wrote that there is a dearth of marriageable women in their area and knowing of yer situation. . . . I thought that. .

. . I thought ye might be amenable to. . . ."

He struggled with his words as she realized what this offer was—a new place to live with the possibility of finding a husband. As in any new place claimed in the wilderness of this land, once settled, men wanted to settle and begin their own families. His cousins must be in that situation now. And Mister Blackwood thought she might find a place there.

"You do not understand, Mister Blackwood," she began to explain the worst of it to him.

"Fin. Please, call me Fin." Now his gaze met hers and the intensity of it made her stomach do some strange quiver.

"Fin." He exhaled as she spoke his name, as though it was something he waited to hear. "I do not think you comprehend the severity of my situation." He looked at her, expectantly, ready and waiting for her to explain it. "I face too many debts to leave here a free woman. And I face debtors' prison or indenture if I try to leave without paying them."

"I ken. . . know that. But, if it is what ye want to do, there is a way."

The quiet words made her world tilt a little then. He offered an escape, from her debts and from Henry's proposition. It could not be legal and it might not be the right thing to do, but it was an escape nonetheless. Her face must have given away the shred of hope she held, for he continued.

"Ye would never be able to return here. Not to Philadelphia or Pennsylvania. And if ye run into trouble with the law again, it could bring ye to the authorities' attention and ye could still be put in prison." He paused then and waited on her to speak.

A thousand questions flooded into her thoughts then. About mundane things and important ones, too. What exactly was he offering her?

"How could this happen?"

"Ye would walk away from these lands and from the people ye ken without a word. Elizabeth Graham must disappear forever." Fin paused then and nodded. "I can send ye to the Virginia colony for now and meet ye to travel the rest of the way with ye when I finish my time here."

This man, this practical stranger, was offering her the help she needed when no one else could or would. When others would stand out of Henry's way and not interfere, Fin Blackwood continued to place himself there. Why?

"Why do you do this, Fin?" she finally asked. A myriad of emotions passed over the masculine lines of his face and in those green eyes.

"Why risk your own freedom when you are so close to reclaiming your life?"

CHAPTER FOUR

D ARE HE TELL HER THE true reason for his actions?
She watched him with those eyes that implored him and promised him and tempted him. All the while, she could not have any idea
of his feelings about her. But all of that, none of that, mattered for he'd
spoken the truth to her—he was not worthy of a woman like her.

He had failed in so many ways and had broken so many laws, of the
king and the land, and she deserved better. Even if she accepted this
offer, the taint of treason and lawlessness that he lived with could not be
allowed to touch her. She would be trying to save her life and had never
harmed anyone while he. . . he taken too many lives to remember.

"My mother, God rest her soul, taught me to help as ye can," he said
instead. "I had word of her death recently and I remembered her words
to me when I learned of yer situation. There is something I can do to
help ye, so I must."

He fought to keep his tone even and measured so that she would not
look too closely at his words. 'Twould be hard enough if she accepted
them as truth and he escorted her south before watching her marry
someone else. But, if she would be safe, he would content himself with
that. And if it took him days or weeks or years to accept that fact, then
so be it. She would be alive and well.

A single tear spilled from the corner of her eye and she shook her head.
"Your mother passed away? I am so sorry for your loss, Fin."

He knew, from the stories she'd shared, that she yet mourned the loss
of her own mother's passing and now she was sharing his own grief. Fin
would have to guard himself or he would find it impossible to control

his feelings in this endeavor to help her.

"Aye, she did," he said. "So I will try to honor her by doing what she said, at least this once." Fin smiled as many memories of his mother's frustrations with him and his antics flitted through his thoughts then. He'd not been the easiest of children to raise. Elizabeth wiped her hand across her cheek and smiled at him.

"I admit that I am overwhelmed by this offer, Fin," she said. "Overwhelmed by this and my circumstances."

She fell silent then and he feared she would refuse him and his plan to get her out from the expectations of Henry Lancaster and his ilk. She looked away then, glancing over at the door, and he watched as she took several deep, slow breaths. When she raised her gaze to his, there was a determination there he had not seen in months.

"What must I do?"

Though he hoped she would accept, he had convinced himself she would not, so Fin stumbled over his words before clearing his throat and nodding.

"I would think that Mister Lancaster would be here early in the morning two days hence to make good on his threat to ye," he began. "So, at first light, bring only what ye must and ride out in yer cart toward the crossing. I will meet ye there."

"And what should I do with. . . ?" She did not finish her words. But when she glanced around the house, her gaze touching on all manner of things, he understood.

"If there is something ye cannot live without, then bring it, Elizabeth," he said. "But the more ye bring, the slower we can travel and the more attention ye risk."

The sadness and loss in her eyes nearly crippled him then. He understood it more than most would, for only six years ago, he'd left home and most of his kin behind never realizing he'd never see them again. Was it kinder that she had these next hours to look over her treasured belongings and choose which to leave? To say her farewells to the home she knew? Or was the way he'd suffered an easier way?

Without further thought, he walked to her and drew her to her feet and into his embrace. Wrapping his arms around her, he held her close and offered her a comfort he'd never been offered when he'd lost everyone and everything. She did not resist and when she rested her cheek on his chest, he whispered to her.

"It will be frightening at first, Elizabeth. That much I ken. But with each step and each new day, ye will find it less and less so."

Her hands slid around him then and she took hold of the back of his jacket, holding on to him. He barely breathed and when he did finally draw in, it was to inhale the warm scent of her. Her still-damp hair smelled of femininity and roses. Her body felt. . . right, somehow there molded against his. He breathed again and realized he wanted this woman as his own, regardless that she could not be.

"Is that how it's been for you then?"

"Aye. Every day is a bit better."

He'd known he'd liked her. Fin admired her strength and perseverance. Her loyalty to those she loved and those in her care. He'd just not recognized until now that they would face the same type of challenge in their lives—losing the life they knew and fighting to regain it, or some of it. He was closer to the end of his journey of reclamation and she was just beginning, but the pain would be the same.

Fin let go his hold and waited for her to release him. Stepping back, he watched as she adjusted her shawl to cover her nightdress and pushed her hair out of her face.

"I will be ready."

"I will be waiting there, where the river road meets the Philadelphia one."

He turned to leave, for there were still many things to do and miles to cross this night, but she stopped him with a touch on his arm. He swore he could feel the heat of her fingers through the layers of cloth.

"What about Nathaniel?" she asked.

Fin had already spoken to the man before approaching Elizabeth with this idea. Born a slave, he had never known another life and would not unless Elizabeth freed him. If she left without doing so, Nathaniel would be owned by whomever Elizabeth owed the most to. Though they'd never spoken on the matter, Fin had strong feelings about the practice of owning people.

"If ye would do so, sign his manumission papers and I will give them to Richard to see them administered to when ye have gone. Or he belongs to whoever claims this farm, to sell or to keep." Disdain entered his voice, even he could hear it, but Elizabeth nodded.

"I would want no one at Henry's questionable mercy, so I will do that, Fin."

His blood roared when she spoke his name. He wished he had a way to make her his, but he would be a penniless traitor with many mortal sins on his soul and she deserved better. There would be many men in the village in the Carolinas who would try to stake their claim on Elizabeth when she was known to them. And he would not, could not, be one of them. With the question of Nathaniel settled for her, Fin walked to the door then.

"I suspect Richard would make a fine Friend out of you if he had more time," she said. 'Twas known that a growing number of Friends' Meetings were denouncing slavery and demanding that it be outlawed in Pennsylvania. Richard was involved in the manumission movement that was active in Philadelphia right now.

"I walk the path with him on many topics and beliefs, but no' all," he admitted. Over the five years, Richard had never forced him to join in his Community or refused him permission to worship in his own faith. It was a founding tenet of William Penn's colony.

Fin reached the door then and faced her before leaving.

"Would ye tell me who yer creditors are? Or does Lancaster hold all of yer debt?" he asked.

Other than a few solicitous remarks from neighbors who worried over the widow's predicament, he'd heard no gossip or bad reports from the other merchants and suppliers with whom he or Richard had accounts or business. Mayhap things were not as dire as he thought?

Elizabeth walked over to the small cabinet and opened it. After glancing over her shoulder at him, she reached in and withdrew a notebook from inside. More than simply a notebook, as she walked toward him, Fin could see it was crammed full with slips and scraps of paper and lists. She inhaled slowly before meeting his gaze and holding it out to him.

It took him but moments of examining the material to discover how deeply in debt she was. The only good thing was that Lancaster held none of it, so far as he knew. Fin suspected that the others would bear the loss in more mercy than the overbearing nobleman's son would. He doubted that any of the men listed on these bills and invoices would track the widow down for their pound of flesh. He closed the book and handed it back to her.

"Why did you ask to see this?"

"Lancaster is a man who would track ye down to extract his payment, but the others are kinder men and not so likely to make matters worse for ye." He nodded and stepped to the door once more. Lifting the latch, he smiled, trying to reassure her. "Though they will no' be happy, they will no' send out bailiffs or trackers to hunt ye down, should ye disappear, say, in two days' time."

Something swirled in the back of his mind as he walked from the house. He'd spoken to Nathaniel earlier about the conditions on the farm and about the other neighbors who Fin did not know. Elizabeth had been late or in arrears for the last six months but, before that, the farm had been solvent. What had changed to make things go so badly so quickly? As he mounted his horse to ride back to the city, he realized it was not something but someone.

Henry Lancaster.

Even the man's name left a bitter taste on Fin's tongue and, now, more so than before. Was the man manipulating things to make it harder for Elizabeth to refuse his ever-insulting offers? He snorted as though he did not already understand the truth or remember old Mister Cooper's refusal of Lancaster's suit for his daughter's hand. This rich, vainglorious bastard was behind it all and Fin knew it.

What could be done though? Now, at this late time, when Elizabeth was so desperate she would agree to leave her whole life behind her to escape his plans? Could anything save what her family had lived and worked so hard for?

Richard Montgomery sat waiting in his house when Fin returned from his late night ride. The man who owned him had never been cruel and had taught Fin many, many things about living and honor and the craft they shared. Although he would not have thought indentured servitude a blessing, this man sitting in the main room watching his arrival had certainly been just that—a blessing.

"Thou hast been on the roads late this night, Finlan. Is there something I should know?" Richard asked, motioning to a nearby chair. "There is ale there in the pitcher if thou hast a thirst or need for such."

Fin did not know what to say or not to say about Elizabeth and their plans. If Richard knew, he would be complicit in the crime they were about to commit. Better to keep him out of it, in true ignorance, in case questions came his way. So, Fin poured a cup of ale for him and for his master and then sat in the proffered chair, still sorting out what to share with the man who had the legal right to know and control both his whereabouts and his actions.

"Thou hast been quiet and thoughtful at Meeting, Finlan. For weeks now. At first, I thought it because of the changes coming to thy life shortly, but now, I suspect that thou hast had an *Opening* and that the widow Graham is at the heart of it."

Fin waited. He'd learned years ago that, when Richard spoke his mind, he spoke in a calm, slow, measured pace. And Fin had found wisdom in the man's words, so he waited once more.

"Thy comings and goings these last days and nights speak of efforts to help her. Is that true, Finlan?"

"Aye, Richard. 'Tis true."

"And what hast thou accomplished on her behalf thus far?"

"I think it best if ye ken no' about this matter, Richard."

"Hast thou offered her marriage and a safe haven with thy relatives in the Carolinas?"

He purposely avoided the real question. "I have told her of the possibilities of marriage there. There are many marriageable men looking for wives and helpmates in the new villages and towns." Richard's expression changed and a slight smile, a mocking one, lifted one corner of his mouth. The man was no fool. When the silence continued, Fin let out a breath and decided to confide the rest.

"Mistress Graham is deeply in debt with no way to pay off her creditors. I offered her a way to escape south, but she must walk away from her life and become another person."

"The widow is a kind, goodhearted woman with much experience at tending a household and a husband. I suspect she will have no problem finding a willing man to take her to wife."

Fin closed his eyes as his stomach clenched then and anger rose within him. He could save her, aye, help her escape, but could not claim her as his. "Aye. There will be many interested among my cousins and the other men building their lives there."

"And thou, Finlan? Wilt thou not claim her hand in marriage since love is already in thy heart for her?"

"I cannot!" He let the words out loudly and clasped his hands into fists. "I have. . . . I have. . . . I. . . ." Fin did not realize he'd jumped to his feet and faced Richard now. "I have too many sins on my soul and too much blood on my hands to claim a woman such as Elizabeth Graham."

His path to this moment in time had been fraught with bloodshed and death, both in the Rising and after it, as he struggled to survive the terrible ordeal of capture and imprisonment. The killing had not stopped on the battlefields and had not been limited to the soldiers they'd faced. Nay, the worst shame lying heavy on his soul did not involve soldiers, but others who'd preyed on him and the other prisoners. Though his youth made him more the target of shameful acts and attacks, his work with his father had made him stronger than many thought and he'd used that strength to kill.

Relentlessly. Many times. Fin glanced at his hands now, certain that the blood he'd spilled marked them even now. Richard stood and walked to him, taking hold of his hands and turning them over.

"No man's hands or soul is free from sin. But the Almighty saw fit to bring thou through trial and tribulation and into the Light, Finlan. Thou hast lived an upright life these last five years, taking His counsel and learning His ways as part of my household. If He has forgiven thy sins, cannot thou forgive thyself?"

Fin looked at Richard and saw nothing but compassion and truth there in the man's eyes. Glancing back down at his hands, he thought on what Richard had said. Fin had prayed for forgiveness so many times but he had never accepted that it could be his.

"Mayhap thou hast had a *Leading* that guides thou to help her? Mayhap thou are worthy of such a woman?"

"I am not of yer faith, Richard, though I respect that ye are faithful to its teachings. There was no revelation on this matter for me." He took in a deep breath and let it out. "She is a God-fearing woman who is forced to flee her life and deserves a man who is no' a traitor and rebel and murderer." Richard would have spoken, but Fin shook his head and pulled from his grasp.

"And more than all that, I am a penniless man who will leave indenture with nothing more than the clothing on my back and the few coins ye have allowed me to earn. I can work to support myself but I can neither pay off her debts nor promise to take responsibility for her life."

Richard stared at him, once more, and did not speak for several minutes then. Tempted to leave now, something held him in place.

"But thou wishes to do that? Pay off her debts and take her as thy wife and helpmate? There is truly love for her in thy traitor's heart?"

Mayhap, knowing that it would make no difference and that she would never learn of his true feelings for her released the truth from within him.

"Aye. I would do whatever was necessary to give her the life she wants. I would take her to wife and cherish her all the days of her life and mine." Fin nodded. "I love her."

"The Light could not live within an evil heart or soul, Finlan. I believe thou hast been called to it and will find what thou seek."

With that pronouncement, Richard nodded and left the room, climbing the stairs up to the second floor.

"I will be working out of the city for the next few days, Richard," he said before the man was too far away. Better to use that excuse so the man did not search for him or expect him here. 'Twould give him time to escort Elizabeth into Virginia and place her with friends there until he was ready to leave for good.

"Go with God, Finlan."

Fin gathered his things together and sought his own room off the kitchen. Had Richard given his blessing then? How much did he know?

CHAPTER FIVE

RICHARD WALKED ON SILENT FEET and entered the room where his wife slept undisturbed. He made his way around the room, undressing and readying himself for sleep as he heard Finlan moving around belowstairs.

The young man who had arrived here in the city those five years ago and the one who would leave his home in just a few weeks were not the same man. God had brought about many changes in Finlan, even if the young man did not realize it.

Richard had experienced a *Leading* when he saw the scrawny, filthy boy stumble out of the hold of the ship and climb up on the platform on that long-ago day. A *Concern* over the treatment of those indentured prisoners led him to claim the young man and the *Leading* that followed brought Finlan into Richard's life and home. God had given him this responsibility and, 'twould seem, He was not done with Richard yet.

Recently, during the quiet moments of their Meeting, Richard had watched as Finlan struggled through some personal challenge and deliberated on a course of action. Though Finlan was not a Friend, Richard believed that God had used their Community to guide the young man and had given him a *Leading* of his own that did, indeed, involve the young widow of Jonah Graham.

So, over the last weeks, Richard had himself paid heed and heard as well and now would do as he was led in this matter. Though the Friends believed that their *Concerns* and *Leadings* were addressed only to them, Richard had seen others so affected and that Finlan had received a *Leading* did not surprise him at all.

As sleep eluded him for the next hours, Richard, once more, opened his heart and listened in the silence before deciding how he could be the instrument he was designed to be in this. By morning, he understood his role and, by the end of the day, he'd set things in motion.

Finlan Blackwood's biggest step would be to realize and accept his own worth. Richard understood that was difficult for a man who had walked the path Fin had. However, Richard had faith, not only in the young man Fin had become, but also in the young widow who Fin loved.

Within a few days, Richard would know if Finlan had heard the Opening given to him. Within a few days, all would be settled.

℅

Elizabeth sat in stunned silence for some time after Fin left her house. The candles sputtered out, leaving her with only the light of one lantern yet burning in the kitchen. It did not matter.

Was her decision the right one? Could she leave everything here behind and begin a new life among strangers? Torn between the obligations for her debts and her inability to meet them, Elizabeth changed her mind several times in the ensuing hours before the sun's light brightened the night's darkness.

She rose from the chair and began her morning chores by rote, cleaning out the remnants of yesterday's fire in the hearth first. Her thoughts churned in her mind as she prepared porridge for her and Nathaniel. She must see to his future and sign the papers for his freedom, whether she ran or stayed. Before any judgement could be entered against her, his fate must be settled.

By midday, she accepted that she would take Fin's offer and leave with him.

By sundown, she was staying.

But, in the dark of that final night when she had a choice, she prayed that her parents and her husband would forgive her the one she made. Over those last hours in the house where she'd been born, grown, married and lived her whole life, she gathered together the most important things she owned and prepared to leave everything else behind.

Her mother's necklace and sewing box.

The quilt she and her mother had sewn in preparation for her wedding to Jonah. 'Twas the same one that covered her marriage bed and the one under which she still slept each night.

Her father's Bible, well-read with dog-eared pages to mark his favorite passages. Even now, she could hear his deep voice reading aloud from it as was his custom to do each night after supper. The book fell open to a page that had been read many, many times and Elizabeth read the first passage, hearing her father's voice in the words there.

> *Trust in the Lord with all your heart and lean not on your own understanding; in all your ways submit to Him, and He will make your paths straight. Do not be wise in your own eyes; fear the Lord and shun evil.*

She let the words pass over her and continued on, hoping and praying that she had done this well. The collection of belongings from which she could not be parted was not a big one, but each choice made the tears flow. Finally, when there were no more tears to shed, she dressed and packed everything in the wagon that stood waiting by the kitchen door.

As she drove the cart down the road, away from her home toward the river road, Elizabeth tried not to look back. She must look forward now and leave her past behind. But, as the road curved along the banks of the Brandywine, she pulled the cart to a halt and turned back.

She would never see the gently-rolling lands that her father had turned into fields or the small house he'd built. The graves of her parents and Jonah lay at the edge of their property, on the hill overlooking the river. Offering up one more prayer as she moved her gaze back to the road that would lead her away, she turned her thoughts to the future that Finlan Blackwood had held out to her.

Anticipation grew with each moment as she approached the place where he would be waiting. Only then did she realize that she was placing her trust in a man about whom she knew little. And yet, her father and Jonah had both respected him and liked him, something they did not do easily or often.

A stranger, truly, and yet he risked his life and freedom to help her now. When she'd questioned his reason, she knew he did not tell her the whole truth. The part about his mother's teachings was certainly true for his words and tone held the soundness of honesty when he spoke of her. Yet, Elizabeth suspected there was more to his reasons than that.

In these moments of brutal honesty, Elizabeth admitted to herself that she'd hoped his offer was more than what it turned out to be. Just as he'd spoken of her worth to those in this new place to which they would travel, she understood his. A young man, trained in a highly-needed skill, would have his choice when he decided to marry.

He'd spoken of not being worthy of her, but mayhap 'twas the other way around? Mayhap there would be a more valuable match for him there? Mayhap he was already betrothed or spoken for?

That would explain much.

Disappointment filled her then, for accepting marriage to a man she knew would be less terrifying than marrying a stranger. She had been fortunate in her first marriage. Jonah Graham and his family had been known to her and her parents had supported her marrying him. Now, she allowed herself a moment to admit that she would have accepted an offer of marriage from Finlan Blackwood.

He was not a rash man. He was not cruel. He worked hard and respected others. Her father had a saying that she thought was true of Fin—a man who could laugh well and often could love just as much.

But he had not offered that. He had, however, offered her a life and she would take it and be grateful. She would be in his debt for this and she would seek a way to pay off this one in full.

When the cart traveled over the last rising before the Philadelphia road, she saw him there and her heart raced. He risked his all to protect her and she would do anything he asked of her. A woman would be lucky to call him her own. Some woman would do that.

"Good morning, Elizabeth," he said softly as she pulled to a stop there beside him. He held out his hand for the reins and she gave them over as she shifted across the seat, allowing him to climb up. He glanced behind into the cart as he tossed his own bag in the back and then met her gaze. "This is everything then?"

"I took only what I could not be parted from, Fin. As you said to do." They settled next to each other and he clucked as he flicked the reins over the horse's back. "The more I leave behind, the more money can be raised at auction to pay back those I owe." A farmstead with a house filled with all necessary furniture and tools was more valuable than an empty one, she knew.

They rode in amiable silence down the road, away from Philadelphia and her life. First they would reach Baltimore and, from there, they would follow the coach road down to Virginia where she would wait for his return. The sun was high in the late morning sky when they stopped to eat and take their ease.

Fin helped her climb down and then found the basket she'd packed for the journey. When she lifted the cover, she found the document she'd signed. She did not want to forget to give it to Fin for Friend Richard's safekeeping.

"If you would take this, they are Nathaniel's papers."

He accepted it and began to tuck it in the pocket inside his jacket. He tried a second time and then handed it back to her. Emptying the pocket of some packet already there, he stared at it before shrugging.

"I did not put this there," he said, turning the packet over to read the front of it. His name was written on the front there in a strong, bold hand. "Richard wrote this."

Elizabeth stepped away to give him privacy. From his guarded expression, he expected some bad news within from his master. She found a spot in the shade of a large willow tree and laid out a small piece of cloth on which to place their food. After unwrapping some meat and cheese, she tore the small loaf of bread into two pieces and found the crock of butter. Then she waited.

"I cannot believe what he has done." Fin walked over to her and knelt there, shaking his head and glancing at the sheet he held in his hand. "I am a free man."

"Friend Richard has freed you now?" she asked. "You had three more weeks left?"

"Aye. Three weeks, but his letter says he has signed the documents within and made me free. I do not have to return to Philadelphia unless I wish to." The joy on his face was a blessing to behold. He held his life in his hands now and could begin anew without anything to fetter him.

"Does he say why now? Why he did not wait for the indenture to finish as scheduled?" Three weeks was not much longer and both men could have waited for Fin to fulfill the requirements.

"Nay. I did not tell him of this journey, only that I would be working out of the city for a few days. I thought the less I shared, the safer he was from any complicity in our plans." He rested his hand on his leg and shook his head once more. "Clearly, he kenned more than I thought."

"What else does he say?" she asked.

"Ah," he said, gazing at the rest of the letter. "Richard has put a price on my early freedom after all."

"Can you pay this cost?" she asked. Friend Richard had allowed him to work for pay, she knew, so he might have enough. "How much does he ask for?"

"Coin would be easier than what he asks of me," Fin admitted before raising his eyes to meet her gaze. "Richard says that to be free now I must tell ye the real reason why I did not offer ye marriage when I arranged this journey."

"Your real reason?" she asked. 'Twas a good thing she already sat on the ground, for that declaration would have knocked her down. If those words had not, then his next words would surely have done so.

"Ye see, Elizabeth, I love ye enough no' to ask ye to tie yerself to a man like me."

CHAPTER SIX

HAVING HER WHOLE LIFE UPROOTED gave Elizabeth a boldness she had not felt before. Having a man express his love for her gave her the strength to reach out to claim that love.

"What kind of man are you, Fin?" she asked. She looked at him across their simple meal and smiled. "I see a man who puts himself at risk to help another. A man who survived when others did not. A respectful man unafraid of hard work. A loyal man who possesses great perseverance. What kind of woman would not wish to tie herself to a man like you if she received such an offer? Or if she heard the words you just spoke?"

Shame, deep, soul-destroying shame, filled his green eyes then and it took only a moment before he looked away. What had he done in his past that caused him such shame?

"I have the blood of dozens on my hands, Elizabeth. I stood during the Rising for the Stuart king and killed many in his name."

"Men fight and kill in wars, Fin. It has been so since the beginning of time."

"I killed others, Elizabeth. Being so young, I was the target of many who used their power over the subjugated to terrorize and punish us. The soldiers who captured us. The guards who imprisoned us. Even other prisoners. They thought I was an easy one to use and torment and never expected that I could and would kill them."

She did not speak at first. His words continued to echo the shame she saw in his expression. Grief and regret mingled there, too. He thought himself too sinful for her.

"How many have you killed since you arrived here five years ago, Fin?"

"What?"

She stood, then brushed off her skirts and asked again. "How many have you killed here?"

"Elizabeth, ye do no' understand." His accent thickened as emotion filled his voice. "I killed them wi' my own hands. No' shot in the battle."

"In times and places where you had no choice, Fin. Kill or be killed. You defended yourself. You lived. You survived." She stepped closer to him and wrapped her fingers around his wrists, lifting his hands up between them.

"Should I be sad that you used your strength to protect yourself? I am not." He stared at her as she held him there and she shook her head now. "What did Friend Richard say about this? He knows?"

"Aye. I told him," Fin said, pulling free of her hold even while wanting to feel the warmth of her touch on him. "He said that I should forgive myself."

"Then I think you should look at his gift of freedom as a chance to do that. To start again. You have given that to me, Fin, so why not accept it for yourself?"

The summer breezes rustled the trees around them as though to agree with her words to him. She could not imagine the suffering he'd lived through and, yet, here he was in fear of her reaction. Because. . . he loved her.

"Promise me that you will try."

"I. . . ." He looked away, gazing over her head into the distance as though remembering his past deeds. "I will try, Elizabeth. For ye."

"Did you mean your words?" she asked. A woman did not hear those words spoken often so she wanted to be certain. Now, her hands trembled and she could not meet his gaze. The touch of his finger under her chin guided her to lift her head and look at him now.

"Aye, Elizabeth. I love ye."

He leaned in and touched his lips to hers in a chaste kiss. Fin smiled then and it erased much of the worry in his gaze.

"But ye are no' beholden to me because of that." He cleared his throat and released her chin. "There will be many clamoring for yer hand when we arrive."

"Finlan Blackwood, I would consider your offer if you think to make one."

She would not only consider it, she would accept it, that much she understood. And he needed to know it, for he had grown into a good man when given the chance to by Friend Richard. A man she suspected she could love in return very easily. If given the chance.

He stuttered then, beginning and stopping to speak several times before he finally did.

"Ye honor me with yer understanding, Elizabeth."

They ate in silence, but it was one filled with happiness instead of foreboding and worry. As she wrapped the remaining food up for later, she noticed Friend Richard's packet. Something had fallen out and lay by its side on the ground.

"Did you read the rest of it, Fin? The other documents that Friend Richard gave to you there?"

She gathered up the cloth, shook it free of crumbs and folded it as he picked up the envelope and the other sheet there. He read a bit more before returning the several sheets to the envelope.

"I will read the rest when we stop again," he said, tucking it inside his jacket pocket where Nathaniel's papers sat.

They packed up the basket and climbed back onto the seat. Tempted to smile and laugh at the strange yet wonderful turn of events and revelations, Elizabeth could not help that her leg brushed his as they traveled down the road south. Not too long after their stop, she began to fall asleep, for she'd gotten little over the last days and nights.

"Lean on me, Elizabeth," he invited. "Get some rest."

Fin had noticed her eyes closing more and more over the last several miles. Shadows under those lovely brown eyes spoke of restless, sleepless nights and the pressures of her plight. He wanted to laugh aloud when she moved closer to him and accepted his offer of support.

Richard had been right in his guidance to speak the truth to her. When he saw the compassion and acceptance in her expression, he began to think he could forgive himself and work to be worthy of her. That she would be open to an offer of marriage was more than he'd dreamt possible, especially since he should be long dead and buried.

He lifted his arm and she snuggled closer to him, resting against him with full trust that he would take care of her. Could it be that easy? Nay, life was not that simple, but together, they could make it work.

If she lived with his cousin and found work while Fin hired out as a blacksmith, he might be able to earn enough to support their own household in a year. The wait would not be so bad and she was worth it to him. Fin would also have to accept, though he would do so begrudgingly, that she might receive better offers from other men who were more established and could offer her everything that she had lost.

He did not realize he'd tensed at such a thought until she stirred beside him. He let himself relax and she slid her arm around his and tucked her head against him once more. In full trust of him. He was in awe of her even as much as he was in love with her. The irony of their situations was not lost on him as he thought on it.

He was about to gain everything he'd ever wanted—his life back, finding his family and being a free man—even while she lost all of that. If only. . . .

Elizabeth woke a few hours later and they stopped again to take their ease and see to the horse's need for food and water as well. He unhooked the animal from the cart and led it to a stream while Elizabeth sought the refuge of the thick trees for her personal comfort. While he waited there in the shadows near the edge of the water, Fin took out the packet and opened it.

He'd not noticed the smaller wrapped packet within the larger envelope or read the second sheet from Richard. Though he wished they could simply travel on together, Fin knew he would have to leave Elizabeth for a short time to retrieve his own tools and the rest of his belongings from Richard's house in the city. Now, he wondered if he should beg off the odd jobs he'd accepted in order to return to her more quickly and finish their journey south.

Caught up in those concerns, he'd not paid heed to the actual words on the paper at first. When he did, he read in stunned silence at Richard's explanation and offer of help. A few calculations gave him several choices he never thought to have. He did not know whether to bless Richard or curse the man.

Nay, Richard had just proven to be a friend in all the best ways possible.

He lingered there, his thoughts scattered, and he had every right to blame the shock at Richard's words for his delay in returning to her at the cart. When he heard her calling his name, he shook himself free and went to her, leaving the horse there to fix his rest.

"Are you well, Fin? You have lost all the color in your face and look pale," she said as she reached up to touch his cheek with the back of her hand. "No fever, thank the Almighty."

He knew what her reaction would be—she would refuse this offer to help her at his own cost. She understood his need, his desire and his plans to be reunited with lost family. What would she say when he turned them around and headed back to her farm on the Brandywine? He grabbed her hand and held it against his face then.

"Ye will marry me?" he asked. Laughing then, he shook his head and asked the question the way it should be asked of a woman by a man who loved her. "Elizabeth, would ye do me the honor of marrying me?"

"Now? Marry you now?" Bewilderment showed in her eyes and in the way her brows crinkled. "I do not understand, Fin. Is there cause to rush in to this?"

"Aye, good cause, Elizabeth. Richard has made it possible to save yer farm," he said, still unable to believe it completely. "If ye would like to try to do that?" Now, 'twas her turn to pale and she stumbled at his offer.

"I have no money, Fin. You know that. I have no way to pay back the debts owed."

"Ah, but I do." Her gaze flitted over his face as she searched for the meaning of his words. "Richard asked me in his letter why I had never inquired about the terms of my indenture. To be honest with ye, I could not read or write when I signed the document that day five years ago and wanted no reminder of how pitiful I was."

"You never asked to see it when you learned?" she asked.

"Nay, 'twas another reminder of my shame. So, just now I read it for the first time and discovered that Richard is far kinder than I kenned. I believed as I'd heard—that I would leave penniless with only the clothing on my back and what he would give me."

"'Tis not so then?"

"Richard has been paying me each month and the earnings have collected over the five years. When I add to that the money I have earned with my extra jobs, we should have enough to pay off most all of yer debt." The shake of her head began as just a small trembling before it became a frank refusal of his words. "He has offered to extend credit to us to pay off the rest. I can work for him and pay it back when I can."

"You? My debts?" she stuttered. "I cannot allow that, Fin. You are fortunate that Richard has provided so well for you but I cannot, I will not, allow you to put yourself back under a contract for me."

He reached out and pulled her to him. Leaning down, he kissed her once, twice and then again. Only when she gave herself over to it did he smile against her lovely and warm lips. His heart pounded and his soul soared when she kissed him back, once and then again. When they were both breathless from those kisses, he lifted his mouth from hers and kissed along the edge of her jaw and on her neck. Her body arched against his, promising joy of another kind between them.

"I told Richard I would do anything and everything I could to give ye the life ye wanted. I ken that losing yer lands is like losing a part of ye. Now, I have the means to prevent that, Elizabeth. Let me do this for ye, I pray ye. Let me."

She stared into his eyes and he waited for what seemed an eternity for her answer. It came as a question, but he would take it.

"How can I ever repay you for this, Fin? What can I offer you to compensate you for giving up your dreams to save mine?"

"I do no' promise an easy path, Elizabeth. We will have to work hard to accomplish all this, but I want to do this. For ye and for us." A tear trickled from the corner of her eye and he reached out to catch it. "Worry no', lass. I can, we can, make our own family here and my kin can visit us. Some could even move up to help us manage the lands. Although I am more than willing to accept yer gratitude, I wish only yer promise that ye will try, just a little, to be happy."

Fin kissed her then, a quick one on her mouth and then he held her close, brushing her temple with his lips. "And I would never demand it of ye, but I would be happy if ye were able to love me just a bit," he whispered.

Elizabeth reached up and slid her hands around him then. This embrace was the same and yet so different from the one when he comforted her just a few nights ago. She turned her head, resting her cheek on his chest and he felt her nod against him.

"I think that is very possible, Finlan Blackwood, and I will do my best to give you what you want as a dutiful wife should."

At her words, his laughter rang out loud and echoed through the woods around them. It would not be easy and it would take years to make the farm and the lands a success once more. But Fin did not doubt that it would be worth every penny spent and every hour worked.

That *she* would be worth it.

Within an hour, their cart was heading north on the Philadelphia road back to the Brandywine River and home.

EPILOGUE

Three Days Later

ELIZABETH STARED DOWN AT THE small package in her hands. Fin had placed it there with a reverence that made her eager to open it. With trembling fingers, she peeled open the paper and then the soft cloth that protected the contents.

A heart-shaped brooch of precious silver lay there before her. Within the heart was a thistle, its flower a purple gem and the leaves were formed by smaller green stones. An engraved crown sat at the top of the heart with more stones decorating the edge of it. It was a costly piece of jewelry, but the look in his eyes told her that this was important in other ways.

"'Tis called a luckenbooth," he explained. "A man gives it to his betrothed to wear at their wedding and then it is worn as protection by their firstborn bairn at the christening."

"Fin, it is beautiful. You did not have to spend your money on such a thing for me. You have given me so much already."

Elizabeth would never be able to repay him for saving her farm and giving her a chance at a life in the place where she'd been born, all of that while giving up so much.

"My mother gave me hers when I left to fight by my father's side. Selling off the stones and the silver of that pin provided me with food that kept me alive through my imprisonment."

She fought off the need to cry at his words and the thought of a boy needing to give up his most precious possession to live. "Was hers the same as this?" His efforts to give her such a thing made it difficult to speak the words.

"The same shape and the stones were the same colors, but this is a bit smaller than hers."

"Oh, Fin," she whispered as he reached out to pin it in place on her dress. "I am honored by this." Touching it, she smiled at him. "Another reason to be so grateful to you."

"If we are blessed with bairns, we can pass it down just as my mother did with hers."

He kissed her then before turning to face the magistrate for the ceremony that would join their lives, their futures and their hearts as one. Surrounded by Richard's family and some friends, they would marry in town and then move out to the farm once their financial arrangements were finished. When he entwined their fingers together, Elizabeth found herself longing for the rest of what was to come.

"A new tradition out of the old," she whispered, squeezing his hand.

"A legacy to pass on to those who come after us," he said.

Soon, words spoken became vows and the separate pasts became one future.

A year later, in July of the Year of Our Lord of 1722, Elias Dougal Blackwood, named after both of his grandfathers, wore the Blackwood luckenbooth at his christening, beginning a legacy that would be handed down through many generations of the family.

TERRI BRISBIN

WHEN NOT LIVING THE GLAMOROUS life of a *USA TODAY* bestselling romance author, **Terri Brisbin** spends her time being a wife, mom/mom-in-law, grandmom and a dental hygienist in the southern NJ suburbs.

A three-time RWA RITA® finalist and award-winning author, Terri has sold more than 2.5 million copies of her historical and paranormal romance novels, novellas and short stories in more than 20 languages since 1998. She's been published by Berkley/Jove, Harlequin, Kensington Books and NAL/Signet as well as indie published and has more romances scheduled release through 2020!

Connect with Terri at *www.terribrisbin.com* or *www.facebook.com/terribrisbinauthor* .

BOOKS BY TERRI BRISBIN

A Love Through Time, 11/1998, 2012
A Matter of Time, 11/1999, 2012
The Queen's Man, 11/2000, 2012
Once Forbidden, 5/2002, 2012
"Taming The Highlander Rogue", digital only, 8/2012
The Highlander's Stolen Touch, 9/2012
"The Forbidden Highlander", HIGHLANDERS, 6/2013
At The Highlander's Mercy, 4/2013
The Highlander's Dangerous Temptation, 11/2013
Yield to The Highlander, 5/2014
Rising Fire – 3/ 2015
Stolen by the Highlander - 4/2015
Raging Sea – 10/2015
The Highlander's Runaway Bride, 3/2016
Blazing Earth – 4/2016
"Upon a Misty Skye" in ONCE UPON A HAUNTED CASTLE,
9/2016
Kidnapped by the Highland Rogue, 10/2016
"Across a Windswept Isle" in THE FORBIDDEN HIGHLANDS,
4/2017
"A Traitor's Heart" in BRANDYWINE BRIDES, 4/2017
Claiming His Highland Bride, 6/2017

For more info, visit: www.terribrisbin.com/books/index.php

A *P*ATRIOT'S HEART

By

GWENDOLYN SCHULER

1779

AS AMERICA'S STRUGGLE FOR INDEPENDENCE draws to a close, Margaret Blackwood's hopes for a peaceful life in the aftermath are cast into renewed turmoil when a grievously wounded British officer is brought to Blackwood Farm for healing and sanctuary. Will she risk her heart and future for a man who could betray her and all she loves?

DEDICATION &

ACKNOWLEDGEMENTS

To the remarkably talented authors
with whom I share this anthology.
You are, each one, a treasured friend.
And to "Margi"- the inspiration.

CHAPTER ONE

Chadds Ford, Pennsylvania
March 1779

"MARGARET. MARGARET, WAKE UP!"

"Papa," Margi whispered on a breath, burrowing deeper beneath her blankets and quilt.

Her father's voice had penetrated but she did not open her eyes.

"Margaret!" A series of loud raps sounded on her door.

The knocking and Elias Blackwood's use of her given name rather than the usually shortened "Margi" roused her. Margi's eyes flew open to see the latched window and night's pitch-blackness beyond the glass panes. A sliver of moon let in light enough to bathe the room in shadowed shapes. Margi blinked. It must be very late. Reluctantly, she pulled herself to a sitting position and rubbed her eyes.

"Daughter, have you wakened?" Her father rattled the doorknob.

"I have, Papa. I'm awake. What is it?" she called.

"I need you. Hurry!" He gave a sharp rap.

Her breathing quickened. "Is it Jamie?"

"Margaret, quick!" her father said, not answering her question.

"I'm coming," she called, tucking escaped tangles of Titian curls into her nightcap. "Papa, answer me. Is Jamie ill?"

Her heart pounded at the thought.

She flipped aside the bedcovers, shivering in the chill, the fire having burned out. Rubbing her arms against the gooseflesh pebbling them, she slid off the bed and snatched up her robe. Winter had been hard on them all, but especially on her ten-year-old nephew, James Josiah Black-wood. He'd been ill with fevers from the fall's first frost.

"Is Charlotte up?" Margi pressed, sliding one foot into her slipper while sliding her other foot under the bed, seeking its mate.

"Your sister-in-law and Jamie are asleep," Elias answered from the hall. "Young Jamie's all right."

What then?

Absolved of fear with her father's words, Margi had dropped to her knees, reaching beneath the bed for her slipper with numb fingers.

"Margi. Quick, now."

"What's wrong, Papa? Are you ill?" Her hands swung in a wide arc and one hand swept over her slipper. Snatching it up, she scrambled to her feet.

"I'm not ill, Daughter," her father answered, his tone sharp.

Margi let out her breath.

"Are you moving, Margaret?"

"I am." She flung open her bedroom door.

Elias Blackwood gave a curt nod, his expression grim. "Follow me."

They heard a door click open.

"What's happened?" Her sister-in-law stepped into the hall.

Elias shook his head. "Charlotte, I'd no wish to wake you or Jamie. You need your rest. It's Margi I need."

Margi exchanged a questioning look with her sister-in-law.

"What's wrong? I've no wish to be coddled, Elias." Charlotte met her father-in-law's gaze while pulling her wrapper around her. "I can help."

Elias hesitated before blowing out a breath. "Very well. I see I'm being tested. Ladies, we're wasting time. Come with me."

"Go ahead." Charlotte shooed them off with a wave of her hands. "I'll check on Jamie and be right down."

The women shared a glance. Margi shrugged, indicating the reason for Elias' summons was unknown to her. She followed her father downstairs and around the curve of the staircase on a trot, heading for the kitchen. A glance at the darkened parlor told her no one waited there. The chill of a winter's night had chased out the downstairs' earlier warmth. Shivering, Margi knotted her robe's belt tighter, hurrying through the downstairs hall, grateful for the warmth of her wool-lined slippers, hoping her father had already stoked the kitchen's fire.

Steps from the doorway, she heard low voices. "Papa?"

Her father put up a hand. Margi dashed the last few steps, catching him at the kitchen's threshold.

"My daughter, Margaret, will help you." Her father pushed her ahead of him. Snatching up her nightgown, she stepped down three steps into the kitchen.

Margi's heart jumped into her throat, stifling her gasp.

Six red-coated soldiers crowded their kitchen, surrounding their over-sized farm table and revealing a long-limbed, brawny soldier, lying bruised and bloodied, across its expanse. In the silence, Margi heard the intermittent pat-pat of blood, dripping onto the stone floor.

She glanced at her father but said nothing, trying to order her thoughts. She had some skill with healing, nursing her nephew and neighbors through the last year, after the county's doctor had left them to follow the Continental Army. Margi had assisted the doctor from the time she'd turned thirteen. Her father believed her gift came from her mother, Emma, while the doc had insisted Margi possessed the intuition and avid interest of a healer. Doc Grove had been gone for over a year. Who would have sent the soldiers to Blackwood Farm, and her?

She stared at her father, who stared at a tall, redcoat standing by the wounded soldier's head. Straight-backed with a ruddy face and tired, reddened eyes, he wore epaulets and carried an air of command.

"He's alive," the officer said in a clipped voice. "The captain's grievously hurt. My men will take only what grain and foodstuffs as we need and leave you, but only if your girl saves him."

A sharp-faced, bearded soldier added, "Your Continentals staged an ambush three miles back. We drove them off, the scum!"

Margi's heart jumped. A half-turn reassured her that Charlotte was not downstairs to hear the exchange. Fear for her Continental soldier brother, Josiah, held her tense and motionless.

"Can you save him?" The officer's face flushed a deeper red.

"God willing," Margi muttered.

"She'll do it." Elias turned to his daughter. "The major has given his word."

And you've given yours, she thought, with a glance at the farm table and the prone man. Giving no quarter, her father's demeanor mirrored the major's. Margi clasped her hands within the folds of her robe and sent up a prayer.

The major crossed the kitchen and gripped her upper arm. "The captain's waiting."

Margi met the major's gaze and gave a curt nod. Thus far, they had escaped the British raids throughout the countryside last fall. She'd not expected a visit in the dead of night, at the end of winter.

Her hands felt clammy as she approached the wounded man. The kitchen was, indeed, warmer. Margi had barely noticed, so intent was she on the British captain. She saw the soldier was not conscious. She watched him, lying with his eyes closed, a jagged, bleeding gash along his hairline, slashed from his forehead to his ear.

Leaning close, Margi's breath caught. For a moment, she was sure the captain was dead.

Stepping between two soldiers, Margi leaned over the captain. Her breath caught, sure the captain was dead. She touched his wrist, nearly recoiling at his skin's coldness. The soldiers on either side of her stood at rigid attention, oblivious to the conclusion that had turned her legs to water. Margi's fingers tightened around the captain's wrist as his face wavered before her eyes. Fighting lightheadedness, she would not retrieve a mirror and signal her fear. Too intent to breath, she bent closer to within an inch of the captain's lips.

Light as air, she felt his breath on her cheek. Her heart leapt. With her upper body touching his, Margi detected the rise and fall of the man's chest.

She let out her breath.

"Gentlemen, please, give me room." Margi waved the captain's guardians away from the table as she circled the patient, assessing the wounds she could see.

"Papa, I'll need clean cloths and hot water, lots of it."

A squat soldier with eyes that crinkled at the corners let out an audible breath, stepping away from his position by the captain's legs, but not before laying a protective hand upon the captain's knee. "Where are your buckets, sir, and the well? We'll need wood pieces for a splint. I fear his leg's broken." He met Margi's gaze. "The captain's a good man, ma'am."

She nodded. No doubt, there were hosts of good men fighting and dying in this war on both sides. Margi's fiancé' had been such a one. Dead nearly two years now, lost at Brandywine Creek, he'd fought with General Washington's army, leaving Margi's dreams to die with him. Margi considered war a cruel choice of men, despite its righteous cause. She prayed against the urge to damn them all. Mourning still, some days she couldn't remember Joseph's features clearly. But she continued to mourn the loss of her future.

The captain gave a low moan. Margi touched his arm, sliding her hand from wrist to elbow over the rough uniform fabric. Her thought was to soothe the man as she took a closer look at the bloodstains.

Her father and the redcoats had gone for buckets and to the well to fill them. Margi crossed the kitchen for her apron. They'd left her alone and the captain still breathed.

Charlotte bustled into the kitchen.

"What can I do for you, Margi?" Charlotte rubbed her hands together before tucking her hair up into her ruffled cap. "Oh," she stepped back, "the man's a British soldier. Why is he here?"

Recognizing the edge in Charlotte's voice, Margi glanced up while tying her apron. "We've not much choice. Papa's struck a bargain with the British major to save us and the farm. If the captain recovers, the soldiers will leave us be, only taking what grain and livestock as they need. If the captain dies, I suspect we'll be burned out."

"God no!" Charlotte whispered, staring at the man on the table. "Is he hurt badly?"

"I don't know yet. Will you help?" Margi asked.

Charlotte hesitated, a frown creasing her brow. "In truth, I should return upstairs. But, yes Margi, I will help you."

Grateful, Margi gave a nod and a weak smile. "The soldiers are outside with Papa. I should have had them remove the captain's coat and shirt. I'm sure he's received multiple wounds. We'll have to get his clothes off ourselves."

"Undress the man ourselves?" Charlotte's frown deepened.

Margi put out a hand to her sister-in-law. "I know, but it's got to be done." She blew out a breath, taking her place by the captain's shoulder.

"Ready?" Margi asked, rolling the unconscious man toward her.

Charlotte shrugged, moving beside Margi and gave the sleeve of the soldier's jacket a tentative tug.

"You'll need to pull harder than that," Margi said.

Charlotte looked up. "You're right." She gave the coat a vicious yank. The captain's arm slid from the sleeve, thumping onto the table. They rolled him together, both pulling the filthy, bloodstained coat from under him. Margi dropped it onto the floor before they tackled the shirt.

Made of fine linen, even stained as it was, Margi was reluctant to cause a tear. Removing it was not easy. Tedious and awkward, they managed to pull the shirt inch by inch up over the captain's chest and arms, finally lifting it over his head. Charlotte dropped the shirt on top of the captain's red coat.

"That's done." Margi drew a breath. "I see a shoulder wound but the blood has dried."

"That's good," Charlotte said. "I'm thinking I should have stayed in bed." She swiped a hand across her forehead. "Will he live, do you think?"

"I can't say. The major said the captain's wounds were grievous," Margi answered in a faint voice. Bent over the unconscious man, she scrutinized the captain's exposed chest for additional blood, signaling another, more serious bullet wound.

A bullet had pierced his shoulder, through and through. Margi saw nor felt any additional wounds through the film of grime covering his chest and belly.

A second bullet had grazed his head but didn't account for his lacerated hairline, which would likely need stitches. It looked to be a cruel gash. Blood still trickled down the captain's face and neck. Margi knew she could clean and stitch up the gash, then bind up his head and shoulder, but the soldiers who'd brought him to her could have done that. Biting her lip. Margi stood, thinking she was missing something.

"This soldier can't travel with a broken leg. They'll be leaving him." Margi spoke to herself.

Charlotte stared at her. "The British can't leave him."

Margi shrugged, feeling uneasy. "I need more light." She headed toward the fireplace and the tallow candle burning on the mantelpiece. "His breeks have to come off, and his boots."

Without a word, Charlotte set herself to tugging off the captain's boot. "There's one off," she announced, stooping to set it down.

"Margi," Charlotte's voice rose, "I see blood dripping beneath him, between the table's planks."

"God help us," Margi mumbled.

She set aside the candle to stoop and see for herself. Her stomach clenched. "Mercy, Charlotte, that's what I was afraid of."

Moving together in silence, they pulled off the other boot and Margi quickly unlaced his breeks.

"Let's turn him, the blood's coming from around his hip." Charlotte snatched the candle from the table Margi had set it on.

His breeks loosened. They turned the captain, seeing the bleeding wound in the fleshy part of his hip.

Margi snatched up a clean cloth, staunching the blood while Charlotte shoved another beneath him.

"Can you hold him, Charlotte? I've got to get that bullet out."

CHAPTER TWO

C HARLOTTE WENT WHITE. "HOLD HIM?"
At seeing the fear in Charlotte's eyes, Margi shook her head. "Not while I remove the bullet. I need to verify where the bullet is. Can you do that?"

Charlotte nodded.

Margi's mouth had gone dry, thinking of what she'd need to do.

She'd need the medical kit Doc Grove had left her. She'd only assisted the doctor in the removal of bullets, the last time days before he'd marched off with the Continentals. Margi needed to recall the process.

She pushed aside her doubts. The wounded captain needed her.

"Lay the captain down," Margi said, thinking there would be more stitching to do. "I'll need my kit and my sewing basket for needle and thread."

Mulling over where she'd put aside her sewing, Margi stepped away from the table, heading for the parlor.

"You stay with him, Margi." Charlotte crossed ahead of her. "The kit Doc Grove left is in the cupboard behind you. Your basket is by the settle. I noticed it before taking Jamie upstairs to bed." Babbling, Charlotte hurried over the threshold and into the hall.

Margi turned to her patient.

Feeling breathless, shyness mingled with hesitancy at the intimacy of their circumstances. She stared at the wounded man. Obviously tall, lean, with a broad chest and shoulders hardened with muscle, his unconscious state concerned her. Glancing toward the kitchen door, she willed her father to hurry. Margi was anxious to begin. Brushing the captain's dirty hair off his forehead, she vowed not to let the captain die.

Her medical kit was where Charlotte had said. Retrieving the carved wooden box, Margi set the kit beside the captain. Lifting the lid, she reached for the instruments, testing their weight before unrolling the soft flannel. Seeing the pieces laid out, she saw Doc Grove's actions in her mind and remembered the process.

Charlotte strode into the kitchen, her color back. "I checked on Jamie. He's fast asleep. Here's your sewing basket."

Margi took it, touching Charlotte's hand in thanks.

"Elias isn't back with the water?" Charlotte frowned. "What's keeping them?"

Margi shook her head. "I've put clean cloths in the cabinet. Will you get them?"

"Of course," Charlotte said.

The kitchen door flew open, letting in a cold night's draft that ruffled the bloody, matted hair on the captain's head. Gooseflesh pebbled across his torso and arms.

"Get a blanket, Charlotte, please."

Charlotte left the cloths and scurried off.

Her father hurried in behind the cold, carrying two brimming buckets, quickly dumping the water into a heavy iron cauldron. It hung alone in the fireplace from a long, iron crane set with hooks of varying heights to accommodate the family's cooking needs. The soldiers followed, lugging their wooden buckets and setting them by the fireplace. The soldiers rubbed their hands close to the crackling fire under the cauldron. Elias filled a smaller pot and added more wood to the flames beneath both pots.

Another look at the captain's pallor and Margi knew that waiting for the water to heat would take too long. The wounded man had made no movement since the soldiers had laid him on the farm table. Margi watched with barely suppressed impatience. Unwilling to waste any more time, she dropped a cloth into the icy water, gasping as her hands followed.

Wringing out the cloth with numb fingers, Margi hurried back to her patient. Charlotte had covered the captain to the waist with a blanket.

"He's not moved a muscle, Margi, has he?" her sister-in-law whispered.

"No." Margi's voice was barely audible as she risked a glimpse at the soldiers watching with tight-lipped censure.

She drew a sharp breath, assembling her thoughts.

"You'll bring him round, I'm sure," Charlotte assured her. "The soldiers left the wood for splints by the door."

"Good." Margi touched her cloth to the captain's face, wiping at the crusted blood edging the gash at his hairline, inches from his eye. He never moved.

"Will Captain Hamilton be all right?" asked the sharp-faced soldier.

"I can't say." Leveling her gaze at the soldier who had addressed her, she said, "There's a bullet in him. It needs to come out."

"Come out?" The soldier's face paled.

"I can see to his other wounds, but you'll need to remove his breeks so I can tend him," Margi said. "That bullet has to be removed. I can do it."

"A woman?" the paunchy soldier questioned.

"I can. Otherwise, he'll die," Margi said.

The soldiers looked at each other. The silence stretched.

Elias Blackwood crossed the room. "You brought your man to Blackwood Farm to have him cared for. My daughter can heal him. She's been an assistant to Doc Grove these last years. I would trust her with my life. You can trust her with your captain."

Touched by her father's sure confidence, she sent him a brief nod.

"She's a woman, sir. I'm afraid we couldn't have it," said a tall, beefy soldier with protruding eyes and a dubious frown.

Elias clucked his tongue. "Then your captain will die. I've opened my home to you. The decision is yours, gentlemen."

Elias went back to heating water while Margi's heart pounded and her fingers tingled to help the man, watching while the soldiers whispered, sending her anxious looks. She did not look away.

"You'd best let my sister-in-law save your captain. You've no one else," Charlotte said.

At that, the captain moaned, low and pain-filled.

"You say you can save him?" questioned the major.

"I will," Margi said, praying she hadn't lied.

The men exchanged looks with the major, nodding as one. "Save him." His jaw set, the major flushed redder than ever.

"You'll hold him." Margi's request came out as an order. The soldiers moved in, positioning themselves to hold the captain motionless. "Papa, I'll need hot water close to hand, please."

Elias set a full pail on a stool by her knee.

Margi probed his side, over his hip. The captain groaned and his eyelids fluttered.

"Hold his head up," Elias said. "Whisky will help dull the pain."

Seconds later, when the captain moaned, Elias tipped the bottle, pouring the contents into the captain's mouth. He coughed and sputtered, managing to swallow what Margi hoped would be enough to keep him still. The remainder coursed down his neck and chest, turning the dripping blood to the color of dusky whisky.

"Are you ready, girl?" Elias asked.

"I'm ready," she said, lifting the long tweezers.

Her father's calm steadied her. She pictured the bullet in her mind, where it lay in the captain's flesh. The instrument slid in quickly but, at her probing, the captain jerked, howling in protest. The soldiers, to a man, nearly lost their grip. Margi lost hers, but she'd felt the bullet. Her tweezers had slid over it. Biting her lip, she prayed to the heavens and probed again. This time, the captain went limp and Margi was grateful. She felt her tweezers close over the bullet. Intent in the moment, her hand steady, Margi drew out the bullet with one hand, while pressing clean cloths hard against the wound.

She heard the soldiers exhale.

Drawing a breath, Margi dropped the bullet onto the cloth Charlotte held. It made no sound. Margi offered a prayer of thanks as intense relief flooded through her. Raising her head, she smiled her first genuine smile since her father had awakened her.

"The captain will live now?" The major smiled at her.

Margi bit her lip. "I pray for it. We've the worry of fever. But, the bullet's out and the bleeding's contained. Now, I've the captain's leg to set."

The sharp-faced soldier stood over the captain. "We'll help with the splinting. He's unconscious. It's best we get it done so he can rest. Am I right?"

"Yes, you're right," Margi agreed.

The splinting had gone as well as could be expected. Roused by pain, the captain had screamed out several times before mercifully passing out.

Margi finished bathing and binding up the captain's remaining wounds. She wrapped clean bandages around his shoulder and head.

Elias and Charlotte took on the job of washing away the battle dirt and grime until Margi was satisfied the captain could be settled into a bedstead brought in from the barn and set up in a shadowed corner of the kitchen. Charlotte had contributed one of her husband's hand-sewn nightshirts.

Margi paused, holding Josiah's nightshirt over the injured man's head. The captain was beautifully formed, in face and body. Long-limbed and muscular, his broad shoulders filled the narrow bed. Clean, his hair blazed a rich chestnut, shot through with gold streaks in the firelight. The gash at his hairline would heal. She suspected any scar would give the captain a rakish air, like a pirate bent on plunder. No woman would be safe.

She observed him for minutes. His color was better, his breathing even and steady. But the captain would need watching. Margi prepared for an even longer night.

"Miss Blackwood, you've my gratitude," said the crinkle-eyed soldier, his concern illustrated by his big hand gentle on the captain's ankle.

"I am obliged to you, as are we all for saving our captain's life," said the major. "Like Edward here says, the captain is a good man."

"It's God who's saved him tonight. Tomorrow, pray again," Margi said.

The bearded, sharp-faced soldier offered his hand. "I thank you, ma'am."

Margi took his hand. "We'll take good care."

"I know you will." A broken front tooth showed through his beard. "Messengers will come with packets for the captain. Meantime, we need to get beyond Philadelphia into New York."

Elias held open the kitchen door. "I've brought your horses around. They've been fed and watered while the ladies tended the captain."

"I thank you, Mr. Blackwood," the major said. "Captain Hamilton lives. We've taken grain but none of your animals. The British Army thanks you. Your home shall remain undamaged. Should you have a need, I am Major Woodhouse. I remain at your service."

With a wave, the major mounted his horse and, turning the animal's head, trotted down Blackwood Farm's winding path, his men following.

Margi and Charlotte stood in the doorway, on either side of Elias Blackwood, watching the soldiers go.

Margi wiped her hands on her apron. The sky was no longer black, but streaked with inky purple. Dawn had broken. The captain had survived the night.

CHAPTER THREE

"HOW IS HE?" ELIAS ASKED, coming up beside Margi. She'd bent to tuck the quilt higher around the captain.

Dawn had not yet reached the darkened kitchen corner, where the captain lay in shadowed profile. His breathing was a little fast but even.

"Well enough," Margi answered. "But, we've days to get through yet. The captain is strong, Papa. That's in his favor."

Elias rested his hand on her shoulder. "You've brought the man through the night, girl. You'll bring him the rest of the way. I'm proud."

Margi twisted her head to meet her father's eyes, her chest tight with emotion at Elias' words. Pressing her cheek against his hand, she closed her eyes.

"Send her upstairs, Pa. Margi's about to topple over." Charlotte glanced up from her vigorous scrubbing of the farmhouse table.

"You've been up, the same as me, Charlotte. Go upstairs. Jamie will need your attention. I'm fine," Margi argued.

"No, Margi. Jamie has plans for the day. I'll have time to rest then," Charlotte said with a conspiring smile at Elias. "Let Margi rest," she urged. "I'll watch over the captain."

"The captain is my responsibility," Margi said.

Her father's calloused hands turned her by her shoulders, a question in his eyes. They were her eyes, holding the rich gold of topaz, ringed in black. Wolf eyes, the Scots called them, intelligent and startling.

"Will you go upstairs, Daughter?" Elias asked.

"No, Papa. I'll stay," Margi said.

Despite an aching back and eyes burning from fatigue, Margi would not leave the captain. Her father knew better than to insist she leave them to rest. Instead, he dragged over a chair, waiting for Margi to sit. Conceding, she sat down. Grateful to be off her feet, she drew a satisfied breath.

"Very well," Charlotte said. "I'll brew us tea."

"I'd be grateful for it, Charlotte," Elias said. "I'll be plowing till dark."

Margi turned, offering a faint smile. "I know. Jaimie's talked of nothing but the plowing for a week."

"Are you sure you want Jamie's help, Pa?" Charlotte's brows went up. "I worry he'll be more hindrance than help,"

"He's ten, Charlotte. Jamie did his part well enough last year." Elias chuckled. "Young Jamie will have help from the neighbor lads. You needn't worry."

"It's a woman's job to worry." Charlotte set down the cups. "I'll ask you now, Elias, while I've the courage."

"Ask me what, Daughter?"

Charlotte lowered her voice to a near whisper. "Blackwood Farm belongs to you. Josiah and I live with our son under your roof. Thus, you deserve our respect and obedience. You know you have mine. I will do whatever you ask."

"Yes?" Elias urged when she hesitated.

Charlotte traced a finger over the tabletop and drew a breath. "Your son, Josiah, is fighting with the Continentals. Yet, you open your doors to the British, even going so far as to have your daughter save your son's enemy's life. Why would you do it?"

Elias Blackwood did not answer right away, looking straight at his daughter-in-law and exhaling through his nose. "As my son's wife, Charlotte, you've the right to an answer. My father, Finlan Blackwood, came to America as a prisoner. He was spared but sent from his homeland as punishment for a defeated rebellion. He'd committed treason. He told me he'd come devoid of hope and found himself indentured for years to a good Quaker blacksmith who treated him well and with respect. That man had no enemies. My father earned his freedom. Coming as he did from Scotland, pacifism was foreign to him. But, the Quaker won out without so much as raising his voice. Every day, that man personified fairness and just consideration for views not his own. The Quaker judged not, but kept his own council. My father embraced the concept, telling me we've no real enemies, only differences of opinion."

"Pa, you can't believe these years of war are over a difference of opinion?" Charlotte's eyes grew wide, unbelieving.

"No, I don't," Elias said. "But, I see there is truth in the Quakers' outlook. When I can, I will avoid conflict. We live under one God. To that end, I'll hold my opinions as to rightness and I'll hold my fire.

"But your son believes otherwise," Charlotte said.

"Josiah's choice is his own, Charlotte. I'll not challenge him."

"Papa." Margi glanced at the rifle hanging over the fireplace, knowing her father's preferred action fell to the altruistic. "Your position is admirable but if Josiah returns before the captain leaves us, what will we tell him?"

"I will tell him what I've told Charlotte," Elias said.

Frowning, Charlotte prepared to pour the tea. "I will think on your words, Pa. Finlan Blackwood's beliefs sound lofty. We've much at stake and much to lose. Though Finlan's ideals are muddled in my mind with what we're living through, I'll accept them."

"Pa," Margi said, "surely you understand Josiah's stance. We've decades of farming this land, not for England, for ourselves and our community. Josiah says it's our hands that are calloused. It's our nails left cracked and bleeding. He thinks of himself as an American, with aspirations no longer tied to England. Those fighting for independence see a different future with a voice in writing laws, solely responsible for our labor without directives from a king."

"Aye, Margi," Elias said. "I know where my son's loyalties lie and I don't disagree. Neither do I consider all Englishman my enemy."

"Charlotte, you'd best leave our father to explain to Josiah and pray he stays away while the captain's healing," Margi said.

A shout from the bed startled them all.

The captain gave a pain-filled cry. Margi jumped to her feet, her body tensing at the sight of the injured man struggling to rise but falling back into the pillow. His eyes flew open.

Margi managed to avoid his flailing hands. Seeing his unfocused eyes, she realized the captain recognized nothing. She seized both his hands, holding them with what strength she had, murmuring calming words.

"Captain Hamilton," she whispered, "listen to me. You've been hurt. Your men have brought you here to Blackwood Farm for safety. I've treated your wounds and set your leg. You need to rest. There's no war here."

What was she thinking? War surrounded them.

They seemed the right words. The captain ceased his struggling and closed his eyes. As she pulled up the quilt, settling him, Margi realized the captain had opened his eyes and they were fixed on hers. He stared from bruised and swollen eyes of the darkest blue. Margi held his gaze for a long moment, the intensity of his gaze pulling her into a realization of her own deepest need.

Feeling color rise in her cheeks at their close proximity, her body tingled. She was grateful for the quilt between them. Margi straightened, taking her hands away. The captain's gaze, no longer unfocused, held hers.

"Are you real?" he asked, his voice deep and raspy.

Her chin came up. "I'm real enough."

He responded with a wince of pain. "How long have I been here?"

"Your men brought you in the night," Margi answered, surprised at his sudden alertness.

A frown creased the part of his forehead not hidden by the bandage. "I don't see them."

"They stayed until I told them you'd heal," she said.

"You told them to leave?" he asked.

Margi wanted to laugh at the thought. "A contingent of six British soldiers? I'm afraid you've transferred more power to me than I possess. Your men held to their duty and left you to us."

The captain rose a few inches, leaning on his undamaged arm. "You say you tended my wounds, set my leg. None of those are small feats."

His breath hitched as a spasm of pain crossed his face. She watched him struggle through it, before managing a lopsided smile.

"I expect you would not hesitate to order my men," he suggested.

Margi cocked her head. "I'll not disagree, Captain."

The captain drew an audible breath. "Ah, tis a rare gift, indeed, to come across a modest woman."

Margi shook her head and bent to tuck the quilt over his shoulders. "You're teasing me. I'd say that's a good sign. You couldn't have ridden anywhere. They're off to New York. I told them you needed care and rest."

"You'll be caring for me?" His mouth curved into a droll smile, until his lips tightened when a pain jolted him.

"Rest now," she whispered.

While smoothing the covers, Margi noticed his speech slowing while his breathing came faster. His spurt of strength had begun to ebb. She watched him in silence for a full minute. Pleased to see good color return to his face, she smiled back. "You're strong, Captain Hamilton. You'll be feeling better soon."

The captain looked to be turning something over in his mind. She found herself absorbed with watching the lines of his face sharpen as they emerged from the night's shadows while the sun rose. Without thinking, she laid a hand over his before leaving him to ponder, needing to distract herself from an attraction so sudden it stunned her.

His name, heard once, had come easily to her lips. *Who was he?* An enemy of sorts, despite what her father had said. Yet, within hours, Margi found herself quite liking the man.

Perhaps the earlier dose of whisky had done its job. He'd been coherent and talking. But, the captain would soon feel the pain. Margi poured the forgotten tea for him, adding what herbs she had to ease pain.

Captain Hamilton had raised his hand, tentatively fingering the swathe of bandage before looking at her. "I can't remember it all. I'm confused. It's hazy in my mind. I felt a searing pain, then burning. I was sure I'd been hit in my side. I fell from my horse…" His voice trailed off.

"Oh, you were hit," Margi said. "The bullet dropped you from your horse, breaking your leg."

"I've a bullet in me?" He lifted his shoulders off the bed.

Margi set the tea cup on the floor and pushed him back gently. "I removed it. Now, you'll heal."

"You?" His eyes widened.

"I did," she said. "Now, drink the tea and sleep. That's a story for another time."

CHAPTER FOUR

BUNCHING THE PILLOW, MARGI HELPED the captain to a sitting position and held the cup to his lips.

"It's hot," he said, wrinkling his nose and sounding like a five-year-old child.

"Of course, it's hot. It's tea," she said. "Drink it down. It will ease the pain."

He drank, then gave her a curious look. "You're a bit of an amazement."

"Am I?" She lifted a brow, wrapping his hand around the cup. "Finish your tea. You can sleep on the thought."

"Sleep on it?" he repeated.

"My gran told me tea is good for what ails you."

"And... you'll tend... me?" His words came with effort.

"Yes, Captain. I'll tend you. Now sleep." She took the cup from his hand.

Tired as she was, the captain's efforts at chat had energized her. Margi knew Captain Hamilton needed to rest but she wanted to hear what else he might say to her.

His eyes were already drooping. She watched them close as he slipped into what she hoped would be a healing slumber.

Minutes later, her eyes grew heavy. The captain's even breathing was the last sound she heard. Until. . . .

"Grandfather, have you breakfast ready?"

Margi jerked awake.

The high-pitched voice of her ten-year-old nephew pealed into the kitchen. Her gaze fixed on the unconscious captain. He never stirred.

"Aye, Jamie. Your mum's about to drop the eggs. Will you have one or two?" Elias called from the fireplace with a wide smile as his grandson swung around the doorsill on a run, his nightshirt flapping around his knees.

"Two, please," he said without slowing. "I'm plowing today."

"James Josiah Blackwood, since when has your grandfather prepared your breakfast?" Charlotte dropped two eggs into a frying pan in the fireplace. "It's me or Aunt Margi who does the cooking in this house."

Jamie shook his head. "We've plowing to get to, Mum. Grandfather fries the bacon. My pa says men fry bacon on the trail all the time. There are no mothers or aunts to cook for them."

"I'll not argue the boy's logic," Elias said, laughing.

"Jamie takes after his father," Charlotte answered, sliding the eggs onto a plate. "Take your place at the table, Son, then eat. You'd best go back upstairs and dress yourself warm if you're plowing this morning. Grandfather's finished his breakfast. He's not about to wait once he's set to go."

Jamie slid into his seat. Charlotte set his eggs in front of him before he'd picked up his fork. "I'll be quick, Ma."

Elias stood with his empty plate in hand.

"Wait for me, Grandfather." Jamie wolfed down the eggs before snatching a handful of greasy bacon waiting on a platter.

"Jamie!" Charlotte admonished.

Jamie crunched into the piece he'd shoved into his mouth, scanning the room for an ally.

"Aunt Margi, tell my ma I've no time to sit proper. My grandfather's waiting," He flittered around the farm table, barely glancing at either his mother or his aunt, edging up the kitchen steps, and stuffing the remainder of his bacon into his mouth.

"Jamie, come back this minute," Charlotte called.

Margi looked at her sister-in-law, then at her nephew. "Jamie, you'd best listen to your mother. Sit at the table and finish your breakfast. Grandfather will wait."

"Well?" Elias teased.

Hesitating but poised to bolt, Jamie swung his gaze from his grandfather to his mother.

Margi rose from her chair by the captain's bedside.

Jamie's eyes went wide at seeing the bed and form beneath the covers.

"Pa!" He hurled himself off the two steps, barreling toward the occupied bed, his eyes alight.

Margi's heart dropped.

His curls bounced over his forehead. Jamie's hands closed around the iron bedstead, stopping his momentum. "Who the hell is he?" Jamie squawked.

CHAPTER FIVE

*W*HO INDEED?
Captain William Roger Hamilton, of His Majesty's Light Dragoons, did not respond to Jamie's indelicate inquiry. He remained dead to the world, sleeping through the remainder of that day and missing the Blackwood's rather awkward explanations for why a wounded British officer was asleep in their kitchen.

Elias had explained it thusly: "Until this war is won, the king is still our king. God expects us to care for all who need our help. Do you understand, Jamie?"

"Aye." Jamie answered, suspicion written across his face.

"That's good, boy," Elias said.

"Grandfather?" Jamie's eyes were fixed on Elias' face. "When will God tell us which side he's on?"

Not nearly soon enough.

(

This early April morning, Margi dug her hands deep into the soil of a flower bed, letting it sift through her fingers, feeling the anticipation of warmer weather and more daylight. Spring had come to Blackwood Farm, warming the frozen earth from winter's biting chill. The mill wheel turned as the sound of rushing water heralded spring. The war appeared distant.

Margi continued to dig, dropping seeds as a dark cloud stole across the sun, leaving its chill behind as the sun disappeared. Margi shivered. Not much had changed since the British fled Philadelphia. The two armies battled on with no clear path for either the British or the American's to be seen as certain victors. News remained sporadic. Impasse appeared to be the general consensus as clashes continued around Pennsylvania. Citizens were worn to the bone. The family had heard nothing from Josiah or his regiment.

Margi sighed. Her optimism had begun to fade. Work on Blackwood Farm continued. Spring planting had always buoyed her spirits, giving her renewed hope. A warming breeze stirred the hair Margi had tied low on her neck. Busy with planting, she let out a sigh. Her hands stilled. She lifted her head to the sun's warmth, remembering Captain Hamilton's first night at Blackwood Farm. The captain remained, becoming integral to the farm's success. Margi had learned to appreciate his kindness and generosity. British or not, Margi found him a welcomed companion.

Weeks later, Captain Hamilton was healing nicely, surviving his wounds, as well as the inevitable fever that shook him within a week of his arrival. Stomach knotted tight, forgoing sleep until the fire and delirium gripping him had passed, Margi had remained by his side. If the captain awoke weakened from his ordeal, Margi found herself left weaker. She'd finally dropped into the sleep of the exhausted.

She had saved the captain's life.

The memory of those days drifted through her mind as Margi tried unsuccessfully to stifle the surge of pride flowing through her. Pride was a sin.

Pressing her hands against her lower back, she drew a deep breath and stretched. Did fondness for Captain Hamilton mean the Blackwoods were traitors?

Jamie's excited whoop echoed across the front lawn, from the side of the stone and clapboard farmhouse. Rising, she shook out her skirt and brushed dirt from her hands, unable to hide her smile at seeing her nephew carom around the side of the house.

Following behind, her father walked with Captain Hamilton, who swung along on the crutches Elias had fitted for him. Despite crutches, Hamilton's bearing held profound self-assurance as, broken leg notwithstanding, he crossed the space.

The corners of the captain's mouth lifted at the sight of her. A near forgotten sweetness drifted through her, warm and honeyed like the spring air. Returning his smile, Margi marveled at how effortless his movement was. Hamilton would bear no lingering limp once he'd put aside his crutches.

A draft of air ruffled the hair curling over his forehead. Liking the bold, clean look of him, Margi knew her expression warmed at the sight. Dressed in a homespun shirt and an old pair of Josiah's breeks, the yellow bruising was gone from around his eyes. Margi longed to know more of what thoughts dwelled behind his fathomless blue eyes. With her father so near, she dropped her gaze to avoid his noticing.

"Pa, it's warming earlier than I'd thought. We'll have a fine garden, I think."

Her father's big hand closed around her shoulder. "My girl's gifted with a green thumb. Her gardens are a glory every year. I hope you'll be at Blackwood Farm to see them, Captain."

Hamilton nodded at them both. "Seeing your gardens would be a pleasure. I see shoots sprouting already." Hamilton looked at her, holding her gaze. "If I've gone, I'll return to see your garden, Miss Blackwood."

Heat suffused her cheeks. She told herself it was the noonday sun. "You are most kind, Captain. But, I'm afraid my father exaggerates."

At the thought of his leaving, an unexpected pain sliced through her.

Hamilton gave a low chuckle. "I've no doubt your garden will be glorious. I've meant to expand my knowledge of horticulture. I'm afraid I'm sadly lacking in that area."

Hamilton's gaze never left her face. Mesmerized, Margi couldn't look away, content to drown in the wild blue intensity of his gaze.

"You're teasing me."

"Not at all, Miss Blackwood. What I say, I mean."

Putting voice to her fears, Margi looked away. "You'll be leaving us soon, Captain. Once you are gone from here, thoughts of horticulture and gardens will be far from your mind."

"Ahem," Elias cleared his throat. "My thoughts are on Captain Hamilton's suggestions for the mill. I'm much obliged. He's a gift for construction, you know, and an eye to business as well."

"I didn't know," Margi said.

"You'd do well to listen more, Daughter. Right now, a bite of food is in order, then we're back to work."

Margi opened her mouth in protest but checked the impulse with a sidelong glance at the captain's smile of pleasure at her father's words of approval. Elias clapped the captain's good shoulder before heading up the slope of lawn, his lengthy stride eating up the grassy expanse. At the porch, he stopped. Lifting his hands to his hips with his battered felt hat pushed back on his head, Elias stood staring up at the porch roof.

Turning, he cupped both hands around his mouth. "We've got carpentry repairs here. Good thing we milled those extra planks," he called out.

"My leg's stronger every day, Mr. Blackwood," Hamilton called.

Elias' voice boomed. "Good. I'll expect the roof fixed by the end of the week." He disappeared through the open front door.

Eyeing Hamilton, Margi breathed in and out. "You'd better not be expecting to be climbing ladders and fixing roofs." She gripped the captain's wrist. "You're not strong enough. You'll not disregard all I did to save you."

Hamilton's eyes narrowed. Jaw tight, he stared at her.

Margi felt the weight of her words, ashamed of the panic making her speak so. She had no desire to see him hurt again. He would ignore her at his peril. Captain Hamilton had arrived at Blackwood Farm a stranger, a British soldier with a life different than her own. *And now?*

Hamilton had become something more. She thought of him in the dead of night before sleep took her. Margi refused to admit her growing attraction, promising herself she'd keep an emotional distance. But her vow was becoming harder to adhere to. She swallowed over the thought that perhaps it was best he leave.

"At the risk of repeating myself, Miss Blackwood, you are an amazement!"

Margi lifted her chin. "So you've said. And, I believe I asked, am I?"

He gave a startled laugh. "You did, I remember. You put me to sleep with tea. You've not a cup hidden somewhere, have you?"

When Hamilton balanced on his crutches to lean in, peeking over her shoulder, her breath caught. So close, his scents of new grass and sunshine weakened her knees.

She stiffened. "I've no tea with me," she said in a voice hardly recognizable as hers.

"I see." Straightening, Hamilton held her gaze with a puckish grin.

She laughed.

"There's the sound I listen for each day," he said. "Be assured, I'll not endanger myself. Weeks in bed are detriment enough." Dropping his crutches, Hamilton offered his arm.

Margi had stooped for the crutches.

"Leave them," Hamilton said.

Surprised, she'd slid her arm through his. Walking slowly beside him, she felt the warmth of his body heat hers.

"I know what you've done for me, Miss Blackwood. It's likely, I'd have died. I know it well."

She hadn't known.

"I've been walking without crutches since last week," Hamilton explained.

He looked utterly pleased with himself. Margi hid her astonishment by offering nothing more than a nod.

"The walk to the mill is a near mile," he continued. "Your pa suggested the crutches. It was to be a surprise, you know, my walking."

"A surprise," she repeated. "You're so well then?"

"I am well, thanks to you," he said.

Smile fixed, her heart dropped. Hamilton would go back to his men.

"Not to worry, Miss Blackwood." His look was intent. "I'll not be leaving quite yet. I'm still unsteady on my feet."

Stumbling for effect, he wobbled against her. Without thought, Margi's arm slid around his waist while his arm went around her. "Careful," she warned.

"I'm always careful, Miss Blackwood." His arm tightened.

His low laugh sent a shiver of anticipation down her spine. She shifted, giving her time to breath.

It was all she could think to do as they slow-walked up the slope. She offered her strength. Margi had seen Hamilton naked, her hands sliding over his muscled body as she'd covered him with cold cloths when he shivered, lost in fever or bathing away grimy sweat. Yet, their walk to the house felt far more intimate with his body leaning into hers, his warmth enveloping her while his breath rippled through her hair. Margi realized she'd fallen in love with Captain Hamilton. At the stunning realization, she stumbled over a jutting rock.

Hamilton's hand splayed across her middle as he drew her tighter against him. "Miss Blackwood," he rasped, "watch your footing. You are keeping me upright. Hubris led me to believe I was further along the road to recovery."

They'd reached the top of the slope with both of them panting. He was drained from the morning's exertions. She was straining from his weight and fighting her need for more of his heat.

A husky hoarseness colored the voice in her ear. "Please know," he said, "I stand corrected."

Margi smiled, urging Hamilton up the porch steps, indicating several hand-hewn chairs. "We'll sit," she said. "It's best."

He straightened to his full height. "Miss Blackwood, much as I long to lower myself onto a chair on this porch, I'm not lacking manners. Seat yourself. When you're comfortable, I'll be pleased to join you."

He swayed. Margi jumped to steady him, quickly taking her seat before Hamilton keeled over.

Over time, they'd become easy with each other. From the first days, Margi had experienced his kindness. Especially Hamilton's generosity to Jamie. Missing his father, the two had bonded after Jamie had taken his grandfather's words to heart. Willing to help, Jamie spent hours at Hamilton's bedside, always ready with a distraction.

Despite the pain Margi had read on Hamilton's face, for Jamie, Hamilton's smile may have been forced and his enthusiasm mustered with effort, but never once did Hamilton send Jamie away. Rewarded for his efforts, Hamilton took his first tentative steps with the assistance of a crutch under one arm and a proud and grinning Jamie under the other.

Sitting together in the quiet, content in silence, Margi's mind drifted.

Once Hamilton became comfortable on his crutches, to her astonishment, Elias had shown Hamilton his blueprints for the house he hoped to build. Margi had watched on a spring's afternoon as, heads together, they poured over the diagrams. She'd served them tea which they'd not touched.

She'd discovered Hamilton had studied architecture before taking a commission in the military. Hamilton had confided his disappointment, explaining that accepting the commission held the better option, given his position as a second son. Her father had nodded, a reminder of shared disappointments not considered during war.

"When do you expect your garden to bloom, Miss Blackwood? I regret my time here is coming to an end."

He'd leaned over, to rest his arms, touching hers, drawing her away from her thoughts.

"I expected as much." Margi forced a shaky smile, glancing away. "The gardens should be at their best in July. You'll be gone by then."

"I will return to see your gardens," Hamilton said. "On my honor, I promise you that."

Margi's heart jumped. She prayed it was so.

It was too soon for him to think of leaving. Margi vowed if he went, she would send him off with a smile and prayers for his safety.

Hamilton promised to return. Margi would focus on that.

She closed her eyes, hearing the titters and chirp of jays over the quiet. Restless in her thoughts, she set her chair rocking with a push of her foot.

She heard his slow intake of breath. He'd taken his arms away. Opening her eyes, Hamilton was staring at the rotted timbers holding up the porch roof. She recognized his expression, familiar and much like her father's when assessing a repair. Despite herself, she smiled.

Without looking at her, Hamilton spoke. "I'll be at Blackwood Farm for a time yet. That wood's gone soft." Lowering his gaze to hers, he smiled, like he'd read her mind. "You've a bigger job here than expected, surely more than a week, I'd say."

Margi's heart lifted as her lips curved in a smile. "We appreciate your help, Captain. More's the work with Josiah gone. I'd not expected this war to last years."

"With no end in sight, it appears." He leaned forward, scanning hills that rolled one into another across the four compass points. "You've much land with no tenants to cultivate the acres. The process is new to me."

"How is that? You've farms in England," Margi said.

"We do," Hamilton said. "Croppers work the land. They plant, tend and harvest. In return, we give them dwellings and small plots for their use. Of course, the tenants have rent to pay but the estates serve to provide them sustenance."

Frowning, Margi said, "I'm not seeing your process as altogether fair."

Hamilton shrugged. "Perhaps, but that's been the way of it. Each to their place."

"There's the crux of my brother's argument," she countered.

"What are you saying?" he asked.

Margi stopped rocking and turned her body to face him. "It seems a reasonable accommodation but what of a man's ambition, his willingness to work harder for a larger reward? Why should a man remain the whole of his life confined in the station he was born to? Josiah and my father spoke often of men deserving a choice."

Hamilton shoved a hand through his hair. "I've had such thoughts after being sent to the colonies. But, I fear such a change is impossible. Royalty's right to rule would never allow it. A king will not give up his power to a cropper working his land."

Margi nodded with real regret. "I fear you're right. Still, I do love the thought of freedom without constraints."

Not hiding his surprise, Hamilton looked at her. "I hadn't believed women had such thoughts."

"And why is that, pray tell?" Margi teased. "Perhaps, because that's been the way of it, each to their place?"

"Touché, Miss Blackwood."

They stared at each other, as though coming to agreement.

CHAPTER SIX

"CAPTAIN HAMILTON, AUNT MARGI!" JAMIE'S high-pitched shout rang out. "Look up!"

They both looked toward the sound.

"Here! I'm up here," Jamie hollered.

Rising, Margi's lips tightened, eyeing the captain. "Do you hear that? Jamie knows he's not to climb trees. He fell out of one last year, managing to knock himself out and break his wrist."

"A boy can't resist a tree, Miss Blackwood."

Her eyes narrowed. "His mother's warned him."

"I'm sure." He rose to follow. "I would suggest her warning has yet to enter his head. A tree to climb is an irresistible lure. I was much the same."

Margi shook her head at him.

"Jamie's up there," Hamilton said.

Margi held his gaze for moment enough to recognize a certain forbearance at her ignorance of boys and trees.

Pointing, he prodded her with a nudge at her waist while she questioned her suitability as Jamie's aunt. She should know such things about her only nephew.

Scanning the trees, she spied Jamie and gasped, her heart giving a convulsive leap at seeing the boy so high in the tallest tree within a stand of tall trees.

"Jamie, what are you doing?" she shrieked.

"Being a boy, fierce and fearless." Admiration colored Hamilton's voice.

Ignoring Hamilton, Margi ran down the porch steps across the grass, stopping at the foot of a massive tree. "Come down here, right now," she ordered.

Newly leafed branches rustled as her nephew hung upside down with his knees bent over a bough, grinning in diabolical delight. "Aunt Margi, I'm watching the road, scouting for soldiers. No one's coming."

"James Josiah, get down before your mother sees you."

From high above, Jamie shook his head. "I'm on watch," he argued. "If I see someone, I'll sound a warning."

Margi swore she heard a low chuckle from Hamilton.

Swallowing her fear, and frustrated, she tried logic. "Jamie, you cannot see anything upside down. Come down. You'll frighten your mother."

"I can't. It's my watch," Jamie insisted.

"Come along down, boy," Hamilton urged. "Do as your aunt says. You've kept us safe this morning."

Then came the crack of a branch and a frenzied rustle of leaves.

"Jamie!" Her hand shading her eyes, Margi couldn't see through the thick leaves and branches. "Answer me!"

"Are you all right up there, James?" Hamilton called.

More rustling of lower branches, Margi squinted to see, afraid to blink. "I won't fall." The voice drifted from the trees. "I climb trees all the time."

"Good heavens," Margi uttered.

Hamilton had lifted the leg Margi knew was not completely healed. Searching for purchase, his booted toe upon the tree trunk, she touched his arm. .

"Don't," she whispered. "He'll come down."

"Jamie, your aunt and I are waiting. Your mother's near to serving dinner," Hamilton cajoled. "I think I smell pie."

He and Margi exchanged looks. Shrugging, Hamilton raised a brow. "I'm coming," Jamie called.

Throat tight, Margi watched as Jamie became visible, lowering himself from one branch to another. Just as Margi was about to breathe again, Jamie paused, locking his legs around another branch to search the long road. He swung with arms outstretched, while his shirt dropped to cover his chin and nose.

"Another look, Captain," Jamie hailed from above their heads. "If someone's coming, we'll know in time to sound a warning."

"We'll wait." Hamilton's smile was conciliatory. "You'll make a fine scout. Take your final scope and come down with your report."

Margi rolled her eyes.

"What's going on out here?" Charlotte swung across the front yard, wiping her hands on her apron.

Neither Margi nor Hamilton responded.

Her nephew scrambled down as Margi watched.

"You'd best slither your way down this tree trunk quickly, your mum's across the grass." She lifted her arms to catch him.

"I'll do it myself, Auntie." Jamie's feet reached the lowest limb, his face shinning with accomplishment as he slid down the tree trunk. Feet on the ground, Jamie turned with military precision. "We're safe, sir. Our road's empty."

"Excellent job." Hamilton gripped the boy's shoulders with both hands. "You've a place in my company when you're old enough."

Jamie beamed.

Charlotte's hand closed around Jamie's arm. "I'm not so fond of my son wearing a red coat," Charlotte softened her comment with a smile. "Jamie's to be a farmer like his father."

Hamilton acknowledged her comment with a slight bow, dropping his hands from Jamie's shoulders. "I concede to a mother's hopes, Mrs. Blackwood. Jamie will do you proud farming Blackwood Farm."

Charlotte tightened her grip on her son's arm until he looked at her. "Jamie, you were in my view the whole time. You are not so safe from discipline, young man. Climbing that tree and to such a height, I couldn't speak for the pounding of my heart watching you. You've frightened me, along with your aunt and Captain Hamilton"

At seeing Jamie's smile fade, Margi moved closer to Hamilton, thinking to take his arm and walk back to the porch, saving her nephew from embarrassment at being chastised in the company of a man he hero-worshipped. She caught Charlotte's eye.

Charlotte indicated with a scant shake of her head they remain. "Jamie, I want Captain Hamilton and Aunt Margi to hear what I'm telling you."

Jamie kept his eye on his mother.

"I will tell you, Son," she said, "both farmers and soldiers need to think. Always. Whether a farmer plows his field or a soldier keeps good watch, thinking through what's expected of you is as much the job as physical strength. It falls to you to protect yourself as well as those within any company you are part of. You did not think today, James Josiah." Charlotte's gaze swung to the captain. "It's important, is it not,

Captain?"

"It is, young Jamie," the captain answered. "Your mother's right. Do you understand what she's telling you?"

"I do, sir. More likely my grandfather will explain it all to me again, so I'll remember and think when I've the impulse to please myself." He looked at his mother. "It's sure I thought of only myself this morning. I wanted to help. I'm sorry, Ma." He hung his head.

"You're a good boy, Jamie," Charlotte said, ruffling his hair. "I'll tell grandfather to go easy. You were trying to help. I trust none of us will see you swinging from trees in the future. Now, go wash up. Dinner's waiting."

A smile broke across his face as Jamie turned on his heel. Margi suspected he'd be back to climbing within a week.

"Captain!" Jamie gave a leap and a shout, pointing. "A rider's coming!"

Sure enough, an unknown rider, his hat pulled low over his forehead, galloped up the dirt road.

Margi squinted into the glare. There was something familiar about the rider, but as close as he galloped, Margi could not name the man. A glance at Hamilton caught his face tightening as he watched the approach. The two men were acquainted. Wondering at their connection, she walked down the slope of lawn to greet the horseman.

"Can I help you, sir?" The rider pulled up his horse, staring down at her as she waited along the grassy edge of the road.

"Miss Blackwood, ma'am, I'm here to speak to Captain Hamilton." He snatched the hat from his head. "Do you remember me?"

Margi gazed up at the man's sharp eyes and sharper features, and remembered. "Yes, yes, I do. You brought the captain to Blackwood Farm."

"My name is Nathaniel Bartlett," he said. "I'd not said as much when we left the captain. The situation was urgent. Forgive me."

Nodding, she said, "The captain's healing well."

"I see. He's looking better than when we left him. We're in your debt, ma'am."

Mr. Bartlett stared past her. Margi turned while the captain swung toward them, his crutches under his arms.

Would the British be calling him back to his company? It was too soon. Margi swallowed around the tightening of her throat.

"Bartlett, what is it?" Captain Hamilton asked.

"I need a word, sir," Bartlett said.

On crutches, Captain Hamilton's hand slid absently down Bartlett's horse's neck and was rewarded with a contented whinny. "You'll have it, Nathaniel. But, can you wait? We were about to sit down for the noon meal."

"I'll wait, Captain." Bartlett gazed toward the stable, then looked at Margi. "Could I water my horse, ma'am?"

"Please do." She waved in the stable's direction. "Forgive my manners, Mr. Bartlett. Water your horse and join us. Can you spare the time?"

Bartlett looked at Captain Hamilton, who nodded.

A smile turned his serious affect into an expression of earnest kindness. "It would be my pleasure, Miss Blackwood."

❦

The ham and biscuits consumed, Margi busied herself clearing the table of the empty plates. Hamilton and Mr. Bartlett had removed themselves from the house, presumably for privacy. From the kitchen window, Margi watched them cross the backyard together. It occurred to her that Mr. Bartlett had arrived not dressed in his uniform. *Why?* He could have been a neighbor come for advice on late spring planting.

Watching the two, deep in conversation, more questions rose than had been answered during their meal.

Mr. Bartlett had gobbled the ham and sweet potatoes in such quantity, Margi nearly asked how long it had been since he'd eaten. She'd remained silent, however. She listened as her father suggested the war could not continue with England battling with France and Spain rattling their sabers. King George had no choice but to concede to America on a number of demands. England needed the moneys coming in a steady stream from America. Either way, Elias planned to farm his land. Whatever the outcome, the farm would prevail. Margi doubted an outcome so simple.

Charlotte passed her a dripping dish to dry as Margi's mind swirled.

She looked at her sister-in-law. "Captain Hamilton will be leaving us soon."

Charlotte paused, lifting her hands from the soapy water. "He's still using his crutches, Margi. He'll be here for a time yet."

Margi frowned, eyeing her sister-in-law. "I only worry Captain Hamilton will hurt himself if he leaves too soon."

"Of course you do, why else?" Charlotte said.

"Nothing I can think of." Margi closed the subject.

Charlotte sighed. "Much as I long to see Josiah home and safe, I've no wish to be party to an encounter between the captain and my husband."

Margi read the agony Charlotte hid so well, feeling an answering pang for her sister-in-law's suffering. "It's been hard for you, Charlotte. I'm sorry. I forget sometimes."

Setting her dish on the table, Margi squeezed Charlotte's wet hand and saw her eyes well.

Charlotte blinked, pulling her hand out of Margi's grasp. "Pay me no mind." She swiped at her eyes. "The feelings come on so sudden, with no warning. Having British soldiers here when Josiah fights them, tears at me. Elias' attitude is hard to understand but I respect him. Blackwood Farm is my home and Jamie's. I've no thought to which way I lean. Am I disloyal to your father or Josiah?"

"You couldn't be disloyal to anyone," Margi said, her heart full. "Charlotte, you're more a sister to me than I deserve. Father's not an easy man to understand. To your credit, you understand him better than I do."

Charlotte said nothing but offered a faint smile.

Margi picked up a platter to dry, realizing she had not thought so much on the conundrum her sister-in-law lived with. Margi had been influenced by her father's stance on the war and, more so, after her fiancé's falling at Brandywine. Neither agreeing nor disagreeing with this war, her thoughts would remain her own. Margi refused to take a side. And she would accept the terms of whichever side won. She told herself it didn't matter.

"Margi," Charlotte said, "you'll rub the design right off that platter. Your words are kind. I've had a moment of weakness that is all. I'm grateful you were the one to hear it."

"You can talk to me, Charlotte. I love you and my brother. I've not thought enough about what this war has taken from you. I'm pained to have been so selfish."

"Some nights, I ache for him," Charlotte blurted. "I see him coming up the road, or in the stables currying our horses, but he's never there." A single tear rolled down her cheek. "Margi, it's often my thoughts become indelicate."

Margi watched the blush rise to ride Charlotte's cheeks.

"I'd thought to be a married woman by now, with a child," Margi confessed. "I have those feelings without having experienced the joy of them. I couldn't imagine which one is the worse predicament."

Unexpectedly, Charlotte laughed. "I'd say our predicaments are much the same. I'd not thought of it. I'm comforted knowing, maid or no, you understand."

"We're of a mind, then," Margi said. "I've had other thoughts today."

"About Captain Hamilton's leaving," Charlotte suggested.

"It's that, yes," Margi said. "There's more, especially today. I'd like your thoughts."

"All right. Tell me." Charlotte glanced out the kitchen window before sliding into a chair at the table and indicated Margi do the same.

Margi clasped her hands on the farm table. "What did you think of Captain Hamilton's reaction to our visitor?"

Charlotte frowned. "What do you mean?"

"Well," Margi hesitated. "I've had a feeling..." She unclasped her hands. "Captain Hamilton is off his crutches. Yet, he used them when Mr. Bartlett showed up."

Charlotte shrugged. "Maybe Captain Hamilton was tired. It could be as simple as that."

"I don't know." Margi closed her eyes. "I felt Captain Hamilton was suggesting his leg was still mending."

"It is, isn't it?" Charlotte countered.

Margi nodded.

She dropped her gaze from Charlotte's searching look. "You don't want Captain Hamilton to leave Blackwood Farm, do you?"

"Honestly? I can't say. Some days, I cannot bear the thought. Nights, I think only of him. We've grown close." Margi blew out a breath, her words coming fast. "I fear my feelings, Charlotte. Sometimes, I wish he'd never come here"

Charlotte folded her hand over Margi's. "Oh, Margi dear, you've fallen in love with Captain Hamilton."

"No! I can't." Margi jumped from the table, her voice rising. "My feelings aren't love. I know nothing about him but that he's a British officer. And, I'm questioning even that."

Surprised, Charlotte asked, "Why? What has he done?"

"There's something not right in all this." Margi took her seat. "Did you notice while we were eating, Mr. Bartlett spoke differently than Hamilton?"

"How?" Charlotte asked.

"Pronunciation and cadence mostly. Mr. Bartlett hasn't as strong an accent as Captain Hamilton. And why was he not in uniform?" Margi got up and began to pace.

"I hadn't thought, until you've mentioned it. But, you're right. Mr. Bartlett speaks more like we do."

"You see?"

It was Charlotte's turn to nod. "Bartlett wore no uniform when he came to see Captain Hamilton a month ago. On his visits before that, I don't remember if he was in uniform."

Margi stopped her pacing. "What did you say? When did Mr. Bartlett come here? I never saw him. No one told me."

"Mr. Bartlett's been here several times over the last few months. I'd forgotten. He didn't stay long enough for me to mention it. I'm sorry."

"No need to apologize," Margi said. "Now, I've more questions."

"Ask the captain," Charlotte said with irrefutable logic.

She would not ask the captain. There were uncharted currents swirling but Margi would be more watchful, discovering the truth on her own. Who was Captain William Hamilton and why was he really at Blackwood Farm?

CHAPTER SEVEN

"WHAT'S THE NEWS?" CAPTAIN HAMILTON asked. Bartlett moved deeper into the woods surrounding Blackwood Farm. He stood at attention while Captain Hamilton leaned against the bark of a tall maple tree. The war they would discuss seemed a long way off. The captain signaled Bartlett to speak.

"There's little, I'm afraid," Bartlett said. "Washington's on the road. The action's moved to New Jersey and the south. I don't trust the quiet."

"Where's General Washington?" Captain Hamilton asked.

"There's talk of troops moving south into the Carolinas and Georgia to cut off supply lines. I've not more to report." Bartlett's assessment came with brisk assurance. "Will you be joining us, sir?"

"I will, but not right away." Thoughts of Margaret Blackwood flooded his mind. His words had come without thought. He'd always put duty first. Moments earlier he'd believed he could remain at Blackwood Farm forever.

The idea caught him off-guard. Confounded, he waved his hand at Bartlett. "Be at ease, Nathaniel."

"Thank you, sir." Relaxing his shoulders, Bartlett's hands went behind his back. "What have you heard here among the neighbors? What are the townspeople saying? And what of Elias Blackwood?"

"I've not much. My information falls more to impressions. Elias is circumspect as a judge. He'll sway to one side enough to believe you're allied. Before you agree, Elias will declare the opposite. Elias Blackwood is a canny man."

Bartlett gave a nod. "I've heard the same. And his neighbors? How does the support fall?"

Hamilton shrugged. "In truth, impossible to know for sure. Blackwood's son fights with the Continentals."

"Does he? I hadn't heard," Bartlett said.

"He does. Josiah Finlan Blackwood is his name. Elias Blackwood doesn't speak of it," the captain added.

"What do you think," Bartlett asked.

Hamilton gave a baffled smile. "I wish I knew. They muddle my mind, the lot of them."

"I'm sympathetic, Captain." Bartlett said with judicious seriousness. "What of the daughter? She appears intelligent enough. What is your impression of her? Has she confided any bits we might use?"

"I think not, Sergeant." Hamilton gave his head a shake while his lips thinned. "Elias' father came from Scotland to be indentured to a Quaker before gaining his freedom."

"Say no more, Captain. The Quaker must have had an abundance of persuasive powers. The Scots are fierce fighters while the Quakers remain neutral. As for Blackwood, no one will say."

"Truly," Hamilton agreed.

"If we're done, sir, with your permission, I'll be off."

At Hamilton's nod, Bartlett turned to go. Pausing, he rummaged in the pockets of his coat. "I'm sorry. I near forgot your packet. I'm ordered to put it into your hand myself."

Taking the slim packet, Hamilton glanced at it before bending over and drawing an envelope from the side of his boot. "I'd thought to hold this but take it now. Tell the general I'll be ready when needed and give him this letter. Go safe, Nathaniel"

Bartlett nodded while mounting his horse. "My best to Miss Blackwood. I'm obliged for the meal." He turned his horse onto the road, away from Blackwood Farm.

Not ready to join the family, Hamilton resumed his walk through the woods, hoping to reclaim the pleasure and ease he'd felt earlier. Evening approached, the woods growing quiet. Ahead, a stand of shade trees beckoned. The walking had tired him.

His packet in hand, Hamilton sought the nearest shade tree. His back to the trunk, Hamilton slid to the ground and stretched out his leg, easing the dull ache. He let out a pleasurable sigh, untied the packet and drew out the papers. Slouching down, he began to read.

"Ah, Captain Hamilton, I thought I might find you here." Margi slid down beside him. "What have you got there? A letter?"

He jerked away, shoving the papers back into the envelope and hearing the pages rip. "Nothing important," he said

It couldn't be helped, he thought. He'd scanned enough to understand the gist.

Margi's bright smile dimmed. "I'm sorry I disturbed you." She edged away, preparing to rise.

A pang ripped through him. He'd disappointed her.

She stood over him. "You've walked far today. When I saw you, I thought you might want a bit of company walking back." She turned on her heel.

"Please, don't go." His hand closed over hers, drawing her back.

"I wasn't out looking for you, Captain Hamilton," she replied with a defensive shrug.

Her smile was gone. Beneath his hand, her fingers were tense and cold. Stabbed with the realization that his action was the cause, he did not release her hand. Margi didn't pull away.

"Your hand is cold," he said, holding her gaze. "I'm sorry. I didn't mean for you to think you'd disturbed me."

She gave a slow nod. Staring into his eyes, her lips curved the slightest bit. Lifting a slim shoulder, Margi countered, "I'll not invade your privacy, Captain Hamilton. I promise you that. You'd have thought I'd discovered you as a spy."

"Precisely," he said, pressing his advantage and drawing her down beside him. "In these times, that was the very thought I had."

She eyed him. "No! That's silly."

"It is," he agreed, her hand warming in his.

"You didn't expect Mr. Bartlett, did you?" It was not a question.

"Truth is, no. You read me well, Miss Blackwood."

Margi had no response, not yet ready to admit Charlotte was right. She had fallen in love with Captain Hamilton.

She dropped her head and, with her free hand, smoothed her skirt over the edge of ruffled petticoat peeking from beneath a wrinkle in the dark blue of homespun. "You've been with us for weeks. It was I who cared for you."

"Considering our circumstances," he said with a smile, "do you suppose you might call me by my first name? It's William, William Roger Hamilton."

She didn't answer. She only looked at him until his throat tightened, sure he'd offended her. "I would like that, William. And it would please me to hear you call me Margi, at least when we're alone."

William Hamilton grinned. "It's decided between us, then?"

"Oh, yes, William. But, you shall be Will to me. It's decided." She placed her hand over his.

Her smile lit her face, capturing his heart.

In that moment, their relationship shifted.

Unprepared, not ready to acknowledge the truth of his feelings, Hamilton preferred they remain undefinable.

No more than a mixture of attraction and gratitude, he assured himself. Had his fondness gone deeper, he would have wrapped her in his arms and declared himself. He'd pull her close to quell the constant ache to touch her. He would have kissed her until they were both dizzy.

Knowing their affinity must remain just that, there were opposite aspects at work between them. He refused to acknowledge what he felt for her, settling for simply answering her smile. Sure he stood on a precipice, feeling himself about to pitch heart-first.

Shifting slightly, careful of his movement, Hamilton kept her hand over his.

"It's getting late." She glanced at the sky. "Charlotte expects me back but I'm tempted to stay here forever."

"I've the same thought," Hamilton agreed, relaxing against the tree's trunk, making no effort to rise.

Watching her, a smile crooked his mouth at realizing he'd seldom seen her still.

Hamilton hadn't noticed winter's pallor had disappeared from her skin. Weeks of working outside had added a sun-kissed glow to her face, warm like the shading of a newly- ripened peach. Glints of late afternoon sun filtering through the trees burnished her hair's copper length in a blaze of reddish-gold. Margi Blackwood quite took his breath.

She beguiled him.

Seeing her eyes were closed, he continued to gaze at her, unconsciously synchronizing his breathing with hers. Closing his eyes, he concentrated on the feel of her palm, calloused and warm, over his. She made no move to rise. The moment was perfect. A thought came, unbidden.

He was happy.

CHAPTER EIGHT

"ELIAS, WAIT," HAMILTON CALLED OUT across the backyard. Elias didn't stop, only lifted a hand over his head and wagged his fingers.

Hamilton sprinted ahead, catching Elias at the door to the stables adjoining the barn. "I'd like a word, sir."

"Yes?" Without slowing, Elias strode over the threshold and straight down the passage between the empty stalls, a pencil and paper in hand. Elias finally paused, jotting on the page while mumbling under his breath.

"What troubles you, sir?" Hamilton asked.

"Jamie's slacking. This stall's not cleaned properly, nor is the one beside it." Elias turned, giving Hamilton his attention for the first time since they'd entered the stable. "Have you seen the boy?"

"No, I haven't seen him all day."

Elias drew an audibly irritated breath. The air lay heavy, heated with the smells of hay and manure. Hamilton's gaze drifted to a hay rake hanging on the wall and offered to finish Jamie's chore.

"More than likely, Jamie got distracted and took off, intending to return later," Hamilton suggested. "I remember doing the same at his age.

Elias eyed him through narrowed eyes. "I cannot abide a slacker. I know the boy's head is full of the war. He spoke only last week about following the troops, offering his services." Elias barked a laugh. "I've no thought what service Jamie could render. Lately, his mind is nowhere near Blackwood Farm. I'm afraid it's time I set him right."

"Would you like me to muck out those stalls, sir? Even if Jamie gets back, there's no time before the women will have supper ready." Elias glanced at the half-mucked stalls. "Are you quick, boy?" Hamilton laughed. "I am, sir."

"Get to it, then. I'm obliged." Elias headed out the stable doors.

Half an hour later, as he pitched a full rake of dirty hay into a wheelbarrow, he realized he'd forgotten to let Elias know he'd be leaving within days.

June had found him fully healed, his broken leg mended and strong as ever. He'd tell Elias tonight, after supper. July was a week away. His orders had come yesterday by a messenger, cleverly disguised as an itinerant peddler. He dreaded telling Margi.

The realization pressed against his sense of duty. His reluctance leaving an acute sense of being crushed on all sides. Had his circumstances been different, a life in Pennsylvania offered a certain enticement. But, Hamilton would do his duty and pray for victory. *Perhaps afterward?*

Drawing a breath, Hamilton leaned over the hay rake. He'd finished mucking stalls and ran a forearm across his sweaty forehead, scrutinizing the fresh, clean straw spread over the floor. The two stalls looked as pristine and orderly as any stable he'd seen. Pleased, he hung up the rake and headed to the house feeling a modicum better.

Bare-chested, Hamilton sluiced himself at the pump before entering the kitchen on a skulk, snatching a fresh shirt from a basket left under his bed in the kitchen. He was suddenly ravenous.

Margi and Charlotte Blackwood both looked up.

"Mucking stalls, were you?" Margi nudged Charlotte. They broke into peals of laughter. "Papa told us."

"I've mucked my share of stalls, ladies," Hamilton said.

"Stalls are Jamie's job. Is Jamie behind you, Captain?" Charlotte asked with an expectant smile.

Hamilton looked behind him by reflex. "No, ladies. I've told Elias I've not seen Jamie all day. I'm afraid he's in for a chewing out from Elias. The boy's left his chores half-done."

"Oh dear," Margi murmured. "Jamie's been distracted throughout the last weeks. Where could he have gone?"

Charlotte stopped stirring the contents of the iron pot simmering in the fireplace. "No doubt exploring, acting a soldier like his pa. He's been fiendish over what Josiah does for the Continental Army. It's all he thinks about."

C

Jamie did not come home for supper. Worry had taken root as Margi and Charlotte cleared away the dishes, supper uneaten. Hamilton noticed Elias' minute-by-minute glances out the kitchen window. Charlotte and Margi spoke in low voices, assuring themselves the boy would return before dark, babbling apologies, having simply lost track of time. The women prepared Jamie's plate to put aside.

"He'll lie down tonight without his supper, Charlotte. Tomorrow, I'll speak to him about shirking his chores." Elias nodded at Hamilton. "You wanted to speak with me, Captain. We'll speak in the parlor. Come along."

Face-to-face in the Blackwood parlor, Hamilton took time to scan the comfortable room, in no rush to impart his news. He rubbed a knuckle over his lips deciding what words he would use. A light breeze through the open window ruffled the curtains in a light-filled room furnished with an elegantly carved divan upholstered in moss green brocade. A set of high-backed chairs, stitched in crewel-work, flanked the fireplace. Hamilton decided to choose one of the high-backed chairs should he be invited to sit, wondering which of the women at Blackwood Farm had thought to anchor the grouping with a multi-shaded, tightly-woven carpet.

The room had the feel of Margi.

Elias waved for Hamilton to seat himself. Hamilton passed a mahogany secretary bulging with letters and stacked correspondence, no doubt having to do with the farm. He edged close for a furtive look but saw nothing indicating coercion with the enemy. No notice of supplying the opposite side with foodstuffs, or worse, ammunition. Yet? Pity he'd not time for this, being proficient at reading upside down.

Elias had taken his seat. Hamilton walked over a tightly-woven rug to sit in the opposite chair flanking the fireplace. He waited while Elias lit his pipe.

"It's order that keeps this farm running smoothly. I strive for it. It appears I've been remiss in stressing the importance of order to my grandson."

Hamilton slid forward. "He misses his father, sir. The boy's infatuation with all things military brings him closer to his father."

Elias blew out a breath. "You're an observant man, Captain. And, right."

"You've made a good life here." Hamilton opened his arm, encompassing the room. "You'll have it again."

"I pray it's so," Elias said.

Hamilton realized Elias must have sensed the importance of Hamilton's news, deeming the parlor appropriate.

"What have you to tell me, Captain?" Elias asked.

"My orders have come," Hamilton said. "I'm summoned to join my company. I'll be leaving Blackwood Farm in three days."

Elias nodded. "I thought as much. Will you tell my daughter or shall I?"

"I'll tell her, sir."

"Good," Elias said. "You're a fine man, Captain." His eyes softened. "She'll miss you."

"And I her, Mr. Blackwood. Your family has been kind to me. I owe you more than I can ever repay. Your daughter saved my life."

The corner of Elias' mouth turned up. "Margi did, indeed." He leaned back in his chair, his smile fading.

Hamilton held Elias Blackwood's gaze and waited.

Elias drew a breath. "The girl's been living these last years with the pain of a cruel loss."

Hamilton gave a nod. "She told me she'd lost her fiancé at Brandywine."

"Margi told you?" Elias' brows shot up.

"She did," Hamilton said.

"Humph," Elias grunted. "She took it hard. It's the regret for what she'd expected that nags her now. She and Joseph were young but they had a plan for their lives. Margi held herself strong but Joseph's death shattered her. She's said little, but my daughter put away her joy of life. It pains me. I see changes in her since you've come. You've given her hope."

"Me?" Surprise, tinged with alarm, jittered through him as he listened.

"Aye," Elias said. "You've brought her back to the living. It does my heart good to see it."

Hamilton hoped not, knowing his departure from Blackwood Farm was for the best. An officer with the British army had little to offer a woman living in America.

"Sir," the captain said, "I'll keep your confidence. But, would you allow me a quite personal question?"

"Ask it," Elias said.

"You're a Scotsman, sir. They're known to be fierce. I'd have thought you'd have sided with the rebels."

Elias sat a moment. "That's fair. So I'll explain my thinking. I was born on Blackwood Farm. My father, Finlan, had put fighting aside. A distrust of the English remains with me. Busy tending my farm, I don't think overmuch. Scots and Irish, Germans, Americans, we're men wanting the best for ourselves and families. In that, we're the same. My father worked his years of indenture and after to acquire this land." He slammed his hand down on his knee. "It's the land, man, the land where the Blackwood freedom lies. It's the land, Captain. Do you understand?"

"Yes, I do," the captain said.

Elias looked doubtful. "You don't see, yet. It's written on your face. You'll be gone from here in three days. Where will you go?"

Hamilton shrugged. "Wherever the army sends me. I've a duty."

"And what of your duty to yourself, sir?" Elias asked. "What life will you have in one year or five, alone, traipsing the world with not a handful of dirt that's yours? A man needs ambition and opportunity to set himself as master of his life. My father strived and succeeded. It's up to me to preserve what Finlan Blackwood left to me. It's good for a man to think of legacies. I'm ambivalent over this war between us and England. We've lived in America through a generation. I need only Blackwood Farm, a neighbor with a ready hand, and no king between me and my God."

Astonished to hear his own feelings so articulated, Hamilton could only think to nod.

The parlor had darkened. Shadows gathered, shading Elias' face.

Hamilton stared. "You've just made the case for the rebels, Mr. Blackwood."

Elias' brows bristled. "I make the case for common sense and the virtue of ambivalence."

"I've not thought ambivalence a virtue," Hamilton countered.

Elias rose. "Think on it, Captain."

A pounding at the front door startled them both

Margi had dashed to open the door. Hamilton rose from his seat. Elias was out of the parlor and into the foyer.

Margi swung open the door. "Mr. Samuels, come inside."

"Is young Jamie home? And is my Ned with him?" Henry Samuels stepped into the foyer, looking anxious.

Hamilton stared at the strapping man with the half-homely face filling the foyer.

"No, the lad's not home yet." Elias shook his head. "Much longer and his mother will skin him within an inch of his life."

"Mary's already in a state." Samuels doffed his straw hat, nodding his greeting to Margi while twisting his hat between his hands. "She's heard the British are on the march through the county. There's been talk of some being taken."

"Not children!" Margi gasped.

A chill snaked up Hamilton's spine, knowing it was possible. With an ongoing war with France and Spain instigating on the quiet, Britain was in need of men. In a pinch, boys would do. Both Jamie and his friend may have been taken. *Surely not.*

Yes, Britain needed recruits. They would take indiscriminately, ignoring both age and station. Jamie was ten.

Hamilton's thoughts turned inward as the discussion swirled around him. Considering his orders, if a company had captured the boys, Hamilton knew where to find them.

Henry Samuels was bolstering his argument. "The boys wouldn't have left their fishing poles. It looked to me like they were dropped, one over the other with the lines tangled."

Elias's appeared skeptical.

Samuels added, "The ground was disturbed. I saw it myself."

"No!" Charlotte's voice echoed down the hall from the kitchen. "Henry, what are you suggesting?" Her voice had turned shrill.

"The British have taken the boys. I want to head after them," Henry Samuels replied.

"Where?" Margi asked.

"The soldiers left tracks by the river," Samuels said.

Elias' rugged face tightened, his decision made. "I'll saddle my horse."

"We may be gone the night, Elias. They've a lead on us," Samuels said.

"Go, then. Hurry and find them, please," Charlotte pleaded. "I'll go to Mary."

The men hurried through the downstairs and out the kitchen door with Margi and Charlotte trailing behind. It was not yet dark.

Inside the stables, Elias unlatched his horse's stall door.

"Sir, I'm going with you to find the boys," Hamilton said. "If you'll point me to a stall…"

Hamilton saw hesitation rise in Elias' eyes. He was a British officer, after all.

"I can help. Let's go," Hamilton urged.

Flexing his hands, Elias shot Hamilton a direct look before he yanked his saddle from the railing and indicated a stall holding a fast, piebald animal.

Hamilton knew Elias hadn't a choice. He quickly saddled his horse, knowing Henry Samuels knew nothing of his position in the British Army. With nothing said, Samuels would assume Hamilton was hired help or a family visitor. They needed to find the boys and Hamilton could help them.

The men and Charlotte rode out at a fast canter. The echo of hoof beats pounded in Hamilton's chest.

At the Samuels' farm, Charlotte remained with Mary, offering what comfort she could. The three men scrutinized the evidence at the fishing hole before riding off in search of Jamie and Ned.

Hoof beats sounded as Hamilton pondered how he would separate from Samuels and Elias. He'd no wish to have Elias and Mr. Samuels captured. The possibility of them being hanged for treason remained fearfully real. His mind swirled. They'd need to separate.

🍖

Margi had watched them go, squinting into the expanding dusk as her father, Hamilton, and Mr. Samuels, along with Charlotte, left her, finally melding into formless shadows and disappearing. She wondered how she'd been left alone to do the waiting. Helpless and anxious, she breathed a heavy sigh, feeling impatient and restless.

The possibility of Jamie and Ned being captured by the British had stunned her. But her father's ready acceptance of Henry Samuel's choice of action kept her silent. Her father believed the boys had been taken off by the British.

Her heart's pounding had drowned out further thought. Real fear clogged her throat.

Not sure how long she'd been standing alone, Margi could no longer hear the hoof beats. With them gone, the tension eased. The hammering of her heart had slowed and she could think. The thought came clear. She knew the area. Margi would go after her nephew and Ned herself.

☾

Night's darkness was not far off. Hamilton should have left Elias and Samuels earlier. They'd been riding over an hour with no sign of the boys or the British. He stared into descending darkness, listening to the silence. Elias and Samuels had kept them searching on parallel tracks, zig-zagging back through the woods. Hamilton found himself not far from the direction of the British camp. He needed to go. His company should be bivouacked to the south. If the British were not holding the boys, he'd obtain what information he could. He was wasting time.

Spurring his horse, Hamilton rode up behind the two men. "Elias, Mr. Samuels, we need to separate, go off in different directions to cover more ground."

"You think so, sir?" Samuels asked.

"I agree," Elias said. "We should widen our search."

"Let's do it, then." Samuels turned his horse's head. "I'll head north."

"Good thought, Samuels," Hamilton agreed. "Heading north is a wide swath to cover. It's more efficient for you and Elias to travel together."

Elias glanced ahead into the dark. "You've a point, Hamilton. We'll head north."

They galloped off together, leaving Hamilton free to nudge his horse in the opposite direction.

An hour's ride south and he saw the camp's lights. Rising to a standing position in his stirrups, the width and length of the camp stupefied him.

"Christ!" he whispered. His blood ran cold.

Left to right, far as his eye could see, glowing pinpricks of light shone across the darkened sky. Hamilton stared. Possibly two companies, comprised of five hundred men each. His jaw tightened as he contemplated the damage one thousand men could do. He lowered himself into the saddle, the rigid leather sounding its protest. Hamilton rubbed a hand across his eyes. The task of locating two boys just became harder. Then, to get them away, his mind spun, shifting through options. He refused to consider the charge impossible.

Dismounting, he pulled his distinctive red coat from his saddlebag, thinking the chance of walking into the camp and coming upon the boys was a sure impossibility. He'd need to go directly to the source.

Tethering his horse to a tree and smoothing what wrinkles he could from his coat, he prepared to walk into the camp, hoping his appearance was not too disreputable.

An unexpected sound rustled the bushes surrounding him. Whirling, he dropped to the ground. His horse whinnied as a boot bounced against his side and a body fell over his, squeaking in surprise. Twisting in one motion, he closed his arms around a soft body confined against his. His heart stopped.

"Margi?"

CHAPTER NINE

"**B**LOODY HELL. WHAT ARE YOU doing?" Hamilton rolled to face her, doubting her presence, even as he felt her warm breath on his cheek and her heart beating against his.

"I came to find Jamie," she said.

He stared, her face shadowed in the dark. "You came to…find Jamie?" Hamilton couldn't comprehend what was said with Margi in his arms.

"I tracked you."

Tracked him.

Lying against him, he held her gaze as she studied his face. Hamilton felt determination in the stiffness of her body. Her voice was even, as if it was nothing to be riding through the woods in the middle of the night and tripping over a British soldier. As if his task was not difficult enough, her attitude irritated him. The woman he'd thought of as eminently sane had taken leave of her senses. No British soldiers would release the boys to a woman riding alone through the night. *Impossible.* Risking her life, she'd added to his charge of finding two boys hidden within a camp of soldiers. She should have considered the danger.

"You haven't found them?" Margi whispered a bit too loud.

Hamilton heard the accusation as he helped her to her feet.

He answered carefully, though irritation had ratcheted to simmering anger. He'd not the time or patience to explain himself.

Hamilton couldn't tear his eyes from the iridescent glow the moon gave her face, the fragile bones delicate beneath her skin. Her vulnerability terrified him. "Isn't it obvious?" He waved a hand. "Do you see Jamie or Ned?"

Margi frowned. In the same tone, she said, "No. I don't."

"Who's there?" An authoritative voice rang out. "Identify yourself!"

Hamilton pushed her down into the bushes, his finger to her lips. "Stay quiet. I'll come for you when I can."

Rising, he leaned in. "Margaret, do not move."

"Dare I breathe?" she quipped.

Hamilton muttered a curse.

"Who's out there? Speak." The voice sounded closer.

Upright, Hamilton's stare unwavering, he backed away from her.

"I am Captain William Roger Hamilton of His Majesty's Light Dragoons," he called out.

"Come forward then. Have you papers?"

"I do." Hamilton pulled his papers from his jacket and, giving her a final look over his shoulder, walked forward holding them up.

"Follow me," the squat patrol guard ordered.

The captain followed.

Captain Hamilton's healed leg ached at the trek across the camp but he'd time to run through his ruse to find the boys.

The guard lifted the tent's flap, motioning Hamilton to enter.

"Come in, it's late," came a familiar voice. "What news have you?"

Captain Hamilton's heart sank. He recognized the voice, ever grumpy and quarrelsome, yet, the general was insightful and able. Hamilton knew he'd need to remain three steps ahead of Sir Henry Clinton, British Commander of North America. His spine ramrod straight, Captain Hamilton walked forward, his demeanor confident.

General Henry Clinton sat, sans uniform coat with his stock untied, looking up as the guard passed Captain Hamilton's papers. General Clinton took little time to read them. "You've arrived early, Captain. You'll be useful tomorrow."

"Tomorrow?" Hamilton repeated.

The commander rose, motioning toward a campaign desk, spread across with an unrolled map, secured at either end with an oil lamp and the commander's sword.

Captain Hamilton stood across the desk at attention, waiting for the commander to speak.

"Yes, Captain, tomorrow." With a wave of his hand at the guard, General Clinton dismissed the man. Once the tent's flap closed, General Clinton set the captain's packet aside, his hands palm down on the desk.

"Captain Hamilton, you've a fine reputation. You'll join the fight,"

Clinton said.

Tomorrow. The thought was dizzying and impossible.

"Our scouts have discovered a contingent of rebels camped in the valley beyond these hills. They've no knowledge of us. We have them outflanked." Snatching his sword, he stabbed its point onto the map.

Hamilton knew the maps and saw the sword point marked an area not far from where they stood.

"We'll strike at dawn," General Clinton said. "We've intelligence the contingent contains a valuable target. I've no verification the general is among them. But, should he be captured, our futures will be assured." He smiled a mirthless smile.

Captain Hamilton nodded. "Commander, I'm at your service. I, too, have heard rumors, most recently that your company may have picked up the information from some farm boys. Actually, I heard they were picked up this morning. I've came to interrogate them."

"Who sent you?"

"My papers don't say?" Hamilton countered.

Clinton gave a wave of dismissal. "We do have a dozen or so prisoners. Our soldiers brought them in this evening. If the boys are there, interrogate them."

Hamilton managed to control any excitement in his voice. "Where are they being held?"

The commander pointed. "Southwest end of the camp, near the artillery. You've time before dawn. Can you do without sleep?"

"I can, sir," Captain Hamilton replied.

"Come back straightaway if you've the information I need." Sir Clinton waved Hamilton out.

"If not, I'll sanction raids in this county not soon forgotten. That's all, Captain."

Hamilton's throat tightened.

Outside, the camp was quiet. Hamilton ran the distance, his heart pounding.

The two boys were tied to the wheel of a mammoth cannon. The cart holding the cannon held the remainder of the prisoners, secured to the rails. Chins on their chests, they slumped with drooping heads, sound asleep. Hamilton couldn't imagine it. Off to the side, Hamilton spied one guard, deep in a stupor. He moved in, soundlessly, beneath the noise of snores and coughing.

Jamie's eyes were wide open, watching him. Finger over his lips,

Hamilton crouched beside the boy, unknotting the ropes, thankful Jamie was the first in the line of captured men.

"Shhh," he whispered.

Unraveling was taking too long. Unsheathing his knife, Hamilton sliced through the rope, freeing both boys. Jamie nudged his friend.

"On three," Hamilton whispered, "run into the woods. Don't stop. Keep running. I'll find you."

Crouching, Jamie and Ned nodded.

Hamilton counted. "One…two…three…"

They were off. Across the dirt and grass, the boys reached the trees and disappeared. The guard and captives slept on. Hamilton let out his breath and followed.

In the woods, he reached them bent over, hands on their knees, panting. They were safe, for the moment.

Hamilton snatched each boy's arm. "Are you both all right, not hurt?"

Ned shook his head while Jamie answered between pants. "No, sir. They didn't hurt us."

"The soldiers took us away," Ned offered.

"Soon, you'll be home," Hamilton said.

They'd need to hurry. Margi added a complication but another horse would take them home faster. In the dark, Hamilton searched for the branches he'd downed earlier. A hand on each boy, he followed the trail he'd set. He prayed she'd remained where he'd left her. His heart was hammering. Hamilton heard a horse's wicker and Margi walked out from behind a tree.

"Aunt Margi," whispered Jamie, awe in his voice.

"Yes," Hamilton's voice was hard. "Your aunt's come to find you and Ned." He stared at the older boy. "Jamie's mother has gone to be with your mum. You've terrified her by putting yourselves in danger."

The boys hung their heads.

Hamilton brought the horses forward. "Mount up, boys. Jamie, you with your aunt. Ned, you're with me. Let's go."

Out of the woods, they cantered down the roadside until Hamilton stopped, putting up a hand. Dismounting, he signaled Ned to join him. Margi came up alongside.

"I've something yet to do." Hamilton looked up at her

Margi balked. "You're leaving us?"

"I've a duty. I'm not leaving you. You're coming with me," Hamilton said. "There's not time to explain. We need to go, now."

The boys stared wide-eyed.

"Where are we going?" she asked.

He stared at his horse, anxious to be off.

He swallowed. "We're riding into the Continental camp."

"What?" Her voice rose.

Hamilton saw her grip the reins, her eyes darting one way and the other as if deciding which way to ride off.

He laid his hand on her knee and felt her muscles tighten. "Listen to me, Margi. We'll bring them home, I promise you."

"I don't understand."

"Trust me," he said.

Margi didn't answer. Hamilton's stomach knotted tighter than the ropes that had tied the boys.

"Aunt Margi, Pa's with the Continentals. Do you think he'll be in the camp?" Jamie piped up.

Hamilton watched the flicker of emotion cross her face as Margi's arms tightened around her nephew and her grip on the reins loosened. She gave him a direct look.

"I trust you, Will." She snapped her reins. "Let's go."

❦

They managed the distance in short time, approaching the dark camp with little disturbance

"Say nothing," Hamilton said to Margi and the boys before giving a sharp whistle.

The crackle of branches and murmur of leaves was heard seconds before two Continental guards on horseback crashed through the woods.

"We heard you creeping in," said a blue-coated soldier. "I was about to challenge your presence, sir. But, I see who you are."

"We're good then," Hamilton said. "I've news for the general."

"I'll take you in," said the Continental's guard.

"We'll follow," Hamilton said.

Leaving a guard behind, they trotted into a quiet camp, so much smaller than the British. Hamilton couldn't help but take notice of the boys' reaction to the shaggy-haired guard, looking enormous astride his horse with shoulders like a bull buffalo. Wide-eyed, Jamie stared while Ned tightened his grip around Hamilton at seeing a large head set upon a thick neck, his hair tied in a straggly tail beneath a battered tricorn, appearing both formidable and frightening. One steely-eyed glance at the boys and they quickly dropped their eyes. Hamilton stifled a smile. "The general's waiting, sir. The woman and boys will come with me." The guard snatched Margi and Ned's horses' reins once Hamilton dismounted, leaving Hamilton alone in front of the largest tent, a dim light glowing past the canvas.

He'd given Margi a reassuring smile that she didn't return. The tent's flap opened.

Well over six feet, standing erect and dignified, looking every inch the part of America's Commander, General George Washington put out his hand. "Join me inside, sir."

"Thank you, General," Hamilton strode into the tent behind Washington.

"General Washington, Colonel William Hamilton, at your service, with information on an imminent attack by General Clinton at dawn."

Hamilton gave what details he knew.

General Washington's eyes narrowed. "We've no choice but to break camp and ride north to New Jersey. We've troops there. One thousand British, you say?"

"I was in the camp," Colonel Hamilton said explaining the rest.

The general sighed. "Get the Blackwoods home, William." He paused, thinking. "I believe we've a Blackwood here. Josiah Blackwood, a good man, returned after a difficult but successful mission. I'll send for him. Take him with you, Colonel. We'll put out information that you've been captured. Your intelligence at Saratoga proved invaluable. You'll join us in the southern campaign. We're going to win this, you know."

"We will, General Washington. I'm sure of it."

"Go, then. Keep them safe. Godspeed."

"Thank you, sir." Hamilton saluted and left, having dispensed his duty.

CHAPTER TEN

THE CONTINENTALS WERE WARNED, ROUSED and already breaking camp when Hamilton found Margi, Jamie and Ned finishing warm coffee in tin cups.

They looked up. A smile curved his lips, feeling both relief and joyful anticipation at the happenstance of finding Josiah and his returning with him. His smile widened and his heart lifted at the thought of Charlotte's reaction.

He'd surpassed his duty. British Commander Clinton would savor no victory today. Hamilton would see them all safely home before heading south to join his men. Word would go out to the British he'd been captured in battle. A spear of relief rose in him, a singular pleasure at his hard-won success. He would share it with Margi.

"Pa! It's Pa!" Jamie flew across the space and into his father's arms.

Margi jumped to follow. "Josiah!"

Josiah ran forward, scooping the boy into his arms. "Ho, boy! How did you get here?"

"Ned and me, we were captured by the redcoats, Pa." Jamie pointed. "Captain Hamilton rescued us!"

Holding Jamie, Josiah put out his hand. "I owe you a great debt, Colonel. I've been told what you did. Your courage humbles me."

"You've no debt, sir. Your sister saved my life," Hamilton said.

Josiah held out an arm for Margi, who walked into it. Her brother's arm closed around her as she laid her head against his shoulder. Hamilton saw her tears and looked away.

Margi rode apart from him, looking ahead, her face blank, appearing detached, uninterested. She rode beside her brother with Jamie, exhausted and asleep, with his father's arms around him. Hamilton watched her reach to touch the boy during their ride.

He'd felt her coldness, a noticeable distance within minutes of their leaving the Continental's camp. She talked in low tones with her brother, sparing him no glance. Certain of Margi's powers of deduction, Hamilton knew by the set of her shoulders and implacable expression, she'd put two and two together. He'd made a dire mistake leaving her in the dark.

He drew a breath, rubbing a hand over his jaw, feeling the beginnings of a day's stubble. Hamilton knew that stubble was the least of it when he was forced to rein his horse away from hers and her brother's when she spurred her animal past his without a word. Back straight, she rode off toward the woods.

"It's best to follow her, sir," Josiah said. "I've no knowledge of what's between you. Spur your horse. Margi will listen."

A sleeping Ned behind him, he'd nothing to do but follow after her.

Hamilton feared she would condemn him for his silence. Secrecy had kept him alive and those few he cared for safe. He cared for the Blackwoods. Silence did not demand an explanation.

Riding through the dark, following after her, he considered his defense while his heart weighed heavy, knowing he'd hurt her. Ned's limp head rolled across his back, emphasizing the weight.

At his approach, Margi ignored him, lost in her thoughts. Helpless, he realized he'd not succeeded after all. The price he would pay was nothing he'd expected. He regretted the Blackwood family's suffering at providing refuge to a British officer who was an enemy to their brother and son. He especially regretted the pain he'd caused Charlotte. He'd acted cowardly. The realization shocked him. He'd never chosen cowardice over right. They'd offered him refuge. He'd received much more.

He edged his horse close to hers. The silence between them stifled, heavy like a suffocating blanket. He stared at her riding beside him. She was not smiling nor would she look at him. The moments stretched as they rode, long, lonely moments.

Hamilton searched for the words to persuade Margi to understand. Her expression remained tight as dawn lightened the sky, the light chasing away shadows.

He swallowed, clearing his throat.

She nudged her horse ahead. "You've lied to me from the beginning," she whispered. "We've nothing to say to each other."

Her stony expression did not alter as he came up beside her. "I did not lie to you, Margi. I simply held my counsel. It was my duty."

She looked at him. "You put my family and all we hold dear in danger without a thought to the consequences. We risked our lives to help you," she hissed.

Hamilton kept himself carefully expressionless, but his fingers had tightened to numbness on the reins as Margi spoke. "I should have told you that I'd sided with the rebels." His words tumbled out. "After the massacre at Germantown in '77, my thinking changed. I was ashamed to call myself a British officer. I spoke up but there was no investigation. I drank to ease the pain and the anger. The Continentals approached me in a tavern. The rebels' cause is right. I believe it to my core. For not trusting you, I am sorry."

"I don't know that I can forgive you, Will," she said.

The use of his name and the break in her voice gave him a sliver of hope. He slowed his horse, letting her ride ahead. He'd leave her to think.

She rode off to join her brother. He watched them speak animatedly to each other. The realization came out of nowhere with a jolt. Hamilton needed Margi Blackwood.

"Margi!" Hamilton caught up to ride beside her. "We're near the farm. I promise I'll answer all your questions. Please, listen to me!"

Margi did not answer.

"Please," Hamilton began, "I am truly sorry. I know you're hurt. I was wrong. I wasn't thinking. I never would have put you or your family in danger. I believed I'd have been gone, but there was you and I…" His voice trailed off.

Her head came up, eyes blazing. "You did put us in danger, Will. You are a spy, after all. I'll not listen to your flattery and more lies. Speak the truth or leave me here, now. I'll find my father and Mr. Samuels. I'll tell them you lied to us, using us for your own motives." She gave a bitter laugh. "My father will say your silence is an English thing to do, should he partake of more whisky than is prudent."

Her words tore through him, damning for their truth, stinging him raw, like a well-aimed whip.

"Margi, forgive me. I… love…"

"Look!" Jamie cried, safe in Josiah's arms. Wide-eyed, he pointed. "Our barn's on fire!"

They spurred their horses under billows of black smoke blowing over the trees while flames leapt into the sky. They reached the yard to see the stables and barn engulfed. Fully ablaze, Hamilton knew there was no hope of saving the buildings. The wild screams of trapped horses echoed across the yard.

"God almighty." Josiah jumped from his horse with Jamie. "Grab a bucket and water, Son!"

"Papa!" Margi screamed, sliding from her horse and running headlong after Elias, who had run into the burning stable after the horses.

The scene was frantic as Henry Samuels lugged a heavy bucket of water toward the barn. The boys ran back and forth, yelling orders while Elias slowed to shout at them to stay put. The buckets were in the barn. The effort was useless.

Hamilton had tied the horses and run for kitchen pots, before spying a bucket overturned near a water trough. Scooping it through the trough, he heard Margi screaming for her father.

"Margi, stop!" Hamilton shouted. "I'll get your father and the horses." On a run, he flung the water into the stable entrance, stomping on what flames he could reach.

The horses pounded their stalls with wildly flailing hooves. Their frightened screams vibrated the air. He couldn't see through the smoke and his burning eyes. Intense heat drove him back. Shouting for Margi and Elias, his eyes watering, he soaked a handkerchief and clamped the cloth over his nose and mouth, trying to move into the stable to find Margi and Elias and reach the horses. Coughing in the smoke, he ran down a shadowed row of empty stalls, hearing the cracking of burning wood.

A horse shrieked. The sound chilled him despite the sweat rolling down his face. Hamilton thought he heard Elias' voice.

"Elias?" he called.

"I'm here," Elias shouted. "Get yourself clear! My hand is on the latch. It's hot, I can't hold it"

"Margi's in here,"

"Lord! It's too late." Elias shouted

A panicked and frantic animal crashed through the stables in a massive blur.

"Margi?" Elias' voice rolled through the barn, hoarse but loud as ever. "Sophie's frantic. If you're near, get out of her way!"

With that, the noise of a charging horse deafened Hamilton as a second animal galloped through on a tear.

Margi screamed. Then, no sound came but the sound of hoof beats.

Frantic, Hamilton scrambled, hunched close to the ground, calling her name.

He found her, crumpled in a heap on the floor, her arms covering her head. Hamilton snatched her into his arms "I have her, Elias!"

"Is she all right?"

Hearing the fear in Elias' voice, Hamilton couldn't answer.

He carried her outside, whispering the words he should have confided weeks ago. Margi lay in his arms, limp and lifeless, neither moving nor making a sound as he laid her beneath the branches of a massive oak bordering the orchard, away from the heat and the fire.

Heart hammering, his throat too tight to speak, Hamilton knelt beside her. He gently probed her for injuries.

"Captain Hamilton, is she..." Soot stained, Elias Blackwood approached slowly, unable to form the words.

Hamilton could only shake his head. He'd begun to shake as he watched relief wash across the older man's face. Elias blinked back tears.

Josiah joined them, bending to touch his sister's hand, saying nothing, shock and fear in his eyes.

"Margi will be fine. She's strong." Elias insisted. Crouching over his daughter, he met Hamilton's eyes. "We were raided. The British rode in, anxious to plunder. It was a rag-tag group. No discipline. They set fire to the barn after they stole most of the horses. Bastards!"

"I'm sorry, sir." It was too little to say, but it was all he could think of at the moment.

"It wasn't you who gave the order." Elias laid his hand on his daughter's head, like a blessing, and continued. "Henry and me, we hid while they did their worst. As the sky lightened, those redcoats threw their torches and rode off, taking all but two horses, leaving the poor animals to burn."

The crash of the falling roof as the structure crumbled in on itself, froze the men in place as wood and sparks flew. Hamilton's heart sank at the sight. He watched with Elias and Josiah, with an unconscious Margi between them. They were struck silent at their last look at the collapsing barn and stables.

Welcome home, Josiah, Hamilton thought with bitter irony.

Elias shook his head, stalwart and resolute. "We'll rebuild, Captain. The house and land remains."

"I curse them all!" Hamilton vowed, fisting his hands.

"We'll manage," Elias said. "And, we'll pray. Curses are futile."

"You're a better man than I, Elias Blackwood."

"He is that, and a better man than I am," Josiah said.

There was nothing more to say. Amid the devastation, they fixed their gazes on Margi, both watching the nearly imperceptible rise and fall of her chest.

"She's breathing," Hamilton whispered.

"Aye," Elias said. "General Washington's messenger reached me and Henry. You were kind to send word the boys and my headstrong daughter were found." Elias' big hand cupped Margi's cheek. "My girl will be all right."

Hamilton gently touched her face with his damp cloth, wiping at the soot.

"Keep watch." Elias rose. "I'm grateful Charlotte's at the Samuels' place. Henry rode to his farm once the redcoats had gone. I told him to tell Charlotte to stay with Mary till morning. It's time I send Ned home."

"Pa, I'll see him home," Josiah said. "I long to see my wife and we'll need Charlotte to tend Margi while we start our rebuild tomorrow."

Margi stirred. Her eyelids fluttered.

"Didn't I tell you?" Elias stared down as his daughter, looking pleased as his lips moved in a silent prayer.

Hamilton breathed his own prayer, gently gathering her close. He let his tears fall unchecked. "Margi, love, wake up for me. Please. Your father's here safe and the horses, too. Stay with us, love."

Hamilton stroked the side of her face before he bent, nestling his head into the curve of her neck, letting what tears he had left drop. "Forgive me," he whispered. "I love you."

Holding her, sure he imagined the feel of her hand sliding into his hair. Hamilton's heart jumped when she pressed him closer and whispered. "I love you, too, Will."

A jolt of pure joy surged through him. "If I were upright, love, I'd be taking a knee and asking you, Margaret Blackwood, to do me the honor of being my wife."

Unable to breathe, Hamilton waited for her answer.

Margi struggled to sit up, her face pale but glowing in the sunlight. "If I were upright, William Roger Hamilton, I'd be accepting your offer. Once you trusted me, I understood your keeping your secrets. I don't wish to be married to a spy. You're done with it, Will, aren't you? I've loved you from the first, though I didn't know it."

"Say you'll marry me, Margi." His heart pounded.

She drew a breath. "I've loved you from the first, though I was loath to admit it. But yes." Her lips curved in a heart-melting smile. "Spy or no, I will marry you. I would be proud to be your wife, Will."

"Kiss her!" Jamie screeched. "The barn's burned down but my pa's home and Aunt Margi's got me an uncle."

Hamilton kissed her, taking his time about it while hearing his new family's happy laughter surrounding him. And he held Margi Black-wood in his arms.

EPILOGUE

Blackwood Farm
August 1779

"AUNT MARGI, THE GENERAL'S HERE!" Jamie flew across the threshold of her open bedroom door, snatching her hand, pulling her to the window and nearly trampling the hem of her silk gown. "Look! Pa's riding with him. See?"

Margi laughed. "I see, yes."

"Jamie, be careful," Charlotte admonished from the doorway.

"I've got to see Pa!" That said, he pushed away from the window on a run as Margi yanked her skirts close as he veered off, avoiding Charlotte's attempt to catch him.

"Margi, I'm sorry. Did Jamie tear your gown?" Frowning, Charlotte moved to scrutinize the hem.

"No," Margi said. "Don't scold him. He's excited. Josiah's arrived with General Washington."

The women gazed out over the front lawn, seeing the general dismount and step onto the lush grass.

"General Washington's done us a great honor," Charlotte said.

"Indeed, he has." Margi glanced at the general but her eyes were on Will. Her breath caught. Achingly handsome in his Continental's uniform, blue suited him. Will stood, an equal, as General Washington clasped his arm, before they walked out of sight with Josiah. Jamie walked by his father's side, subdued for once.

The general had put a request to the two men. They had decided to accept. Neither the war nor the danger was over. But, she'd not think of that today. Margi smiled at Charlotte.

"I never thought to see Jamie so serious," Charlotte laughed. "I wish you happiness, Margi. You're beautiful in that gown. I've not seen lavender in a shade that pale. You should always wear silk and lace, tucked and shirred just so." She emphasized her words with her thumb touching her forefinger. "It's perfect for a bride."

"Thank you. I am happy." Smiling, Margi turned from the window. "Where's father?"

"I'm here, Margaret." From the doorway, dressed in his Sunday finery, her father gave her a long look.

Margi's throat closed at seeing his heart in his eyes. She recognized the velvet pouch in his hands.

"I've brought the Blackwood's blessing for your wedding, my girl."

Eyes tearing, she forced out the words in a whisper. "The Luckenbooth."

Charlotte put her handkerchief into Margi's hand. "Will you wear it? Josiah and I would be pleased."

Margi dabbed her eyes. "I'd be honored."

Her father pinned the brooch over the lace edging her bodice. "You're the image of your mother when she wore the Luckenbooth on our wedding day." He caught her dropping tear with his forefinger. "She's blessing you on this day."

"I never thought to wear...." Her voice trailed off as she stared at the brooch's sparkle, then up at her father.

Elias cleared his throat. "You were born a Blackwood. I'm proud of you." He offered an arm to each woman. "It's time. We're not about to keep William waiting."

Glorious this day, the gardens glinted in the sun, blooming with color and filled with friends and neighbors. She would always be a Blackwood with her and Will remaining on land beyond the creek that her father had recently deeded to them. The newly-raised barn and stables lent the underlying smell of fresh-milled wood to mingle in the air with the scent of the roses she'd continue to baby. Their life would be good here.

She blinked and saw Will under the arbor waiting for her. Tonight, she'd be a Hamilton.

On her father's arm, Margi walked toward Will, head high, her heart soaring. She was clutching the flowers Charlotte had picked, violets of deep purple, like the stones in her borrowed brooch. Smiling at Will, she breathed the flower-scented air when the brooch's truths struck her.

Her grandfather had sold his brooch to survive. Made of stones and silver, Finlan kept its image in his heart. A piece of Scotland to sustain him, thoughts of the Luckenbooth brooch held the truth of his memories, giving him his motivation for hope. Finlan had replaced the remembered brooch when he could. Different stones, new silver but what the Luckenbooth brooch represents remains the same. It held a legacy of hope.

Margi locked eyes with Will. Her father squeezed her hand before placing it in Will's. She heard the words, answering in a joyful voice. Her eyes never left Will's as he slipped a gold ring on her finger. She welcomed its feel and promise.

They were pronounced man and wife. Turning to their family and friends, cheers went up. Calls wishing them joy and happiness rang in the air, Jamie's being the loudest.

"Uncle Will, kiss Aunt Margi," he shouted.

Will's lips slid over hers, soft with love. Their breaths mingled, sending shivers through her as she kissed her husband back. Her heart swelled with love for this man as she pulled him closer. He was hers and she was his.

His lips slid to her ear. "I love you beyond life, Margaret Blackwood Hamilton."

Margi's joy-filled laugh rang out as she gifted her husband with the smile of a well-loved wife.

GWENDOLYN SCHULER

GROWING UP IN SALEM, MASSACHUSETTS fueled Gwen Schuler's love of history and the sea. Fortune or fate set her upon the deck of her own sailboat as she took her readers with her via her blog as associate editor of Seaboat.com at its inception. Her pieces for the Chesapeake's, Nor'easter magazine featured the cruising life and the personalities she met in her travels between the Chesapeake and the Bahamas. "A Patriot Heart" as part of "Brandywine Brides" is Gwen's second anthology.

BOOKS BY GWENDOLYN SCHULER:

Any Earl Will Do in THE MARRIAGE COIN, 2014

$\mathcal{W}$OUNDED HEART

By

MARTHA SCHROEDER

1865

ESCAPING CONFINEMENT AT A MILITARY hospital as America's Civil War ends, Charles Blackwood seeks Blackwood Farm's solace hoping to reclaim his life and end the hallucinations that plague him. He finds his farm on the brink of ruin but he also rediscovers his first love struggling to save his family's legacy. Will Charles find the strength to admit his love for her and will she find enough trust to return that love?

DEDICATION

&

ACKNOWLEDGEMENTS

To old friends and new—

The Writers Who Lunch who finally had a chance
to write something together after all these years,
And the new friends at Waverly Heights who are
making sunset the nicest time of life!

With profound thanks to Laurel O'Connor, for her
editing and equine expertise and to Robert O'Connor for his
patience and profound technological knowledge.
I owe you both more than I can say.

CHAPTER ONE

THE SLIGHT RISE IN THE deep green hillside felt familiar beneath his feet. He paused for a moment, resting his hand on the neck of the horse he had found wandering on the road and brought along. Two battle-scarred, ragged loners trying to find their way out of the dark and fiery nightmare of war. Maybe this serene landscape that seemed familiar, yet not at all what he was used to seeing, would do it.

The mingled smells of clover and hay were so familiar he felt for a moment as if the door to the past was about to swing open. With it, the chaotic shards of memory would arrange themselves like puzzle pieces and make everything clear once again.

"Hey, you!" The rough voice jerked him back to the confused present. "What are you doing around here? You looking for a job?"

Charles Blackwood blinked as if he were just waking up. "Where am I?" he muttered. Then, as if realizing that was a strange question, he cleared his throat and said, in a stronger voice, "Is this Blackwood's place?"

"Yeah." The rough sounding farm hand squinted into the sun as he stared at Charles. "You know the Blackwoods?"

"Charles and his sister." Charles looked around. The barnyard was raked and the chickens picked their way through fresh corn.

"You know Miss Louisa?" The man sounded suspicious.

"Yes, I grew up around here."

"Oh, yeah?" The man stepped closer, looking ever more suspicious. "And who might you be?"

Charles was deciding what semi-truth to offer up when he heard the whisper of a woman's shoes on the barnyard dirt. "Charles!" He recognized that voice but it wasn't his sister's.

He looked up and stared directly into the clear blue eyes of his childhood friend and partner in untold mischief. Tessa. Tessa—he cast about for the rest of her name but, like so much of his past, it stuck just on the cloudy side of memory. Then it came to him. Tessa King. For a moment, Charles forgot where he was, who he had become. A smile formed before he could stop it and he felt the deep scar on his left cheek tighten and pull sharply upward, twisting his face into a sort of parody of a smile. He held up his hand in an instinctive gesture to keep her at her distance.

"I don't know who you think I am, ma'am," he said, a cold frown replacing the instinctive smile. He took a step backward. He always kept his distance from people before they could turn from him in revulsion.

Tessa's smile became uncertain for a moment. But she shook her head as if clearing cobwebs from her brain and held out both her hands. "Don't be absurd, Charles. What game are you playing?" She took his hands in hers. He was surprised to feel them firm and work-worn. When he looked down at them, he saw they were well-tended but bore unmistakable signs of hard work.

"Are you thinking I do not look as pretty as I used to?" She pulled her hands from his grasp and put them behind her back. She flushed as she looked down at her faded cotton dress.

"Few of us remained the same if we stayed around to do the work." She raised her chin and looked at him closely, but Charles could see no hint of pity or revulsion in her gaze. "I guess we have both changed." She smiled wistfully. "But I would know you anywhere."

Reassured by her apparent acceptance of his appearance, Charles returned her smile. Yes, they had changed. Tessa, the merry, quicksilver sprite, was older, more serious. The carefree light that had brightened every room she entered had dimmed.

"What are you doing here, Tessa?" he asked. "I've been...ill for... awhile and I haven't had any letters from Louisa. Do you know where she is?"

He took a step back from her. He hated lying but it was necessary when he didn't know or couldn't reveal the truth. He had no idea how long he had been in the hospital and had lost some days on the road since he had walked out with the clothes on his back and the hundred dollar bill he had sewn in the sole of his right boot. He had heard the doctors talking about sending him to Saint Elizabeth's Hospital outside Washington. He knew what that meant. St. Elizabeth's was the lunatic asylum. Once you were in there, you did not come out.

From that moment, he had thought only of hiding his condition by avoiding people and thus not revealing the hallucinations and nightmares. He had made his way by instinct alone to the place he could not name but where he knew he would be safe.

"Louisa isn't here." Tessa's voice was clipped and her face cold. It was so unlike the sunny expression he remembered that Charles stepped backward. "I'm running your farm now. Have been since she left."

Charles took a deep breath and planted his feet solidly, in an attempt to find his footing in this uncertain world. Louisa gone? He couldn't believe it. The dream that had kept him going all these long, nightmarish months had been the thought of Louisa and him working on their horse farm together.

"What drove her away?" Instinctively his hand tightened on the rope with which he was leading the tired, uncared for horse that stood patiently waiting. Now he butted his head gently again Charles's shoulder—a bid for attention and an offer of comfort.

Tessa reached her hand out to stroke the horse's neck. "What a good boy," she crooned. "We'll have to find you some fresh hay and a dry stall to sleep in. What's his name?" she asked Charles.

An embarrassing question. He didn't really want to tell her the simple name he used. But she looked as if he might be able to trust her, at least a little. "Buddy," he said. The horse *was* his buddy, his only friend during the long trek from the hospital to this place that he had thought was home. He feared Tessa might laugh at the idea of such a plain, uncared for animal being his friend. He didn't know what people would think. But then he didn't look much better than his friend.

Tessa put her hand on his arm. "Let's go into the house. I'll have Casey take care of Buddy. I have a lot to tell you."

Charles felt the nerves just beneath his skin jump. She was going to tell him something he didn't want to hear, something he feared would make the waking nightmares come back, perhaps even the visions that were so real they convinced him he was back on the battlefield, could smell the smoke, see the fire, hear the cries of the wounded.

Still, this was home and he had nowhere else to go. He shrugged and braced his shoulders. He looked after Buddy as the man led him away. Louisa might have gone away but he still had his friend.

He looked at the woman by his side. Perhaps Tessa would truly be his friend as she had been when they were children. They entered the house through the back door, rather than the porch his mother had added to the front and had always insisted they use.

A pot of something savory simmered on the back burner, coffee in the old spatterware coffee pot steamed on the front of the stove and a fresh loaf of bread rested on the cutting board. "Sit down," Tessa said, wiping her hands on her apron. "I'll pour us some coffee and we can talk."

She seemed nervous. Within a few minutes there was a cup of steaming coffee set before him and Charles inhaled the familiar scent. "Thank you," he said. "This smells like home."

"You are home, Charles." She looked down at her hands as they rested on the scrubbed pine table. "I'm the one who doesn't belong."

"Tell me what happened. Why are you doing farm work instead of living in that big fancy place your brother built down the road?" He smiled at her. He had often teased her about the large, white mansion Jackson was so proud of.

Tessa smiled but it was a stiff and ironic smile, not the open happy expression he remembered. "Well, the war happened and you may remember Jackson was never one to get his elegant embroidered waistcoats mussed. So, when the guns started firing, he began packing and getting ready to leave."

She had kept her voice light and ironic but Charles could tell she was embarrassed and angry. "He wasn't drafted?" Charles asked.

"He convinced the army that he would be more useful brokering cotton and raising money for the Union in England." The words fell like stones.

"And did he?" Charles couldn't keep the contempt out of his voice.

"I believe so." She looked down at the table top. "The army didn't seem to think I needed to know what Jackson was doing." She circled her coffee cup on the table, paying strict attention to every circle. "Jackson didn't think so either. But Louisa left me a letter when she left for New York and another short one when they left for London. She told me they had married before they sailed. That's the last I heard from either of them. I would have written that I had moved into your house so I could look after the horses if I had known where to write."

"Why did you move here?" Charles looked at her. He wasn't sure the Tessa he remembered was as tough and principled as this formidable girl.

She looked up. There was a sheen of tears in her cornflower blue eyes. "I had nowhere else to go. Jackson sold Hedgemere out from under me. He thought that without money or a home I would have to go along with them to New York. After all, what else could I do?"

"Why didn't you?" Charles didn't think he sounded accusatory, but Tessa flinched.

"I couldn't join the army, but I wasn't going to tuck tail and run away." She raised her chin. "Taking care of your place was the only thing I could think of that would help the army." She looked up at him. "Help you." It was almost a whisper.

She straightened her shoulders and looked proud. "And it did help. The army came by soon after and bought the horses. Paid me for them. A good thing, too, because not long after that, Confederate raiders came and took everything that wasn't nailed down. All the crops, the two milk cows, the chickens. Afterward, some of the neighbors sold me some chickens and some seed corn they'd hidden and I planted the vegetables. So we got by."

Charles was amazed. He had always known that Tessa had a sharp brain under those blonde curls, but he had never seen her steely resolve before.

"Didn't you have anything from Jackson? From your place?"

Tessa rose and went to the stove. "Are you hungry?" she asked. "Would you like a bowl of stew? It's really not half bad. Maisie Alcott has taught me a few simple recipes so she doesn't have to do all the cooking."

"Maisie's moved in here with you?"

"Yes, Charles. There were Confederate raiders before the battle and some stragglers Lee left behind afterward. It was safer for both of us to be here together. And she found some money in the Alcott house. Her brother left it for her when he went with the army. We closed up her house and tried to do what farming we could on both places."

"Did anyone other than Jackson leave?" Charles could hear the accusation in his voice when he mentioned Jackson.

Tessa's tone turned frosty. "Yes, Charles. Your sister."

"She must have been forced," he said again, his chin set in a stubborn line Tessa used to laugh at when they were children. "Louisa wouldn't have left all the animals and implements and crops and just walked off."

Tessa gave him a pitying look. "Jackson can be very persuasive, when he waves silks and furs and jewels at a girl. Particularly when an enemy army is marching toward her."

Charles shook his head, as if trying to get rid of an annoying insect buzzing in his ear. "But, Tessa, we won at Gettysburg. Didn't it all end then?"

"Surely you knew what was happening. You were in the army. Someone said your unit was at Gettysburg. Didn't you see what happened? Don't you know?"

The vise-like band around his skull began to tighten and the sounds of artillery and rifle fire began to sound from over the hill. He closed his eyes and began to pray that he be allowed to avoid the hallucinations this time.

"You don't see much when you're in a battle," he said. "Bullets and artillery fire and screams. And it goes on and on. I remember my unit going forward. We got to the crest of a hill on what I remember was the second day." He had never talked about Gettysburg. He could feel reality start to slip sideways and he gripped his coffee cup tightly. It was real, something he could believe in. "Or I think I remember," he whispered to himself.

Tessa looked at him and Charles tensed. He had been travelling alone, with only Buddy for company, for so long that he had gotten used to talking to himself or the horse as they walked the endless miles. What would Tessa, his old friend, do? Would that simple sentence make her suspect that Charles suffered from what he had heard the doctors call "soldier's heart"? A kind description for having gone insane in the aftermath of battle.

But Tessa smiled and extended her hand. "Come upstairs and let's get you settled. You look like you could use a good long sleep."

Charles looked down at himself. "What I would really like is a bath. Doesn't have to be hot, just clean water and lots of soap."

Tessa nodded. "Of course. Do you remember where the pump is? Out by the well, under the cherry tree."

He closed his eyes. For just a minute, as she spoke, he could see the well and picture himself and Tessa running around it, throwing water at each other, screaming with laughter. He smiled. He was home. This was the place where he belonged.

"Is the wash tub still in the milk house?" he asked.

"Yes, just where it's always been. And the soap is in the stone crock by the bucket." She moved towards the small stone house where they kept the milk to keep it cool. "I'll get it."

"No, you've done enough for me." Charles put his hand on her arm.

"And you've been working all day. I can get my own bath ready, if you can tell me where the towels are."

"I'll get some." Tessa slipped out of the room and returned a few minutes later with clean towels that smelled like sunshine. They must have hung on the line that had always been strung between two ash trees in the side yard.

"Thank you," Charles said, breathing deeply. "This is wonderful." He closed his eyes. Maybe if there were enough things here that struck chords of home he would lose those screaming visions of the battlefields filled with smoke and flame and dying men and animals.

Charles moved off toward the pump and Tessa turned back toward the house, her hands clenched tight to keep sobs from bursting from her throat. She could not prevent the tears from running down her cheeks. Charles, so tired and dirty and wary, even of his oldest playmate and friend. That hurt her more than anything, even more than the defection of Jackson and Louisa. But the haunted look in his eyes and the fear when he looked at her told her that Charles had suffered greatly and was still not free of the memories of war.

Tessa followed the sounds of Buddy's nervous whinny to find the horse in the small pen at the back of the barn. Casey was standing without moving, armed only with a soft brush and a bucket of water. The horse wasn't threatening him, merely tossing his head and looking from side to side as if trying to find out how he could escape if he had to. But Tessa feared that any sharp movement on Casey's part might frighten Buddy. She moved closer, her tread quiet and her voice soft. "Now, Buddy, no one wants to hurt you. No one at all." Her voice a sing-song cadence, she looked at him in the eyes and smiled. She reached for the bucket and brush. At that movement, Buddy tossed his head and whinnied. His eyes rolled and Tessa put the bucket down without a sound. "It's all right, you good fella," she said. "I won't do anything you don't want. We'll just wait until you get used to us and to the barn and the stalls."

Buddy was not reassured. His eyes rolled and his feet danced nervously. Tessa inched back away from him. "Let's just move away and let him have the pen to himself until Charles comes."

She spoke softly and Casey nodded. "Yes, ma'am, that's fine by me." He moved quietly toward the door from the outdoor pen to the stable and slipped through. Tessa reached out a peaceful hand and stroked the horse's neck. She used the soapy brush in a soothing motion down his body. At that moment, there was a movement and Tessa turned her head slightly to see Charles enter the stable. He was grinning.

"Are you giving these nice folks a hard time, Buddy-o?" he asked. He walked forward and stroked the horse's nose and said, "See, I had a bath and I feel much better. I promise you, you'll like being clean once you get used to it." Buddy nudged Charles' shoulder and stood patiently while Charles dipped the brush in the soapy water and began to finish washing him. Tessa could have sworn that the horse sighed and began to relax as Charles stroked down his body. "Doesn't that feel nice? You feel much lighter without all that mud and dirt, don't you?" Charles continued to talk soothingly as he washed rhythmically.

Tessa saw what was needed and she left to get another bucket of clean water and place it near the horse. She could see that the animal was already looking much more presentable. "He's a dappled gray, Charles, not mud colored. Once he's fed and groomed he'll be a very handsome boy." She nodded at Charles, who was looking much better, as well, despite the water spots and dirt splotches on his pants. His black hair was gleaming as it used to and his blue eyes, though tired, were brighter, not the dull blue they had been when he and Buddy arrived. He even seemed to be standing a little taller and a faint smile played around his long, mobile mouth. "You may need another bath and another pair of Jackson's britches once you get Buddy clean, but you'll be a handsome boy, too. I promise you." She gave him one of her old cheeky smiles.

Charles smiled back. "Well, we'll both look a lot better. Handsome, I don't promise."

Tessa dipped the brush in the bucket of clean water and handed it to Charles. "Come inside once you finish putting Buddy's hay in his stall. I'll make up a bedroom for you. You can have your old one at the top of the stairs, though Maisie—"

The door she had referred to suddenly swung open with a bang and a tall, large-boned woman stood frowning in the doorway, holding a rifle across her body. "What's going on? Who are you?" she demanded.

Charles took a breath and managed not to reach for a nonexistent weapon when faced with someone who was armed and sounded angry. The woman might not know him but fortunately he knew her.

"Hello, Maisie." He forced himself to extend a hand. "I'm Charles Blackwood."

CHAPTER TWO

"YOU'RE NOT." THE DEEP, RASPY voice was accusatory. "You can't be."

"But of course he is, Maisie." Tessa sounded surprised. "I recognized him even before he opened his mouth. How can you not see it?"

Maisie stared at Tessa for a moment, then at Charles. When she spoke, she sounded strained but friendly. "I'm sorry, Charles. You surprised me and the sun was in my eyes. Of course, it's you. Welcome home."

Charles was used to studying people who were trying to sound friendly. Maisie was smiling now, but her eyes were cool and wary. He'd seen that same look in the eyes of the army doctor who'd pretended to be his sympathetic friend just before he'd stood in the hall and spoke of sending Charles to a locked ward.

Before he could respond, Tessa spoke up. "I'm going to make up a bedroom for Charles. Since you're already settled in the second bedroom, Maisie, I thought I would make up the third floor room for him. Then we can discuss plans over dinner. Isn't it lucky I made a big pot of stew? Plenty for everyone. Casey can stay, too." She smiled at both her friends, and appeared not to notice that neither of them seemed very comfortable with the idea.

Before Charles could think of a friendly but cool response, Buddy stamped his right front foot and let out a loud snort. "That's a serious bid for attention," Charles said. "I'd better see if I can untangle his mane and tail." He turned away from the two women and looked around for a comb.

"I'll go find Casey and see if he can find a comb." Tessa slipped out the door, leaving Charles and Maisie staring at each other. Maisie was still armed, but Buddy stood between them and that gave Charles some protection, a guardian. As he recalled, the Alcotts weren't horsemen and Maisie was looking at Buddy very warily. Charles breathed a little easier.

"I'm glad you were here with Tessa during the fighting particularly," he said, rummaging around the shelves and finding a ragged old towel. He began to rub Buddy down with it. He looked around again. "Is there a blanket here? I wouldn't want Buddy to get cold."

"I don't know." Maisie sounded impatient. "We haven't had horses here since the last Confederate raid." She narrowed her eyes. "You seem to be making yourself right at home in a mighty quick hurry."

"You forget." He gave her a cool, level look. "I *am* home. But you are most welcome to stay on with Tessa. There is plenty of room for all, and she shouldn't be by herself."

Maisie gave him a sour smile. "What about me? Don't you think I need protection?"

Charles nodded toward the rifle she still held cradled across her body. "Seems to me you have a good amount already. Shouldn't Tessa have a gun, too?"

"Can she shoot?"

"Of course she can. But if you had any doubts you could have asked her. Even had a little target practice if you wanted a demonstration."

Maisie tried another smile and a more conciliatory tone. "No need for rifles now, Charles. The war's been over since last year. Which reminds me…" Her voice sharpened. "Where have you been all this time?"

Charles consciously relaxed his muscles and continued to rub Buddy slowly and rhythmically. "Why do you ask?"

"I like to know who's putting his feet under my table. And what they've been doing."

Charles raised his eyebrows but said nothing, letting her words hang in the air. Maisie tried to stare him down but Charles shook his head ruefully. "I thought we had established they are Charles Blackwood's feet and they will be under Charles Blackwood's table. You seem to have trouble keeping that thought in mind."

Maisie drew herself up to her full height, which was close to Charles' six feet. "I will leave in the morning if you want me to." Her voice was a challenge, but Charles refused to be drawn in to her argument.

He shook his head. "I've told you I would like you to stay on as a companion to Tessa. I don't think she should be alone out here without another woman."

At that moment, the door opened and Casey came in, carrying a wide-toothed comb and a well-worn blanket. "Here we are. Haven't needed this for some time." He went over to the stall he had filled with hay and clover. "It'll be nice having an animal around again. I'll get started on this fellow's mane and tail. Gonna take some doing to get him back in shape, but the shape of his head, way his ears are set—he'll look real good." Without waiting for a reply, Casey started to work.

Maisie gave a derisive sneer and turned away. "I'll go see if Tessa needs any help in the house. Set of his ears, indeed," she muttered. "As if you knew anything about horses." She slammed out of the stable.

"Seems a bit tetchy," Charles remarked. "I don't remember her much from before the war. How did she come to live here, do you know?"

"No. She just showed up, I guess. I think she came just a few weeks before I got here." Without another word, Casey rolled up his left pant leg, revealing a long, red scar, puckered and making his leg twist to the inside. "In case you wondered why I wasn't in the army at Gettysburg. I've learned to walk pretty straight so long as I don't have to stand for too long at a stretch."

"I caught the hitch in your step," Charles said without a grimace at the sight of the scar. "How long were you in?"

"July of sixty-two to January of sixty-three. Hardly long enough to get my uniform dirty."

"Long enough to get that scar. That's plenty long enough." Charles took the bucket of water he'd used to rinse Buddy's coat and tossed it out the door.

"Thanks," said Casey.

"What for? Just telling the truth."

"That's not the way some people see it. When I got out of the hospital, I was mustered out and came back here. There were a lot of whispers about deserters and such like."

"A lot of people who never saw a gun fired in a battle have a lot of opinions about war. You shouldn't pay them any mind, Casey."

"Thanks," Casey said again."Let's let this fellow have some peace to eat his dinner and get some rest." Charles put Buddy in his stall, gave him a pat and turned to leave.

❧

Meantime, Tessa was having an awkward conversation with Maisie. Until today, she had taken Maisie's quirks and sharp opinions in stride. Tessa's brother, Jackson, had been high-handed and insisted on things being done his way. She had usually taken the easy way out, giving way and seeming to agree when she did not.

Now, she was aware that she had taken the same path with Maisie. But no more. Perhaps it was because Charles had returned and she had confronted him about Louisa. Later, she had watched him face down Maisie in a calm and reasonable way that left no room for Maisie to bluster and continue to argue. Tessa thought she could hold her own if she could do it calmly, not be drawn into a loud argument or forced to flee the sound of Maisie's loud, abrasive voice.

"How long are you going to let this Charles person stay here?" Maisie slapped some silverware on the table in no particular order.

Tessa folded napkins neatly and straightened the knives and forks. "It's not for me to say, Maisie. Or you either," she added when Maisie opened her mouth and frowned. "It is his house. I don't know why you act as if you had never seen him before."

"I don't remember him," Maisie mumbled. "I'm not sure he's Charles Blackwood. Could be anyone. Someone who picked up Charles' army papers on the battlefield. You hear of that happening."

Tessa stared at her. "I'm amazed you don't recognize him. It's Charles Blackwood, no mistake and no stolen papers. I don't know how you don't see it, Maisie. But you'll just have to take my word for it. It's Charles." She smiled. "It's wonderful he made it through the war. I'll have to write Louisa. I have her address in London. She'll be so excited."

Maisie didn't look excited as one should if a neighbor had come back from being presumed dead. She looked as if Charles didn't belong at the Blackwood farm. Tessa shrugged. "I don't understand you. I know people around here have thought Charles was dead, but they'll be delighted that he's home, safe and sound. And you'll just have to get used to it and stop talking as if he's some stranger."

Maisie began to spoon stew into a big white china serving bowl. "I'd still like to know where he's been all this time."

Tessa turned to face Maisie and put her hands on her hips. "You listen to me. This is Charles, come through the war and home in one piece, thank the good lord. Just accept it and treat him like the returning hero he is." If she sounded angry it was probably because she, too, wondered where Charles had been since the Battle of Gettysburg had ended in July of 1863. And he didn't seem likely to tell her any time soon.

Maisie looked startled. Tessa thought she probably had never heard mild-mannered Tessa speak in that no-nonsense tone of voice. But she wasn't about to give in without a last attempt to cast doubt on him. "Even if it is Charles, you don't know he was a hero. Lots of men were in the army and didn't shine in battle."

Casey stood in the open doorway. "You're right about that, Miz Alcott. Some got shot up without the chance to fire back." He nodded to Tessa. "I'll take my stew in the stable with Buddy. He doesn't care how I got wounded, or where."

"Casey, don't be silly. You'll eat at the table, same as always. Sit down and have some stew and some of this bread I baked this afternoon."

Her voice was low and calm but it held a note of steel and Casey sat down without more argument. "Thank you, Miss Tessa."

They could hear Charles moving around the third floor. No one spoke for a moment while his footsteps sounded. Tessa broke the spell first. She moved to serve Casey and then Maisie. "Come and start supper. Charles will be down in a few minutes. He had to change his clothes."

"I didn't see any men's clothes left in the closets here." Maisie looked up from her dinner.

Tessa stared at her. "And I didn't know you had searched through this house."

Maisie shrugged. "I didn't search exactly. Just while I was cleaning sometimes I happened to look."

Tessa was tempted to drop the subject but she thought of how Charles managed to say what he had to say without raising a ruckus. "You never cleaned." She kept her voice firm and quiet. "I did it or Casey's mother came over to help. You worked the fields. How did you come to look through the drawers and closets?"

Maisie shrugged again but didn't answer. After a moment's silence, she asked Casey to pass the bread. Tessa picked up the bread board but held it in front of her tightly, her knuckles white. "I'd like to know how you found out there weren't any of Charles' clothes here."

Maisie stared at her, her jaw set in a stubborn line, her eyes hooded. "I don't remember. For heaven's sake, Tessa, you are making such a fuss about a pair of pants."

"It's not about pants, Maisie. It's about you snooping."

"I wasn't snooping!" Maisie's voice had risen to a near shout. It was at this point that Tessa usually gave way or left the room.

This time, she didn't have to decide how to stand her ground. Charles had entered the room and seemed to grasp the situation at once. He went to stand beside Tessa, who gave a slight sigh. She felt safer with Charles there.

"What were you looking for, Maisie?" he asked. His voice was low and pleasant but his expression was stern. "When you didn't find my pants."

"Nothing. I don't know what all the fuss is about." She shoved her plate back and got to her feet. "I'm not hungry. Good night."

She might not be hungry, Tessa thought, but she'd grabbed two slices of bread before stalking out of the room.

Charles calmly sat down and smiled at Tessa. "This looks wonderful. It's been a long time since I've had a hot meal at a real table. And been able to share it with friends. Except for Buddy, of course." He grinned at Tessa and Casey and picked up his fork. "And he wasn't much of a conversationalist."

The meal was hot and tasty, just what Charles said he hadn't had in a long while. Tessa smiled. She could cook well enough to make a really good dinner. And this was the most pleasant company she'd had for a long time. Years ago, before the war, there had been parties at the King home. Her mother and father had entertained lavishly and Tessa had been allowed to stay up and peer through the banisters at the grownups below as they moved through the rooms in their colorful dresses and well-tailored formal suits. She smiled a little wistfully. She hadn't thought about those days in a long time. In fact, she hadn't even thought about her parents in weeks, maybe even months. Her pre-war life, with its laughter and wine glasses and sparkling chandeliers, seemed like a dream and she consigned it to that part of her life that she dwelt in just before she slept.

She noticed that she had lost track of the conversation and looked up, startled. Both Charles and Casey were looking at her. "What have I done?" she asked. "Have I missed something?"

"No," Charles said. "But I think you need some fresh air. Let's us go for a walk, just up to the roadway and back."

Casey rose and inclined his head. "I'll say goodnight then." And he went out the back door toward the house he lived in with his mother.

Charles held out his hand and Tessa put hers into it. "Where is your shawl, Tessa? It's chilly out there."

Tessa reached to a row of hooks on the wall by the back door. "I'm afraid it's a bit shabby. For a long time, I haven't thought about clothes or much of anything but putting one foot in front of the other." She took a blue knit shawl from one of the hooks. Gently, Charles took it out of her hands and smoothed it over her shoulders. He handled the faded blue folds as if they were the finest silk and Tessa an aristocratic beauty. She sighed. "I've managed to keep things going but we've only scraped by. I don't know if you can understand how hard it's been."

"Tessa, of course I can. You've been wonderful. I am amazed that the place hasn't fallen to pieces. I've passed many that have on my way back here. I can't believe what you've done. Where did you find the money to make repairs and keep up with the crops? You're amazing."

She ducked her head in embarrassment. "Oh, it was mostly Maisie. She had some money, I guess from her brother, and she spent it on Blackwood since Jackson sold Hedgemere."

"Who bought it? Do you know them?" They had come to the end of the path and paused to lean against the picket fence.

Tessa shook her head. "No, actually, I've never met them. As far as I know, they've never even come to look at it. I guess after the battle they decided Pennsylvania wasn't such a healthy place to live."

"Strange." Charles looked down at Tessa's face. Illuminated as it was by moonlight, it was mysterious and beautiful. He couldn't resist. He had to reach out and touch the rose petal softness of her cheek. He moved slowly, as if mesmerized. "Lovely. You are a picture of a beautiful girl by moonlight."

Tessa shook her head and ducked. "You're being silly. I'm not lovely. Jackson told me once that I would never be anywhere near as pretty as Louisa."

Charles smiled. "Well, I guess Jackson and I admire each other's sister. I think Louisa is nice looking but nothing close to as lovely as you are. So, I guess he and I will just have to agree to disagree." He stroked her cheek and she raised her eyes. What he read in their depths was irresistible. He pulled her closer with a gentle tug and touched her lips with his. Tessa had never been kissed with anything like the tenderness she felt from Charles. The farm, the bone-deep fatigue that dogged her steps every day, the daily grind of work that never was finished and never ended—all faded away. Instead, she was enveloped in warmth and strength and happiness. In a single instant, she felt her world, her life take on new color and meaning.

"Oh, Charles." It was all she could say, more than she should have said.

"My darling girl." He rubbed her arms and put his arm around her. "Forgive me. You are shivering. Let's get you inside before you catch your death."

The concern in his voice was sweeter than the loveliest love song.

"Yes, Charles."

"I shouldn't have kissed you. No one is here to protect you."

"Protect me from you?" Tessa gave a quiet, musical laugh. "That is very chivalrous of you, Charles, but I don't think I need protection from you. And if I should, by some mischance, I have a pistol always with me." She smiled at him again, kissed her forefinger and placed it on his lips. "Good night, dear Charles. Rest well."

CHAPTER THREE

CHARLES SPENT A FEW MINUTES wandering about the first-floor rooms. He hadn't been in the house in over three years. His memories were eroded by his wounds and his illness and the harsh pain of battle. He looked around his family home and breathed in the scent of wax on wooden furniture and starch on clean linen. Home. He smiled. But something tugged at his consciousness. He closed his eyes to see if he could call it up more clearly. There it was—a second floor window. He couldn't see exactly what had startled him, seemed out of place. Then he saw it, a shadow of a human being that had stood quietly at the window looking down at them.

He was still unclear as to what or who it was. Slowly he turned his head to see if he could see what had caused the shadow to stand still. What was it staring at? He had no idea. If he had been still at Gettysburg or having one of his waking nightmares of those three days of hell, he would have said the shadow was looking down at one of the houses scattered around the town.

He shook his head impatiently. It was absurd to try to fit everything he saw into his past experiences. This fleeting shadow might not relate to anything in the war. Impatiently, he continued down the hall and mounted the stairs to the second floor as silently as he could. On impulse, he looked around the second floor and saw an open bedroom door. A quiet figure stood by a window. He drew back, away from the door. Maisie was at the window. It was she who had stared down at Charles and Tessa as they had kissed.

What difference did that make? Impatiently he moved toward the stairs to the third floor where his small bedroom was waiting for him. He mounted the stairs, making as little noise as he could. When he arrived at his room, he entered to find a great sense of peace. The bed had been made up with sheets and a blanket that were well-worn but clean and soft. The walls were close and he felt safe. A deep breath. This was home. Without doing more than slipping out of his clothes and climbing into the bed, Charles was ready for sleep. No more tossing and turning and attempting to think of peaceful things to ward off nightmare memories. Here, he was surrounded by peaceful things. Smiling quietly, he slid into sleep.

The next day he awoke with the sun and enjoyed several precious minutes of silence and quiet before getting up and dressing. He smoothed his bed and looked around to make sure that everything was in order. He gave a quiet nod of approval and started downstairs. On the second floor, everything was quiet and he continued to the first. He felt as if any noise he made would shatter the peace of the morning. He looked into the kitchen. No one was there, but the back door was ajar so he went over and looked out. Tessa was feeding the chickens and filling the water dishes with fresh water. When she looked up, she saw him at the doorway and came over to him.

"Good morning, Charles." Her voice held a smile and he couldn't help but smile back. "I've got some eggs for breakfast for you and Casey and me. Maisie wanted to go see her family and she's left already. She seemed to be in a big hurry. I don't think anyone is ill, but she wanted to go before first light."

"When will she be back?" Something tickled at the back of his mind.

"I'm not exactly sure. She thought maybe by the end of the week."

"Does she do this very often?"

Tessa looked at him with a faint frown marring her forehead. "No, not often at all. But when she does want to go see them I can't stand in her way."

Charles smiled, banishing the vague worries about Maisie's disappearance. "How did she go?" He couldn't help his questions.

Tessa began beating eggs for scrambling. "She walks to the road and gets a ride with a farmer and his wagon. She's known hereabouts so it probably won't take her more than a few hours to get to end of Chester County where her family lives."

There seemed to be nothing suspicious about Maisie's activities, so Charles went about his chores, ate breakfast, complimented Tessa on the fluffiness of the omelet and Casey on the coffee when he found out that the handyman had prepared it. Then he set out to see what needed to be done around the place.

When he went into the stable to see to Buddy, he noticed that the horse was missing a shoe. Probably had been for some days but both Charles and Buddy had been so tired as they pushed themselves on toward Charles' home, that they hadn't paid attention to a missing shoe.

Later that morning, he and Casey took Buddy to the blacksmith whose shop was in the nearby village. The smith took a good look at Buddy's hoof and told Charles he was lucky he'd brought Buddy in before his hoof cracked. That would have made it much harder to mend. He appeared to be curious about how Charles had found the animal. Charles was always leery when anyone took an interest in either where he had been before he came home or how he and Buddy had become travelling companions. It made him nervous and he couldn't help but wonder if the army was looking for him and who might be seeking Buddy. He hadn't thought much about it before they had gotten home to Blackwood. They had looked like any pair of poor strays, leftovers from the war, no different from any other wandering man and horse. But the war was over and questions now seemed more pointed.

With a civil reply and a cash payment of the bill, Charles moved quietly and politely to cut off the conversation and head back to the farm. After they had led Buddy down the road for a mile or so, Casey said quietly, "Are you running from the law or something, Charles? Miss Tessa knows you. You seem to own the farm but you get very nervous when people want to know about you."

"You asking questions, Casey?" Charles picked up his pace a little. "Because there are a lot of men like me, who didn't end the war where they started out. I'm not sure all of us can account for every hour or defend every action."

Casey held up his hands. "I'm not asking anything. I'm just saying, I'll be happy to back up any account you choose to give. I'm on your side. I just wanted you to know that you can count on me."

"Thanks, Casey. Let's hope I don't have to take you up on it. I confess I've been getting an itchy feeling recently, like someone is watching me from behind a barn or up a tree. Used to feel that way a lot when Jeb Stuart was nosing around Pennsylvania and the battle was coming on. Don't know why it's getting bad now."

Casey looked at him with clear eyes. "Maybe it's not a holdover from the war. Maybe somebody *is* watching you or getting ready to. Let's keep an eye out for anyone asking questions or any stranger. Can't hurt to be careful."

Charles felt a great sense of gratitude to Casey for taking his fears seriously but matter-of-factly. He breathed easier as they continued back to the farm. When they arrived, however, the peace suddenly disappeared. Standing at the doorway, talking to Tessa, were two men. They weren't dressed for the country but wore plain dark suits and carried large briefcases.

"Not army," Casey breathed.

Charles took a deep breath. "Pinkertons." Private detectives who had served the government during the war but now did private investigations for those who could afford them. He debated what his course of action should be. Should he face them now or try to evade them? What would the point be? If he ran, where would he go? He was home. This was where he wanted to be. His fear was of the doctors and the threat of those locked doors in St. Elizabeth's hospital and the sobs and cries that came from behind them. He did not fear a Pinkerton investigation. It was not a police force.

Still, the fear of being taken back to the army hospital turned his stomach to ice. He squared his shoulders and went up the steps where he saw Tessa smiling at the detectives. "Here he is, gentlemen. Charles," she beamed at him, "these men are here to tell you that you have been awarded a purple heart for the wounds you suffered at Gettysburg. Isn't that right, gentlemen?"

"Well, it will be awarded at a later date. Right now, we would like Lieutenant Blackwood to come with us to the Army Hospital. Lieutenant?" The two men circled around Charles and each went to take an arm. But Tessa stepped up and put her arm around Charles' waist.

"Why, gentlemen, you didn't tell me that you wanted to take my fiancé away with you. Why do you want to do that?" Tessa smiled at them, but her arm tightened around Charles. "I will have to insist on going with you. We are only recently engaged and I cannot allow him out of my sight. You know how we newly engaged girls are." She managed a girlish giggle that was very unlike her. The look in her eyes was worried, but she continued to play her part. Charles was happy to go along.

"Of course, dear," he said with what he hoped was a doting smile. "Everywhere we go, we go together. The war parted us long enough.

We don't want the army to keep us apart any longer." He leaned over her and placed a tender kiss on her brow.

The Pinkertons looked at each other. Charles was happy to see that they looked a little confused. "Don't worry, detectives," he said. "I'm not going anywhere. I'm home and so is my fiancée. We'll be here when you come back with a warrant."

"We'll be back, sir," said one of the detectives. "We need to confer with our principal."

"And who is that?" asked Tessa, her voice still sweet and calm. "And what do they want?"

The two detectives turned and left the property at a brisk walk without another word. Tessa and Charles turned to each other. "What happened, Tessa? When did those men appear and what did they say they wanted?" He knew his expression was cold and worried, not warm and grateful. He felt those emotions but this large secret had festered within him for so long he did not know how to begin to talk to Tessa.

"They said you could be a deserter and they needed to find you and see if you were the Charles Blackwood who had left the Satterlee Hospital in Philadelphia without authorization." Tessa looked worried and frightened. Was she frightened of him? Charles couldn't blame her if she were.

He would tell her everything. She had a right to know. She had lied to the detectives for him without knowing whether he deserved her protection. "I guess," he began, "that technically I am a deserter. The war was over and I was in the hospital though my wound was almost healed."

Tessa's face looked drawn and pale. "Why did you leave, Charles? Why didn't you wait to be discharged like everyone else?"

Now the truth had to be told. "I had nightmares. In the daytime when I was awake. I would hear cannons firing and men screaming. It was absolutely real, Tessa. I could have sworn that a battle was going on right outside the window. In fact, I probably did swear there was fighting." He paused, fighting the sense that one of his nightmares was about to overtake him. "I can't describe it any other way. Living nightmares, as real as sunlight and corn in the field."

Tessa looked at him gravely. "Do you know they aren't real or do you think you have to fight them?"

"At first I thought they were real, even though I saw the hospital and doctors and nurses and knew there wasn't a battle going on. I can't explain it. Except that, slowly, I realized the difference. Although, at first I had to tell myself that what I saw and heard wasn't true. Slowly, I began to know the difference even though, every so often, I still hear and see what isn't there. Now I know it isn't."

"Why did you run away?"

Could he bring himself to reveal the truth about what had awaited him if he had stayed? The calm trust in Tessa's eyes told him he could. She laid her hand on his arm. "You can tell me. I will understand."

He believed her. His heart lightened at the idea of sharing the nightmare truth with her. "The doctors knew that I had these dreams. I tried to hide them, but I couldn't. The screams came out, particularly when I heard the other men's screams." His voice grew lower and quieter, as if he was afraid to be heard.

"What did you think would happen to you?"

He turned to her, anger sharpening his voice. She didn't understand; no normal person could. "I didn't just think I knew, I absolutely did know what would happen to me. It had happened to others. I would be locked away for years, probably forever if I continued to have the waking nightmares. I couldn't stand the idea. I thought for a while that because my wounds were healing they would let me go. Then I heard them talking about me. They said I was hopeless and they would have to lock me away in St. Elizabeth's, the Army hospital and lunatic asylum in Washington. So, that afternoon, I put on my uniform jacket and my boots and walked out the door during exercise hour. The hospital wasn't heavily guarded. Most patients were too sick to leave or do any harm, so I just walked off and headed for home."

Tessa stared at him. "You are the bravest man I know. You could have been shot before you got outside the gates. Or any time while you were on the road." She leaned forward and kissed him. "I am so glad you and Buddy made it home."

He took her hand and smiled back at her, the lightness in his heart even greater now that she had kissed him. He felt happiness growing. "You are pretty intrepid yourself, Miss King. Claiming I was your fiancé to those Pinkertons without a blink. Very quick thinking. What if Casey had said it wasn't true? Or Maisie had come back. She would have denied it in a heartbeat." He frowned a little. "Though now that I think of it, I can't think why she would."

"She hates me." Tessa spoke as calmly as if she were announcing what they would have for dinner. "She's always been in love with you and if she couldn't have you, she would take Jackson. He wasn't as wonderful as you were but he had money and looked as if he could rule the world. She'd take that."

Charles gave an incredulous laugh. He was preferable to Jackson with his money, golden good looks and social position? Unbelievable. He shook his head. "You are perhaps just a little prejudiced towards me because Jackson is your brother and you don't see him as special."

Tessa just smiled at him. "You always were modest, Charles. But believe me, you have Maisie in the palm of your hand. She's just angry because you don't see her that way."

"It's not important, at any rate," he said, shrugging the whole question aside. "What is important is who is trying to send me back to the army hospital and is willing to spend good money to find me and do it. And why would they want to? But thanks to your quick thinking, I'm not sure they will come back. You've made it clear to them that I have friends and they can't just whisk me away without a trace." Charles shuddered. The very thought of being put in a locked ward for the insane was too horrifying to contemplate. His mouth went dry and his hands began to shake. "I can't tell you how grateful I am." At the thought of what he had escaped, his eyes filled and he lowered his head to his hands.

Tessa looked at him. "Come with me. Let's take a walk. We'll go out to the stable and take Buddy a carrot." She held out her hand and smiled.

Charles rose and took her arm. Life was precarious, the war had made that clear, but it was also precious and every moment was golden. This one with Tessa was a particularly rich gold.

The stable was dark, but they had brought an oil lamp and they could see Buddy standing tall, expression alert. "Aren't you a handsome boy?" asked Charles with a smile. Indeed, Buddy was a different animal. He was groomed and his coat was shining and his mane and tail were in perfect order. He stepped over to Charles and pushed against his jacket pocket. Charles laughed. "You think I have a treat for you, do you?" He reached in a pocket and withdrew a carrot. Buddy munched happily. "You've fallen into a tub of butter, haven't you, old friend?" Buddy butted his shoulder and Charles flung an arm around his neck. "Well, yes, you are right. So have I."

CHAPTER FOUR

THE NEXT TWO DAYS SEEMED to pass in a sort of pastoral dream. The farm was still barely functional. There were no large fields planted, just small areas of vegetables. He saw no horses in the stables. Tessa explained that she still did not have the money to care for them so the two horses they did have had remained at the neighbors' farms. Charles was grateful that the place did not look prosperous, since that might cause whoever was hunting him to look harder to find him. They fed the chickens and Buddy and then they weeded the path that led to the house. Tessa baked a pie on the second day and they ate it at lunch with Casey. It was he who brought them back to earth.

"Have you heard anything from Maisie?" he asked. They shook their heads and he frowned. "What about the Pinkertons?" he asked. "Have they been around asking questions of any of the neighbors?"

When Charles and Tessa again shook their heads, he looked at them sternly. "You two are behaving like a couple of gapeseeds. Get your heads on straight." He pointed at Charles. "How could you stay here alone with an unmarried woman? What do you think the Pinkertons could make of her reputation? Won't even need them to do it," he added. "Maisie will do the job on you both all by herself."

Charles felt as if a bucket of cold water had been poured over him. He wondered how he could have been so blind. "You're absolutely right, Casey. Tessa's reputation will be lost. What can I do about it? Can we get your mother to come and stay?"

"That might look even worse to all the neighbors." Casey looked at both of them and shook his head again. "It will just point out that no respectable female has been here for days."

"We've already told the Pinkertons that we are engaged," Tessa said. "Won't that help?"

"You know the people around here. That's not going to do any good. You're not behaving like an engaged couple. No parties, no calling the banns in church. No ring. Charles hasn't even been around to see the neighbors since he came back. It won't work. They'll think you are living together without a wedding. Which," he added, "in fact, you are."

"What can we do?" Charles asked.

Casey looked at him as if he were too stupid to come in out of the rain. "Marry the girl, of course."

Charles looked at Casey. He was appalled. He didn't want to force Tessa into a wedding she might not want. He had told her about his mental problems, problems the army might well view as requiring incarceration in a locked ward for years. She might feel the same. He remained silent. He looked over at Tessa—her face dead white with two bright red spots on her cheeks and he realized that his silence said to her that he didn't want to marry her. Well, he asked himself, did he? Did they still know each other after the separation and upheaval of the war? Was he the same carefree young man he'd been when he'd joined in 1862? He didn't know if he could offer her his life to share with her, as broken and badly mended as he was. As opposed to letting her be gossiped about, of course, he could.

Casey glared at him. "If you won't marry a girl you know is as virtuous as any in the world, then I certainly will." He bowed to Tessa, a strangely courtly gesture from the farm hand. "And honored if she would accept me."

Charles stood and went to take Tessa's hand, but she quickly put both hands behind her back. "Don't say anything, Charles." Her voice was thick with unshed tears. "Anything you say now would mean nothing. You have made it very plain how you feel and I won't marry anyone who had to be shamed into offering for me. Please—" She held up her hand, palm out, as he opened his mouth. "Don't say another word." As she turned on her heel, her blue cotton skirt swirled around her.

The door suddenly opened and Maisie swept in. She looked windblown, her dress collar twisted, her hair uncombed. Her gaze darted all over the room. "Aha!" she said. "So you are all here together. It's worse than I thought! The three of you all staying here. I've never heard of such a thing!" She pointed her finger at Tessa, as if she were the villain in a stage melodrama. "Wait until your brother hears about this. And with you, Charles. Jackson's best friend. Disgraceful!"

At the mention of Jackson, in a tone that said being her brother gave him jurisdiction over Tessa, several things became suddenly clear to Charles. "What do you think Jackson is going to do? She's of age and we are engaged. Besides, he left her here without any means of support or place to live. He has nothing to say about what she does."

Maisie glared at Charles. "After the harm you have done to this poor child, I am surprised you dare even offer her your name. Not that it is worth much. I've heard about what you did in the hospital. Crazy antics and then deserting the army. You are worse than useless."

Charles stared at her. "How do you know what happened to me in the hospital?"

"The Pinkertons told me." Maisie said it proudly. "It will be all over the Commonwealth before nightfall."

"I wouldn't be surprised." He sounded disgusted. "Anyone the Pinkertons don't tell, you will. Explain to me how they knew where to find you, Maisie." Charles spoke slowly. He was thinking his way through a number of things that had puzzled him since he had arrived home.

She looked surprised at the demand and didn't answer for a moment. "I don't know. They just found me. That organization has all sorts of methods. I don't know what they are."

"Oh, in this case, I think you know very well. Because they didn't find you, did they? You found them. The minute you left here, you got in touch with them. But why?"

At this moment, Tessa spoke up. "Because Jackson asked you to. Right, Maisie? He gave you the money you had when you came here asking for a place to stay. Jackson, not your brother."

Maisie raised her chin and spoke as if daring the three of them to find fault. "So what if he did. Why shouldn't he? We've always been friends. He asked me to stay with you. Like a chaperone."

Tessa's gaze was clear and cold. "Then why didn't you tell me what had happened? You pretended you needed a place to stay and said we would live together, sharing our pennies. But you could have asked Jackson for money any time. And you could have told me the truth."

Maisie looked uncomfortable and gazed around, her eyes nervous, like an animal seeking escape.

Charles had been thinking of Maisie. "Where is Louisa, Maisie?" he asked at last. "London? New York? Or right next door at Hedgemere, perhaps. It never was sold, was it?"

"I don't know, Charles. I was to leave messages for Jackson in the hollow tree at the end of the drive. That's all I know." She shrugged as if she had no interest in where Jackson was. Perhaps, as long as she was paid, she didn't.

"What kind of messages?" Charles thought he could make a pretty good guess but he wanted to hear it.

"What Tessa was doing, if she'd met any young men. Things like that. He was interested in his sister. It was only natural." Again, that defensive whine.

"Did he leave anything for you besides questions about Tessa?"

"Money." Maisie had the grace to look ashamed at last. "He would leave me money in the tree if I wrote him we needed it. Not much. Jackson said if I had too much it would look suspicious."

"So you let Tessa scrape along when, all the time, Jackson was getting richer, making bullets and cannons. And getting you to pretend you were in need of money." He stared at Maisie with a cold glare. "You are almost as despicable as he is."

Maisie tossed her head and glared back at Charles. "At least I am not crazy and living alone on a farm with two men, like Tessa."

Charles gave her a frigid smile. "You are confused. *I* am the one who's crazy. Tessa is not crazy and she is not lacking in virtue in any degree whatsoever. And we are to be married as soon as I can convince her that I love her and will work all my life to be worthy of her."

Maisie's eyes gleamed. "So you haven't been able to persuade her you're sane. I am not sure you are, Lieutenant Blackwood. And she might be a bit nutty, too. Anyone who lives as she is doing is probably as crazy as you are." Her eyes gleamed with malice. "Wait until Jackson hears about this."

"It will be some time before news can reach him in London. That is where he is, isn't it?" Charles took two steps toward Maisie and, like the frightened animal she had resembled when she'd entered the house, she gave a strangled shriek and fled out the door.

"Where do you think she'll go?" Tessa looked concerned. "Should you follow her and see that she is somewhere safe?" Charles shook his head.

"Not necessary. She's probably gone to find Jackson or the Pinkertons," he said.

"But if Jackson is in London, it will be weeks before he can get here.

What will she do until then?"

"If Jackson really is in London, she'll stay with neighbors. Or in a hotel. I'm sure she can afford it. I have a feeling our friend, Maisie, has plenty of money." When Tessa shook her head and frowned, he added, "She wouldn't want you to know she'd been squirrelling away a tidy sum while you were pinching every penny."

Tessa stared at him. "Is she that devious? Am I that naïve?"

"Yes and no," said Charles with a smile. "You have a hard time believing that anyone is not only a sneak but malicious. I'm sorry to tell you, but Maisie is both. She's always been jealous of you and I think she enjoyed watching you worry and took great pleasure in the idea that your brother watched while it happened."

Tessa looked stunned. "Stupid," she said at last. "I deserved to be taken advantage of. I've known the woman most of my life and, while I never liked her, it never occurred to me she would steal from me."

"Don't forget she had help from your brother and probably my sister, as well."

Tessa looked dazed, as if someone had struck her. "I don't know what to do."

Casey had come and gone into the house from the barn and the stable, listening to the conversation, but he had relaxed his watchful stance once Maisie had fled the house. Now he looked at his friends and said, "I think you had better stop worrying about what has already happened and start to think about what is going to happen. You have forgotten that Maisie still has a tongue like a rattlesnake and knows how to use it. And your brother has friends among the lawyers in the county seat."

"What could I have left that he'd want now?"

"Money," said Charles.

"Land," said Casey.

❧

Tessa stumbled out to the front steps. She felt as if she had misread the entire world most of her life. Her brother wanted her property and her money? And she had not even been aware that she had any. She thought that money and land was the province of men. Jackson had taken care of it and she had let him, assuming he would know what was best for his little sister. That was what the world told her. If he had said he wanted to sell all their property, she would have nodded and signed whatever he had put in front of her, sure that he knew best.

It had taken this confused mess in the aftermath of war to wake her up. What must Charles think of her? He had been through so much and had come out tougher and stronger than ever, while she, Tessa, had merely looked after his farm as best she could. That was all. And she had come out as simple as she had gone in. She shook her head in disgust.

Charles came up to her and she saw that his expression was sharper than it had been in the last few days. He had come down to earth, Tessa thought with an inward smile. What did he think now?

"I want you to marry me tomorrow," he said, his tone crisp and businesslike. "It is the sensible thing to do. In fact, it is the only thing to do if you and Casey are right about what Jackson intends."

Tessa couldn't help herself. She laughed. Charles was proposing as if he were asking her to sell him a heifer or some bushels of corn. "I'm not going to marry anyone as if I were entering into a business deal. Jackson may do things that way and I may be a fool, but I need a little moonlight and romance. After all, even a marriage of convenience is designed to last a very long time."

Charles came up to her and took her hands. His look was no longer businesslike and determined. Instead, he gave her an uncertain smile. "You don't understand," he said. "I'm not sure I do, not completely at any rate."

"Well, I think I do. You have gotten yourself and, incidentally, me into a mess and the only way out seems to be marriage. But marriage when you have just gotten free from hospitals and doctors must seem like one more iron door clanging shut." She clenched her fists and fought to keep her voice level. "I won't do that to you."

Charles looked at her as if she were not making sense. "Don't be silly."

It was as if he had slapped her. Jackson used to say those same words to her, dismissing her needs and desires as the unimportant thoughts of an empty-headed female. Tessa sprang to her feet and stood on the step. They were almost eye to eye and she felt suddenly strong, an equal. She could say what she needed to say. "I am not silly. I am not going to be married off to fit someone else's idea of a well-arranged life."

Charles looked alarmed. "I don't know what you are talking about. I didn't mean you are silly or not worth listening to. I have never thought that. I only meant that you are not an encumbrance to me and it surprised me that you could think it." He took a deep breath. "I won't put words in your mouth if you won't do the same to me. I have always loved you. No, don't interrupt," he added as she opened her mouth to protest. "I have always loved you. When we were growing up it was a boy-and-girl feeling. But it was real. And when I arrived back here a few days ago, exhausted and barely able to put one foot in front of the other, I found you running the place, keeping everything going. And suddenly, everything was clear for the first time in almost four years."

Tessa could hardly breathe. For the first time, she saw Charles without the hero worship of a young girl for a soldier in a dashing blue uniform. And Charles, the grown-up, tempered by war and injury, with lines of suffering on his face and weariness lurking in his eyes, was a man to be loved and understood.

"I understand, Charles," she said, her heart in her eyes and a scratchy lump in her throat. "And I love you, too. We have been through the fire of war and we each know what the other has endured."

At last, Charles felt as if he were truly home. Tessa was his home. "Yes," he said with a heartfelt sigh. "We have grown together though we have been apart."

Without another word, they melted into each other's arms. Words were not necessary, Tessa thought, and could not encompass their feelings. It was a moment to be cherished for all the years to come. A moment for silence and touch. They had found each other and now they managed to fit into each other's bodies and hearts despite the way the world had tried to separate them.

"Yes." Tessa had never felt so peaceful and yet so strong. No matter what happened, she could meet it and withstand it because Charles was beside her.

A moment like that was too precious to last. Into the silence of the Pennsylvania countryside came the clatter of horses' hooves and the jingle of a harness. From around the corner of the lane came a shining black carriage, its metalwork gleaming. A coachman in a handsome black and white livery cracked a whip over the heads of two fast-stepping matched chestnuts.

Neither Tessa nor Charles had a moment's doubt of who was breaking their peace. The carriage came to a sharp halt just in front of them and the coachman sprang down to open the door and let down the steps. They stood in the doorway with their arms around each other and smiled and spoke as one.

"Welcome." Their voices laden with irony, Charles and Tessa smiled at the fashionably clad pair that stood in the roadway. "Do come in."

"Jackson," said Tessa.

"Louisa," said Charles.

CHAPTER FIVE

TESSA HARDLY RECOGNIZED JACKSON. WHY had she never noticed that the fashionable clothes he always wore resembled a bird's plumage and the way he stood, with his chest thrust out and his legs locked and spread apart, made the likeness even more pronounced. Jackson, the strutting peacock, Tessa thought. Somehow, the idea made her feel more confident, less like the admiring younger sister.

Jackson strode over to her, looked her up and down and shook his head. "Where did you find that dress?" he asked with a sneer. "Mrs. Blackwood's rag bag? I must take you to get your wardrobe refurbished. You are a very pretty girl when you make an effort. Very pretty." He looked at her, Tessa thought, as if she were a prized filly. "We'll go to Philadelphia or, perhaps, even New York."

"I can pick out my own clothes, Jackson," she said, stepping back from his cool appraisal. "Thank you just the same."

"No, really, Tessa, you need guidance. Just look at Louisa. That's stylish. Before I took her in hand she looked almost as dowdy as you."

Everyone's gaze swiveled to Louisa. She was dressed in the latest fashion, silk and taffeta and lace. And feathers on her hat, which was tipped rakishly over one eye. Everything was made of royal purple. How could they have overlooked her, Tessa asked herself. Then she studied her childhood friend and saw that she stood as still and frozen as a mannequin, no expression on her face, no personality shining from her eyes. A statue could not have looked more perfect. Or more lifeless.

Tessa smiled at her old friend and went over to embrace her. It was exactly like hugging a statue. "Louisa," she said, "how are you? You look beautiful. Welcome home." She leaned toward Louisa and kissed her cheek. She wasn't sure if anyone else noticed but Louisa withdrew, shuddered a little, as if touching Tessa were somehow physically frightening.

Charles had stood a little apart, as if waiting to see what Jackson and Louisa wanted. Now he turned to look carefully at Louisa. He smiled faintly. "Sister," he said making no move to touch her or go any closer. "Welcome home."

Louisa said nothing, as if waiting to see what else Charles would say or do, but Charles merely stood looking at her, quiet and watchful. Tessa thought Louisa wanted Charles to touch her, put his arms around her but could not reach out herself. Well, she could break this logjam if no one else would.

She turned to her brother. "Jackson, where have you both been and what are you doing back here? I heard you were in London. Is that true? Is that where you both bought these astonishing clothes?" She smiled at him then turned her smile to Louisa. "Tell us all about your adventures." She made her smile as warm and welcoming as she could manage in the cold and watchful atmosphere that surrounded the Kings.

Jackson ignored her. He turned to Charles, his eyes so dark blue and unwinking they seemed to absorb all the light in the room. He stood in front of Charles and eyed him up and down as if he were a specimen in a zoo. "So, Charles," he began. Charles did not move and his expression did not change. It was a duel of statues, Tessa thought. Jackson had clearly expected to make Charles nervous but there was no sign of that in Charles' hooded gaze. "So," Jackson began again, "what is this I hear about your losing your wits in the war?" He looked at Charles' threadbare uniform jacket and smiled, a humorless, shark-like smile. "Feeling better now, I hope."

At last, an expression flitted across Charles' face. It was a sardonic smile. "The war was…difficult. Particularly Gettysburg. You were wise to leave town." His grin was as humorless and icy as Jackson's smile. "Clever to avoid all the mess and noise and flying body parts. Especially when you could pick up such colorful clothing instead of wearing a uniform like mine. Apt to get messy. Tell us, why did you come back?"

Jackson's large white teeth gleamed. "Just checking on the lurid stories we heard."

"Well, as you see, you should not trust paid informants like the Pinkertons," Charles said. "What did they tell you? That I was a raving lunatic and likely to stay that way for the rest of my life?" He gave a confident grin directed at Jackson's angry face and shook his head in mock pity. "Sorry to disappoint you. Doesn't pay to be too trusting when you are paying for information." He clapped his hand on Jackson's shoulder. "Next time, be more careful."

Jackson shrugged off Charles' hand and turned on Louisa. "What are you gaping at? There's nothing funny here." His voice was a snarl and he raised his hand to her. Louisa cringed back and lifted a hand to shield her face.

Charles moved with the speed of a cat, confronting Jackson, one hand holding Jackson's wrist hard enough to make him wince, the other resting on the waistband of his own trousers where a small pistol was nestled out of sight. "Keep your hands to yourself, Jackson." Charles released Jackson's wrist.

"Louisa's my wife. I can discipline her if she needs it." Jackson rubbed his wrist and turned his back on Charles, who reached out and spun him around.

"Louisa is my sister and you will not touch her." The words fell like cold stones. Jackson opened his mouth and Charles raised his hand to forestall any words. "Do you understand me? You will not touch my sister."

"Or what will you do?" Jackson puffed out his chest and faced Charles with a sneer.

Charles nodded toward the wrist Jackson was still rubbing. "You don't want to discover the answer to that question. I'd be very careful. Perhaps Louisa should stay here with Tessa. You can go to Hedgemere."

"Don't be absurd. My wife stays with me."

"How long do you plan to stay here?"

"Who knows? What are your plans now that you are out of the locked ward of the hospital? Are you and my sister married? I haven't heard of any nuptials or seen any ring. When did they take place?"

"You haven't heard of a great many things. Those expensive informants of yours haven't been doing their job."

Tessa raised her hands and shook her head. "How can you two behave this way? Like a couple of tomcats fighting over a garbage pail!" She turned to Louisa and laid gentle palms on her friend's hands. "Come, Lou, let's go upstairs and leave these two to their nonsense." Louisa's eyes filled with tears and a glimmer of hope. Tessa put her arm around Louisa's waist and led her away, murmuring about cups of tea and warm afghans.

The atmosphere in the downstairs room chilled. Jackson's eyes held a calculating gleam. "So you are not married."

"I do not see why that makes any difference to you." Charles' voice was as cool as ever but his eyes followed Jackson's every move. "You have shown no interest in Tessa since you ran out and left her before Gettysburg. Why the sudden concern?"

Jackson shrugged. "No reason. Brotherly affection, that is all." At Charles' incredulous laugh, Jackson grinned. "Well, all right, I wanted to see if there was any chance of persuading her to sell her half of Hedgemere to me since she's not living there. I thought she might be interested in making some quick money."

"Especially since you were trying to starve her out with Maisie Alcott's help." Scorn laced Charles' voice.

"You'll never prove that," Jackson said quickly. "It was hard to get money from England to the scene of the battle in Pennsylvania try though I did." The look of pious concern he pasted on his face would have told anyone that he was lying.

"Well, now you know she's safe and with friends and not interested in selling. In fact, we may be interested in dividing Hedgemere by deed so that Blackwood and Tessa's half of Hedgemere could be combined." Charles had spoken almost at random. He had not thought of combining Tessa's property and his own but the murderous look on Jackson's face alerted him to the existence of some plot. Every instinct said to guard Tessa and Louisa from Jackson.

"No, that can never happen." Jackson spoke softly but there was menace in every syllable. He turned to Charles and smiled his jackal's smile. "It is really too bad the Rebs didn't put an end to you in '63. Would have saved a great deal of trouble."

Charles knew he meant every word. So did he when he answered. "Their whole army couldn't do it and God knows they tried. If I were you, I wouldn't be fool enough to think I could, even with the help of those bully-boys you hired."

Jackson raised both hands in a gesture of surrender. "I wouldn't dream of trying to best a seasoned warrior like yourself. Even one who had to be locked in the crazy ward." He gave a short, delighted laugh. "But they didn't lock you up tight enough. You ran away. Not only crazy but a coward!"

"I tell you again, you were misinformed. I was never locked up anywhere. And I ran nowhere. I just decided I was well enough to go home, so I did."

Standing in the doorway, Charles moved toward Jackson, who hurriedly picked up his hat and coat. "Don't bother to see me out," he said with another chuckle. "You might mistake me for a lion or a ghost or whatever you see in your delirium." Jackson moved casually out the door until Charles began to stride heavily after him. Then he gave up his pretense of a carefree stroll and began to run.

Charles stood in the doorway and watched Jackson swing into the carriage and order the coachman to spring the horses. He didn't move until the carriage disappeared down the lane and he was sure Jackson was gone.

❧

Charles stood in the darkened parlor trying to make sense of what he had learned. From her days in pigtails and a pinafore, Louisa had cherished a schoolgirl crush on Jackson. He had always been handsome and charming, shining and blonde, but there had been something about him that Charles could not like. Now he had discovered what that was—the hidden cruelty and callousness.

Jackson had harmed Louisa, emotionally if not physically. Charles would have to discover how deep that cruelty went and do what he could to help his sister heal. Meantime, she must be kept away from her husband. Tessa's kindness and warmth had healed Charles and had already started to ease Louisa's frozen pain. She, too, would heal.

But the larger problem remained. He would have to persuade Tessa to marry him even if she thought he was doing it just to save her from gossip. Jackson had all but admitted that he wanted Charles dead. The only possible reason was so Louisa would inherit Charles' half of Blackwood. The avaricious gleam in Jackson's eyes had told Charles that he probably wanted the whole of Blackwood and might not hesitate to arrange Louisa's death as well as Charles' incarceration in the insane ward to get it.

He felt a cold chill down his back. Could this kind of cold-blooded murder for gain really be the work of people he had known all his life? He thought of the Confederate soldiers he had seen charge after him and his men, yelling like hyenas and swinging swords around their heads. Probably perfectly normal farmers and planters in civilian life, he was

sure, murderous as jackals in wartime. Yes, anyone was capable of anything, given the right circumstances.

He rubbed his cold arms and went to the back of the house to be sure
all the windows and doors were locked. His gaze swept over the yard
and paused at the stable. He stood for a moment, looking at the door.
Something was moving inside. Buddy, perhaps. No, it was a light. An
unshaded lamp, he thought.

"Charles." It was the merest whisper.

He turned toward the shadow of Casey who had come into the house
without a sound. "Who's in the stable? Did you see?" Charles asked.

"Too dark. But that's an open flame near the hay."

"We'd better go and take care of our arsonist."

Casey nodded. "I'll check on the carriage first. See if the Pinkertons
and King have circled back here."

"I'd better go see about the stable. The flame may be Jackson returned
to burn us out. Simple and less risk to him." Charles was amazed at how
unemotional he was about the idea of Jackson trying to kill him and
possibly Tessa and Louisa, as well. The war had deadened some emotions and sharpened some fighting instincts.

"Be careful. I'll be back as soon as I can." With that, Casey slipped out
the door, silent as a shadow.

Charles waited a few moments then noticed that the lamp in the stable
was moving more quickly, making erratic shadows on the walls. Unable
to wait passively in the house, he slid in his stocking feet to the front hall
and carefully opened the closet door.

He looked at the lantern shadows and decided against loading the
family rifle that stood in the closet. He could handle Jackson unarmed,
as he already had today. He tugged on his boots. He could see and hear
nothing. The carriage seemed to have disappeared, as had the Pinkertons. He shrugged and headed for the back door.

As he slipped outside, he heard the jingle of horses' harnesses toward
the front lane. Casey had apparently managed to cause some problems
for the Pinkertons and they were leaving. He couldn't stop to wonder
or inspect the landscape. The light in the stable was more erratic now.
Charles tried to stay in the shadow of the trees as he crept towards the
stable as fast as could.

Suddenly, there was a snort from Buddy that sounded as if it came
from the open pen just outside the rear of the stable. Then a shot rang
out. Charles broke into a run and burst through the stable door. Inside,

chaos greeted him. Buddy's eyes were rolling as he pulled against a rope Jackson was using to drag him toward one of the stalls. Jackson was trying to aim his pistol at Buddy but the lantern still smoldered in the hay and could burst into flame at any moment.

Charles grabbed the water bucket in Buddy's stall and flung its contents over the hay that still showed occasional flickers of flame. Buddy was still pulling against the rope and Jackson was trying to pull him into the stall and aim the pistol at the same time, but it was wavering uncontrollably in his grasp.

Where was Casey? Charles looked around as if the farmer should be somewhere nearby, but he saw no one. At that moment, he heard approaching footsteps.

He looked about him ready to take the pistol from Jackson and crack him with it when the footsteps, whether of Casey or the Pinkertons, entered the stable. But it was neither. Instead, Tessa and Louisa entered, each fully dressed. Tessa carried a pistol.

She took in the scene at a glance. Putting the pistol in her pocket, she said, "Fill the bucket at the well, Lou, and bring it back." She headed toward Buddy, talking in a low voice, trying to calm the frightened animal. But Jackson waved his arms, one holding the pistol which was still casting erratic shadows on the wall. He yelled at the horse, trying to force him back into his stall, but instead keeping him excited and still shying away from Jackson. Buddy came closer and Jackson, always nervous around animals, dropped the gun in the hay.

At that moment, Louisa reentered the stable. The swing of the door as she came in fanned the flame in the smoldering hay and it flared suddenly. Louisa dropped the bucket, spilling the water on the ground without drenching the burning hay. She then fanned the flames with her skirt, trying to put out the fire but instead ensuring the flame and smoke would grow.

Charles could see catastrophe looming and he took control of himself and the situation. Whatever fears fire held for him because of his memories of the burning farm buildings at Gettysburg, he stifled them and took command. "Tessa, give me your pistol, cover Buddy's eyes and take him out. Jackson, don't move or I'll fire. If I don't kill you, I'll leave you in here wounded. Louisa, go fill the bucket again and pour the water on the fire."

Tessa put a towel over Buddy's head and, speaking to him in calm, soft tones, handed the pistol to Charles and led Buddy outside. The sudden cessation of the noise and erratic movement gave Jackson the respite he needed. He rose up from his crouch in the corner and shook himself, trying to regain control. He looked around and saw that his wife was present. He frowned at Charles, who was looking at him with silent watchfulness, Tessa's gun held down at his side. He did not want to risk fire and gunfire if the girls and Buddy could get to safety before he had to tackle Jackson. Jackson clearly thought he was in charge of the situation. He stood as straight as he could and spoke in a deep, loud voice.

"Louisa, take that pistol from Charles. I see it in his waistband. Give it to me. Never mind the fire. We're going to leave in one minute." He held out his hand and snapped his fingers. "Now, Louisa! I want the pistol now. You can see that Charles is threatening me. I may have to shoot him."

Louisa took the pistol from Charles' pants. Charles did not want to risk injury to his sister so he remained quiet as Jackson stepped toward Louisa. Then Charles took the bucket from Buddy's stall. Jackson grinned, thinking Charles was heading toward the door, which would leave Jackson alone with Louisa. He took the shoulder of her arm holding the pistol in a punishing grip. Louisa gave a gasp of pain and attempted to wrench herself free. Charles aimed the bucket at Jackson's head, but Jackson pushed Louisa and grabbed for the gun. It went off with a loud report as she fell on top of Jackson, her hand reaching for the pistol. Jackson pushed her aside and tried to stand. He looked down at his hand in shocked surprise. It was covered with blood, which was pouring from his stomach. He swayed for a moment and sank to the floor. Louisa scrambled to her feet, still holding the pistol. Charles ran to Louisa. "Are you hurt?" He began to reach for her to see if she had been shot but he stopped dead when he saw Louisa looking down at the smoking gun as if it were a snake.

She stared at Charles as if she had never seen him before. Her bloodless lips moved soundlessly. "What have I done?" she whispered.

CHAPTER SIX

TWO WEEKS LATER, TESSA STOOD quietly at the back of the Blackwood farm parlor, watching to see if Jackson's memorial service was going smoothly and checking on Louisa who was still silent and shaky. The chairs had been pulled in from all the other rooms and two benches borrowed from Hedgemere stood at right angles. As the large group gradually filled the room, Charles had murmured in her ear that the crowded room seemed to be cheering Louisa up.

Glancing around, Tessa thought he was right. Louisa looked better today than she had since before that dreadful night that seemed to have sliced her life in two. There was color in her cheeks, her shoulders were straight and her eyes met those of visitors without shifting away and dissolving into tears.

Most of the group had arrived by now. Tessa signaled Charles and then went to sit at the small piano they had borrowed from Hedgemere and began to play "Our God, Our Help in Ages Past". Charles went to sit beside his sister. One of Jackson's classmates at the university who had become an Anglican minister rose to speak.

Tessa hoped his words comforted at least some of the crowd. No one blamed Louisa. Everyone understood that she had not meant to harm Jackson. They could see how much she had loved her handsome husband. In spite of everything he had done, Louisa had loved him and had tried to show him what she felt for him as they tried to show her their love. It seemed to help that Louisa could see the magic circle of their love and its healing power. Now they depended on time, the great healer, to complete the cure.

The short service was at an end. Jackson had not lived long enough or been close enough to any of the people of Chadds Ford for them to offer testimonials for him. But Tessa heard more than one neighbor say Louisa was young and, they hoped, someday might become a valued friend and neighbor. Tessa hoped so, too

Tessa drifted around the room, listening to her neighbors and refilling cookie plates with their best recipes. They couldn't help but observe her empty left hand. Some of the nosier old gossips raised their eyebrows and Mrs. Elderwaite, who loved to embarrass the young, came right out and asked when she and that nice, young man were going to marry. Stifling an almost overwhelming urge to say "whenever it is, we won't invite you," just to see the old lady's jaw drop, Tessa, instead, smiled a neutral sort of smile, murmured something noncommittal and moved on.

A few minutes later, there were still neighbors gathered around the cookie and tea table, having been unable to tear themselves away from each other's company.

"You can stand here forever waiting for this gossipy group to go home." Charles leaned over Tessa and murmured persuasively, "Can't you stop for just one minute and come outside and look at the moon?" He nuzzled the side of her neck. "Or better yet, look at me. I can't stop looking at you. Pretty as a bouquet of spring flowers in that flowery dress."

Tessa let the towel drop and arched her neck. She gave a little shiver and leaned back against him with a smile. "I feel almost happy when you do that."

He turned her around with a frown. "Almost?"

"I thought we had a solid life, but now I'm feeling it will always be shaky. Do you understand?"

He took her head in his hands and bent low to look in her eyes. "If you mean our love can't withstand a little fire and chaos, then you don't know what it's made of. Our love goes deep and grows strong. Look at what you have done for me already. You've saved my home." He kissed her softly. "Brought light to my soul." He brushed kisses over her eyelids. Now his voice grew husky and she knew he spoke the deepest truth he knew. "You have healed my wounded heart."

They stood in rapt silence for a long moment, looking around them at what would be their home. Charles held her close and spoke as surely as if he could see the future. "I think we should marry right now. Today.

We have the guests, the minister." He grinned at her. "The cookies and tea. Let's do it! We've waited and planned like a couple of old folks. But we're not old folks, Tessa. We're young and we have our lives in front of us. What do you say?" He grabbed her arm and swung it the way they used to do when they were children. Tessa knew she wore her heart on her sleeve for Charles and she didn't care who knew it. She flung one arm around his neck.

He smiled down at her, looking for the first time, she thought, totally healed and whole. The nightmare shadows were gone from his eyes. And she was sure she could see a sunlit, happy future ahead of them.

"I think it's time for us to make Mrs. Elderwaite eat her gossip. Marry me, Tessa King. I will always love you, but now I need for us to ring bells and sing and tell the world." His arms closed around her and he bent his head until his lips claimed hers. "And now is the perfect moment! Please. Today, this second. We haven't a moment to waste!"

Tessa felt her heart swell with such love and certainty she thought she might burst. She reached up and hugged Charles and caught her breath on a sob. "Oh, my dearest, I do love you so. And I believe, or I will believe if you'll kiss me a few dozen more times, that we will be happy and strong in this place for generations to come."

"Happy to do my best to convince you, dear heart." Charles picked her up with a smothered laugh and whirled her around. "Now let us go and get our friends and neighbors ready to be happy with us." He grinned that same mischievous boyish grin she had thought was gone forever. "I'm going to tell Mrs. Elderwaite the news. I can't wait to see her face when I tell her I have to marry you so I can get you into bed without further ado!"

"Charles!"

Louisa, her eyes curious, came up to them and looked at their beaming faces. "What are you two up to? It looks like one of your games that always ended with both of you messy and laughing." Louisa smiled at them both. "Those were wonderful times. What are you up to now?"

"Well," Charles drawled the word, "as a matter of fact we are planning an elopement."

Louisa clearly thought they were joking. She smiled indulgently. "Really? Whose?"

"Ours," Charles announced. "Only we are more efficient than everyone else. We brought our guests here and will have them stay."

As usual, Louisa's first thought was of Tessa's wedding dress. "You're wearing that? Well, it's pretty enough." She tapped her chin and smiled. "Don't move until I get back. I have just the thing to finish your outfit." She hurried from the room, her step lighter and her expression happier than Tessa had seen it since she had arrived home. While Tessa straightened her hair and smoothed her dress, Charles moved through the room, stopping to talk with first one group of guests then another. He spent a particularly long time with the minister, who seemed at first doubtful but after hearing their story, smiled and shook Charles' hand heartily.

Mrs. Elderwaite's expression was stunned, but after a few minutes, it melted into an indulgent smile. Tessa couldn't imagine what Charles had found to say that would cause that. At that moment, Louisa hurried back into the room. In her arms was a beautiful while lace shawl which she draped with loving care around Tessa's shoulders. "You look beautiful and I am so happy that you will be happy. It makes up for all the sorrow I've caused you." Louisa reached into her pocket and drew out the Blackwood family's ancestral brooch. "For you," she whispered, feathering the lightest of kisses on Tessa's cheek. "I want it to be with you and Charles, with the branch of the family that is strong enough to be happy."

"Someday you will be as happy as we are, I know it!" Tessa couldn't help her expression straying to Casey, standing with his mother looking at Louisa.

Louisa saw Tessa's face and shook her head. "No matchmaking, Tessa. I warn you!" She shook her finger in her friend's face. Her expression sobered for a moment and she hugged Tessa hard. "You both deserve all the happiness in the world." She looked around. "I'd better get to the piano and begin the service." She smiled at the minister and Tessa thought that Louisa didn't need any matchmaking!

"Here we are, the Blackwoods," Charles whispered in her ear, "home and happy forever!"

MARTHA SCHROEDER

A FORMER WALL STREET LAWYER, MARTHA has written thirteen novels—historicals, contemporaries and Regencies, that have been published by Kensington, Ballantine and Harlequin. For more information, connect with Martha at *www.facebook.com/martha.schroeder.18*

BOOKS BY MARTHA SCHROEDER:

The Bronze Talisman in THE MARRIAGE COIN, 2014
A Merry Little Christmas
A Rose for Julian
True to Her Heart
More Than A Dream
Guarding An Angel
Twice Shy

ℋEART'S SONG

by

GEORGIA DICKSON

1919

ETHAN BLACKWOOD LOVED THREE THINGS - his family, his farm and his blessed bachelorhood. Then Serena Jordan appeared on the scene. Serena…beautiful, talented, and bruised, was looking for a place to call home and Chadds Ford seemed to have just what she needed. Ethan and Serena weren't looking for love, but the moment they met changed them – and the plans they'd made – forever.

DEDICATION

&

ACKNOWLEDGEMENTS

To *The Writers Who Lunch* for their unwavering support and help, especially Kate and Martha who guided this first-time author through the complex and sometimes bewildering process of creating a story that people would actually want to read.

And to Mariah Stewart, my BFF and mentor, who has always known that I could do this. She had faith in me when I didn't. And she didn't give up...even if it did take ten years for me to actually write a story with a beginning, a middle and – best of all – a happy ending. With love and eternal gratitude.

CHAPTER ONE

May 1919

ETHAN BLACKWOOD SWORE SOFTLY AS he fitted the horses to the rigging and prepared the carriage for the five mile journey to the county's Spring Social. He was glad to be home especially on so beautiful a spring evening but he wasn't happy at that particular moment.

Aurelia Blackwood hurried across the yard. "Ethan Blackwood. Are you ready? I don't want to be late but I don't want to rush you if you need more time."

Ethan knew his mother worried about him. He just smiled, took the large basket, which no doubt contained her famous butter pound cake, set it on the floor behind the bench seat and easily lifted her up into the carriage with the strength and confidence of old.

Ethan smiled up at her. "All set, Ma. Fix your bonnet and let's go. I'm hungry!"

He joined her in the carriage a moment later. When he reached to take up the reins, her hand covered his. "Ethan, please. I know something isn't *fine* as you've been promising me for the two weeks you've been home. Is life in the country not for you any longer?"

Pretending all was fine not only hadn't stopped her from worrying, he'd given her the wrong impression entirely. Perhaps honesty was the best policy, after all. "Life here is a life I love, Mother. I can't imagine another. And I love the work here. In fact, Tom and I were talking this morning about modernizing. But losing part of my leg in France makes for a few struggles and frustrations."

"I knew you should stop in to see Doctor Blake."

"The military doctors and nurses were wonderful and I had excellent care. I've been assured that, with my knee intact, I should be able to take up my old life with little difficulty. For the most part, they were right but there are still struggles. I'm simply impatient."

"Patience was never easy for you." A small, secret smile tipped her lips. No doubt, she was remembering one incident or another from his boyhood. "What else? Come on. I know it's more. You eventually mastered even patience."

"I'm also having a bit of a problem with all the curious, but kindly stares and questions from neighbors and friends. Though I know they are genuinely concerned about me. I'm an oddity. Farming accidents are common but not having an amputation caused by German shrapnel and infection. And they also see me as a hero."

"To all of us you are, Son."

"I don't feel I deserve it. I left many friends behind. They are the heroes but they'll never hear themselves lauded. They'll never see loved ones again or go to a social. Never marry or see a child to carry on their names. It weighs on me sometimes but I've at least decided how I will deal with that aspect of the aftermath of war. I am going to do all those things for them as well as myself. The social tonight will be a good start on the rest of my life."

"You are right. And, young man, I think your attitude is commendable even if you feel your service to the country wasn't and don't argue. I never lose a battle I care about."

He held up his hands in surrender and laughed as he was nearly sure he was meant to. Aurelia Blackwood was the fiercest of defenders when she needed to be.

"Now, is any of this looking forward about Lillie Price?"

"I'm anxious to see her, of course. I can't tell you how relieved I was when she wrote to say her parents had insisted she leave Philadelphia while the influenza pandemic was raging there."

His mother nodded. "They were in a panic, no doubt about it. The Spanish Flu would worry any parent. But, of course, after the danger had passed, Lillie returned to Philadelphia to complete her studies. And now it's on to a professional career."

Ethan couldn't fight the smile. "To think she was once the tomboy who could keep up with us boys no matter the challenge."

"No one was more shocked than I was the day she got up at that church social and sang *Shall We Gather at the River,"* his mother admitted and shook her head. "I still can't believe that voice came from a seven year old."

"But after that, things were never quite the same. Lillie was always having a lesson – voice, piano, or dance. I might have lost my best friend that day but Lillie remained a steadfast friend all these years."

His mother touched his sleeve. "She was. Right up until the day she came over to tell you Jessie Lovejoy, who was the Dean at the Philadelphia Conservatory of Music, had heard her singing at the county fair and that she'd been offered a place at the Conservatory."

Did he still see pity in his mother's eyes? Or hope? "I *was* happy for her. I mean it. We are friends. *Only* friends. Lillie was never meant to live her life in a farming community. Now she'll be doing what she was born to do. And so will I."

"It would have been so lovely to join the Blackwood and Price families." She sighed a bit. "But, as you say, it wasn't meant to be. Oh! Did I tell you Lillie's brought a friend with her? A young woman, Serena, I believe that's her name. Apparently, they met at the Conservatory and Serena has been Lillie's friend and accompanist since."

Ethan only half-listened as his mother chatted on about Lillie and her friend. He was focused on the countryside he'd missed so much, glad they had taken the buggy and not the car. And he was enjoying the newly green trees and grass and the wild flowers that had begun to spring up along the roadside.

He sighed softly as he recalled spring on the battlefields of France. Death and destruction had been everywhere he'd looked, with fields burned and forests destroyed. Only his memories of home and the beautiful Chester County countryside and Blackwood Farm had sustained him and kept him from losing his mind on the horrors of the battlefield. Ethan had always been physically strong, but he'd found reserves of emotional strength he hadn't even imagined he possessed.

". . . with Lillie traveling to Europe, now that the war is over and that dreadful flu seems to have run its course."

His mother's voice brought him back into the moment. Ethan realized he really hadn't been listening but he wasn't worried. His mother would be sure to repeat the story to the women who would be joining them at the social so he was bound to hear it several times over.

The county social hall was brightly lit and the field adjacent to it already filling with buggies, cars and several new Ford trucks, which really piqued Ethan's interest. He had been perfectly content with horse power on the farm before he left for France but, with his injury, he thought having a truck to get around the property might make it easier. He knew it was time to modernize and he had been talking with his foreman Tom Appleton about it only this morning.

He helped his mother down from her seat and retrieved her basket. The two of them set off for the gaily decorated entrance.

Several neighbors were there and greeted the Blackwoods like the old friends they were, taking special care to shake Ethan's hand or hug him while offering a sincere "thank you" and "will done, Son." Many of the women were teary and more than one man retrieved his handkerchief from a breast pocket. The depth of their emotion wasn't lost on Ethan and he greeted them with equal warmth and friendship.

"Well, if it isn't Ethan Blackwood home from the war!"

Ethan turned in the direction of the voice to find Ada and Dora Grimshaw, mother and daughter, greeting him just inside the entrance into the hall.

"Ladies, pleased to see you." Ethan tipped his hat and smiled.

"Mother and I'd heard you were home but, you naughty boy, you didn't even find time to pay us a call." Dora waved her hanky at Ethan. "Why we were simply shocked, yes shocked, I tell you, to hear about your dreadful injury. How will you *ever* manage the farm? We know Tom Appleton took care of things while you were away but, really, how will you resume your old life?"

Ethan listened politely but seethed inside. Dora Grimshaw had had her cap set for him for as long as he could remember and without a shred of encouragement from him. Even his mother, who genuinely wanted Ethan to find a girl to love, marry and settle down with, hadn't encouraged Dora in the slightest. But here she was, prattling to him about his leg, the war, his farm. He was astonished that she didn't pass out from lack of air because he was sure she hadn't taken a breath.

"Well, Dora, I'll tell you. Uncle Sam did a mighty fine job building this new leg for me," reaching down to give his lower leg a solid rap with his knuckles, "and the training I got – you know walking, climbing, running - well, it was just the best in the world. Why, I can do everything I did before. I just have to approach it a little more carefully. After all, I wouldn't want the leg to fly off in the middle of, I don't know, a dance. You will honor me with one tonight, won't you, Dora?"

Ethan grinned as Dora's expression went from dismay to confusion to understanding.

"Well, I never," she scolded. "You shouldn't tease like that, Ethan. It isn't nice. Of course, I'd love to dance with you later. We have *so much* to talk about."

"We do? I mean, I look forward to it, Dora."

"Well, I see Dora Grimshaw hasn't wasted any time," said his mother when she caught up with him.

Ethan related the whole conversation, including sound effects, to his mother.

"I've promised to dance with her later this evening. She said we have a lot to talk about. I hope she doesn't start pestering me about us seeing each other. I swear the woman is as dense as an Army mule. I have never given her the slightest bit of encouragement but she doesn't seem to understand the meaning of the word no." Ethan laughed as he shook his head

"You have a point there, Son. Well, I'm glad you can see the humor in the situation, but I'd be careful of Dora. You know she's had her cap set for you since you were babies and Dora usually gets what she wants."

"Not this time, Ma, I've faced more determined foes on the battle-field. Dora Grimshaw doesn't scare me."

Ethan took his mother's arm in his as they headed into the ballroom.

"Now let's get a table, find our friends and get this party started."

CHAPTER TWO

"WHAT IN THE NAME OF all that's holy happened here?" Ethan asked his mother. The century-old building had been reborn. "I can't believe my eyes. How did this happen? I thought the old place was slated for demolition."

"You wouldn't have believed it, Son."

He turned to his mother when she spoke.

"Folks were on fire with ideas to renovate the place." Aurelia continued. "I think the war had something to do with the change of heart. With so many landmarks destroyed in Europe, people here realized that we should hold on to a bit of our own history."

"You mean new is not always better," he said to indicate that he understood his mother's explanation.

"Yes. Just look around."

Ethan followed his mother's hand as she gestured.

"The battered old floors have been refinished. Doesn't that walnut inlay look beautiful against the old oak? Everything has been redone or replaced. You can see that horrible green paint is gone. I picked out the new paint colors," said Aurelia proudly.

"You made great choices, Ma." Ethan patted his mother's back as he looked around. The wainscoting was painted a soft dark gray and the walls above painted in a lighter gray, while the ceiling had been painted a soft, pale blue.

"Joseph Burns and his carpenters designed and manufactured the new plantation-style shutters. They can be opened and closed to adjust to the light at any time of day. He insisted that we add the crown molding, and placed it to give added dimension to the ceiling."

Several of the men who had stopped by to say hello to Ethan listened to Aurelia and then joined in.

"Hello, Ethan, it's good to see you." Phil Cobane, an electrician, slapped Ethan's shoulder in greeting. "I couldn't let old Joe Burns take all the credit, so we electrified the place, updated all the lighting and fitted it with the those glass and bronze chandeliers. Don't they look better than those old gas fixtures?" He looked up and smiled. "After that, we figured the matching wall sconces would finish the space and really show off the windows. What do you think?" He gestured, pointing to the new 16-pane windows.

"The change is remarkable and you all should be very proud of what you accomplished," said Ethan. "The building couldn't be more beautiful. What is it you're so fond of saying, Mother? Wait, I've got it. It's simply stunning!" He laughed, gently mocking his mother's frequent use of the phrase. And after a few seconds, everyone joined in, with Aurelia laughing the loudest.

Ethan noticed that the windows were open to the soft evening breeze. The fragrance of spring in the country mingled with the floral arrangements and lighted candles dressing the tables.

"Gosh, it's good to be home. I don't know what could have made this evening any better," said Ethan as they made their way to a nearby table.

"Hello, everyone." He smiled as he shook hands with the friends who were already seated. Looking around, he saw that the stage at the front of the room was set for the small orchestra that would provide the evening's entertainment and a parlor grand piano had been added which meant that Lillie would definitely be singing tonight.

Ethan smiled at his mother who was already deeply engaged in conversation. "If you ladies and gentlemen will excuse me, I think I'll get something to eat. Ma, are you coming along?" asked Ethan.

"That's all right, Ethan. I'll get something a little later. I haven't seen Bill and Sara for a month of Sundays. Why don't you go on ahead?"

He nodded and left them to their conversation.

As he made his way back to the building's library, which housed the buffet for the event, he greeted friends and neighbors, stopped to talk, and answered their questions about the farm and his health. It was just like old times and it felt wonderful. *Thank you, Lord, for bringing me safely home. I am so grateful to be here with my mother and all of our friends.* It was a prayer Ethan had offered many times since arriving home and he knew it wouldn't be the last.

Walking to the buffet line, Ethan noticed a young woman helping some of the servers. He didn't recognize her so he assumed she was a new neighbor. Her face reminded him of the many portraits of the Madonna he had seen in churches and hospitals in France and when she laughed at something, he noticed the laugh didn't quite reach her eyes. Beautiful, serene, and sad, her heart holding a secret she would probably never tell, leaving him to wonder about the tragedy that marred so lovely a face.

He would ask his mother about her after dinner. Right now, he was hungry and the aroma of home-cooked food was too enticing to put off the trip to the buffet any longer.

❧

Dinner was over and the men had begun to rearrange the room for the evening's entertainment and dancing.

"Here, let me get these chairs. I've been on vacation long enough," he teased when several of the men assured Ethan that he didn't need to help.

"That's right. We don't want him to go soft from sitting around watching us do all the work." Ethan laughed as his friend and Blackwood Farm foreman, Tom Appleton, chimed in with the others. The men continued to joke and laugh as they worked and, before long, the room was set.

As the musicians began to take their places on the stage, Ethan saw Lillie and made his way the across the room to greet her.

"Lillie! Lillie!" he called over the crowd. Lillie turned to the sound of his voice, and he saw the mysterious young woman step away from Lillie.

"Ethan!" cried Lillie as she ran to meet him.

Ethan laughed as he caught Lillie in his arms. He spun her around while they hugged fiercely as old friends do after a long separation.

"But you look wonderful," cried Lillie. "Even though your letters were always full of jokes about your injury, I was worried beyond reason. Ethan Blackwood, I should be angry with you for worrying me so, but I just can't be. I am so glad to see you!"

"Don't cry Lillie-Beth," soothed Ethan, calling her by his pet name for her. "It's really all right. I'm really all right. As good as new, I promise. So dry your tears and tell me what you've been doing. I want to know everything."

"We don't have enough time for that tonight. There's so much I want to tell you, it will take *weeks* to explain everything. But wait, I'm forgetting my manners. I'd like you meet my very dear friend, Serena Jordan."

Ethan turned to meet Lillie's friend only to see the mysterious young woman step forward, her hand outstretched in greeting.

"I'm so pleased to meet you, Ethan. Lillie has spoken of you so often I feel I know you already."

For a few seconds, he just stared. Serena Jordan was not only beautiful, but her voice was pure music. Soft, gentle and there was something else...an accent? But he realized he didn't care, he just wanted her to keep talking.

Ethan shook himself slightly and took her hand.

"I'm very pleased to meet you, Serena. Welcome to Chester County. I'm sure Lillie has been showing you the countryside and introducing you to all of our friends. Have you been here long? Will you be staying the summer? Have you seen Blackwood Farm?"

Ethan stopped. He was babbling and, thank God, he knew it. Ethan Blackwood, confirmed bachelor was...smitten. *Get a grip, man. She's just a friend of Lillie's. No need to go overboard.*

He realized he was still holding her hand and he quickly dropped it.

Serena laughed and Ethan noticed that, this time, the laughter reached her eyes.

Her name, he thought, was perfect for her.

"I came back with Lillie a few weeks ago. I'm not only Lillie's friend but I'm also her accompanist and I've been working with Lillie on her repertoire. Lillie has a real gift which means she must work very hard, doesn't it, Lillie?" Serena turned to her friend for confirmation.

"That is correct," Lillie answered frowning. "Did I mention that Serena is a very tough taskmaster? She won't let me take a day off. So no, we haven't done much socializing, apart from helping with the food and flowers for tonight. Well, Serena did most of that. She's an absolutely wonderful cook and baker and she's a wizard in the garden."

"Lillie, please don't exaggerate. I helped a little, that's all."

"I am not exaggerating! You are marvelous at everything you do and don't you dare deny it!"

"Ladies, ladies." he held up his hands in mock-surrender. "No need to argue. Let me be the judge. Dinner was wonderful but I haven't had dessert. Why don't we head back to the buffet to see what we can find? Serena, you can point out your desserts and Lillie, you can watch me eat them. Does that sound like a reasonable compromise?"

Laughing, the trio made their way to the library and the dessert buffet.

CHAPTER THREE

WHILE THE AUDIENCE SETTLED IN their seats and the musicians made their way to the stage, Emily Higgins, president of the Chester County Women's Guild, made her way to center stage and called for their attention.

"Ladies and gentlemen. Friends and guests. Welcome to the spring celebration of the Chester County Women's Guild. We hope you have enjoyed the evening thus far." She waited for the applause to stop and then continued.

"As you know, tonight's celebration is twofold. We are, of course, celebrating the annual tradition of a Spring Social but we are also welcoming home so many of our own boys who served in the Great War. And while we are relieved and heartened to see so many of them here tonight, we must not forget those who were lost. Let us bow our heads in silent prayer for all."

After a moment, she continued. "We want to thank all the men and women who made tonight's celebration possible, especially those who gave their time, talent and, let's not forget, the funds to refurbish this wonderful old landmark." She gestured to the audience in recognition.

"You know who you are, so please give yourselves an extra round of applause." Then holding out her hands to quiet the audience, she continued her speech.

"Of course, we have music and dancing this evening, but we also have a very special treat planned for you. Our very own Lillie Price will be singing for us. As you know, Lillie will be leaving us in September to begin her professional career. We feel privileged to have her with us this evening. Lillie, accompanied by her friend, Serena Jordan, will be performing several arias and a few of the songs recently made popular during the war."

The audience erupted in thunderous applause as Lillie took center stage.

Serena took her place at the piano and, as Lillie nodded, Serena played the opening chords of *One Fine Day*, the popular aria from *Madame Butterfly*, and the magic of Lillie Price's voice filled the hushed room.

☾

Ethan waited while the audience crowded around Lillie and Serena, congratulating them on the concert.

Lillie's singing was, as usual, breathtaking. Her voice was always beautiful but four years of study and practice had refined and strengthened it. He'd heard many people wonder how such a "little lady" could generate so much sound. Lillie's performance was no surprise to hm. He'd known from the start that she had the talent and will to make a successful career. His best friend would, in the not too distant future, become a world-famous soprano.

This night, it was Serena Jordan who had totally captivated Ethan. She played beautifully and her accompaniment of Lillie was brilliantly nuanced. He watched Serena's face as she moved through the arias to the popular songs, which had given him the time to really study her.

Serena Jordan was a beautiful woman. She was taller than most of the women he knew and her figure slender but with a womanly fullness that was enticing. Her oval face was accented with high cheekbones and a deep cleft in her chin. Her hair, pulled into a knot at the back of her head, was chestnut with copper highlights that gleamed under the stage lights. Her clear, ivory complexion, now flushed by her efforts at the keyboard, was luminous. Her mouth was perfectly shaped with full lips and small, even teeth that showed when she smiled. But it was her eyes that he found arresting. They were large, slightly almond-shaped and the color a black-rimmed golden hazel. Long, dark eyelashes and elegantly arched brows completed the "portrait" that was Serena Jordan. She was a goddess.

Ethan Blackwood didn't believe in love at first sight. He'd scoffed at the idea when his buddies had talked of some beautiful mademoiselle they'd met who they had been sure they couldn't live without. He'd always cautioned them not to rush into something they would regret when it was time to move on. Some listened and those who hadn't were often sorry. But tonight, he was unsure of everything. He might be falling in love with a woman he'd met two hours before.

For the first time in his adult life, Ethan Blackwood was truly terrified.

CHAPTER FOUR

THE CARRIAGE CARRYING SERENA JOLTED her awake when it stopped at the entrance of the Price residence.

"Come on, sleepyhead." Serena heard the laughter in Lillie's voice. Serena loved music but performing often exhausted her while it energized Lillie. Her friend was exhilarated and wouldn't be ready to sleep for hours, one of the many reasons that Lillie Price would have a brilliant career and she, Serena Jordan, would not.

"I'm awake, thank you very much." Serena smiled in spite of the late hour and her own fatigue. "You should have been home and in bed hours ago. You have to conserve your voice, missy, and you can't do that by dancing and singing George M. Cohan's entire song book."

"Well, *missy*, you could have ended the whole affair by not agreeing to play. Who's showing off now? You've studied classical music your whole life yet you live to play George M. Cohan, Scott Joplin and Irving Berlin. That last chorus of *Over There* nearly sent me over the edge."

"Let's not forget, you're the one who agreed to perform at the benefit for the county veteran's association."

Serena was deep in thought as the friends made their way up the path into the house. Serena was ready for bed, but she knew Lillie and her mother and father would be hours yet, as they settled into the library enjoying a sherry, talking and laughing as they recalled this evening's events.

Not tonight for Serena. She was ready for sleep.

"Good night, Mr. and Mrs. Price, Lillie," said Serena. "Thank you for a lovely evening. And Lillie, please don't stay up too late. We have work tomorrow." Serena laughed as Lillie, in a manner befitting the diva she would become, stuck out her tongue in response.

As Serena closed the library doors and made her way to her room, she thought about the events that had brought her to Chester County, the many wonderful people she had met in the last several weeks and, rather startling to her, the man who was Lillie's childhood friend, Ethan Blackwood. His looks were arresting - with his easy smile, electric blue eyes, and dark blond hair. This male perfection, topped off by chiseled good looks and a tall, muscled frame, was the last thing she needed to think about at the moment. So Serena forced her thoughts from Ethan Blackwood to less unsettling thoughts of what would become of Serena Jordan.

♁

Serena had been enjoying her stay with Lillie. She loved the soft, clean air, the quiet and the slower pace that country life provided. Best of all, it was spring. The countryside was exploding with colors and scents and her city-weary senses couldn't get enough. Lillie's invitation couldn't have come at a better time.

Philadelphia, where Serena and her family lived, was hit hard by the Spanish Flu pandemic. A city of two million people in 1918, some 500,000 contracted the disease, spread by sailors arriving at the Philadelphia Navy Yard. Experts reported that 16,000 people died. Her family was luckier than most but they didn't escape the flu altogether.

Her Aunt Nicki, her grandfather's sister, had survived but her beloved grandparents succumbed to the flu within days of each other in October. The vaccine that would soon save thousands of lives came too late for them. Serena was heartbroken by their deaths. They were the last links to her mother, who'd died shortly after giving birth to Serena. They were both parents and grandparents. It was they who soothed her when children teased that she was an orphan. And finally, when they felt she was old enough to understand, her Nonna Lucy and Poppa Giuseppe, or Poppa Joe as she called him, they explained what had happened to her parents.

Serena smiled at the memories of her childhood.

Her Nonna Lucy had taught her to cook and bake, while Aunt Nicki, an expert dress designer and seamstress, had taught her to sew. Serena smiled as she recalled the happy hours spent with these women who were always patient, never scolding, while Serena mastered the secrets of kitchen and workroom.

Poppa Joe had been a shoe maker and saddle maker whose shop had been just down the street from their home in South Philadelphia. He hadn't been able to ride a horse, but wealthy Philadelphians and their suburban counterparts relied on him for saddles, riding boots and accessories.

Serena had loved his shop, where the window that showcased Poppa's goods featured a life-sized white horse named Caruso after the famous Italian tenor. There was also a Victrola, like the one in the parlor at home, where Poppa sang along as he played his beloved recordings of opera and classical music.

What a happy childhood I had with such a loving and generous family. I'm here tonight through their care and encouragement. I'm having a wonderful time here but I'm looking forward to getting back to Philadelphia and the Conservatory. I miss my students. I miss Aunt Nicki.

Serena let her thoughts drift back to the evening. Everything was perfect - the decorations, the food, the music. She'd also enjoyed meeting the people Lillie had been talking about as long as Serena had known her. She especially enjoyed meeting Ethan Blackwood, who Lillie had described as her best friend growing up. *I wonder why she didn't tell me he was so handsome. I think he's the handsomest man I've ever seen. And he's still single. Imagine, so handsome, polite and...likeable. I must ask Lillie tomorrow why Ethan isn't married.*

"*Stop that,*" Serena told herself, forcing Ethan's handsome face from her mind. One thing that Lillie did mention – several times – was that he was a confirmed bachelor, despite the efforts of many mothers and daughters of the county to change that fact. Obviously, they'd all failed miserably, which was some comfort to Serena as she settled herself to sleep.

Really, Serena, this is nonsense. Stop wondering about Ethan Blackwood's marital status. You have much more important things to think about...like preparing Lillie for her tour. Now go to sleep!

CHAPTER FIVE

SUNDAY AFTERNOON WAS THE TIME to catch up on the business of running the farm and that's what Ethan was doing when his mother called him to lunch. He'd been gone more than two years and, although he knew the farm was safe in the capable hands of Aurelia Blackwood and the foreman, Tom Appleton, Ethan wanted to look at things just to confirm that fact. Both the physical property and the balance sheet of Blackwood Farm were in excellent condition.

"Well, I guess I can retire to the life of a gentleman farmer. From the look of things, you and Tom did a masterful job running the place while I was gone. Of course, I didn't worry for a minute, you know." He smiled at Aurelia as he found his place at the scrubbed pine kitchen table.

"Really? Just when I thought *I* could retire. You would scandalize the county putting your old mother out to work while you sit on the veranda smoking your pipe and giving orders."

Ethan laughed as his mother set a plate before him and took her own place at the table.

"I'm almost serious, Ma. I know you had to make adjustments for the war, but everything is in great shape, from the buildings to the balance sheet. You and Tom managed very well without me."

"That's because we knew you would be back to run the place. We had to keep it going. You learned well from your daddy and granddaddy. Tom's been farming Blackwood since he was a boy, so he and I just followed the Blackwood way of doing things. That doesn't mean you weren't missed every single day, because you were."

Ethan smiled again at the emotion in his mother's voice and noticed that she was reaching for her handkerchief.

"Now Ma, don't start crying again. I swear, for a woman who's always claimed she never cries, you've been weeping almost constantly since I got home."

"Well, a mother has a right to tears when her only son comes home from the war, doesn't she?"

"I'll give you that," said Ethan, "but could you try to stop at least until I get my dessert? The crust on the cobbler will go soggy if you keep this up."

"Very funny, Ethan Blackwood, very funny, indeed. If you've finished teasing your poor mother, I'd like to talk about the dinner party I have planned for this evening."

Ethan's first bite of apple cobbler never made it to his mouth. He put the spoon back in the bowl.

"What plans for dinner this evening? I thought we'd agreed to keep things quiet for a couple of weeks until I was feeling stronger and more settled in."

He watched as his mother got up from her place to start clearing the table. Aurelia Blackwood had always moved around when she wanted to make her point. *Here it comes,* Ethan thought.

"It's nothing very grand. I've invited the Prices and their houseguest for dinner this evening. I just thought you'd enjoy seeing Lillie. You haven't had any time to catch up with her - last night was so rushed with the performance and all - and I thought dinner this evening would be perfect. And I noticed that you seemed quite taken with Miss Jordan."

Ethan shook his head and laughed. "Ma, you are quite impossible. Lillie and I had already planned an evening to catch up. And as for Miss Jordan…"

He stopped. What about Serena Jordan? She'd hardly been out of his thoughts since last evening. Her face had replaced the columns of numbers on the balance sheets and the sound of her voice had drifted through his thoughts as he tried to work this morning. He'd spent hours thinking of excuses to see Serena but each new one sounded more ridiculous to him than the one he'd just discarded. And then, just like that, his sainted mother had given it to him as easily as inviting her to dinner on Sunday evening.

"You were saying, Ethan?"

"Uh, I think dinner would be great."

❦

Serena Jordan was fussing. Something she rarely did. She was fussing about what to wear tonight. Should she wear the blue silk chiffon, the yellow silk with velvet trim or the dove gray faille? Maybe she would wear the white silk and lace blouse with the black skirt? And she was fussing about her hair. Should she wear it up or should she pull back into the low knot she usually wore?

She was being ridiculous, working herself into a schoolgirl's frenzy because she was dining with Ethan Blackwood tonight. It was ridiculous because she wasn't dining *with* Ethan. She was dining with his mother, her friend and her friend's parents. This wasn't an engagement, for heaven's sake, it was a family dinner. Why this reaction? Not for the first time today did the word *schoolgirl* cross her mind when she thought of her reaction to Ethan. Earlier, when Lillie had mentioned the invitation, Serena realized that Lillie had seen immediately the situation for what it was.

"Serena Jordan, tell the truth, you are wildly attracted to Ethan Blackwood. It's as plain as the nose on your face, silly. And why not? He's the catch of the county and you're beautiful and smart. Why, you're perfect for each other." Serena had been shocked by Lily's frank assessment. But Serena wasn't a girl any longer. She had to face the facts. She was attracted to Ethan Blackwood.

Living in Philadelphia had afforded many opportunities to socialize. She wasn't so different from any of her friends. She had enjoyed many outings to picture shows and musical events. There were lunch parties and dinner parties. Yes, she'd had admirers, some of whom could have become serious. They were all very pleasant, but nothing more so she'd never allowed the relationships to go beyond friendship.

Ethan was something else. Serena hadn't stopped thinking about him. Or his smile. Or the sound of his voice. Or the way he'd looked. She blushed.

As the clock on her dresser chimed five, Serena realized that she'd been daydreaming for nearly an hour. In that moment, two decisions were made: the dove gray faille and her hair dressed in a knot at the back of her head.

Her decision on Ethan Blackwood would have to wait.

CHAPTER SIX

ETHAN HAD JUST REACHED THE front hall as John Price's car appeared around the final curve of the drive. As he stole a look in the pier mirror in the hall to check he appearance, he heard his mother chuckle.

"You're perfect. I'm sure the Prices and Serena will appreciate your sartorial efforts but I would be most appreciative if you would greet our guests and take them to the parlor. I just have to make a final check on dinner."

Ethan heard his mother laugh as she made her way back to the kitchen. He groaned softly and wished the floor would open and swallow him. *Why am I so nervous? Hell, man. You faced the enemy line with a cooler head. Serena Jordan isn't the enemy. She's a woman and you've had dinner with a woman before. Why is Serena Jordan different?* He turned from the mirror. *Oh right, you met this woman only last night and you've been on pins and needles all day just waiting to see her again. Maybe you think you're falling in love with her, that's what's different.*

He plastered a smile on his face and opened the door. "Hello everyone and welcome," Ethan said and greeted his guests one by one.

"It's lovely to see you again so soon," Letty Price said and smiled as she handed Ethan her wrap. "It was so kind of Aurelia to invite us for supper. We hope you're not too tired after last evening."

"Not at all," he replied. "I think with a few more weeks of Ma's good care, I'll be ready to get back to work full-time."

He turned his attention to Lillie and Serena.

"Hello Lillie, Serena. You both look lovely this evening. I see you are quite recovered from the party."

"Of course, silly." Lillie smiled as she tipped her cheek for a kiss. "Last night was a picnic compared to singing a full opera. Now that's hard work, isn't it Serena?"

Ethan turned to Serena and had to remind himself to breathe. She was that beautiful.

"That's a fact, although Lillie makes it seem easy. She thrives on the hard work it takes to make a great singer."

Serena paused for a moment. "Forgive me. I'm forgetting my manners," Serena said, holding her hand out to Ethan. "Thank you for the invitation. I'm pleased to see you and your mother again so soon. And I've wanted to see Blackwood Farm and your home. Lillie has told me so much about it. The house is lovely and so much different than the houses in Philadelphia, where everything is so tall and narrow. I've so enjoyed the openness and light of the country. I sometimes feel I could stay here forever." She stopped suddenly, as if she thought she'd said too much.

"Well, the house has been in my family for almost 200 years," he said as he led his guests into the parlor. "It's been enlarged some over time, but not much has changed since my great-grandmother, Meredith, came here as a bride. My parents added electricity and indoor plumbing. Modern conveniences, I am unashamed to say, I could not live without."

They all laughed and as Ethan was about to offer something to drink, he heard his mother's voice.

"Good evening, everyone. It's good of you to come." Aurelia beamed as she moved through the little group with hugs and kisses. "Now, don't get too comfortable. Dinner is ready. We can save the sherry for after. Let's get to the table while the food's still hot. Ethan, would you take Serena and Lillie in?"

He smiled as he offered his arms to each of the women and thought, not for the first time, that his mother's instincts for romance had not dulled in the years since his father's death. And, for once, he was not unhappy about it. He was going to need all the help he could get if he was going to court Serena Jordan. The thought brought him up short. Feeling his mother's gaze on his back, he tuned his head just in time to see Aurelia and Letty share the unmistakable smile of female conspiracy.

Ethan thoroughly enjoyed the dinner. Conversation was lively and the only talk was of life in the county and the local farms. Something for which he was truly grateful.

"Mrs. Blackwood, dinner was delicious," said Serena. "And this chocolate cake is simply the best I've ever eaten. Would you share the recipe? I would love to be able to bake it for my family when I return to Philadelphia. My Aunt Nicki loves anything chocolate. This cake would cause her to swoon."

Ethan smiled at Serena's genuine enthusiasm. He realized that she was the most direct woman he'd ever met. She didn't...what was the word so popular now? Gush. Dora Grimshaw came to mind. Now there was a gusher.

"I don't know, Serena. That depends on whether Ma can pry the recipe from Rachel Appleton. She's our foreman's mother and her chocolate cake recipe is a county secret. What do you think?" He turned to his mother for confirmation.

"As a matter of fact, Rachel said she would be happy to share her recipe with Serena," Aurelia turned to Serena and smiled.

"Why just this afternoon, Rachel told me she had tasted several of Serena's baked goods at the party and declared her baking to be heavenly. And she went on to say that anyone who could bake as well as Serena deserved to have the secret chocolate cake recipe.

"Of course, Rachel said she would have to personally dictate the recipe to her and only if Serena would share *her* recipe for the cookies – I believed you called them biscotti, Serena – and only if you visited Rachel at the cabin. Mata Hari had nothing on Rachel Appleton," continued Aurelia, referring to the notorious German spy.

"Let's go into the parlor, shall we? Perhaps we can persuade Serena to play for us. It's been some time since Grandmother Meredith's piano was really played. An hour or so of Christmas carols doesn't really count. Serena, that's her portrait hanging over the piano."

As the others settled into their chairs, Ethan followed Serena to the piano.

Serena looked up at Meredith's portrait then seated herself and opened the lid to the keyboard. Looking up at him, she asked, "What would you like to hear? I can play just about anything you like. Classical, jazz, ragtime?"

"Do you know Scott Joplin?" he asked. "I really enjoy his music and even have a favorite. It's called *Solace*. Do you know that one?"

He watched her eyes light up in recognition.

"I do! It's one of my favorites, too! How lovely that you know it. His rags are so much more familiar to people. You know, *The Entertainer* and the *Maple Leaf Rag*. They're wonderful, but there's something about *Solace* that really speaks to me."

Ethan understood what she meant. The piece was so unlike Joplin's other compositions and he was transported as she began to play. He couldn't take his eyes from her hands as they glided over the keys. Everything about her was beautiful. He couldn't believe the force of his emotions. It seemed that after just 24 hours and a casual dinner with family and friends, he was actually falling in love with Serena Jordan. How in the world would he be able to tell her? She was going to think he was crazy, maybe shell-shocked.

"Serena, would you like to see a motion picture on Saturday evening? We could have dinner before and then see the film at the Grand in West Chester. The feature film is *Daddy-Long-Legs*. It's the latest Mary Pickford film. I believe they're also showing a new Charlie Chaplin short. Do you think you would enjoy that? Lillie said you enjoyed…"

He looked away from Serena when he realized that everyone was looking at him, waiting for him to finish the sentence. As he looked back to her he saw that she was smiling up at him.

His heart thudded so loudly in his ears he almost missed her whispered reply.

"Yes, Ethan, I would love nothing more."

CHAPTER SEVEN

"LILLIE, LILLIE, CAN I COME in? I know it's late, but I just have to talk with you."

"I knew he would ask you for a date." Lillie squealed as she threw open the door and pulled Serena into the room. "Tell me everything."

"There's not much to tell. Wait…how did you know he was going to ask me for a date?" Serena narrowed her eyes at Lillie who was bouncing on her bed like a four-year-old girl.

"I've known Ethan Blackwood my entire life, silly. I knew he was smitten the first time he clapped eyes on you. He has *never* looked at a woman the way he looked at you. It was inevitable. I didn't think it would happen so quickly. That's the surprise."

"What do you mean, so quickly?"

Lillie continued. "Ethan has always been one of the most deliberate men I've ever known. He's been that way since we were children. Even then, he planned and deliberated. There was no such thing as a spontaneous swim in the pond. Forget it. He had to make a list of pros and cons. That's what I mean about quickly. Don't misunderstand, he was never dull, he knew how to have fun. He just liked to think about it. You have made quite an impression on him, Serena. Told you."

"I swear, Lillie Price, sticking out your tongue to prove a point is going to get you in trouble one of these days." Serena laughed. "I can see the headlines now – Famous opera star dismissed. Sticks tongue out at conductor."

"I'm as serious as a missed entrance. Ethan Blackwood is in love with you, or he's falling in love. I have never seen him like this. He blushes, stammers, grins and is all out silly around you. This is not the man I know and love like a brother. When all the boys in the county were courting and getting married, he always stood back, never getting serious even about the most eligible – and by that I mean rich and pretty – girls in Chester County. At least a dozen prominent families would have loved to join their names – and farms – with the Blackwood's. In a word, my love, Ethan Blackwood is a catch."

"Don't I know it." Serena sighed. "These feelings are unfamiliar to me, too, you know. I was so sure I would be going back to Philadelphia in July but now I'm not sure of anything. I have a good job waiting for me at the Conservatory... senior instructor. Imagine! At 23, I would be the youngest women ever appointed. I would have a steady income, enough to keep my grandparents' house which is large enough so I could take in students who couldn't afford the board at the Conservatory. The extra income that provides would allow me to travel. You know I've always wanted to visit family in Italy. And I could visit you. What am I going to do?"

"Do? You will do nothing yet. But I have a feeling you will be having a serious conversation with him before long. In the meantime, you have Saturday to look forward to. You can borrow my new pale green chiffon – it's perfect with your eyes and hair. In fact, I don't even know why I bought it," Lillie mused to herself. "And beyond that, you are going to enjoy the summer here which will give you plenty of time to get to know Ethan. If what you feel right now is genuine, those feelings won't change and, most important, my friend, you will know exactly what you should do come the end of July."

"You know, for a flighty soprano, you are pretty level-headed, Lillie Price. I am so glad you're my best friend."

"Me, too. Someone has to talk sense into you. Stop being so serious about everything and enjoy yourself! You, better than most, know that life is too short to waste dithering – is that the word you've used with students? Enough! Talk to me, Serena. I want details."

A mile away, Ethan sat on the porch rocking and smoking his pipe while recalling every detail of the evening with Serena. Her smile, her scent – vanilla and lemons – her laughter, the way she participated in the conversation at dinner. He loved that she was self-assured but not in an impolite way. She didn't interrupt or try to call attention to herself, but time and time again, he found himself turning to her for conversation. Most of all, he couldn't forget the jolt of electricity he felt when he touched her arm as he took her in to dinner and again as he helped her into John Price's car while they said their goodbyes.

He turned to the sound of his mother's footsteps as she joined him. He grinned as she set a small tray with coffee and chocolate cake on the table before them.

"Well, that was quite an evening. I think everyone had a good time. Serena seemed to feel right at home with us, didn't she? I'm glad of that. The war brought so much sadness, it was good to have laughter and music in the house again, wasn't it, Son?"

"Yes, Ma, it certainly was. John and Letty are looking well and it's clear they are delighted to have Lillie at home with them for the summer. And I'm so happy to see that Lillie hasn't changed, except now she's a woman, not the girl who left us four years ago. Serena said Lillie has a tremendous career ahead and that she will be successful on par with some of the greats. It's almost beyond belief. I still see her in mud up to her ankles trying to catch tadpoles." He chuckled but his thoughts turned serious again. "Serena said the kind of career Lillie wants will take years more study and work and will be often lonely. That makes me feel bad and I said so to Serena. But Serena just smiled and told me not to worry. Lillie knows what she wants and is willing to make the sacrifices to achieve it."

"Serena says? Is that right? Ethan Blackwood, you've said Serena's name three times in as many sentences. In your whole life, I've never heard you do that before. Ever. Do you want to talk about it?"

"I can't believe it, Ma, but I think I'm falling in love."

He heard her intake of breath and turned to face her.

"Well, well. I beat you to it, didn't I? You can take that innocent look off your face, Ma. You've been trying to match me with one of the county girls for years. It wasn't easy, but I ignored you and thwarted your plans at every turn. Let's face it, determination is your greatest strength. And now you're dumbfounded because I've found the woman I think I want to spend the rest of my life with and you didn't even help. Ok, you did invite her to dinner. There is that."

He took his mother's hand and waited. "Aren't you going to say something?" He watched as her still lovely face glowed in the moonlight. He was sure she would cry but as she turned to him, he saw only happiness.

"Ethan Blackwood, you are full of surprises tonight. Do you think Serena feels the same way about you?"

"Well, I know how she looks at me and if I've learned nothing from your years of matchmaking, I know when a woman is interested." He sighed. "She accepted my invitation to dinner and the pictures on Saturday evening without hesitation and I'm taking that as a good sign. Say your prayers, Ma, this could be it. I can't believe I'm saying this, but I'm falling for a beautiful woman who is perfect and perfect for me."

"That's wonderful."

"Maybe not so wonderful. She's perfect in every way. I'm an amputee. I have no way of knowing how she will feel about getting involved with a man who is…disfigured. I do know that, before this goes too far, I'm going to talk with her about it."

"Surely, it won't be a surprise. Lillie must have told her about it."

"Hell, the whole county knows about it."

"What are you going to do?"

"Find a way to talk about it."

CHAPTER EIGHT

"SERENA, IF YOU'RE GOING TO keep daydreaming, we'll never get through this piece."

Serena blinked and looked up at Lillie who stood, hands on hips, scowling at her.

"It's only Wednesday. Your date with Ethan isn't until Saturday. We're going to lose the whole week if this keeps up."

Serena knew her friend wasn't really angry as Lillie's lips quivered and then finally broke in to a full-blown smile.

"I'm so sorry, Lillie. I just can't help it. My concentration is completely gone. This is such a new feeling for me. Honestly, I don't think I've ever felt this way. I can't think of anything else. I think I'm falling in love."

"Fallen's more like it," Lillie smiled. "It's alright, Serena, we've been working since nine this morning. It's time to stop for lunch. And Ma reminded me I'm to take you to the cabin this afternoon so you and Rachel Appleton can share recipes. You'll be the envy of at least a dozen county women who have coveted that chocolate cake recipe for decades."

Serena laughed as she gathered up music and closed the keyboard lid. "I am honored. My grandmother shared almost all of her recipes but she always had one or two she held back. They were given out like royal warrants as a reward for a good deed or in return for a really spectacular recipe she couldn't get any other way."

"I can't imagine wanting a recipe that much. I've never cared much about baking or cooking except that I know what I like to eat. I guess I take after my mother. She really doesn't like to bake or cook, much to my father's displeasure. Fortunately, the man has an iron constitution and the means to hire a good cook to prepare the meals. We'd all starve if we had to eat my mother's cooking all the time. But for goodness' sake, don't tell Mother I said that. She thinks she's gotten better over the years."

"Well, you did learn about fashion from Letty and that's something all well-dressed divas absolutely need to know. You have to look as good as you sound." Serena laughed. "And that reminds me, we still haven't decided for certain on the green dress. I'd like to try it on again."

"Why don't we plan to do that this afternoon when you get back from your recipe exchange? I'll drop you off at the cabin at Blackwood Farm and come back for you in a couple of hours. I can use the time to study scores." Lillie yawned. "Or take a nap."

&

"It's such a lovely afternoon, Lillie. We should have walked."

"One must never walk when one can drive," Lillie quipped. "Honestly, you are taking country living to heart, aren't you?"

Serena blushed. She knew her friend wasn't fooled by her sudden interest in walking for health. Serena hoped that she'd run into Ethan as she set out for each walk. She'd started walking on Sunday after lunch but had had no success and it was already Wednesday. Maybe tomorrow would be her lucky day.

"You're humming again, Serena. You're humming *Solace*. What is it with you and that song? You've been humming it or playing it whenever you have the chance. I love Joplin as much as you but I only just got it out of my head and now it's back. Can't you hum some Puccini?"

"I'm so sorry." Serena sighed. "I played it for Ethan on Saturday evening and when I hum it, I can still see his face. I think it moved him as much as it did me. I thought humming it might bring him to me. Will you listen to me? I am being totally ridiculous."

"I don't think so." Lillie sighed in turn. "I'm happy with the path I've chosen but, let's face it, my happily-ever-after will come in the form of curtain calls for the next couple of decades, if I'm lucky. If Ethan feels about you the way I think he does, you won't need a song to bring him to you."

Lillie pointed out the window. "Well, here we are. The cabin is just ahead on the other side of the pond and Rachel is waiting for you. It's 1:30 now. I'll be back around three. Will that be time enough for the recipe exchange?" asked Lillie.

"I'm sure it will be. Both Aurelia and Letty said Rachel enjoys a good talk and that I should be prepared to stay awhile. Apparently, she offers a lot of good advice with her recipes."

"Don't I know it? I thought Rachel would be the one person to tell me not to waste my time and parents' money on such tomfoolery as singing. Thought she would tell me to stay here and marry Ethan Blackwood, but she didn't. She told me to go out and find my dream. She said love would find me when I was ready." Lillie stopped and stared for a bit. "I haven't thought about that for years. Funny what comes to mind when you least expect it. Have a good time. I'll be back at three to escort you back to the house. You'll have a veritable state secret on your person."

Serena laughed and waved as her friend tooted her horn and drove off. As she turned on the path to the cabin, Serena recalled Rachel's words to Lillie. Perhaps that's what had happened to her. Serena wasn't looking for love but, just maybe, love had found her.

CHAPTER NINE

"HELLO THERE, SERENA. I'M MIGHTY pleased to meet you." Rachel Appleton waved her hello from the door of the cabin. "I'm so glad you could find the time to share recipes. Young women today are all so busy what with jobs and such. It's not like the old days when a woman stayed on the farm to help." Rachel clasped Serena's hand in her own and led her into the cabin.

In the few moments it took Serena's eyes to adjust to the light, Rachel had set out a plate of cookies and poured them a cup of her special herbal tea.

"Come sit by me." Rachel patted the chair next to hers at a long pine table. "You've quite a hand at baking, I can tell. The crumb on your biscuit cookies was as tender as soft butter and I would be pleased to know how you do it."

"My grandmother taught me." Serena smiled at the memories of the hours spent in her Nonna's large kitchen. The big, black stove with its ovens warming the room on even the coldest winter days.

Rachel noticed the change on Serena's face, patted her hand and said gently, "Sorry, I didn't mean to bring back sad memories."

"Oh, no, please don't. I loved baking with my Nonna, my grand-mother," she corrected. "I miss her and my grandfather so much. You see, they both died during the influenza epidemic."

"I'm very sorry to hear that. It must have been very hard for you. You don't have family close by, do you?" Rachel asked kindly.

"How did you know? I don't think anyone but the Prices know the whole story. My, word does travel fast in a small town."

"No, child, it's not that," Rachel said gently. "It just seems to me that a pretty young woman like you would have been married with children by now. The fact that you're here with Lillie for the summer means that you don't have family close by." Rachel again patted Serena's hand and waited.

"Why, you're right, of course." Serena laughed in spite of the sudden sadness she felt. "I have an aunt, Nicki, who lives with me in Philadelphia. She was eager for me to spend time in the country. The rest of my family lives in Maryland and New Jersey. We haven't seen each other for some time, mostly because of the flu. It made travel very difficult. I hope I will be able to visit them before I start back to school in September."

Rachel's eyes widened at this. "You're still studying?"

"Oh no." Serena laughed again in reply. "I will be teaching voice and piano at the Philadelphia Conservatory of Music. Lillie and I met there some years ago and we've become good friends, as you know. I am so pleased to be staying with her and her family here. It's so beautiful here, so different from the city."

"Well, who knows? A lot can happen in two or three months. Maybe you'll find something to keep you right here in Chester County. There's the school nearby and we could use a *good* music teacher." Rachel winked and continued. "Old Mrs. Clive has been at it for too many years so it might do some good to have a new teacher at the school. Church choir could use some help, too."

Serena was stunned. Before she could reply, Rachel got up to retrieve paper and pencil from the nearby sideboard.

"Ready?" Rachel asked and started right in with the recipe. "Butter and flour two cake pans..."

℈

Serena startled as the regulator clock chimed three. "I had no idea it was so late. We've been talking and laughing so, I'd completely forgotten the time. It was good to be able to talk about baking and cooking this afternoon. And I loved hearing stories about the Blackwoods and the Prices. It's been like spending time with my grandmother and hearing stories about her childhood in Italy." Serena blushed at the familiarity of her comments.

"No need to blush, child. I am old enough to be your grandmother."

Rachel laughed. "I enjoyed the time, too. Not too many young things around here want to spend time trading recipes and stories with an old woman, so the pleasure was mine, as well."

Serena rose to clear the table of tea cups and cookie plates and paused. "Rachel, will you let me come visit you again before I go? I so enjoyed talking with you and it wasn't just to get the chocolate cake recipe. Honest."

"You can come by any time you like. I always have time for a friend, especially a young one." Rachel's eyes shone with affection as she rose and gave Serena a warm embrace. "But don't rush off, Serena. You may find a lot more to keep you here than you think."

Serena was deep in thought as she walked toward the road where Lillie waited. *What in the world is the old woman talking about? I'm due back in Philadelphia at the end of July. Surely, she couldn't know about my feelings for Ethan. Lillie's the only one I've told and Lillie wouldn't tell anyone else. I'm sure of that, so what does she mean?*

Serena got to the road but Lillie was nowhere in sight. No matter, it was still a lovely afternoon and, although some dark clouds had started to appear in the distance, the sun still shone brightly so Serena decided to start walking. Lillie would probably come along at any minute.

She heard the motor before she saw the car, but it wasn't a car, it was a truck and her heart started pounding wildly when she saw Ethan Blackwood was driving it.

"Looks like you could use a ride." he smiled as he leaned over to open the passenger side door.

"Why, thank you, sir, but my grandma told me never to get into a truck, even a brand new truck, with a strange man." Serena batted her eyelashes so theatrically, that Ethan burst out laughing.

"Never fear, my dear, your hero is here. And I think it's going to rain." He had barely finished the sentence when the spring storm was upon them.

Serena stepped up onto the running board and into the truck. She seated herself comfortably next to him.

"That was wonderful timing, Ethan. Lillie was supposed to come for me at three o'clock but I guess she was so engrossed in studying her score, she just forgot."

Serena frowned and then laughed as she finished the sentence. "Or, she fell asleep. She did say something about a nap."

"Knowing our darling Lillie, my guess is the latter. She always did love an afternoon nap."

"I know," she said shivering slightly as the afternoon had suddenly turned cool. "Lillie is a dynamo but when she stops," Serena searched for the right words, "she does just that. I've never seen anything like it. It's like someone has flicked a switch."

Serena mimicked the effect, her eyes bright and blinking, her smile artificially bright, her hands up and framing her face. In the next instant, her chin was on her chest, shoulders slumped, eyes closed, hands down. The speed of the transformation sent him into another fit of laughing so hard that he had to pull the truck to the side of the road.

"Oh, Serena," he said, wiping the tears from his eyes. "Lillie would be furious if she saw you right now."

Just as he managed to catch his breath, Serena started laughing again.

"I know, so let's not tell her, shall we? It can be our secret." She pursed her lips and put her finger to them in confirmation of their secret pact.

Ethan was sitting so close to Serena that her light scent of vanilla and lemons enveloped his senses. Without thinking, he leaned in and kissed her very gently on her pursed lips.

When Serena returned the kiss, the effect was electrifying, as if a current had passed between them.

"Serena, I'm so sorry. I don't know what came over me. Wait...I ah...I do," he stammered. "I've wanted to kiss you since the moment I saw you at the party. Can you ever forgive me?"

"There's nothing to forgive. We're both adults. This is 1919." Serena reached up to touch his cheek. "I've wanted you to do that since I first saw you on Saturday night. How nice that Lillie and Mother Nature conspired so thoughtfully. I will be forever grateful to Lillie's naps and spring storms. Won't you?"

Ethan leaned in and kissed her again, this time taking her in his arms, never wanting to let her go.

Reluctantly breaking the embrace, they looked at each other and knew that a crossroads had been reached. Where it would take them was yet to be determined.

Riding along in silence, Serena was the first to speak. "So, Ethan, why don't you tell me about the truck?"

Ethan knew in that moment his bachelor days were over.

CHAPTER TEN

LILLIE WATCHED FROM HER BEDROOM as Ethan helped Serena down from the truck and noted that he didn't let go of her hand as he walked her to the front door. Seconds later, Lillie watched him drive away as Serena's footsteps sounded in the hall. But she was left disappointed when Serena didn't come bursting in.

"Well, if the bee won't come to the honey, then the honey will have to go to the bee, or something like that," Lillie said aloud.

"May I come in?" Lillie used her most soothing voice as she tapped on Serena's door.

"Could I stop you? This is your house, or are you too muddle-headed from your nap to recall that fact?"

Uh oh, she's really angry. Her friend rarely lost her temper, but Lillie recognized the *tone* as the same one Serena used with overzealous suitors and lazy students.

"I'm so sorry. I meant to close my eyes for just five minutes and before I knew it, it was 3:30 and pouring." Lillie braced herself for Serena's wrath as she entered the room.

"Save your late entrance for your next conductor. I am not amused." Serena *sounded* angry. Turning to face her friend, Serena suddenly grabbed both of Lillie's hands and began to twirl her around. Turning and turning until they were breathless.

"What has gotten into you? I'm sorry I was late." Lillie stopped. "Wait, you're not wet! Why aren't you wet? You should be wet." Lillie shook her head as though still clearing the cobwebs from her nap.

"How very observant of you." Serena laughed, threw herself down on the feather-filled mattress and laughed even harder.

"Wait. Ethan drove you home. What happened? Why are you so happy and why aren't you wet? I thought you would be furious with me because you'd gotten wet walking home from Rachel's, which I knew you would do."

"First of all, you were *supposed* to pick me up at 3 o'clock. I will never understand how someone who can make an entrance exactly on the right note in an aria neglects to remember the time of an engagement." Serena sat up and held up her hand to fend off the barrage of questions she knew was about to burst from Lillie's mouth.

"Second, I am not wet because I started walking home from Rachel's at 3:05, just about the time Ethan was coming home from buying his new truck and *before* the rain started." Now holding up both hands, Serena continued.

"Third, we kissed." Serena sat back on the bed.

"Wait. You mean to tell me that Ethan Blackwood, the man who deliberates and ponders every decision in his life whether it's over which tie to wear to church or which feed to give his horses, kissed you? Just like that? In the truck? In the middle of the road?"

Lillie sat down next to Serena, still dizzy from all the twirling.

"Syntax, Lillie." Serena laughed despite trying to keep a straight face. "No, he didn't kiss me in the middle of the road. He kissed me on the middle of the mouth. Right here," Serena tapped her lips with her forefinger and then burst out laughing. Again.

"How?" Lillie couldn't believe it. Ethan Blackwood kissed her best friend this afternoon.

"Well, when you didn't show up at 3 o'clock, it was still a beautiful day so I decided to walk. About ten minutes into my walk, Ethan just happened to be driving in from town and thought I would like a ride. I'd never ridden in a brand new truck and it did look like it was going to rain, so I said yes. And then it happened."

"Oh no, you don't." Lillie jumped up and persisted. "There had to be something more. What did he say? What did you say? You two are about the most serious, deliberate people I know. You just don't go around kissing people in the middle of the road, for heaven's sake."

"I told you we didn't kiss in the middle of the road, we kissed on the lips." Serena started laughing again and then stopped. She looked up at her friend.

"I'm waiting." Lillie demanded

Serena noticed that Lillie was tapping her foot. Perhaps it was time to be serious for a few moments. "We laughed. That's all, we laughed and then we kissed."

"You laughed? About what?" Serena watched as Lillie's eyes narrowed and she knew Lillie was sure she was hiding something.

"It's a secret. I can't tell you.."

"Well, whatever it is, I'm sure it's a doozy. Promise you'll tell me some day?"

"I will. I promise. Now, will you help me finally decide on the dress? Ethan said we're having dinner at the Colonial Restaurant, then going to the pictures at the Grand. I love the green chiffon, but will it be too much? West Chester isn't Philadelphia. I mean, that's not, oh I don't know what I mean."

Serena sighed again as Lillie left her room to fetch the dress.

○

The rain had stopped by the time Ethan arrived home with the new truck. He spotted his mother working in the kitchen garden as he parked. He sounded the horn and called, "Ma, come take a look. She's a beauty." He got out of the truck, took out his handkerchief and started wiping rainwater off the hood and fenders.

"Really, Ethan. I'll never understand men and their machines. Women and babies are beautiful. Sunsets and sunrises are beautiful. Horses are beautiful. But trucks? What is this fascination with all things mechanical? Your father, God rest his soul, was just the same."

"I think it's a man's prerogative." He stopped wiping and turned to face her. "Just as it is a woman's to change her mind," he teased and then turned serious before his mother could respond.

"I happened upon Serena on the way home. She was walking back to the Prices' after visiting with Rachel. Lucky for me, Lillie had forgotten to collect her. I was her knight in shining armor today. I saved her from the drenching rain. And she was most appreciative and told me so by telling me the truck was beautiful."

"Well, Son, I'm glad you got to spend a little time with Serena. You've been mooning around since Sunday, playing that Scott Joplin record on the Victrola over and over again until I'm about to lose my mind. I was going to ask you to move to the barn but I have a better idea."

He heard the laughter in her voice and then felt his mother's hand on his cheek.

"Why wait until Saturday evening? Take the girl on a picnic. I'll even pack the basket for you. Just telephone her and ask her. There's no law saying you can't take her on a picnic and out to dinner and the motion pictures in the same week. Unless something has changed since your father and I went courting."

Not for the first time that week did Ethan hear his mother laughing as she walked away from him. What was it about love that made everyone laugh? He decided right there to take his mother's advice. She was right. There was no point in waiting until Saturday to see Serena.

He whistled as he went up to the house and the telephone.

CHAPTER ELEVEN

THURSDAY HAD ARRIVED AND IT was a perfect day for a picnic. Ethan kissed his mother good morning and grinned as she shooed him away to continue her preparations.

"I do believe I smell fried chicken and I spy a jar of your prize-winning bread and butter pickles. What other ambrosia can we expect?"

"Don't be fresh, young man, or you'll be preparing your own potato salad and cornbread." He had his hand smacked as he reached for a chicken leg. "That chicken is for your lunch with Serena. Your breakfast is warming on the stove. And if you behave yourself, you can expect one of Rachel's butterscotch apple pies." He watched his mother smile as she mentioned Rachel Appleton.

"Rachel's apple pie. This is a special occasion, indeed. Wait, how did Rachel know about the picnic? Serena only accepted yesterday. Mother, have you been talking to Rachel?"

"Of course, I've been talking to Rachel. I talk to Rachel every day of my life. In fact, I'll see her later today when we drive into town together for some supplies. There's nothing unusual about that."

"What's unusual, Ma, is one of Rachel's butterscotch apple pies landing in my picnic basket not twenty-four hours after said picnic was planned."

"It's not your picnic basket until I give it to you. So eat your breakfast and then please get out of the way. I have too much to do this morning without having you underfoot."

Ethan got up from his place at the breakfast table and hugged his mother. "Thanks, Ma. That's the first time you've raised your voice to me since I've been home. Feels like things are getting back to normal around here. I'll be back around eleven. I told Serena I'd pick her up at eleven-thirty."

He laughed as his mother snapped her kitchen towel at him as he walked by. It felt just like old times to leave her muttering under her breath.

☾

Serena had been awake for hours after a mostly sleepless night. As the dawn broke, she found she was hopelessly confused.

Only yesterday, Serena had been thrilled by Ethan's kiss and delighted with his invitation to a picnic but as she tossed and turned through the night, her misgivings had solidified into serious doubts that her relationship with him was deepening much too quickly. They'd met only five days ago. How could she be in love? She had so much to think about. She wished Aunt Nicki was here to talk to. Perhaps she should go back to the city to talk things out with her. Nicki always had the perfect solution to any problem.

"Serena, are you awake?"

Serena groaned inwardly at the sound of Lillie's voice. She really didn't want to talk with Lillie just now. The conversation was bound to turn to her feelings for him and she knew Lillie would tell her not to be foolish. That she knew her feelings for Ethan were real and to grab on to this opportunity with both hands and hold on.

"Yes, Lillie, I'm awake. Come on in."

Serena stretched and sat up in bed, patting the space next to her as Lillie sat.

"It's so early for you. Couldn't you sleep either?"

"What do you mean either? You should have slept like a baby. Why couldn't you sleep? What's wrong?"

Serena watched as Lillie's clear blue eyes clouded with worry.

"I had a little trouble, yes, but I think it's because I'm excited about seeing Ethan today. It'll be the first time we'll be alone and, quite honestly, I think he might ask me to marry him." Serena pulled nervously at the coverlet. "And I don't know what I'll say."

"You love him, don't you? You did yesterday. What's happened since then?"

"I don't know Lillie. I guess nothing's really changed, but I can't get past the feeling that it's all going too fast. Life isn't a fairy tale and I'm not a princess waiting to be rescued from the wicked queen. What I do have is a career waiting for me back in Philadelphia." Serena paused to give Lillie a chance to say something. When she didn't, Serena continued. "I've worked long and hard for this opportunity. If he does ask me to marry him, I'll have to give up teaching at the Conservatory. And then what will I do? I am totally unprepared for the life of a farm wife."

Serena looked at Lillie.

"I know you have something to say, so please just say it."

"Serena, for once in my life, I am almost speechless. As usual, you are complicating things. You don't know if Ethan is going to ask you to marry him today or any day, for that matter."

Serena put her head in her hands as Lillie continued.

"But for what it's worth, I think you two are a match made in heaven, with a once in a lifetime chance for love and true happiness - something that most people never find. Just like a skinny tenor."

Serena smiled at Lillie's little joke and then hugged her friend and got herself out of bed.

"Once again, you're right. I've worked myself into fits because I never learned to just take it all one day at a time." Serena stretched and yawned. "I can't help it. I've always been a planner and Ethan Blackwood was never part of that plan. Well, the sun is shining and it's going to be a beautiful day. How about a walk before breakfast?"

Serena laughed and ducked as the pillow Lillie aimed at her flew across the room.

CHAPTER TWELVE

E THAN'S HEART SWELLED AS SERENA made her way to the truck. She looked so beautiful this morning, more beautiful than yesterday, if that were possible.

"Well, good morning." He had come around to the passenger side door. As he opened it and took Serena's hand to help her up into the truck, he felt the familiar jolt of electricity. He wondered if she felt it, too. "Sorry about the truck but Mother took the car for her shopping expedition into West Chester. She and Rachel make the trip a couple of times a month. I think Ma enjoys it as much as Rachel does. Although she would never admit it, my mother loves to drive. I know she can't wait to get her hands on this beauty." He suddenly stopped talking and grinned. "My mother warned me not to make too much of the new truck. She reminded me that it's *just* a truck, not a new baby. She said men care too much about machines. Personally, I think she's being unfair about it. What do you think?"

"Well, I don't know your mother well enough to judge, but I'm not sure that's an accurate assessment. My Aunt Nicki was the first woman in the family who learned to drive and own her own car. And she knows how to make minor repairs. She's more enthusiastic about her precious 1915 Model T than almost anything else, except perhaps her passion for clothing design. She thinks every woman should know how to drive. She taught me when I was nineteen."

"You can drive? Is there no end to your talent? What else are you keeping from me?"

Before Serena could answer, Ethan pulled into a narrow lane and announced that they were just a few minutes away from their destination.

"There's a great spot just along the Brandywine Creek that I've been going to since I was a boy. It's always been a great spot to fish or have a picnic. I think you'll like it."

Serena's delight was evident as she clapped her hands. "Oh, Ethan, it's just beautiful, so green and peaceful. And look at the wildflowers along the bank of the creek. What are they?" Serena asked, pointing to the pale blue and white blooms.

"They're called Virginia bluebells. Ma has them up at the house. She's always liked them because they were among the first to bloom. There's phlox and foamflower, too. There'll be lots more to see as the season matures. It's pretty early days yet. Wait 'til you see it in July. It's really beautiful then." He stopped and turned to Serena who was staring him.

"What? I'm a farmer. I should know about flowers, right? My mother made sure I always knew the difference between a weed and a flower. She figured if I knew what it was I wouldn't step on it."

"I'd be surprised if you *couldn't* name them. It's your enthusiasm that's so surprising."

"Well, I'm just as surprised to find out you can drive and you have an aunt who's an auto mechanic."

"Don't be silly." Serena laughed. "I didn't say she was an auto mechanic. I said she could make minor repairs. She's a fashion designer, for heaven's sake. She designed and made the dress I'm wearing today." Serena gestured to her pale pink dress. "In fact, she's made most of my clothes since I was a little girl."

Ethan parked the truck and, as he came around to help Serena out of the truck, he was struck again by her loveliness. She wore her chestnut hair down and tied with a ribbon. A few softly curled wisps framed her face. The pale pink ribbon matched the faint blush in her cheeks and the color of her dress.

"Do you have a blanket?" Serena asked.

"Right here," he said, handing Serena a faded gingham quilt. "This is the official Blackwood picnic blanket. Why don't you choose a place and I'll get the basket and follow."

Serena looked around for the perfect spot and saw it almost immediately, just ahead, under a dogwood tree covered in soft pink blossoms. As Serena turned to seek his approval, she realized he had followed her right to the spot and had just lowered the basket to the ground.

"Here, let me help you with the blanket." Ethan's voice was soft and as he reached for the blanket, he took Serena in his arms and kissed her passionately. Serena dropped the blanket and stood on tiptoes. She reached up and wrapped her arms around his neck and kissed him with a passion that matched his own.

"We have to stop meeting like this," said Ethan, "because I don't ever want to stop kissing you and that could be very dangerous."

"Then how about some lunch? I'm Italian and we believe that any dangerous situation can be defused with food, especially an all-American picnic lunch."

His laughter broke the tension. "You know, I recall reading that in a history book. I didn't believe it at the time but I hadn't met you. I'm convinced. Let's eat."

❦

"I don't think I will be able to eat for a week," said Serena. "You mother makes the best fried chicken I've ever tasted. Do you think she will share the recipe?"

"Probably. I think Ma would share every family recipe with you if you asked. She really likes you, you know. More lemonade?" He raised the thermos jug and waited.

"How do you know that?" Serena raised her glass for a refill. "Your mother met me about ten minutes before you did."

"The proof, my dear, is in this picnic basket," he said, pointing to the wicker hamper. "She prepared her very best, most treasured picnic fare for us. Fried chicken, potato salad, cornbread and," he held up a mason jar, "her very, very special prize-winning bread and butter pickles which, according to the experts at the county fair, are more precious than emeralds."

"More precious than emeralds?" Serena raised an eyebrow in mock skepticism. "Well, that's some very strong evidence, Mr. Blackwood, but what additional proof can you offer? Surely, there must be more."

"I give you the final piece of evidence." He reached into the picnic basket, lifted the covered plate and, with a flourish befitting a magician, removed the red and white checked cloth. "Voila! Rachel Appleton's butterscotch apple pie - truly food of the gods!"

"You still haven't answered my question. How do you know your mother likes me?"

"I just told you. Ma prepared this entire picnic and asked Rachel to bake the pie. She wouldn't have done that if she didn't like you. Nor would Rachel have baked the pie, so they both like you." Ethan cut a generous slice of pie and handed the plate to Serena.

"I must be city-stupid because I still don't see how that proves anything."

"If Ma didn't like you, she would have suggested the picnic but *you* would have been expected to prepare the lunch. You don't have anything to prove. She knows you can cook and bake. And the fact that Rachel asked for your recipes is significant."

He stopped to take a bite of pie. "If you could get this recipe from Rachel and duplicate it, I'd marry you next week."

"What did you say?" she stopped eating and put her plate down on the blanket. "Did you just say something about marriage?"

"Yeah, I guess I did. But pie or no pie, I'd marry you tomorrow if you'd have me." He laughed then turned serious. "But I shouldn't have said anything because...you know that I'm an amputee, right?"

"Lillie told me after she got your letter. She was so worried about you. And I worried with her."

"I don't know if I can ask you to live the rest of your life with me. But I do know that I can love you and care for you as well as a man with two good legs. The doctors and nurses may have taught me everything I needed to know about living life as an amputee, but they never said anything about what to do or say when you fall in love."

"Please tell me how it happened. I would really like to know." Serena reached across the blanket and took Ethan's hand.

"It was near the end of October, just a few weeks before the Armistice was declared." He cleared his throat and went on.

"By that time, the American troops were out of the Argonne Forest and we'd begun our advance toward the south. The objective was to stop the German troops to allow the French to capture Sedan, a railway center critical to the transport of enemy troops and supplies. In the end, the combined Allied Forces were successful and the French captured Sedan which all but finished the Germans."

Ethan had stopped talking and was staring ahead then closed his eyes and shook his head.

"Ethan, come back to me. You were a million miles away," Serena said softly. "Tell me what happened next."

"The fighting was horrific, Serena, something I hope never to experience again."

He took a deep breath and continued.

"Most people really don't understand what it means to be in a battle. It's more than a series of explosions and gunfire. It's the sound of flesh being torn apart by rifle fire and shells. It's the sight of men racing toward each other, bayonets fixed and ready to stab and rend. It's the cries of officers leading their men into the skirmish. And above that, you hear the men screaming in agony as they are hit. After what seems like an eternity, the shooting and shelling stop and an eerie silence falls over the battlefield, broken only by the cries of the wounded as the medics and priests minister to them.

Ethan's eyes never left Serena's face as he told the story. He thought his heart would break when he saw that she was weeping.

"I can stop if this is too much for you," he whispered as he wiped away her tears.

"No, please go on. I want to hear it all."

"The day I was wounded, our platoon was heading toward an embankment not far from the font line of battle. The plan was to stand ground and hold off the German troops and force them back. The fighting was pretty fierce and the barrages never stopped but we were holding our own and advancing steadily toward the German line, forcing them back."

Ethan took a deep breath. "It happened in a heartbeat. I heard the buzz of the shell just before it hit. The concussion of the shell knocked me out and the next thing I knew, I was in a field hospital and a nurse was telling me that I had been wounded. She explained the extent of my injuries. I was pretty banged up but my left leg got the worst of it. She told me that I would need surgery but that it would be several hours at least because the more severely injured soldiers were taken care of first. To be honest, I felt pretty lucky. I was so happy to be alive that I didn't care about being wounded. Well, almost."

Ethan reached into his shirt and pulled out a small, silver, heart-shaped medallion on a thin chain and held it out to Serena.

"Do you remember the portrait of my great-grandmother, Meredith, that Ma pointed out on Saturday night?"

"Yes. I remember thinking that you must have inherited your blue eyes from your great-grandmother."

"In the portrait, she's wearing a brooch called a luckenbooth. It's been in my family since 1721 when Finlan, the founder of the Blackwood clan here in America, gave it to his beloved Elizabeth just before they were married. Since that day, it has been worn by every Blackwood bride at her wedding."

"That's so romantic. Did your mother wear it, too?"

"She did, and so did I. The Blackwood babies wear it at their christening."

"So the medallion you're wearing is a replica of the Blackwood luckenbooth."

"Well, not exactly." He pointed to the medallion in his hand. "The actual brooch has an amethyst in the center and the leaves are made up of small emeralds. But for that, it's a pretty fair replica."

"Is the medallion a family heirloom as well?" Serena asked.

"Not at all. Here, look at the back."

He removed the medallion and chain and handed it to Serena.

"The print is so small, I can barely read it." Serena squinted as she looked more closely at the little medal.

"Wait, it says 'God speed. AB'."

He watched the expression on her face change from puzzlement to understanding.

"Your mother had it made for you when she knew you were going into the Army and signed it AB instead of *Mother* because there wasn't room. Am I right?"

"Give the little lady a kewpie doll." He imitated a carnival barker awarding a prize.

Serena placed the chain around Ethan's neck and kissed his cheek as she did so.

"So it was your good luck charm."

Ethan offered Serena more lemonade. When she shook her head, he poured himself a glass, drank it in one long pull and continued

"Battlefield wounds are especially dangerous because of the conditions and it's often hours, sometimes days before proper treatment can begin. And although I was transported to a field hospital pretty quickly, my leg got infected and the surgeons had no other treatment choice but amputation. All things considered, I was pretty lucky."

"How does that make you lucky?"

"I still have my knee. It sounds simple, but having a working knee-joint made my recovery and rehabilitation much easier. Once the wound healed, I was fitted with my prosthesis and trained to use it as effectively as the original."

"Does it still hurt?"

"It does, sometimes. But not so much that I can't work. And I meant what I said earlier about being able to love you and care for you as well as any man with two good legs. That's what's really important, isn't it?"

"Yes, it is. I'm so glad you told me about the war and how you were hurt because I can tell you with absolute certainty that your injury makes no difference to me. You've said all I need to know...that you love me." She smiled and took his hands in hers. "And I feel the same way about you, but I don't think we're ready to talk about marriage. You don't know anything about me. And while I know more about you than I did earlier today, I still know only what Lillie has told me."

"But I do know about you," Ethan said gently. "Lillie's letters were always about you. She described how you befriended her when she first arrived in Philadelphia and that you were one of the kindest people she'd ever met. I know everything. Lillie told me about your childhood and how you lost both parents before you were a year old. I know your grandparents raised you and encouraged your musical studies but that they taught you the practical lessons of life so you could be independent. She said you were funny, talented and smart – you speak Italian *and* French. The only thing Lillie didn't describe was how beautiful you are."

Ethan caressed Serena's blushing cheek and then took her hand in his

"I don't know what to say, Ethan, except that when Lillie wasn't studying, she was either talking about you or writing to you. I had no idea she was telling you about me in her letters."

"I told you. Lillie wrote about how hard she was working and you." He leaned back on his elbows and stretched his legs.

"Lillie made you sound like some kind of hero from a fairy tale you know - shining armor, white horse – the whole picture. I would laugh and tell her that no one could be so wonderful but she would just shake her head and tell me another story. Now that I think about it, she never stopped talking about you."

Serena thought for a moment. "At first I thought she was in love with you and then I realized that she did love you, but like a brother. Do you understand what she was doing? She *wanted* us to know each other before we actually met. She didn't want us to waste any time once we did. Lillie planned this whole thing. She wanted the two people she loved most to love each other."

"Don't cry, darlin'." Ethan sat up and pulled a handkerchief from his pocket and gently wiped away Serena's tears. "It's clear now why I felt comfortable with you from the first moment we met."

"I know. I didn't think it was possible. I mean, this just doesn't happen, does it?"

"It must, because it has." He smiled but grew serious. "You haven't answered my question, Serena. Will you marry me?"

"I want to say yes, Ethan. With all my heart, I want to say yes. But I think we have to slow down, spend more time together. You've just come home and there's so much you need to do at the farm." Serena continued before he could interrupt. "And I have a lot to think about, too, the position at the Conservatory for one. And I still haven't decided what I'm going to do about my grandparents' house and my grandfather's shop in Philadelphia. I just need some time."

"Well, you haven't said no and that's encouraging. I'll give you whatever time you need but, please, don't take too much time, Serena. I love you and want to marry you. Please remember that."

"Of course I will. I honestly don't see how I'll be able to think about anything else. I've never been asked such an important question before."

Please, God, I will never ask you for another blessing as long as I live but that you grant me the honor of having this woman as my wife. I promise I will love her and provide for her and the children you send as long as I have breath in my body.

With this silent prayer in his heart, he pulled her into his arms and kissed her passionately. He was elated by her equally passionate response.

Ethan was filled with wanting her but he broke the embrace before he lost himself completely to the longing that was flooding his entire being.

"More pie?" he asked, his voice husky with desire. "Or do you think we should pack up and head back? We don't want to miss dinner, after all."

"Don't you ever think about anything but food?"

"As a matter of fact I do, but it wouldn't be polite to say what, exactly." He grinned as a blush spread across her cheeks.

"Stop grinning, Ethan Blackwood, or I'll..."

"Tell me, Serena, what will you do?" His heart thudded in his chest as he gathered Serena in his arms and kissed her again.

"Ah...I'll go for a walk, that's what. It' such a lovely day and there's not a rain cloud in sight. The exercise would be nice after all that food. Would you like to join me or are you going to sit here all afternoon and eat yourself sick?" Serena stood and looked down at Ethan as she straightened her skirts and patted her hair "Well?"

"A walk sounds just fine," he said as he joined her on the grassy bank. "I can show you more of the creek and where we played as kids. In fact, this was a great place to play hide and seek. Now that I think of it, with the weather being so fine, we could play a little hide and seek ourselves. How does that sound?"

"It sounds like you want to play Catch and Kiss," said Serena, referring to a popular children's kissing game. "I loved playing hide and seek...when I was six years old. But I have to admit it might be fun. And since I'm your guest, I get to hide and you get to seek which means you have to count to one hundred in *French*."

"Wait. I can only count to twenty in French," he called after her as she made her way towards the woods.

"Then count to twenty five times, silly. We can have a French lesson after you've found me," Serena teased.

"Ok, Mademoiselle, have it your way. You go on and try to hide. I'll find you and when I do..."

"You'll have another piece of pie, right?"

Ethan laughed and started counting. "Un, deux, trois..."

CHAPTER THIRTEEN

❝THIS WAS AN EXCELLENT IDEA, Lillie," Serena said as they walked along Gay Street in downtown West Chester. "I love looking in shop windows, especially millinery shops. I've seen at least four hats I can't live without. Wait, make that five. I've just seen the hat I'm going to wear tomorrow night. It will be perfect." Serena pointed to a cloche hat woven from silk in several different shades of green and gold, with bands of green silk running through the weave. The same silk lined the hat and formed the crown. A flower woven from the silk ribbon completed the design. "I just have to try it on," said Serena as she pulled Lillie to the door of the shop.

"Wait, I have to finish my ice cream," laughed Lillie. "I hate to waste a perfectly good strawberry cone. That hat isn't going anywhere."

But Serena was already in the shop, speaking to the sales woman and pointing to the window. "I'd like to try on the silk cloche with the green ribbon trim, please."

"Of course, madam. Let me get that for you. Why hello, Lillie. What a surprise. I'd heard you were back from Philadelphia," the woman said. "I missed your performance last week. I understand it was very well received."

"Hello, Louise. How nice to see you," Lillie replied. "I didn't know you work at Purcell's."

"Yes. I've been here about a year now. I've even started to design some hats for Mrs. Purcell's clients. In fact, I was just about to show one of my hats to this young woman," Louise told her as she pointed at Serena.

"This is my friend Serena Jordan, Louise. She is staying with me this summer. Serena is helping me prepare for my concert tour this fall. We were at school together. In fact, Serena will be joining the faculty of the Conservatory this fall. We are all very proud of her."

Serena noticed that while the two women smiled as they made polite conversation, their smiles were frozen in place. She couldn't wait to ask Lillie what was going on *after* she tried on the hat.

"Oh, yes. I'd heard something about that. I think Dora Grimshaw mentioned your tour at bridge last night. How nice for you, Lillie."

Louise turned to Serena. "Will you be staying long?"

Before Serena could answer, Louise moved to the window and removed the hat from the display.

"If madam would sit here." Louise pointed to a chair in front of a dressing table and mirror.

"Oh Lillie! I just love it," said Serena, as she fitted the hat on her head. "It's perfect! I love the effect of the woven silk and the ribbon trim is a perfect match for the dress I'm wearing to dinner tomorrow. Don't you think?"

Serena turned to look at Lillie and caught the warning in her eyes. "I'll take it, thank you," said Serena as she removed the hat and handed it to Louise.

"Of course. I'll just get a box. I won't be a minute." Louise disappeared into the back of the shop as Serena turned to Lillie.

"What is going on?" Serena demanded.

"Hush!" Lillie whispered. "I'll tell you outside. The walls have ears and Louise Asher is the last person you want to know your business. She has a direct line to Dora Grimshaw who, I am sorry to say, is the second biggest gossip in Chester County."

"Who's the first?" Serena giggled.

"Her mother, Ada. Now stop laughing, pay for your hat and let's get out of here."

Within minutes, Serena had paid for her hat and said goodbye to Louise Asher. As they reached the door, Serena noticed the sales girl was already making a phone call. Once outside as they walked away from the shop, Serena burst into laughter. "Lillie, who is that dreadful woman? It's hard to believe someone so…gruesome could design such a beautiful hat."

"Louise Asher is one of Dora Grimshaw's 'ghouls'," Lillie explained.

"Girls?" Serena asked.

"No, *ghouls*. When we were in school, there were about six girls, including Louise, who spent their free time and a lot of class time, as I remember, making our lives miserable. Dora bought their loyalty with invitations to parties and expensive gifts, things like that. Poor Dora was never secure enough to make friends the usual way, and it didn't help that she always had to be the center of attention."

"What *are* you talking about? I'm not from here, remember? Please do tell."

"Be patient. Let's get the car and I will reveal all on the drive home."

℅

"Thank you, Louise. Dinner tomorrow night you said." Dora Grimshaw smiled into the telephone receiver. "It was most fortunate that after lunch, Lillie and this Serena Jordan person stopped at Brown's soda fountain for an ice cream where Edith Hatcher just happened to overhear something about the Colonial Restaurant and the Mary Pickford film at the Grand. They must be going to dinner and the pictures. Well, I'll just have to see what I can do to make sure that Ethan Blackwood and Miss Serena Jordan have a lovely evening."

CHAPTER FOURTEEN

"THIS HAS BEEN LOVELY," SERENA told Ethan as she sipped her coffee. "Dinner was perfectly delicious. As good as any you could find in Philadelphia. And I can't get over how much this restaurant looks like Wanamaker's Crystal Tearoom."

"I've enjoyed it, too. I'm glad we were able to get a window table. It's a pleasure to see folks enjoying themselves." He gestured toward the people strolling along the sidewalk. "All of this seems so far from France."

He shook his head. "Have I told you how beautiful you look tonight?"

"Yes, you have. And have I told you how handsome you look? That blue suit really brings out the color of your eyes."

"Stop! You'll make me blush," he teased.

"Well, now you know how I feel. Honestly, the way you look at me. It isn't...decent."

"I can't help it. This is a new experience for me and I can't believe my good fortune. Just think, a week ago, I was a confirmed bachelor. Then I met you and, in an instant, I fell in love. I would tell the world if I could, and as soon as you give me the word, I will."

"Oh, I want to. We've talked about this and you've promised to give me time. I have to go back to Philadelphia to settle my grandparents' affairs. Then there's my post at the Conservatory. I've made a commitment to teach the entire year. If we marry as soon as you want to, I would have to resign almost as soon as the semester begins and I fear that would put a strain on the staff, not to mention my professional reputation. Don't you see?"

"I understand, sweetheart, and I promise not to bring it up again tonight. Let's just enjoy the rest of the evening. We still have the pictures to look forward to." He gestured for the waiter to bring the check. "We'll have almost the whole summer together. I won't have to go back to Philadelphia until the end of July and, if I need to, I can always go back to the city for a day or two at a time to take care of family affairs." Serena smiled at Ethan's boyish expression. "Now don't pout. We both have work to do. I have my work with Lillie and you have the farm. You can't spend the next two months taking me on picnics and to romantic dinners."

"Who says I can't? I'm a genuine war hero," he countered then continued, "but you're right. I need to get back to work. After all, I'll have a wife and five children to support. You can't do that sitting on your... ah...laurels all day."

"Five children," Serena said solemnly. "How did you know I wanted five children?" When he didn't say anything, she continued, "I spent so much time alone growing up, I promised myself that when I got married I would have lots of children to make up for the loneliness." She blinked away the tears. "You are serious, aren't you?"

"Darlin', I'm as serious as a judge at a country fair. A man can't get much more serious than that." He winked. "Charlie Chaplin and Mary Pickford await our company. Shall we go?"

⦿

The house lights came up as the Charlie Chaplin short ended. "I just love him, don't you?" Serena laughed as she turned to Ethan.

"Well, I'm not sure I *love* him but he does make me laugh. Do you want to get a drink or some popcorn before the main event? I noticed a vendor set up across the street." He looked at his watch. "There's time if you like."

"Thank you, no. I couldn't eat or drink another thing. But I would like to powder my nose. Why don't you get your popcorn?" She then looked at her watch and said, "I'll meet you in the lobby in ten minutes, all right?"

In the powder room, Serena liked what she saw when she looked in the mirror. *Every woman needs a beautiful hat. Aren't I the clever one to have found this one?*

"Excuse me, but aren't you Serena Jordan, Lillie's friend?"

Serena turned away from the mirror to the sound of the voice.

"Why, yes, but I don't believe I've had the pleasure…" Serena stopped as the woman stepped into the glow of the lamplight to face her.

"I'm Dora Grimshaw, an old friend of the Blackwood family. Ethan Blackwood and I have known each other since we were babies."

"It's good to meet you, Miss Grimshaw. I've heard so much about you." Serena extended her hand in greeting.

"Really? Well then you must know that Ethan and I have an understanding."

"Pardon me?" Serena dropped her hand. "I don't understand."

"You will, Miss Jordan. Ethan and I were promised to each other as children. You can ask anyone in Chadds Ford. I should think a well-bred young woman such as yourself would know better than to steal another woman's intended."

"You are correct in that, Miss Grimshaw. I would never steal another woman's *intended*. However, I have it on very good authority that you and Ethan were never promised to each other," Serena said stonily.

"Surely, you don't mean Lillie Price. Why, everyone knows that Lillie went nearly mad when Ethan refused her attentions. All of that singing nonsense was just a ruse to remove her from polite society. She simply fled to Philadelphia to avoid the scandal."

Serena couldn't believe what she as hearing as Dora continued.

"Ethan and I agreed that we would give him some time to readjust to life here at home before we announced our engagement. So you see, you are merely a… how shall I say it, a diversion, something to amuse him before he settles down to his responsibilities."

"I don't believe a word you're saying, Miss Grimshaw," Serena said with as much calm as her rising temper would allow. "Ethan Blackwood would never misrepresent himself to me, or to anyone. How dare you even suggest such an impropriety?"

"Well, why don't we find Ethan and ask him?" Dora asked. "Surely, that would be the most appropriate action, don't you agree?"

"I couldn't agree more," said Serena, "after you, Miss Grimshaw. He should be waiting in the lobby."

Serena turned to gather her belongings then left the powder room to find Ethan waiting for her in the lobby, Dora Grimshaw holding tightly on to his arm. Serena noticed that Ethan, to his credit and her immense relief, looked extremely uncomfortable.

"I see you two have met," Ethan said, disengaging Dora as gently as he could.

"Yes, we have," Serena smiled as she turned to her. "Dora has something she wants to tell you, don't you, dear?"

"Why, whatever do you mean, Serena?" Dora started to back away but Serena took Dora's arm in her firm grasp before the woman could get away. She'd been told by more than one overly enthusiastic gentleman that hers was an iron grip.

"Come now, Dora. Don't be shy. Let's tell Ethan about our conversation, shall we?"

"What conversation, Serena?" he asked. "I don't mean to be impolite, but what in the hell could the two of you had to talk about? You've only just met."

"In a word? You. Dora told me all about your childhood betrothal. It sounded just like a fairy tale, really,"
Serena continued sweetly.

"Then she told me how Lillie nearly went mad with jealousy and had to – what did you say, Dora? – *flee* to Philadelphia to avoid the scandal. Then she told me that you and she – Dora that is – agreed that you could have some time to adjust to being home from the war and that I was a diversion. Did I miss anything, dear?"

Serena turned to Dora and waited. And waited.

Finally, Serena could no longer contain herself.

"Dora, you poor, misguided woman. Lillie told me all about you and your girlfriends – ghouls she called them – and how you delighted in making trouble for anyone who wouldn't do exactly what you wanted them to. I know all about your failed efforts to snag Ethan and that even his mother, who wanted him settled happily more than anyone, never encouraged you in the slightest." Serena's laughter died on her lips. "You're the most pitiful creature I think I've ever met. I feel sorry for you."

When neither Ethan nor Dona spoke, Serena continued.

"You thought your little speech would fool me into thinking that he was being dishonest about his feelings, didn't you? You thought I would run back to Philadelphia. Well, I'm here to tell you that this city girl isn't easily fooled and if Ethan Blackwood says he loves me, then he loves me!"

"Why Serena," Dora said when she found her voice, "I'm sure there must be some misunderstanding. I would *never* say anything to hurt Ethan or anyone he cared about. Isn't that right, Ethan?"

"Dora," he said turning to her, "you have been a thorn in my side since we were three years old. I have tried being polite. I have tried to ignore you. And tonight, I am here to tell you that if you were a man, I'd punch you in the nose. Do I make myself clear?" Ethan's voice was quiet yet filled with anger.

"Of course, Ethan. I'm sure Serena just misunderstood what I was..."

He held up his hand.

"Not another word, Dora. Please. Just leave." He pointed to the door.

"Well, goodnight, you two lovebirds. See you at the wedding," Dora trilled.

"What in the hell...I think we should leave, Serena." He turned and saw that a small crowd had gathered and had been patiently watching the exchange.

"Show's over folks. Well, this one is anyway. The main event is starting in the theatre," he said as he took Serena's arm and led her from the theatre. "People will be talking about this for years. I don't think anyone has ever had the courage to stand up to Dora Grimshaw. How in the world did you do it?"

As they walked hand in hand, Serena explained. "It wasn't easy, believe me. That woman is terrifying." She laughed. "I forget who said it, but forewarned is forearmed."

Seeing the puzzled expression on his face, Serena continued, "Lillie declared yesterday afternoon a holiday. We drove into West Chester and had a lovely time. We had lunch at Taylor's Tea Room, ice cream from Brown's soda fountain and spent a lot of time window shopping. That's how I found this hat." Serena pointed to her head.

"Well, it just happened that Louise Asher, one of Dora's ghouls, as Lillie calls them, works in the shop where I bought the hat. When I started to mention dinner, Lillie hushed me and got me out of there as soon as I could pay for my hat. Did I mention that I love this hat?"

She giggled as he became more impatient.

"Well, what I didn't know was that Lillie spotted every one of Dora's friends along the way. The woman has spies all over town. And when Lillie saw Louise rush to the phone as we were leaving the shop, she realized that Dora would likely plan some kind of ambush in a final attempt to get you for herself. You've got to hand it to Lillie, years of studying complicated opera plots have certainly paid off."

"Hell's bells, woman," Ethan shouted as he picked up Serena and spun her around. "Do you realize that you've done in one evening what none of us have been able do in a lifetime? You have disarmed Dora Grimshaw. You should have been a diplomat, not a pianist."

He kissed her as he put her down and they continued to walk.

"Lillie deserves the credit, not me. I just followed her direction. She warned me that Dora would try something and she was right. At the very least, Lillie deserves flowers and candy." Serena laughed. "They should have had her at Versailles. The treaty that ended the war would have been drafted in a snap." She grew serious again. "It seems we're right back where we started, aren't we, Ethan?"

"I guess so. What are we going to do?"

"Well, I've come to a decision." She turned to face him. "I'll spend the next two months working with Lillie. Then I'm going home to settle my family's affairs. Aunt Nicki can stay in the house and the students I was planning to board to help with expenses can still do that. Nicki will have the time of her life taking care of them. While I'm there, I'll meet with the head of the Conservatory to see what adjustments we can make to my teaching schedule. If we can't come to an agreement, I'll find work in Chester County. I have my teaching degree and good teachers are always in demand as Rachel reminded me the other day."

Serena stopped to catch her breath.

"Does this mean yes?" he asked hopefully.

"It does, my love. Life is too short to wait for the plans we've made to come to fruition." Serena took Ethan's face in her hands and, standing on tiptoe, kissed him gently. "Some decisions have to be made with the heart, not the head. And when your heart is so filled with love that it sings, you have to listen."

EPILOGUE

THE FOLLOWING ANNOUNCEMENT WAS PUBLISHED in the July 5, 1919 editions of the Philadelphia Inquirer, the Village Record and The Daily Local News:

The families of Miss Serena Lucia Jordan of Philadelphia, Pennsylvania and Mr. Ethan Blackwood of Chadds Ford, Pennsylvania proudly announce their engagement. Miss Jordan is an instructor in piano and voice at the Philadelphia Conservatory of Music. Mr. Blackwood is the owner/proprietor of Blackwood Farm, Chadds Ford, Pennsylvania.

A December wedding is planned.

GEORGIA DICKSON

DEBUT AUTHOR GEORGIA DICKSON IS delighted to contribute to the Brandywine Brides. Georgia has been playing around with two romance novels for the last fifteen, maybe even twenty years and, after her BFF Mariah Stewart made an offer she couldn't refuse, Georgia finally decided stop sitting on the brains that God gave her and use them to write her contribution to the Brandywine Brides anthology.

PLEASE, PLEASE like her story so she won't be barred from participating in the next anthology or going to lunch with the other Brandywine Brides authors. They're a great group and they have a really fun time!

You can write to Georgia at *www.georgiad614@gmail.com*

℘AINTED PROMISES

By

KATE WELSH

1943

HEIR TO THE BLACKWOOD NAME, Callum has stayed on the family farm to help support the war effort, though he'd rather be fighting with the soldiers than feeding them. Meri Johansson, hunted as a spy across war-torn Europe, is finally safe but haunted by memories. Can Callum's love free her of the grip they have on her soul?

DEDICATION

&

ACKNOWLEDGEMENTS

This book is dedicated to friends who have had my back lately:

To the Brandywine authors who got me writing again, especially Martha.

To Lyn Cote who helped me when I was panicking about my current "downsizing" life with her great suggestion for where to find the perfect apartment.

And to Andy and Paul. Without your generosity over the years I would not have been able to write this part of the Brandywine anthology and I'd be stuck in an overwhelming life. Now John and I can move on, leaving many worries behind. Many thanks to all of you

CHAPTER ONE

Blackwood Farm
July 1, 1943

CALLUM BLACKWOOD LISTENED TO HIS mother, Serena, while fighting with the antique water wheel. Even though it had started out a rusted mess, he'd decided to get it working again. He needed to save gasoline somehow because they'd nearly run out of their ration last month. It needed to be working by the busy season or they'd never get the corn ground.

When she asked how it was going, his frustration spilled out. "If Pop had stayed home instead of joining the War Department, the harvest and this damned wheel would be his problem. I warned him I'd be better suited to shooting Germans than running Blackwood. I can tell he's worried that I'm in charge here."

"Your father has complete faith in you. Plus he doesn't want you being cannon fodder. One soldier more or less won't do a thing for the war effort. You've turned a horse farm into meals for the fighting men and done a great job of it. That's just as important."

He knew she was right but this was hard. Nearly every one of his friends and cousins had enlisted and he was home, safe and sound. Hard as it was, he stayed silent and went inside to scrub his hands at the utility sink, trying to hide his frustration. The smell of water and loam filled his senses as his mother's heels tapped behind him on the wide plank floors.

She cleared her throat. "Callum, I need to tell you something. I hope you aren't angry but...I rented the cabin."

"My cabin? I just spent months fixing it up. Adding a bath and a kitchen. And the porch."

"I know. But her grandparents were friends of your grandparents. The Vandergrifts. Remember? Meri's their sole heir. Her mother, Sarah, died giving birth to her. Sarah was their only child. You remember her. Audrey became her pen pal after she visited late that summer."

"Wasn't that after I'd left for college?"

"Oh, right. Well, Meri arrives in less than two hours." His mother touched his shoulder. "She was in Europe, Son."

"Europe?"

"Meri had gone there to study art. But we were pulled into the war and she got trapped there."

Callum blinked. "Whoa. What else do you know?"

"Very little. I imagine she'll have crates of paintings and a steamer trunk. Please go fetch her in the wagon. We need the pickup to deliver Harriet's preserves."

Callum stared, his mind trying to work out the logistics of this whole situation. The preserves he'd known about, but trunks and crates? That made no sense but something nagged him more. "How did this happen so quickly?"

"Stanley Arthurs who runs the art school in Chadds Ford stopped by. There was a mix-up about her using a student apartment. So he asked us to put her up. And, of course, we must."

Callum sighed. Unless he wanted to be an ogre and cast a quasi-orphan into the streets, he was in a no-win situation. But he had to try. "Why can't she stay at the Vandergrifts' house?"

He looked up from his now clean hands. His mother gave him the look. She'd rarely disciplined her children and, though he was too old for that, the look said, "I'm so disappointed." It still stung. He stuck his head under the water and soaped up his face and hair. When he came up for air, Serena Blackwood ended his protests. "She learned of Josiah's death and the sale of the family home when she got to the states a few days ago. She's quite wealthy now but very alone at twenty-two years of age." She handed him a towel.

He dried his hair then surrendered. "I'll go get her."

"Perfect," Serena Blackwood said and gifted him with one of her beatific smiles. She looked happier than the sad woman his father's sudden departure left in its wake. With Ethan Blackwood in Washington,

D.C., where he faced long days and nights of important War Department work, they were mostly on their own without his day-to-day involvement and wise counsel.

Remembering his last conversation with his father, it was suddenly less important to find a little autonomy than to do as he'd been asked—take care of their family. Callum forced himself to smile back and his mother turned happily and walked out the door.

God help him. What did this artist's arrival make so "perfect" for his mother?

Why was she always involving him in her plans to help his sister's friends? He had enough on his plate trying to keep up the Blackwoods' part in the war effort.

CHAPTER TWO

MERI JOHANSSON SETTLED ON THE train station bench and took a deep breath. The air so far from the fighting smelled sweeter. The summer sun warmed her as she hadn't been in too long. Her father had stolen this feeling of security and peace from her and she would never forgive him. Summer in this part of the country was just what she needed. She finally felt…safe.

She finally was safe. But not as safe as she would have been in her grandfather's arms.

She'd been in the United States for seventy-two hours and all that was left of her world had disintegrated yesterday. It felt as if nothing would ever be all right again. It hurt. Like a knife in her heart. How was she still alive and breathing when she knew his death was her fault?

Their family lawyer told her Josiah Vandergrift had been in a panic over her since the attack on Pearl Harbor. Then at the news on the 11th of December that Germany had declared war on the U.S., Grandfather had suffered a fatal stroke, her name on his lips.

She tried to take heart. He had loved her, provided for her and pro-tected her…until no one could…the day she'd entered the war right along with her countrymen. Her anger at Adolf Hitler, the destroyer, burned bright in her heart again for just a moment. He had even figured a way to kill her grandfather half a world away.

Until that moment, at this country train station with a summer breeze blowing and the scent of honeysuckle wafting past, all she'd had to hold her together was anger. Army Air Corps General Arnold and Franklin Roosevelt had managed to quench much of it with a promise to try to protect Europe's art and architecture as the bulwark of civilization it was.

Meri leaned her head back against the wall behind the bench and breathed in deeply, trying to reach for the calm serenity that painting used to give her. She let out the breath. *I've done all I can.*

"Miss Johansson?"

Meri jumped off the bench, ready to fight or run. She hadn't decided which when she looked up and focused on a handsome, very surprised man towering a foot over her. "Sorry," she managed as she covered her pounding heart with her hand.

"No. I'm sorry. You looked lost in thought but I didn't mean to startle you. Are you Miss Meri Johansson?"

Needing a bit more space, she stepped back and dropped clumsily onto the bench. This handsome fellow probably thought she was as peculiar as she'd begun to believe she was. Had the war made her someone unable to fit in at home? Well, she had no choice. She stood again. "Yes, I'm Meri Johansson."

He gifted her with a small smile. My but he really was handsome— more so when he smiled. It made his blue eyes sparkle. "I'm sure you're exhausted," he said, his voice playing over her nerve endings. "Where is your luggage? My mother sent me prepared for crates of paintings and trunks."

"My paintings are gone. I'll most likely never see them again, but considering the world may never see the *Mona Lisa* again, my work is pretty inconsequential."

"What do you mean?"

"Why are my paintings gone or why do I think the *Mona Lisa* is?"

"Both I suppose."

"Mine because the Germans took them when they ransacked the Villa il Palimerino where I lived with my grandfather's friend, Lola Costa." Her voice cracked at the thought of Grandfather but she stiffened her back. He was gone and she was alone. It was vital to hold it together. If not, and her father found her, she'd wind up in his control, possibly locked away in an asylum. It was her greatest fear since the nightmares began in London. Her father wanted her money and would declare her incompetent to get it. She was of age now so that was the only weapon at his disposal. She had to be ever vigilant.

Meri forced herself to continue in a calm, controlled voice. "We'd been warned the Gestapo was coming. There was a passageway between rooms where Lola had me hide. Calling me a spy was their excuse to search the house and confiscate any art they deemed forbidden and degenerate. Or of good taste and worthy. I could hear them searching. Divvying it all up. What to keep. What to burn. But they got so greedy and judgmental, taking everything they could lay their grasping hands on, they missed the passageway."

Meri saw his handsome countenance change. His amazing blue eyes narrowed and darkened. "They stole your work? You had to hide or they'd have arrested you? As a *spy?*"

He clearly understood she could have been executed if found. Meri just nodded. It felt like an ancient story now. A faraway tale told again and again as she'd tried to get help for the people and civilization's art and architecture. She wished it was a forgotten story but it haunted her. "My landscapes and portraits were acceptable to their Führer. The better an officer's collection, the more influence he gained within The Third Reich. Gestapo officer, Muller, coveted mine. That and my U.S. citizenship made me a target."

Meri paused and took a deep breath. "All over Europe, it's the same. They're taking all the art they can cart off to Germany. That's what I meant about the *Mona Lisa.* When the museum staff at the Louvre realized invasion was imminent, they tried to hide the art. Even French Resistance leaders don't know where it is. I tried to send a painting home not long before Pearl Harbor but it didn't make it. That day, I could tell something about shipping a painting upset the postal clerk. But I was desperate." Her voice hitched again and she clenched her shaking hands. That had been a scary day. "After Muller's raid, I understood the painting was lost."

"Here. Sit," he said his smooth tenor voice full of gentle kindness. The man reached out to touch her arm near her shoulder.

A zing shot down Meri's arm. She wasn't sure she liked it or feared it. She'd cut herself off from feelings a long time ago but they were all rushing in now and she couldn't seem to keep them at bay anymore.

"You look upset. Please, take a few minutes. Collect yourself." He pointed toward the bench she'd been so contented sitting on before he'd materialized at her side. "It must have been hard to get out."

Not sure if he'd said who he was, Meri realized she might have been baring her soul to a cabbie. Thank God she'd been vague enough to not give away how much more she'd done—so many unforgettable, haunting things. "No. I'm fine. It's fine. I'm sure your meter's running and—"

His bark of laughter halted her words. "There's no meter, so no hurry. You're on Brandywine time now. We try to keep things serene around here." His lips tipped up into a secret, little smile. "Oh, and there isn't a taxi within miles of here. I'm Callum Blackwood. You'll be staying with us. I understand you know my sister, Audrey."

She felt the color drain from her face and she finally sank onto the bench. If she stayed with Audrey's family, they'd hear her screaming from one nightmare to the next throughout the night. And they'd see how her mind wandered at inappropriate times. "I-I thought I was to stay in an apartment Mr. Arthurs arranged for me."

"Arthurs stopped to see Mama. There's a mix-up with that apartment. He knows we have an ancient cabin you can stay in. It was built by one of our ancestors in the early 1800s. It's been well taken care of and it's even newly renovated. All the spiders and such were sent packing so you needn't worry about livestock. Well, except horses, two ponies, one cow, three pigs and too damned many sheep for my liking. Those are as far from the houses and outbuildings as possible. Mother thought you'd prefer the cabin rather than be saddled with the Alphabets all day. Every day."

An unexpected bubble of laughter erupted from somewhere deep inside Meri. She covered her mouth in surprise. "I'm sorry. Audrey hates that you came up with that nickname for her and the rest of your sisters." Audrey *claimed* to hate it but Meri had always heard a note of affection for Callum's sobriquet.

He smiled and the light seemed to glow in his surprising eyes. It was as if the irises contained a thousand prisms. She had the sudden urge to paint him. And to get the color of those eyes just right.

She hadn't painted since that awful night—her latest watercolor, still damp, clutched in her fingers as she'd cowered in the passageway listening to Lola being grilled—for hours. She'd relentlessly parroted the intricate fabrication they'd come up with in case time ran out before the resistance executed their escape plan for Meri. Lola had finally managed to convince the Gestapo officer that Meri had slipped away in the night with a young male artist—a man who didn't exist.

All she could do now was pray she hadn't left Lola in jeopardy and that she and the villa would survive all that lay ahead. After passing through Italy, France and Spain, having seen evidence of the atrocities being committed against the civilian populations, her imagination ran wild with her fear for her dear friend.

CHAPTER THREE

CALLUM EASED DOWN NEXT TO Meri Johansson. Her rose and jasmine scent seemed to mix with the aroma the honeysuckle growing wild along the tracks. That scent drew him like the bees to those fragrant, delicate-looking wildflowers.

He leaned forward and peered again into her stunning blue-green eyes and saw only vacant inattention. He'd seen this before. His heart dropped because in the days ahead, he knew this petite young woman could be in for the fight of her life. Actually a fight for her life. He was pretty darn sure she'd have to be as strong and tenacious as honeysuckle. Because Meri Johansson wasn't with him at that moment. Were he a betting man, he'd say she was about four thousand miles away, still in danger.

Joe Kellogg, Blackwood's trainer and his right hand man, faded into his thoughts. His pop had hired the World War I veteran before Callum was born. When Callum was a young pup tearing into the stables, thinking only of seeing his pony, Patches, he'd often jar Joe out of his thoughts. Callum had always felt bad, seeing the man's hands shake as he'd saddled Patches.

In those early years his father would sit with Joe, sometimes for hours, talking and pulling stories out of him about the trenches, the poison gas and the screams of dying men and horses. In that way Pop had helped a genuinely nice man fight his demons.

Joe had a wife and two growing sons now. They all lived a happy, secure life in a house at the edge of the northwest corner of Blackwood Farm. Joe could talk about war now and no longer fall headlong into what he called waking nightmares that felt too real to be only in his mind. If war had done that to a strong man like Joe Kellogg, Callum couldn't imagine what it must have done to a young woman who'd been trapped and fighting for her life.

Callum watched in still silence as Meri stared blankly across the tracks. Her features were so pale, at that moment, they looked carved from marble—an angel fallen to earth. The affect was made all the more poignant by the meaning of the black dress she wore.

His oath to stay away from her to thwart his mother's plans for him to once again help one of Audrey's friends washed away with the tears that rolled down her cheeks. He reached into his back pocket for his clean hanky, making a mental note to talk to mama and Audrey. They'd need to draw her out carefully the way Pop had with Joe. He didn't think he should be involved but, right then, he had no choice.

"Miss Johansson?" he said softly and touched her shoulder. Nothing. He cleared his throat and pressed his handkerchief in her hand, saying her name a bit louder. This time, her hand did tighten on the hanky as more tears followed the first. "Meri," he called louder with a slightly sharp tone.

She blinked. A gush of tears fell as she turned her head to stare at him. A blush stole across her wet cheeks. "Oh? You were saying?" she asked, clearly aware she'd missed something but just as unaware how long she'd stared into space.

He pointed to the hanky in her hand. "You're crying, miss."

She quickly swiped it across her face. "Oh, I'm so sorry. I was thinking about Lola Costa. I lived with her at her villa. She was my grandfather's friend. My mother's friend. My teacher. She became my friend." She shook her head. "More." She took a shaky breath. "She was like a mother to me. I'm so afraid I put her in danger and that, now, she's in one of those horrible concentration camps."

He'd heard speculation about them. "I'm sure she's fine," he told her quickly. Probably too quickly. "Hitler likes artists, I hear. We should get you to Blackwood. You'll feel better surrounded by things that remind you of the good old U.S. of A. Nothing's more American than a log cabin, right?"

She stared at him in gratitude. But that look quickly changed to horror. He realized he'd said too much and that she had figured out he knew she had a problem with her mind.

Damn!

CHAPTER FOUR

MERI FOLLOWED CALLUM ALONG THE wooden platform and down the stairs to the gravel lot. He led the way, carrying the messenger bag of necessities a few nurses had put together for her at Burtonwood Air Base in England. She looked down at the only thing the nurses hadn't gathered for her—the dress Mrs. Arnold had kindly set out for her the morning after news of Grandfather's death reached them.

The Arnolds couldn't have been kinder but she'd wanted to get away from Washington where her father might catch wind of her return. She repeated the words in her mind that should ground her and calm her. "You're safe, Meri. Stop acting as if a boogie man is going to jump out from behind every bush."

"Excuse me?" Callum asked.

Meri walked headlong into the hard wall of his chest. He'd stopped and turned back to her. She'd been so lost in thought she hadn't noticed. "What?"

"You said something—about boogie men and bushes. I haven't heard that name since Dottie hit eight."

She huffed out a breath. "Ignore me. It's hard to get used to being out in the open during daylight. We operated and traveled mostly at night. I'm afraid I'm still having problems with my nights, days and continents getting mixed up."

He shot her a grin. "Ah. That was Carrie until she turned one. Screamed for attention every night and slept like an angel all day. I should have known then she'd be trouble."

Meri relaxed a bit. He'd obviously missed her slip up. *We operated?*

Really, Meri.

It took her a few seconds of staring at his even, white teeth and those full, turned-up lips to realize he'd been teasing about his sister. She forced a smile but knew it was only a vague imitation of a real one. Callum looked a bit unnerved as he led the way to his vehicle. Like most men he was probably afraid she'd start crying again.

"This is General. And this is Sergeant," he said, introducing his team.

Meri blinked and stopped short of running into his back this time. Somehow she had to stop thinking. It was clearly bad for her. A low guttural wuffel and being knocked backward a step or two brought her completely out of her thoughts.

The hopeful look in the bay's velvety eyes wrapped around her like a cloak of serenity. She felt a rusty chuckle rise through her chest. She reached up and stroked the bay's muzzle as Callum grabbed its halter. "Sergeant, behave," he warned.

"No, he's fine." Her laughter felt less rusty this time. "He's just saying hello. Aren't you, fella?"

The other big bay at Sergeant's side tossed his head with a loud snort and a jangle of the harness. She moved to the side and grazed her hand down the bright white blaze on General's forehead. "Hello to you, too, sir. I seem to be meeting Generals of all sorts these days. The last one was a handsome older fellow, too. He's got your smile beat but you look much cuddlier."

"You figured this one out." Callum chuckled and his hand bumped into hers as he, too, stroked General's blaze.

Somehow, Meri managed not to gasp but quickly moved her hand to the horse's neck. "Good boy," she murmured and moved back to Sergeant. "I grew up around horses," she explained and switched her attention back to General. "At school I used to sneak off to the stables all the time. My father would have had a cow if he'd learned how much time I spent there. The headmistress understood, though. These are your horses? You run the horse farm now?"

"It was primarily a horse farm till the war." He shrugged his wide shoulders. "May well be one again. I know my pop would like that but who knows what the post-war years will even look like. It's bound to change nearly everything. Right now, we only have seven full-size horses in the two stables along with two ponies. We use the barn for the cow and the tractor and other farm equipment. I'm growing crops mostly for the Army, Navy and for locals who need help."

Callum glanced at his watch, reminding her of the passage of time. He probably had things to attend. So with a final pat to each equine neck, she moved over to the wagon. She looked up at the wooden bench then at the skirt of her dress. It had four pleats in front so she'd be able to climb but she missed the boy's pants she'd worn most of the time since Italian partisans rescued her from the villa.

She heard Callum's sigh from behind. "I should never have listened to my mother. You couldn't have traveled with trunks or crates. We could have had a fast comfortable ride in my car."

Meri turned back. "It's okay. I kind of like the wagon. General and Sergeant must have more personality than your car."

He shot her a grin and shrugged. "It's a 1939 Mercury Club Coupe convertible so... "

Once again, he drew a smile from deep within her. Each one felt less rusty. The man was some sort of magician where her emotions were concerned. She wasn't sure if she liked that or being attracted to him but she'd have plenty of alone time in the Blackwoods' cabin to figure it out. "This is fine," she told him and turned away to plot her path upward. "I spent days in a hay wagon traveling through Spain. Could you go up first and steady me if I need help with that last big step?"

Callum nodded. "Whatever you need," he said quietly but seemed to be talking to himself. Then, agile as a leopard she'd once sketched at the Philadelphia Zoo, he moved upward to the seat with an enviable, attractive economy of movement.

Meri got a good grip on the wagon, put her saddle shoe on the hub and climbed. When she arrived at eye level with Callum, he looked a bit surprised. "I'm...uh...stronger than I look."

"Glad to hear it," he said with a smile and a look of gentle understanding. What he understood, she wasn't sure she wanted to know any more than she wanted to explore his implied offer of help moments earlier. But his gentleness enticed her as he helped her onto the bench.

They sat in silence as the jingle of harness and the placid clip-clop of the hooves created a peaceful and serene journey. She smiled, remembering his description of his town. Like his mother's name, Serena. Tranquility and security wrapped around her and her eyelids grew heavy.

CHAPTER FIVE

CALLUM LOOKED AT MERI JOHANSSON resting against his side, her sweet face and her long, dark lashes lying on her cheeks. Her golden blonde hair was such a stark contrast to her dark eyebrows and lashes he'd bet folks thought she bleached it. This close, he could see nearly every hair color from a few light brown threads to copper to bright arctic white woven among the plentiful golden strands. It was an unmistakably natural effect he found especially captivating with her rose scent floating around him.

He pulled the team to a stop and glanced down at Meri's pale cheeks. He hated to wake her. Her deep slumber spoke more of exhaustion than tiredness. She'd fallen against him about half an hour ago and he'd put his arm around her—to keep her safe. He'd had to jostle her pretty good while turning the team into the lane and pulling them to a stop but she hadn't flinched.

Audrey's happy shriek, however, had Meri jumping as if stuck with a pin. Right out of his arms. Which left him feeling worryingly bereft. A greater worry, though, was Meri's terrified expression.

Callum reached out a hand to cup her shoulder, hoping to give her a frame of reference. "Glory be, Audrey!" he scolded. "You're loud enough to wake the dead. You scared the daylights out of poor Meri."

"Meri, is it," his mother said as she came around the big Bridal Veil bush at the end of the walk. Her elegantly arched left eye brow rose to accompany the knowing look in her eyes. "You two certainly became fast friends."

Callum jumped to the ground and landed less than a yard from his

BRANDYWINE BRIDES ANTHOLOGY 249

mother. "Don't," he ordered through gritted teeth then went around the wagon to assist Meri down. She didn't know his mother had a habit of roping him in to situations he found uncomfortable. He knew that much about Meri Johansson already.

"We had lots of time, plodding along the roads in an empty wagon. We could have gotten here in a quarter the time if I'd used my car. Not to mention our sore behinds from an old wagon bench. Maybe you and the girls should take it to the market next time. Think of all the gas you'll save."

Trying to look innocent and failing, Serena Blackwood said, "How would I know she'd arrive with nothing? I thought you'd need the room."

He leaned down and said quietly, under the sound of his sisters on the other side of the wagon excitedly greeting their guest, "You don't know what a disaster this may be. Especially for her. She's been outrunning the Gestapo for a year and a half to keep from being arrested and shot as a spy. You and Audrey have quite a job ahead of you. Meri Johansson is holding on to sanity by a thread. You have to help her."

"Me?"

"Well, not me. I just can't." Then in a louder voice as he climbed back to the uncomfortable seat, he added. "I have a full schedule for the rest of the day, ladies. So deal me out of dinner. No doubt, I'll still be work-ing by bedtime." He slapped the reins and left his mother to handle the sweet little time bomb that WWII and Stanley Arthurs had dropped on them.

He didn't blame Meri even a little but his mother had meddled in his life for the last time. And she'd have to handle the damage control this time. Unlike the time she'd roped him in to taking his sister's star-ry-eyed school friend to the prom. After which, followed three months of surprise visits at all hours of the day and night before their father had given up and told her to stay away. Or when a neighbor's daughter needed a date for an ex-beau's wedding so she could show the county she was doing just fine. Unfortunately, the groom's drunken brother had insulted her and Callum had been forced to defend the brokenhearted young woman's honor.

And it wasn't that he didn't want to help Meri. But as he'd watched the angel in his arms sleeping, he'd known he couldn't handle coaxing her to face her demons the way his father had Joe Kellogg. He wouldn't mind comforting her but he couldn't be the one to draw out the pain he knew those lovely eyes of hers revealed. He didn't have it in him.

🚐

Callum pulled out the stop just after the light failed. He lit his lighter, happy to see the river grab the wheel's blades to start it turning. He sighed in relief that he'd gotten the ancient technology working before the first harvest. He was nearly there. Tomorrow, he'd hook up the rest of the gears and the mill stone would be ready to grind on water power.

Tonight he'd write Pop a note for the morning mail. He'd be happy this idea had worked and as far as the other things that had happened that day, Pop would understand why he had no time for dating or romance.

As he pocketed the lighter, a quiet voice behind him whispered, "It's a soothing sound. Almost like a waterfall."

Meri.

And there went his resolve. Looking over his shoulder, Callum squinted. He couldn't see her but he knew her voice already. The new moon kept even the white collar of her dress from being illuminated.

"It can get pretty loud when the river runs faster."

"I guess I'll find out."

So, she didn't plan to move on quickly from there. He wished he knew if he was annoyed or happy about that. Either way, he would finish transferring his office to the mill building in the morning. At least that way her perfume wouldn't distract him while he was trying to work. His sisters and their spats were bad enough. Meri's close proximity would shoot his concentration all to hell.

"Right. Arthurs' school is open year round, now. I'm a little confused though. Aren't you already an artist? You said your paintings were in a gallery in Florence?"

"I took lessons from Mr. Arthurs in the summer of '38. He took me on as a favor to my grandfather." She let out a small chuckled, "No one says no to Grandfather because anyone who ever met him likes—." Her voice broke. She cleared her throat and went on, "...liked him. Grandfather knew Mr. Arthurs because he taught my mother. He helped Mr. Arthurs when he bought the school from Howard Pyle's widow. I learned a lot that summer and a lot from Lola Costa. But Lola's fine art style and the Brandywine School are very different forms of expression. I want to try to incorporate her fine art nuances with his pictorial exactness. Fuse both schools somehow."

"Is that possible?"

"Damned if I know."

He sputtered out a shocked laugh at her mild expletive.

"Oops. Sorry. Tramping across Europe in the company of desperate men and women isn't good practice for life in polite society. Your mother will ban me from being around her daughters if I forget myself like that at dinner."

"You don't know my mama. She isn't as sheltered as you might think. Then again, our Bernie is a little too wild already. Please don't encourage her in that direction. Mama's nearly despaired of making her into a lady."

"I would have thought Carrie was the older of the two middlings but I got the idea they were born in order." She laughed.

The full-throated, musical sound played along Callum's spine and swirled south of his belt. Damn. A happy Meri sounded more irresistible than anything he'd ever heard.

"I meant like A-the oldest, B-the next born and so forth," she went on to explain. "So how old are they?"

Callum cleared his throat. "Well, Audrey's your age, of course. Bernie's eighteen but a tomboy so she seems younger than Carrie's sixteen. You'll run into Bernie and nine-year-old Dottie at the stables a lot. They're horse crazy and help Joe a lot."

"What about you?"

He heard her step closer. That beautiful scent of hers mingled with the wildflowers that bloomed nearby. Combined with the tinkling sound of her laughter, it made her too tempting. He cleared his throat again. "Oh, I have my own chores."

She laughed again as he'd hoped she would. "I meant, do you like the horses?"

"Bernie used to help me gentle the misbehaved rejects in the area then I'd sell them at a good profit. And Pop and I ran a breeding and training program. All that changed with the war, though. I don't have time for any of that now. Running a full-scale farming operation is too time consuming, but it's rewarding in its own way. Where do you fall?"

Silence met his light question. He wished he could see her. As the silence stretched, Callum began to wonder if his innocent question had somehow pushed Meri's head under to drown in a bad memory.

CHAPTER SIX

STANDING IN THE PITCH BLACKNESS, Meri fought to stay in the conversation by pressing her thumbs into the plate in her hands. She finally won the battle. "....so thanks," she heard Callum say.

"Here's your dinner." Damn it. She'd sounded rushed and nearly desperate. And hadn't there been a question? Double damn it, and he was thankful for something, too. What, she didn't know.

When she'd managed to stay present in her conversations with General and Mrs. Arnold and with President Roosevelt, she'd thought she was okay. But she was quickly realizing that hadn't been normal life and she was failing spectacularly at fitting in.

"I imagine dinner was my mother's idea," Callum said.

"Oh. Right-o. And no thanks necessary. I'll enjoy fetching and carrying for your mum. She's a sweetie."

"Could you carry it inside the mill? I put up blackout curtains so I can put a light on in there and wash up. I don't think I'd enjoy axle grease mixed with my food."

Meri followed him inside the board and batten building she'd noticed on the way to and from the house. It smelled of wood and the nearness of water. The water must be cooling the interior.

She waited by the door wondering what it would look like, then the lights flickered on. It was a large, rustic room with a stone fireplace at the far right. To the left, she could hear the wheel moving and splashing but it was walled off from his office space. Besides the board and batten walls, it had open rafters that showed off a cedar shake roof. It was quaint, just like the barn and the log cabin across the pond where she'd be staying. All three buildings were on her list of subjects to sketch. They radiated the uncomplicated tranquility her soul craved.

"So have you ever been scared off by a problem horse?" he asked, flipping up the faucet handles hanging on the wall over a large cement work sink.

That was his question. Double dang it! He'd noticed she'd dropped the conversational ball. "Uh, sorry. I got distracted by your supper. And no. I've never been afraid around a horse."

She'd leave out how afraid she'd been of the two-legged fascist variety who'd been hunting her and her friends. And how angry she'd been.

Fear and anger.

In retrospect, not a good combination—for her actions or her sanity. She wished she could unsee some of the things she'd witnessed but she couldn't regret all of the lives she'd helped take. They'd been the enemy of everything she believed in. Unfortunately, other faces—the inno-cents—still haunted her.

"Maybe I'm too stupid to be afraid enough to hesitate when I should," she muttered, not sure if it was an animal or the enemy she spoke of.

"I'd bet you're just confident with them. Animals know when they can count on someone. Insecurity is usually the problem unless a horse has been abused. My father's mount, Champ, is a little off right now. He's probably feeling deserted by Pop and I don't have much chance to ride these days so he's getting restive."

"I'll chat up Champ then. Give him a bit of extra attention. I'm miss-ing Grandfather a lot and having a four-footed friend might help. They tend to listen and not offer unwanted advice."

He nodded. "I'm sorry about your grandfather, Meri. I guess you don't even know how much you'll miss him, yet. His death is so recent for you. I noticed you switched from present to past tense earlier when you were talking about him."

She blinked back tears and turned away, trying to compose herself. "Thing is," she began, "I've been missing Grandfather for years—living off his letters and his voice in my head. It kept me going. I must have read them each a hundred times. I'll be happy to chat up Champ."

"Or me. I promise to listen and not butt in. I take it dinner wasn't rest-ful." Callum smiled a little. "Do you know that every once in a while you sound more English than American?"

"I lived, traveled and fought with expat artists from all over Europe and the British Isles for two years making our way across Italy, France then Spain. I supposed they rubbed off on me a bit."

He grinned again. "I wondered how that 'damn' you uttered was in English."

She felt her face heat. "I promise to sound more ladylike in the future."

Callum's expression changed from teasing to serious in a heartbeat. "Don't bother being careful around me, okay? It isn't necessary. You're dealing with enough without guarding your words for every Black-wood. Consider me a respite from proper behavior. Come over and muck out the stalls in britches and curse all you want if that's what you need to do. I'll have Joe Kellogg's wife, Harriet, send you a pair of their son's old pants. Raymond was about your height six months ago. Okay?"

Callum Blackwood was a thoughtful man and great to talk with but she didn't quite fit in at the house. She was a quiet person. And the Alphabets had been in rare form earlier, chatting to beat the band. Meri laughed.

"What?" Callum asked, sending her another handsome, white-toothed grin.

"I thought of your sisters as the Alphabets. I'm afraid you've infected me. Carrie would quite possibly smack me. But I think Audrey actually views it as if her brother coined it just for them." She felt a smile stretch her lips upward. "But we aren't to notice the pretense, understand?"

"Wouldn't breathe a word," he promised with another killer grin.

Finally, a co-conspirator she wasn't afraid to disobey and whose grin was the only thing in the *killer* category about him.

CHAPTER SEVEN

CALLUM WALKED OUT OF THE barn into the early morning to
face his first task of the day. That, after a long talk with Patches about
the night of thought, resolution and, finally, restless sleep that he'd just put
in. He had no time for Meri even though every time he ran into her, he
found himself drawn to her and offering all manner of encouragement
and help. So he'd avoid her. He'd be pleasant but busy when they did run
into each other. It shouldn't be too hard to avoid one tiny woman among
the others. He'd stick to his route of fields, his new office in the mill and
his room in the house, once they were all in bed. Harriet liked feeding
him so he'd just steer clear of his sisters, Mama, Meri and dinner.

"Off to a busy day in the fields?" Meri's voice floated to him from the
direction of the pond. He turned and there she stood—up awfully early
for someone as tired as she'd been.

"Not sleeping in?"

She shook her head. "I don't need much sleep."

He ambled toward her. For someone who didn't need sleep, she looked
downright exhausted and like she'd been that way for some time. Worried in spite of all he'd told himself, he said, "Don't forget riding. Maybe
you need to tire yourself out some more."

"That's what I thought. So I thought I'd take a walk. It's so quiet here.
Peaceful. Maybe it's too quiet to sleep."

"Or for breakfast? You're up pretty early to eat at the house."

"Oh, I'm not hungry. When you have to make do with what the
enemy doesn't want or what little farmers manage to hide away, your
brain gets used to not telling you it's meal time."

Still, she was rail thin and needed to eat more. "Time to learn to eat on time then. Let's go see what the kitchen has to offer." He put his hand out in invitation. She took it then looked startled when he clasped her small hand in his. Trying to act as if he hadn't just grabbed a live wire, Callum said, "I haven't eaten, either." He dropped her hand like the hot potato it was as soon as they were on their way. "Harriet'll have my head if I don't eat what she left for me. Have you met her? Like Mama, she's a great cook—scary woman though. Mama has her cook for us so we have an excuse to pay her more. Those boys of theirs are eating us all out of house and home now that they hit their teens."

"Your mother's very kind. I feel badly that I'm not going to fit with her plans."

Callum about choked on his tongue. "Plans?" he asked hoping he'd sounded more nonchalant than he felt.

"I think she saw me as a companion for Audrey to attend USO dances. I can't do that. Dancing with freshly-minted, young soldiers isn't for me. I know the evil they'll fight. How can I smile and flirt, knowing how many of them will die in the coming year? And I need to mourn Grandfather." She hugged herself. "I went to Florence a child, following my mother's steps in the art world. Now I just feel old. After she left Italy, my mother came back here, too. But I gave up on thinking I'd learn anything about her. I only remembered how peaceful and lovely and quiet it was here. And I needed that."

She looked so sad and disillusioned. He fought the urge to put his arm around her as she kept pace with him. "I'll talk to Mama about the USO," he found himself promising. "Just do what you need to do for you. Do you drive?"

"I do. I plan to see if Grandfather's car is stored for me somewhere. Grandfather loved that car. I can't imagine Mr. Butler selling it. I think I'll call him. He's my grandfather's attorney...my attorney now, I suppose. He'll know what happened to it."

"If you need a ride to pick it up, let me know. You could even drive the Mercury there to get your feet wet. You're used to driving on the right?"

She turned and walked backward keeping pace with him. He could almost see her as a little girl walking to school with friends, dancing along in the sunshine. Then he remembered her childhood in girls' schools and his heart sank. Apparently, Meri had lost the only person other than her long dead grandmother who'd ever cared about her.

His life had been so much better than hers. He made a mental note to give his mother a break. So what if she'd tried to play matchmaker? At least she did it out of love and wanting to see him as happy as she and his father were.

"I can't risk an accident by driving your car, Callum. It sounds like it's almost your pet."

He ignored that last bit. A man and his car were sacrosanct but he'd never admit it. With everything going on in the world, it sounded foolish. "But you do drive?"

"I can even drive in Rome. If you can drive there, you can drive anywhere. Those people are crazy but your car's important to you."

He shrugged. "It's a piece of machinery," he lied as smoothly as he could. "It sounds as if you can handle a few country roads and Wilmington isn't exactly a bustling city. If you don't come up with a car, you can borrow mine. You need to get to the studio. You need your art right now. Just like I need to keep this farm producing well for the war effort. Like Bernie needs to ride. Like Mama needs to take care of all of us and our less fortunate neighbors. Having a calling feeds the soul."

She nodded. "I never met anyone but my grandparents who understood an artist's need to work. You must miss your work with the horses. I bet that's what feeds your soul and not crop rotation."

It was like she could see into his soul...and like he could see hers. What the hell! "Right now, fighting this war the only way left to me is what I need. I can take a ride and visit the horses on the way past the barn. My soul is fed just fine. We need to see you get to Arthurs' studio and we need to feed you for real. And here we are." He gestured her up the back steps. "Breakfast awaits in some form or other." His second of the day but she needn't know. Then he was done with their guest...

Except for taking her for her car.

After that, she'd be all settled in and on her own.

But then he looked down at her as she passed him in the doorway. That jasmine scent wrapped itself around him and the look of utter gratitude in those magnificent eyes did something deeper. They wrapped themselves around his heart and, apparently, all protest to the contrary, right around his soul.

He admitted it then, at least to himself. Callum Finlan Blackwood was a goner. There just didn't seem to be a thing he could do to resist this sprite who'd entered his life only yesterday. He wondered if he was the only Blackwood male to have ever experienced such utter defeat so quickly. Or had they all faced similar dilemmas?

He was drawn to her each time he encountered her. They'd talked in his office for two hours the night before about art, horses, history... so many topics linked together by the finest of threads he couldn't even remember how they'd gone from one subject to the next without a break in conversation. What was that about?

She fascinated him. Impressed him. Worried him. And thoughts of her haunted him when she was nowhere in sight. Try though he might, he didn't think he'd be able to resist her for long. Worse or maybe better—he had no idea why he'd even try.

CHAPTER EIGHT

M ERI STROLLED ALONG THE LANE toward the house on the main road. She anticipated the scenery around the next bend because, as the season moved onward, Blackwood's landscape was an ever-changing treat for the senses. Wildflowers. Fields of corn, beans and berries. The trees of the orchard were pregnant with an abundant variety of fruits. She smiled as she spied a deer feasting off something in one of Callum's neat and tidy rows. Her sketchbook was filling up with Blackwood Farm. But her paintings were a disappointment to her teacher. Even the rest of the students didn't seem to grasp how vital they were to her. She'd begun to think, perhaps, she'd made a mistake, not in coming to Chester County, but in enrolling in classes.

She forced all that out of her mind and focused on the scenery. Callum certainly had a green thumb. She opened the book to her favorite picture of him and couldn't fight a smile. He'd stood just out of her hearing, talking to the blind, ageing pony named Patches as Callum took the old boy for a walk like an oversized pooch. She sighed and closed the book on the sketch and started wandering, restlessly this time. Nature receded and her thoughts took her inside her mind.

What a kind man Callum was. She'd felt better just being around him that first day. But she was broken. Too broken to seek him out even if she longed for and might even need him. So for the last two weeks, she'd stayed in the shadows of all of the Blackwoods' lives.

That first morning there, she'd even instinctively lied to him about the reason she'd gone to Florence. How did you tell someone with a wonderful family like Callum's that your father—a man who'd spent her first seventeen years ignoring her—had decided to sell her in marriage to his forty-two-year-old business partner as soon as she graduated high school?

Finding someone like Callum, who embodied all the good qualities her grandfather had possessed, who would see she stayed safe from her father's treachery, could be an answer to her prayers. But it would be so terribly unfair to him. They could be nothing more than ships passing each other on a stormy sea. Fitting and so very sad, Paul Laurence Dunbar's poem rose in her memory. Yes...They were ships passing in the night.

Maybe meeting Callum and not being the unstained soul he deserved was her penance for the lives she'd helped take. She'd been so very angry that she hadn't thought about all the ramifications of her actions. Until evil men weren't the only ones to die.

"Miss? Are you okay?"

Meri whirled and found a small boy staring at her from the dark interior of what looked like an animal's den. A sob burst past her lips and she shuddered. Wiping her eyes and cheeks with the back of her hand, she tried to compose herself as she looked around. She'd wandered off the lane at some point and was deep in the woods. She was quite possibly lost.

She realized then that the boy knelt in front of an old wooden crate the size of a refrigerator. It sat tucked between two trees and was covered in tarpaper and heaped with leaves and branches, perfectly camouflaged by the deep Pennsylvania woods. The boy crawled forward. "It ain't much but you're welcome to come sit a while," the small voice said.

"Are you one of Joe Kellogg's boys?"

"Oh, no, miss. I ain't no one's boy. I live here. It's all mine. And pretty okay all in all. Plenty to eat now that the crops are coming in, too. But I don't steal. I pay by weeding the rows when no one's around. So it's okay. You'll keep my secret, won't you?"

His high-pitched voice, full of hope and loneliness tugged at her heart. He wasn't the first displaced boy she'd found in the woods but she'd never expected to find one in America. Boys like this were a great help to the resistance. They carried messages and took food to freedom fighters unable to be seen in towns. But they'd been displaced by war and death.

Here, children were supposed to be cared for. She hadn't thought this kind of deprivation existing in America. Then again, she hadn't thought the world could become so dangerous a place for innocents.

Like a lifeline thrown from above, she grabbed hold of this child's circumstances. He needed her. He gave her purpose. She nodded and crawled behind him into his little bower. Inside, she found a blanket, a sawn log he gestured proudly toward—his stool and a three-legged table. She sat on the stool not wanting to diminish his prized possession and set her sketch book gingerly on the table. She found the table was sturdy.

He must have seen her surprise. "I borrowed his hammer and swiped a nail one night when he was still buildin' on to that old cabin where you live. I figured if I nailed it to the crate, it would stand with only three legs."

"You're quite resourceful. How is it possible the Blackwoods don't know you're here?"

"I'm guessing this is too close to the river for horses. Too many chuck holes and real squishy ground to ride through. A few times, the river's come up pretty close, to here. I got nervous in spring about my place but it worked out."

"I'm Meri Johansson. What's your name? And how old are you?"

"Me? Oh, I'm Mickey.

"Mickey, it's nice to know you. Thanks so much for your hospitality."

He tilted his head and reddish hair fell into his green eyes as he screwed up his little face, clearly thinking hard about something of vital importance. "My what-a-tality, miss?"

"Hospitality means you have a nice little place here and you kindly offered me your stool. I really needed to sit. I think I'm a bit lost. I left the lane and wandered. I think pretty deeply sometimes."

He nodded sagely. "Been watching. I was afraid you was plannin'' to jump in the river just now. That's where you was headed, crying and all. Nothing's worth being so sad over, if you don't mind me saying." He gestured around him. "I didn't have nothing till spring. Look how good I have it now."

His simple statement knocked the wind out of her. If this was a palace, where had he been before finding refuge here? "What's your last name, Mickey? And you never said how old you are."

The boy just shrugged. "Not rightly sure."

Had she missed something again? Well, there was nothing but to ask. "Not sure about what, Mickey?"

"Nine maybe ten I guess. And I never had a real last name. We get given the name of the orphanage we start in. But then they sent me to a different one and," he shrugged again then continued, "maybe it'll seem silly...they was real mean at the second. And those who pretended to care but sent me away...I don't want to use their name, neither."

"I see. It doesn't sound silly at all. You know, I don't like my father." At least Mickey didn't lack the bravery to do what he thought was right. "Suppose I'm just plain Meri to you since you'd understand how I feel."

"Okay, Plain Meri." He stuck out his grubby hand. Refusing to cringe, she took it and smiled into his sweet, thin face. She found she needed to blink back tears as Mickey pulled back. "Want an apple?" he asked in a whisper as if the contact had been too much for him, too. "I swiped them out of their old cellar last month. Just took about a dozen but I weeded two rows for each one I swiped."

What to do? Take some of his hard-won nutrition or risk hurting his feelings. She finally nodded. "An apple sounds wonderful."

Mickey grinned and passed her the apple as if it were the finest cuisine in the world. His straight, yellowing teeth showed beneath his slightly full lips. This child needed care. Maybe she'd buy him some soap, a tooth brush and tooth powder. He'd need a towel, too. She looked at his too short pants and stained polo shirt. She'd find a way to help while trying to get him to accept even more. It felt so good to look outside herself. It was as if God Himself had sent this needy child into her life to put her on the path back to living, past being pulled inside her head and trapped by her own mind. A spontaneous smile tipped Meri's lips as plans crowded her mind. She took a bite of the apple Mickey had given her. Nothing had tasted as good for months.

CHAPTER NINE

"CALLUM, STAND STILL FOR A minute."
Callum turned back toward the barn. "After that wild thunderstorm last night, I thought I should go check on the sheep, Mama."

"Now I know you're avoiding me. You hate those sheep."

He knew he'd wait but still said, "That doesn't mean I don't look out for them."

"I want to talk to my first born. We scarcely see you these days. Do you even know what's going on?"

He glanced at his sister behind his mother. "Are you girls giving Mama trouble, Bernadetta?"

"No." She stood there looking ready to chew nails at his use of her real name.

"Then how about you let Mama and me visit for a few minutes. You were supposed to help Joe with Champ, weren't you?"

"Fine. And it's *Bernie!*"

Callum laughed and motioned her back toward the barn. She stalked off but winked at him over her shoulder. Uh-oh. This was more than a how-are-you talk. Terrific. "So, what can I do for you, Mrs. Blackwood?"

"Come to dinner. Please. I'm so worried about Meri. Have you seen her at all?"

"Not so often as I thought I would. Our schedules must conflict." Though he did see her walking in the distance most mornings and in the evenings, too. He had the idea she was being as careful to avoid him as he'd intended to be with her. That actually stung. Be careful what you wish for, huh? She'd even managed to get hold of her car by herself. He ate in his office or at the Kelloggs' most nights so they could plan the next day. He'd only seen her at Sunday dinners in the last two months. "What's going on?"

"She looked simply awful when I saw her this morning. But she did, at least, finally admit she's afraid of storms." His mother shook her head. "The girl's wasting away. I swear she's lost more weight and I didn't think that was possible."

No. He hadn't noticed. Maybe because he'd studiously avoided looking at her the times he'd been at the same table with her. He didn't feel proud of himself. Point of fact, he felt like a damned coward.

"She picks at her meals," his mother went on. "Politely excuses herself, taking her nearly full plate to the kitchen, then disappears like the ghost she very nearly is. I'm worried, Son. What you said comparing her to Joe Kellogg when he first came here...it was spot on. She simply won't open up to me or Audrey. I had to practically pull this morning's admission from her word by word. When Stanley Arthurs asked us to put Meri up, I had no idea she'd arrive so troubled. I know I'm constantly involving you in helping neighbors and friends and that sometimes it hasn't been as easy as I'd assumed it would be but, Callum, if you developed any rapport with her, please try to get her to talk to you."

He'd thought she'd begin to feel safe with Audrey and his mother and be able to share her troubling memories. Apparently not. "Is she at least going to the art school every other day?"

"I believe so but she only paints there. Perhaps, you could let her know it would be fine to use the cabin as a studio. Maybe more painting would help. But I don't believe she even has an easel to use at the cabin."

Callum shrugged. "I can cobble something together and take it over. It'll be a conversation starter. In the meantime, I'll start coming to dinner."

"Thank you, Son." His mama covered his hand and squeezed. It was a gesture he remembered from as far back as he could remember when her hand had engulfed his in size and in love. Now, small as hers were compared to his, the gesture still said love. "I knew you'd help, honey. Meri is a sweet soul in need and I just can't fill the bill on this one."

He leaned in and kissed her cheek. "Thanks for letting me know, Mama." Then he glanced over at the cabin. Meri's art lessons didn't seem to be helping the way he'd thought they would. His sheep mission abandoned, Callum headed for his workshop to build an easel. On the way, he remembered the rockers in the attic he'd meant to put on the new porch. He'd been so busy running away from Meri that he'd put everything out of his head regarding her and the cabin.

(

"Suppose I walk you home tonight, Meri?" Callum suggested when she excused herself at dinner.

She looked like a deer caught in the headlights of a fast approaching car. "Oh, you don't have to. I walk there alone all the time."

"I know but I've got a sort of a belated welcome gift for you."

She bit her lip and fiddled with her flatware. "Sure. I'll just take care of my plate and meet you outside."

Callum frowned at her retreating back. "You don't think she's afraid of me do you?" he asked no one in particular.

"Well, you can be a tad overwhelming," Carrie said.

"Honestly, Carrie, you are so nasty," Bernie snapped. "Callum is a nice guy and nice is a good thing. Those fellas you go around with from school are shallow and thoughtless. They're social climbers who have a love affair going on with their mirrors."

"Bernadetta Ann Blackwood," Mama gasped. "A young lady does not talk of love affairs."

"It's a figure of speech, Mama," Bernie countered.

"Not at my dinner table and not by my daughter. We all know you have had a low opinion of every boy your sister has ever liked. But you needn't lower yourself to their level to describe them. And that is all I want to hear on this subject. "

"Yes, Mama," Bernie said. "At least you agree they're low class."

"Miss Goody Two-Shoes, you say something rotten then apologize and all is forgiven. Well, I'm sick of it. And I'm sick of you," Carrie shouted.

"And I'm sick of both of you wrecking every meal for Meri," Audrey put in.

Callum moved toward the kitchen but stopped at the tired plea in his mother's eyes. Audrey was right but so was Bernie. He'd seen one kid hand off a heavily-lathered animal for Bernie to unsaddle and rub down like she was a servant. Then Carrie had followed suit. Callum had grabbed them both by the scruffs of their necks and ordered them to care for the horses they'd treated so badly and he'd had Bernie super-vise them. Callum was pretty sure that was one fellow they'd never see again. Carrie, however, continued her offhanded abuse.

Bernie and Dottie had black hair like him and gorgeous green eyes. On the tall side, in his opinion, Bernie was as beautiful as their mother. He was sick of seeing her hurt by thoughtless young men who treated her as if she were invisible. But mostly, Carrie's treatment really burned him. He sighed as he watched the arguing continue. Thank God his sisters were mostly his mama's problem.

Meri Johansson was about to become his. But for now, he gave a loud whistle and the room fell into shocked silence. "The arguments at mama's table end now. For good. Got it?" He didn't even wait for their response. The continued silence spoke volumes—dinners with him there were going to be calmer at least.

He found Meri at the foot of the steps, facing the rear door. She looked sweet with her hands behind her back as she rocked from heel to toe, impatient to see what was afoot. But she wore a hand-caught-in-the-cookie-jar kind of expression, making him wonder what was afoot with her.

"So, how are your art lessons coming along?" he asked, hoping to get her to relax.

"I'm not sure."

Her answer had him zeroing in on her wellbeing. "Do you only work over at Arthurs' place?"

She shrugged. "I sketch here but painting can get messy so that's what I do in class."

"A bit of paint here and there on the cabin floor would just add to its history. Everyone who stays there would be impressed that a famous artist once worked there."

She looked at the ground looking sad. "I don't think famous is going to happen. Luckily, Grandfather left me well off enough that I can paint for myself if not others. To hear Mr. Arthurs, that's a good thing."

"Maybe you could show me some of your work. Get the opinion of a common man." He shrugged. "Can't get much more common than a farmer."

"I see you as more of a gentleman farmer. Do you like this kind of farming? Or can you not wait to get back to just having horses?"

"The jury is still out. I enjoy watching the fields and the orchard bloom and then produce fruit and vegetables. But I miss training horses.

And riding," he added, an idea occurring to him. He remembered something his pop had said about Joe Kellogg. He'd been hired as a handyman but Pop had noticed Joe's affinity for the horses. Apparently, he'd done much better mentally after beginning to work with them.

Callum sighed and hoped he hadn't sounded too dramatic. "It's not much fun riding with the girls. I just had to squash an argument between the three oldest. I'm too dammed young to be their father. I need to relax once in a while. Maybe you could ride with me? Joe said you've only gone once. Champ really needs exercising. As does Captain. He's mine and a handful or I'd let you ride him."

"I could fit it in before I go to class a few mornings a week." He glanced her way and thought he'd glimpsed a napkin tucked behind her back. Why would she feel the need to hide taking her dinner with her? She was probably eating at the cabin to avoid his sisters and their bickering.

"If you worked at the cabin, would you still go to class every day?"

"Maybe not. I have to keep an eye on my ration book and Mr. Arthurs seems underwhelmed with my talent so it's discouraging. I still want to take lessons but I'd love the chance to work out this idea I have and not be judged before I'm ready."

"In that case, I'll meet you at the cabin. I have to pick up that welcome gift I mentioned." He separated from her and headed to his workshop. He glanced back in time to see her cup a hand under the napkin she'd kept hidden. He'd see to it she felt comfortable at the dinner table or his middle sisters would be the ones skipping dinners.

CHAPTER TEN

M ERI REACHED THE CABIN AND stopped short at the porch where the scent of fresh cedar always greeted her. But, this time, she found herself blinking back tears. Two rockers filled her vision. They reminded her of how she thought the porch should look. Her chest hurt with a desperate longing to belong right there for the rest of her days. It wasn't just the perfection of the scene the cabin created sitting between the woods and the pond and the barn or the storybook family who owned it all. It was mostly Callum and his kindness toward a stranger who'd suddenly come along to scotch all his plans for moving into the cabin.

Before her thoughts strayed into even more dangerous, impossible ter-ritory, Meri rushed inside and through the cabin to the compact kitchen recently added on to the back. After tucking the rest of her dinner aside for Mickey, as she'd been doing since finding him, she went back to the porch and settled on the rocker furthest from the door.

Thoughts of Mickey had her pondering the logistics of feeding him. For once, she was thankful for Carrie and Bernie and their penchant for bickering because she'd nearly been found out tonight when Callum almost followed her into the kitchen. She didn't think the Blackwoods would toss a poor boy off their land but they'd feel responsible. And Mickey was liable to run off rather than feel like a burden.

Her campaign to make life better for the little urchin would be much easier if she began cooking for herself. It wasn't as if she hadn't gotten a ration booklet to use if she decided to buy her own food. But Serena Blackwood had asked her to please show up at six each night, dressed for dinner. She'd said she was trying to instill ladylike behavior in her younger daughters. Serena tried to see that dinner was an exercise in decorum but it seemed to wear on her and those middle two got on worse than oil and water. Meri smiled. More like gasoline and a lit match!

"You like the rockers?" Callum asked.

"The porch needed them," she told him. "It seemed lonely without them."

"I'd meant to raid the attic but I got busy." He stopped by the remaining rocker. "It never stops around here."

"All work and no play, Callum," she teased. How was it he got her in such a good mood just by showing up? She looked at the small pile of lumber in his hand. "So that's what you stopped off for?"

He grinned. Then with a few flips of his hands, the slats magically transformed into an easel. "Callum, this is wonderful. Thank you. Wherever did you see one like this?"

He shrugged, looking embarrassed. "I just tossed it together out of a few old bed slats, an old hinge, a chain, some bolts and a couple wing nuts that were lying around the workshop. So do you have any work done this gentleman farmer could take a look at?"

She gestured inside. "Come tell me what you think. And please don't lie."

Her hands shook as she pulled out the paintings she'd completed. Each was different, yet all projected the same feelings. It was those feelings Mr. Arthurs objected to. But really, wasn't a painting supposed to evoke a feeling?

The first was of plowed acreage turned battlefield. The ground was stained with blood but the dead and wounded were gone. Just the bloody, ruined field, a bombed out church, and an old priest weeping as he cradled a rugged-looking, wooden crucifix against his chest. He'd stooped down, reaching his hand toward a piece of sheet music—dirtied and trod upon, lying limp across a furrow. Looking closer still, she'd carefully drawn the words and musical notes of *The Old Rugged Cross*.

Callum's eyes filled with tears. "Your teacher's blind."

"It isn't commercial. It'll never sell," she said, dismissing its value as Arthurs had.

"Who cares? War should hurt. We should all know how horrible it is."

The next was not of war. It was Mickey, cleaner than she'd seen him until he'd scrubbed in her tub the night she'd done the sketch. She'd drawn him kneeling in front of his little bower. Callum thought it was of a French child displaced by war. Meri didn't correct him but she wanted to. Keeping him a secret was hard. She hoped Mickey would warm to the idea of the Blackwoods learning of his circumstances.

"This last one is of the Zone Rouge in the forest near Verdun. The battle ended in December 1916," she explained. "The battle lasted ten months and was the longest battle in history. Three hundred thousand died. A million shells exploded there. They say it will still be too full of arsenic for the land to be usable after a century. France left it as it was, hoping it would be reclaimed by nature, eventually. But only a few trees survived and the only thing growing still is this sparse carpet of green. It covers some of the damage but if you look closely, you see some unexploded shells, rusting barbed wire but not the bodies buried there. That's why I added those misty, uniformed ghosts lurking at the edges. It felt wrong not to represent them...not to remember them."

Meri paused, as if lost in thought. "If you stand there for even a moment, you feel them." She pressed her lips together and shook her head. "What Germany wanted so badly is now worthless to anyone and will stay that way when their grandchildren contemplate war. Now Germany wants the whole world. Will everywhere look like this before they're done?"

She tapped the edge of the painting. "This is war, Callum. Feed the soldiers and stop wishing yourself there. Your father was right to make you stay here to run the farm while he uses his knowledge to help stop them before they come here. He'll accomplish more than one soldier."

"I'm sorry, Meri. I must sound foolish about serving. You saw too much of the ugliness of humanity. You've painted your feelings and memories into these. They're haunting. But you've gotten thinner and I didn't think that was possible. You're trying to get a handle on the memories but you're floundering, aren't you?"

She nodded and bit her lip. He was so sensitive yet so strong. The perfect man but she was so unworthy of him. "I wasn't alone when I was painting them but it felt like it."

"How did they not see your pain? It oozes from every brush stroke."

As always Callum overwhelmed her with his empathy. How on earth was she supposed to resist him? "You understand," she whispered.

He shrugged those strong, wide shoulders. "Some, I guess. I want to buy this one," Callum said and lifted *Zone Rouge*. "So much for it not being sellable."

"Callum, you don't have—"

He cut her off with a look. "I want to send it to my pop. It'll remind anyone at the War Department who sees it that they're working to prevent this from happening here. It's very powerful."

He grimaced. "But I'm afraid it's a little too powerful where you're concerned. Don't do this alone even in a crowd at class. You don't have to. I get why you don't want to tell my mother or sisters about your experiences. But you need to talk it out, so share it with me. Drag it into the light. I can be there if you need me. I'm not offering out of gory curiosity. I just can't stand to think of you, alone in these dark places. Sometimes I think your mind is still there."

"Sometimes it is," she admitted. "Do you really want me to ride with you? I love being with Champ."

"I do." He pointed at the painting now lying on the table in front of him. "Joe was in this war. He came home a shadow of the man you see now. Talking to Pop and working with the horses helped him. It'll help you. You can come down to the mill with your easel and paint while I'm working in my office. It's cooler there during the days anyway. And if you want, you can trudge out to the fields and paint while I'm checking on things." He winked at her. "I'll even carry your easel, but you have to promise to talk about anything that upsets you."

Paint with him only a few yards away? Well, at least the attraction she was nearly sure was mutual would die a quick death on his part. He'd see how broken she was. And she'd accept the impossibility of them once she saw his reaction. She'd spent enough wasted daylight hours hoping for a glimpse of him and nights with thoughts of him keeping her awake. Then she'd finally get to sleep and the nightmares came to haunt her and remind her she was too broken.

Who knew? Maybe if she managed to face the past with his help, it would make them friends. She'd need one if her father showed up. She didn't think she'd do much better than having Callum Blackwood in her corner.

CHAPTER ELEVEN

CALLUM GLANCED OVER WHEN THE doors to the mill rattled. Meri! He jumped up and rushed to take the unwieldy easel from her arms. "Darn it, Meri. I was supposed to carry all this."

She looked up at him. The sun slanted in, flooding the room and making her blue-green eyes shimmer. Then her lips drew his gaze and everything inside the mill and outside behind her stilled. Thick silence reigned. She swallowed and stepped back a step breaking part of the connection. "I've handled a lot." Her words severed it completely, reminding him she was still in no shape to deal with all he'd begun to feel for her.

He forced a grin. "Well, you look like a horsefly could pick you up and carry you off so..."

"Then, I'd punch him right in the nose if he tried." She grinned.

God Almighty, she was gorgeous. He swallowed. How did a man fight feelings this strong? He'd been trying and failing for nearly six weeks. "Noses on a fly? I do know they have sharp little mouths." He tapped her parted lips then forced himself to turn away, the contact had sparks shooting through his body. "Near the window?"

"The light there should be marvelous for a few hours." She plunked down a blank canvas then looked around the place. "Can I borrow that chair for my supplies?"

"Sure but I found an old card table in the attic." It was cherry or mahogany and stood on two sets of gracefully curved legs that closed like pairs of scissors when the top was folded down. "I remember there was a painting on it but years of jigsaw puzzles, coloring books and Lincoln Logs must have worn it off. Mama said it was the first furniture my mother's grandmother bought in America."

Standing there looking down at it, her head tipped at an adorable angle, Meri was nearly irresistible. "It needs a picture," she said and looked up, her expression full of excitement. "Can I put one back for her?"

"Sure. She said it was just an old table but she sounded a little sad about it."

Meri squinted and pulled the table next to the windows. "It really is barely there. It's a landscape but of anywhere specific?"

He shook his head. "There was a huge willow near a stream or small river with a meadow of wildflowers in the foreground. And a little boy and girl. She sat on a blanket under the tree making a daisy chain and he was skipping rocks."

Meri smiled and stared.

"What? It was there for years. I used to build log houses and arranged them around it like it was the scenery for my homestead."

"You may think you aren't artistic but you just painted with words. Between that and what's left, I can do this. Maybe I found a way to thank your mother for her hospitality."

"A Meri Johansson original will be pretty valuable one day."

She shot him a perturbed look. "That makes you an assemblage of one."

"Your teacher is a commercial illustrator. Your work is fine art. Lola Costa clearly saw your talent and helped you develop it. Why not just paint? Paint your feelings. Paint what you love. Even paint what you hate like *Zone Rouge* if it frees your soul of the pain. I have bills to pay all the way over there but we can talk anytime if you need to. And take that ride later. How's that sound?"

Another beatific smile lit his heart and made it soar. He couldn't help but smile back. Keeping to just being friends wasn't going to happen. Callum saw that now. But he'd wait for her to be healthy enough to reciprocate his feelings. That was his only answer.

⟨⟨

The clock on his desk struck eleven, a few hours later. Somehow he'd managed to get his mind on his work and keep it there. With one last pen stroke, he closed his ledger. So far so good. The operation was turning a tidy profit, not equal to what breeding and training horses had brought in, but that wasn't the aim. It was about helping the war effort while maintaining family assets.

He looked over at Meri who stood chewing on the top of her paintbrush. Once he'd detached the tabletop and put it onto her easel, she'd shooed him away and gone to work. She was disciplined, he'd give her that.

He tidied the desk then sauntered over. The painting wasn't exactly what he remembered but near enough. The boy had dark hair and the girl blonde. He thought they'd both been blonde. The clothes weren't as old-fashioned but what struck him most was the quality of the light. You couldn't see the sun but its rays seemed to filter through the willow's branches high above striking each leaf differently among the wispy weepers just over the children at play. It also cast here and there into the meadow, forming a magical juxtaposition of shadow and sunshine.

Meri put her brush down. "What do you think?"

"I think you've ruined a perfectly good card table…and made it a work of art. She'll never fold it open again."

At the first phrase she looked crestfallen then when he continued her eyes narrowed and she slugged his upper arm at the shoulder.

"Ow!" He grabbed her fist in his, then pretended to examine it, studiously ignoring every bit of need spearing through him. "Darned, boney, little fist! You really are stronger than you look."

Then he looked from her hand into her eyes. Yearning and need was as clear in her gaze as a message written on a marquee in foot-high letters. He glanced at her lips, drawn there against his will. He moved closer, pulled forward by that silent communication of longing.

"Hey, Callum. Here's the lunch you asked Miss Harriet to make," Dottie called and had them springing apart like a two kids caught with their sneaky mitts in a cookie jar. He glanced at Meri…yep…perfect analogy. She looked good enough to gobble whole.

"A picnic?" Meri asked, her voice just this side of rusty.

"Yeah. I thought it might be added incentive to get you riding."

Dottie stood looking up at him seeming oblivious to the electricity arching around the room. "Callum, Karen's daddy has puppies for sale. I thought you should you know 'cause you did promise. So well," she stammered as she backed out the door. "I'm ready. Well…gotta run." And she was off racing toward the house.

"Did Dottie just ask for a dog?"

He smiled. "Her dog died not long before you came. I told her when she was ready to speak up. I guess she just did."

"So you may get her one. So you know, Carrie threatened—"

He put his hand up. "Say no more. I wish that girl would get permanent laryngitis. One puppy added to my shopping list. I'm glad Dottie's still a little girl. I hope she stays one till Pop can be home. I hate him missing the last of her childhood. I wish he could see them all more. This Labor Day weekend in D.C. is going to do them a lot of good."

"Your mother's really looking forward to it. It's a shame she can't go more often."

Callum's heart sank. Nit wit! Why hadn't he seen it? "If I were to insist Mama go down to D.C. once in a while, would you help me referee?"

She looked worried for a long moment. "I'll take the day shift. We'll share dinners then you get them till bedtime." Then she smiled and saluted. "Happy to assist your piece of the war effort, sir."

He chuckled. "Which one? The war between Allies and the Axis Powers or Carrie versus the rest of the Alphabets because, with the advent of the pup, Dottie's going to enter the fray?" She laughed. "Thanks. We'll suggest it at dinner tonight. But for now, let's saddle the horses and take that ride."

CHAPTER TWELVE

"SO HOW DO YOU LIKE Champ now that you've ridden him again," Callum asked.

Meri smiled over at him then looked over toward where the horses grazed, chomping on grass. Their manes and tails wafted about in the crisp September 1st breeze. "Thanks for the pointers," she said and went back to her sketching. "I didn't even realize I was holding the reins too tight."

"It's a common problem. You aren't afraid, so I guessed you have a hard time relaxing."

"He handles wonderfully. Tell me more about him."

"Champ, short for Champion, is descended from the horse our ancestor rode home from the Civil War. His name was Buddy. Bernie's black is another in Buddy's bloodline through Gabriel, Pop's first horse. She loves the lineage story, so she calls him Buddy, short for Gabriel's Buddy. She watched him born when she was ten and they've been buddies ever since."

"And your Captain. Tell me about him and his unusual coloring."

"He's a liver chestnut. That deep, dark auburn coat and his copper-colored mane and tail about knocked me over when I first laid eyes on him at an auction."

She looked up from her painting. "I hope you know how lucky you are. This is a wonderful legacy and I don't mean the prestige of knowing your ancestry back to the early 1700s. I mean the love your family is about."

"I know. Believe me, I appreciate it. I never wanted anything but to stay here, continue the Blackwood name and keep the property in the family. Leaving for adventure's sake isn't why I wanted to enlist. I saw it as my duty but now I know this is another way to answer the call."

"I'm glad you didn't go. It's...." She looked around. It was so peaceful there. It was hard to explain how rural areas of Italy, France and even Spain had felt so different. "Traveling through the countryside to get off the continent, no matter how beautiful each farm, meadow or mountain was, there wasn't a moment that wasn't disquieting. You never knew when a touring car full of German officers would come around the next bend and demand to see your papers. I'd wanted to head for Switzerland and we tried. But the closer we got, the more patrols there were. Finally, the group I was with decided we'd never get across the border safely. We backtracked and started for Spain."

She looked to see that Callum was listening intently. "We'd been told Franco made so many demands before he'd enter the war that Hitler walked out of their meeting, leaving Spain out of the conflict. No one is sure if Franco was trying for that or not. Whichever it was, Spain meant a relatively safe a place to go. The rest of my group stayed in Spain, in fact, but that word 'spy' hung over my head like the sword of Damocles. Had Germany demanded my extradition, Franco would have handed me over. I've come to cherish the peace of this place."

Callum leaned over and covered her hand. "And Pop will help see it stays peaceful. I don't think they'll make it on shore. And I really think we'll win. We have right on our side."

She shook her head. "An awful lot of men and women had right on their sides, too, and they're dead now. I haven't said much but, Callum, Jews are disappearing. The Germans claim they had to be forced to work for a living, as if they hadn't been. Hitler has made them the scape-goats for everything that has gone wrong in Europe since the depression started. But Abraham Isaacs was just a gallery owner. His wife was a sweet, tiny woman who wouldn't hurt a fly or pass a beggar without giving him everything she had to give. They were gone one morning, their house stripped to the walls along with about fifty other Jewish families. And their businesses were gone, as well. Neighbors said it was the Germans that took them. They didn't just up and leave the way some believe. It isn't going to be good when we find out what happened to them all. What could three and five-year-old and even seven-year-old children do in a work camp? It makes no sense."

Callum looked at her, sadness and worry in his gaze. "No. Hate for hate's sake never makes sense. All any of us can do is help the war effort and pray. You did more than most by finding a way to reach a well-placed general and, finally, the president."

She had to tell him. It would be better to get it out there. Better to see him turn away now. "I did more. I did...things. There's blood on my hands, Callum. They'll never be clean again."

He picked up her hand and turned it this way and that. "They look plenty clean to me. I've never met a purer soul in my life than you, Meri Johansson. Whatever you did, you did it for the right reasons."

"No!" she shouted, destroying the quiet of riverbank. "I did it because I hated them." She couldn't hold back the rage and tears. "I hated them for making me so afraid and for destroying everything good in my world."

Callum didn't get mad or shout back. He just said, very quietly as if trying to restore order and peace to their world, "You know what this whole experience has taught me? Sometimes, we don't get to decide who fights and who doesn't. Or how we fight. We can only do the best we can with the hand dealt us."

He nodded in understanding. "Maybe some of the men fighting for the other side aren't evil and didn't want to fight, but they could have refused to be used by evil. They could have let themselves be arrested. I'll bet there are some who have and they're in those work camps, too. They all had a choice. You and your friends didn't. Your only choice was fight evil or give up and die. I'm so thankful you fought." He cupped her cheek and dried her tears with his thumbs. "But I am sorry it hurt your heart so deeply."

Then he leaned over and covered her lips with his. She could have sworn she felt her heart start mending right then and there. But she was so broken inside.

He moved back and smiled. "Now, why don't you get back to your sketch of those two characters over there eating the rest of our wild-flowers? If you want to talk more about this, I'm here."

So she did. "On Christmas Eve, we were supposed to sink a barge. It was packed to the hilt with crates. We had no idea at the time, but we later found out the crates were full of winter uniforms and ammu-nition for the German occupation forces. We watched as the explosion tore through what should have been the silent night. None of us were caught and we snuck back to the farm and had a little Christmas between ourselves. But some of the nearby townspeople were rounded up and eventually sent to a work camp. The Germans needed someone to blame and innocents paid."

"This war was Germany's fault entirely. Rounding up those villagers was their doing, too." He held out his arms. "Come here, honey," he said and gathered her into those outstretched arms as she cried out her guilt for those who'd had no part in their work that night but who had lost everything. When she stopped her stupid, futile tears, he smiled sweetly and wiped her cheeks with his thumbs. "You're a wonderful, brave girl. You know that, don't you?" But he didn't wait for an answer. Instead, he covered her lips with his again. She wanted to believe him—almost believed him.

When he broke the kiss, he laid back and brought her head to rest on his shoulder. The peace, quiet and the sound of his kind heart beating lulled her to sleep...

She waited in the dark cold for the flyer she was to meet and take to the church where he would hide until the next night when the next one in the Resistance chain would take him a bit further. But suddenly, a hand grabbed her and it wasn't the American flyer's. It was a German soldier's. He pressed her into the wall, his hand around her throat. He touched her breast and she kneed him hard. He yelped in pain but his grip only tightened and he laughed. But then his eyes widened with a gasp. She felt warm liquid seep into her shirt. At first, she thought he'd stabbed her but then his face was replaced by another. This man wore an American flyer's jacket. "You're the one supposed to be rescuing me," he quipped with a crooked-toothed grin.

A shot rang out then and he, too, fell. But with his last moment of strength, he twisted as he fell and his blade found a home in the heart of the soldier who'd attacked her and shot him. He'd died protecting her with his final breath.

She ran, crying silently, knowing she'd let that soldier sneak up on her and that her mistake had cost that brave, good American his life. He would never show that sweet, crooked grin to his mother or sweetheart again. Behind her, the shouts of German soldiers told her they'd found their comrade. And the body of the American flyer, whose dog tags she'd managed to snag before running off into the night. At least his family would have something of his to hold and mourn over.

Meri bolted upright, wide awake, her breathing was panicked breathing. Blinded by tears, she was completely disoriented but then there was Callum, rubbing her back and pulling that story out of her, too. He discounted her guilt and assigned it where she knew it truly belonged. With the brutal soldier who had planned to take more than her peace of mind that night.

The next three weeks passed much like that day. With painting after painting. Some light, sunny landscapes. Horses on the hoof, manes and tails flying in the fall breeze. Some were darker even than *Zone Rouge* and, always, those had a story that needed to be told. She usually painted over those with a lighter landscape. Little by little, the nightmares lessened and she found restful sleep, at last. She managed to eat without guilt. She could smile and laugh, too. Especially with Callum.

The younger girls returned to school after their Washington weekend and were busy with all manner of activities. Serena planned to go visit her husband again at the end of September and, as that day grew closer, Meri heard her singing while she made her last batch of tomato gravy.

Meri kept trying to get Mickey to let her do more for him but he'd accept little more than a warm sweater, a new pair of pants that covered his ankles and a couple pairs of socks and underwear. She started cooking and had Callum over to eat every few nights, leading to more and more talk of her time in Europe. The nights she ate dinner at the house, she fed Mickey leftovers of her own cooking. He still refused to let her reveal his presence at Blackwood. She'd tried to get him to sleep in the small half-story room above hers but he'd shaken his head. Something had to give soon.

CHAPTER THIRTEEN

CALLUM HAD DRIVEN HIS MOTHER to Philadelphia's 30th Street Station because it was raining heavily and he'd wanted to see her safely on the train his father would meet in the nation's capital. He smiled. Mama had been as excited as Dottie was picking out her pup.

But the ride home was a nightmare. He'd started off listening to Glen Miller, then Bing Crosby's new single, *Sunday, Monday or Always* started playing. But the music abruptly stopped and an emergency warning came across the airwaves. The storm had turned into a particularly nasty nor'easter that had stalled over the entire tri-state area. There was a flash flood warning forecasting higher winds to come and continued heavy rain.

Three hours later, he finally turned into Blackwood's lane with the sound of Benny Goodman's Orchestra with Helen Forest singing *Taking a Chance on Love* filling the car. He pressed the accelerator closer to the floor, anxious to finally see Meri for the first time since dinner the night before. She was doing much better—talking more openly about her days in Italy and France. During their early afternoon rides, she'd become a more responsive rider. She still cried sometimes, occasionally mentioned a nightmare and even shouted at him once or twice. But the tears and the anger seemed more cleansing than tortured.

He shook his head ruefully. Her smile lit his life. And her kisses ignited his need to do more than hold her long into the night. But her understanding of his own temper and impatience at those moments warmed his heart and made him smile.

A din suddenly filled the car and the earth trembled enough to take

Callum by surprise. The car skidded on the wet surface and nearly sent him into a tree before he got it under control and to a stop. He jumped out and stood staring in disbelief, rain pelting him. An oak that had probably been a sapling when Finlan Blackwood married his Elizabeth had come down across the drive not ten yards behind him. The trunk had to be at least five feet in diameter. If he hadn't sped up in his impatience to see Meri when he had...

Another gust of wind knocked him back a step. He took the hint, got back into the car and drove to the house to make sure everyone knew to stay inside. After changing into a dry shirt, he grabbed a slicker and ran to check on Meri. Though a tree had never hit the cabin, it wasn't in the safest place if they started toppling. He wanted her out of danger at the house with his sisters, Harriet and her two boys. His father had taught him Mother Nature in a fury was not to be messed with.

He raised his fist to knock when the cabin's door flew open. Meri stepped back, just as surprised as he was. "Thank God you're ready," he told her. "Come on. Let's get you up to the house. Pop and I have kept the trees far enough back that they won't hit the house if they come down. I just had a close call. A huge oak just landed feet from the back of my car." He reached for her. "Let's get going."

She pulled back. "I can't."

Was this another fear to deal with? "Why the heck not?"

"I have to find Mickey," she cried. "He's out in this. All alone. I heard on the radio that there's a flood warning."

He heard her worry and fear—for someone else. "Who in the hell is Mickey?"

"He lives in a crate near the river."

Callum bristled, jealousy like nothing he'd ever felt flooded his mind and body. Sure, he hadn't exactly declared his undying love but that was to make sure she was ready for a relationship after all she'd been though. Had she turned to some vagrant, trying to cling to that old secret kind of life? The wind tossed rain down his neck, ending his deliberation.

No matter. Callum Blackwood could be just as stubborn as Meri Johansson. Who this Mickey was and what her secret relationship was with him made no difference. She couldn't put her life in danger to look in the woods for anyone. Not on his watch. He reached for her hand, tugged her onto the porch and shouted, "I don't care if FDR and Churchill are camped out waiting for Stalin to show up to discuss the invasion, you're coming up to the house where it's safe."

Meri's eyes shot fire and she wrenched her hand free. "I'm a big girl, Callum Finlan Blackwood and I go where I want. Right now, I'm going to get Mickey and make him come here where he's not likely to drown."

With that, she twisted away and ran into the woods and, for a startled second, Callum watched her clawing her way through the underbrush as she headed in the direction of the rising river. He shook free from his confusion. His heart and his honor left him with no choice but to follow.

CHAPTER FOURTEEN

MERI RAN TOWARD THE RIVER, the thick brush sweeping the hood off her head and pulling her hair. But she ignored the pain and the rain trickling down her back. She had to get to Mickey. She had to keep him safe—see him safely settled somewhere before her father did more than send a letter through her lawyer.

She'd stared at it for hours, unable to open the sealed envelope. Finally, she'd torn open the missive, refusing to let fear rule her. Until she'd read his determined words.

Return to New York where you belong. Joseph Hallstead is impatient for his promised wife. It is time you stop these ridiculous art lessons and do your duty to your family.

Family? She'd been so angry she'd balled up the letter and aimed it at the cabin's hearth. He dared call their cold, empty association a family? Callum had a family. Grandfather had been her family. George and Susan Johansson and their three over-privileged children were in no way Meri's family. But if Father found out about the flashbacks, the threat of an arranged marriage would be the least of her worries.

Then, fear for Mickey had changed her focus. Within seconds, she'd scooped up the letter so none of the Blackwoods would see how little her father cared for her. She'd tossed on her slicker, stuffed the letter in her pocket and threw the door open. And found Callum on the threshold. When he got angry because she refused to go along with him, she quickly assumed he wouldn't help her save Mickey. Maybe too quickly, but she didn't have time to go back and ask. At that point, a mere minute could be the difference between life and death.

She knew why her mind had gone to mistrust. Being wrong about people was nothing new to her. It was like a familiar ugly sweater she knew she needed to throw out but clung to as familiar in a new and different world—like needing to survive on her own. She was used to it. So she forced herself farther into the deepening shadows with a heavy heart. The farther she ran, the more desperate she got. When a branch snagged her hair, yanking her to a stop, another stormy day exploded into her thoughts...

She and André ran through the dense woodland along the Garonne River, the wind and rain lashing them. They'd set the charges and Fernando was still near the riverbed manning the plunger. The plant meant to build a secret weapon for Hitler would be long gone before the forced laborers arrived.

Today Fos was empty, the villagers honoring the 1515 agreement between Spain and France would be safe on the bridge overlooking the dam the German engineers had built. She checked her watch. The power plant, the dam and the factory would be gone in seconds.

Just as they reached the overlook, small steps clamored up behind them. "André, the commandant refused permission," the boy gasped in his Pyrenees dialect. "Everyone is in the village and will be killed. You must stop it."

Horror flooded her veins. There was no time. A boom rolled over them and, as if in slow motion, the dam, then the hydroelectric plant, and finally the factory exploded in millions of pieces. Next, a wall of water and refuse swept over the village wiping it off the map along with any human life in its path.

André's hands fell on her shoulders. "Calm yourself. There was a plan for this, too. The elders would keep about their business while the rest fled."

Horrified, she stared at André—so cold...so calculating. Yes, the Germans and their evil plant had been swept away, but at what cost?

André shook her.

"Meri, look at me. At me. It's Callum!"

Meri blinked tear-filled eyes. Callum. Her thoughts had gone into the past. Again. Then she remembered. She hadn't lost her friends in Fos today but she had lost him. But there was still a life to save. She couldn't fail again. "I have to find Mickey!" she yelled.

"To hell with your Mickey! I'm sure he's a big boy and plenty able to take care of himself."

Oh...He didn't realize Mickey was a child. "He's a little child."

He took hold of her shoulders again. "A child?" he demanded. "How old a child?"

"He thinks he's nine or ten," she snapped and glared at his hands holding her still.

"Thinks?" For the first time Callum used language she wouldn't consider repeating. Then he took a breath and continued. "Where the hell is this crate he lives in?"

"Near the river where the ground is always soft."

"That's the flood plain. Let's go, but we *will* talk later."

She nodded. He could shout the house down if he found Mickey and got him to safety.

Callum turned and moved off at a full run, upping her anxiety about Mickey's safety. It was a difficult trek as the wind whipped the brush around, slapping it in their faces as the ground grabbed hold of their boots. Finally, she heard the angry river, roaring over the sound of the wind and rain. She stopped. Turned in a circle. "There," she pointed toward the disheveled crate.

Callum barreled ahead—no time for explanations—and pulled a protesting Mickey from his collapsing little home.

When Callum reached her, he wore an impatient expression but he had Mickey firmly tucked under one muscular arm. He swung Mickey up onto his forearm and grabbed her hand with his free one and they started toward the house.

His anger, she guessed, was probably more over her flashback than over Mickey considering how protectively he carried the boy. She knew the flashbacks were the reason he'd held back from pursuing her originally. And she couldn't blame him. What man wanted a broken woman?

"I'm sorry," she told him once they mounted the front porch. And she was. She'd never meant to hurt him.

Mickey, his blanket wrapped around his shoulders, looked frightened. Callum set the boy on his feet but he kept a grip on Mickey's thin shoulder. "Look, kid. That river was about to drown you." Callum's gaze followed Mickey's angry glance in her direction. "She had to tell me."

"I did, Mickey. You could have been killed out there today."

Mickey bit his lip and nodded, hugging his thin blanket to himself. Callum gestured them inside where they stood side by side, dripping on the foyer floor. That's when Harriet took charge.

An hour later, warm from a bath, Meri wore Carrie's dress and house slippers and sat across from Mickey with a cup of tea warming her hands. Wearing clothes unearthed from the attic and Callum's childhood, Mickey tucked into a bowl of Harriet's stew as she fussed over him, occasionally rubbing his back which clearly reassured him that he was in good hands.

Callum came into the kitchen. "Can we talk?"

Meri nodded and he motioned for her to follow him. The long walk to Ethan Blackwood's office felt like a walk to a firing squad. It was pretty simple. The flashback had to have demonstrated that she was just too broken to love. She probably always had been. Why else had her father never cared enough to keep her around? He had never treated his other children that way.

Callum stopped at the double doors and motioned her inside. And something surprising happened. She didn't know what to call it. It was as if a spirit wrapped invisible, comforting arms around her, lending her the courage to face the end of a beautiful, impossible dream. She stood in front of the fireplace, staring into the flames. After a second or two, she glanced up. There, hanging above the mantel was the painting of the original house he'd asked her to do from an old drawing.

She still had her talent, a gift passed to her from the mother she'd never known. Her life would go on. But it would be so much poorer for the loss of Callum.

The sound of the doors closing had her steeling herself to turn and look into his wonderful eyes as he told her she had to leave Blackwood. But instead, his arms engulfed her from behind. She blinked back tears as he whispered against her ear, "I love you so much. I don't know what to do with all the feelings you make me feel. I can't tell you how thankful I am Mama rented you that cabin."

Meri had only ever felt love in the arms of her grandparents before Callum. But Callum's love was different.

It felt complete. Unconditional. Limitless.

She turned within his arms and gazed into his eyes. Kindness and tenderness shone there, along with a sparkle she didn't understand. "I love you, too. I was afraid you wanted me to leave," she told him. "You were mad at me about Mickey."

Red flags appeared on his cheeks. "Well, I'm an idiot so..."

"Then was it the flashback? Because—"

"Sh-sh." He pressed his index finger against her lips then replaced it with his own, his hands drifting into her hair. The kiss went on and on until he broke it and tightened his arms, drawing her against him, holding her tight. "I was so terrified. The tree came down and then there you were and you wanted to go chasing off after some guy."

She stepped back in disbelief. "Callum Blackwood, you were jealous?"

He huffed out a breath and gave her a rueful grin. "Like I said. I'm an idiot and my rival is a seven year old with a mouth like a drunken sailor."

She giggled. "He did use some choice words when you scooped him up. But he's nine or ten."

He shook his head. "No older than eight and I doubt that. He padded out the years so you wouldn't worry. Did you know he's been weeding the rows to make up for any food he ate?" She nodded. "So I'm not such a good farmer, after all?" She laughed at his disgusted expression.

"Harriet isn't about to let loose of the kid. The words 'bonus baby' floated between her and Joe while you were in the bath. How do you think Mickey will feel about that?"

"He'd love somewhere to belong. He's never had anyone or even a last name."

"He told me I should marry you because you don't like yours. Or your father."

Meri laughed but felt her face heat. "I never know what he'll say next."

He grinned. "I thought he had a pretty good idea."

She turned away. "Callum, that isn't an appropriate thing to tease about. I had another flashback out there."

"I know." He tapped her on the shoulder. She turned back to find him on one knee holding a ring. "Who was teasing? I've wanted to ask for weeks but I worried you'd feel overwhelmed by marriage so soon after Europe. But I was wrong. You're brave enough to face the future, Meri. You ran into a storm to help Mickey even though storms clearly haunt you. So, Meri Johansson, will you marry me?"

Her heart felt like it might explode. She didn't know if it was from happiness or heartbreak. "There's also my father to deal with. He—"

"Life is messy sometimes, Meri. Stay and be messy with me. Marry me."

"Okay," she whispered and he slid a gorgeous diamond ring, set in a filigree band, on her finger.

He stood then and swept her into a jubilant kiss. Then he released her and reached over her shoulder and took something off the mantel. "This is a family tradition. It's called a luckenbooth."

She stared down at the lovely silver brooch where it lay on his finger-tips. It was heart-shaped and edged with stones with a crown at the top. A thistle with what looked like an amethyst as the flower and smaller green stones as its leaves lay within the heart. It looked as old as it was delicate. She reached out and touched it gently and looked up at him. "It's beautiful."

"It was presented to Elizabeth Cooper Graham by Finland Blackwood in 1721 at their wedding. And it's been presented to the intended of each first born male in the Blackwood family since. It's now yours to pass on." He fumbled a bit as he pinned it to her collar then he swept her into another kiss, this one longer than the first. When he came up for air, he said casually, "So, speaking of parents...there's your father to deal with."

He stepped back and pulled a crushed piece of paper from his pocket. The letter. "Harriet said this fell out of your pocket. The steam coming out of her ears told me it was trouble. Look, I can deal with your father, Meri. What I don't think I can deal with is losing you."

"I won't let him come between us. I'll send a response through my lawyer."

"Good idea. But I already called him."

She nearly choked. "What?"

"I had planned to be civil and ask for your hand but then Harriet gave me that letter. I told him we were getting married and that his business partner had better find someone else. So I'd like us to make you my bride as quickly as you're comfortable with. I also let him know your painting promises great things ahead for Meri Blackwood's career."

Meri smiled and moved into his arms again. "Meri Blackwood. I love how that sounds. But not nearly as much as I love you. Let's not put it off. That would just give my father time to cause trouble."

Callum grinned. "Then let's get on with the planning."

EPILOGUE

CALLUM SHIFTED FROM ONE FOOT to the other as his sisters filed past him. Audrey, Meri's maid of honor, graced him with a wink and a grin. Or was it for his best man, Jeff King. Jeff was their distant cousin who'd grown up visiting his grandparents on the estate next door. He was luckily home on leave and able to do best man duty that day. Now they all stood at the front of the church full of neighbors and friends awaiting Meri's walk down the aisle. He looked around. How the simple ceremony he and Meri had planned became a morale boosting celebration for the locals, he had no idea. But his mother was the prime suspect.

A long period of absolute silence seemed to fall over the church, turning up his anticipation, making him jittery for the first time all day. It was probably only a few seconds later, though, when the organist began to play again Wagner's *Bridal Chorus*.

And at long last, his father and Meri finally stepped into view. Wearing a creamy satin and lace floor-length gown with fluttery little sleeves and long, white gloves, she was a vision stepped out of his dreams. And now he understood why his mama had babied those last roses of summer. They were now all in a crown atop Meri's blonde locks with fine tulle veiling that trailed behind her like a morning mist. She had to be the most beautiful woman in the world.

Pop patted her hand after she looked around the crowded church and said something. Probably all the folks his family had invited to the ceremony had her on edge. But then she looked ahead and the music faded as their eyes locked. Somehow, someone was talking then someone cleared his throat and Callum realized she was right there next to him. "Welcome back, Son," Pop whispered and chuckled. "And do I ever know *exactly* what you're feeling."

Then, he left to go sit with the love of his life and Callum and Meri turned as one to greet the uncertain but joy-filled future the way they were meant to go forward...together.

KATE WELSH

KATE WELSH, A LOVER OF all things romantic, started writing when showering love on her husband, children, and family wasn't enough to fulfill her. She's been writing romance ever since. Her first published novel hit the stands in 1998. Kate is the author of twenty-seven romances from inspirational, to contemporary to historical and paranormal with over one million books in print and in multiple languages. She is a two-time RWA Golden Heart® winner and a RWA RITA® nominee. Kate was also nominated several times by RT reviewers for best book in her category. When not creating happily-ever-afters for her characters, she lives her own happy-ever-after in suburban Philadelphia as wife, mother and now a doting grandmom.

BOOKS BY KATE WELSH:

LOVE INSPIRED/STEEPLE HILL
For the Sake of Her Child
Never Lie to an Angel
A Family for Christmas
Small-Town Dreams
Their Forever Love
The Girl Next Door
Silver Lining
Mountain Laurel
Her Perfect Match
A Love Beyond
Abiding Love
Autumn Promises
Joy in His Heart
Home to Safe Harbor
Redeeming Travis
A Time for Grace
SILHOUETTE SPECIAL EDITION
Substitute Daddy
The Doctor's Secret Child
A Bargain Called Marriage
For Jessie's Sake
HARLEQUIN HISTORICAL
Questions of Honor
His Californian Countess
A Texan's Honor
The Bride Wore Britches
The Texas Ranger's Heiress wife
OTHERS
Footprints in Time
The Power of Hope- The Marriage Coin Anthology

WE'VE ONLY JUST BEGUN

By

CARA MARSI

1971

STEPHEN BLACKWOOD RETURNS FROM THE Vietnam War a damaged man, one his family doesn't understand. Free-spirited jewelry designer Elena Delgado's love could heal him. But her fear of commitment threatens to tear them apart. Can Stephen convince Elena he's her happily-ever-after?

DEDICATION

&

ACKNOWLEDGEMENTS

To my husband, a veteran of the Vietnam War, who survived the Tet Offensive—thank you for your service to our country and for your help with the military details in my story.

And to my cousin Johnny, a medic with a Marine unit in Vietnam. Johnny was killed helping a wounded soldier days before Christmas in 1968. We'll never forget you, Johnny.

We've Only Just Begun is my first "historical" romance. The year of my story, 1971, is the year I started dating my husband. Now, it's considered "historical." I loved revisiting 1971, which was one of the best years of my life. Those days were something I'll never forget. I wrote a lot of my story from memory, and there are bits of me throughout it.

I want to thank the other authors in this anthology for inviting me. I'm humbled and honored to be included with such talented authors, whom I also call friends. The Writers Who Lunch rock!

CHAPTER ONE

West Chester Arts Festival,
A park outside Philadelphia, 1971

"THIS DESIGN BELONGS TO MY family."

At the harsh male voice, Elena Delgado looked up into stormy blue eyes. The guy who'd spoken scooped up one of her newest designs, a sterling silver brooch with a citrine stone, from her display table and held it out to her.

Stiffening, she swallowed the angry words that sprang to her lips. The man was a possible customer. Composing her response, she scanned him. Tall, with close-cropped dark blond hair, a straight nose, and firm chin, his expression suggested an uptight personality. His white button-down shirt stretched across broad shoulders and was tucked into the slim waist of his pressed jeans. The total effect screamed money, arrogance, and prestige. Far different from the mellow, long-haired hippie guys she usually hung around with.

"What are you talking about?" Her words came out slow and measured.

Features stern, he said, "My family has jewelry with this design passed down from my ancestor who came from Scotland over 200 years ago."

Elena raised her chin. "That's a luckenbooth and, to my knowledge, the design isn't proprietary. If you think I stole it, then maybe you should find a lawyer and we'll work this out before a judge."

Releasing an audible breath, he dropped the brooch into her waiting hand. His features softened, giving him an air of vulnerability that arrowed straight to her heart. The stirrings of attraction made Elena's knees wobble. Setting down the brooch, she placed her palms on the table for support.

"I didn't mean to imply you'd stolen it," he said. "I thought my family owned the design."

She smiled. "Guess you were wrong."

He returned her smile, showing even, white teeth and a small dimple in his left cheek. That smile and that dimple almost made up for his earlier rudeness.

She picked up one of her cards and handed it to him. "Here's my card with my telephone number. If you decide you'd like this brooch, or another piece of jewelry, for your wife or girlfriend, give me a call." *What a clumsy way to find out if he's married, Elena.*

He slipped the card into his jeans pocket. "Thanks."

As he strode away, she admired his long-legged gait. She still didn't know if he was married or had a girlfriend. She hoped he didn't have either and that she'd see him again.

"Excuse me. Do these come in other stones?"

Turning her attention from Mr. Uptight and Gorgeous, Elena smiled at the woman who'd come to her table and was examining a pair of earrings. "Yes, they do. Let me show you."

As the woman considered the earrings, Elena glanced over again to her intriguing accuser. He leaned against the trunk of a large tree not far from her, scrubbing his hand down his tanned face, which had taken on an ashen sheen. As she watched, he started to shake. Her heart pounded with sympathy.

She stepped from behind her table, ready to go help him, then stopped when she saw a blonde woman come up to him and grab his arm.

❦

When he'd arrived at the park where the arts festival was being held, Stephen Blackwood's attention had focused immediately on the black-haired, olive-skinned woman manning one of the nearby tables. He'd barely acknowledged Karen telling him she'd see him later. As she'd walked off, he'd made a beeline for the exotic beauty selling jewelry. His immediate attraction to the woman had given him an unexpected punch in the gut. He usually went for more conservatively dressed women, not a hippie wearing a leather band circling her head, holding back her long, straight, black hair. Fascinated, he'd studied her as he'd walked toward her table. Her deep purple, gauzy dress with a low-slung macramé belt skimmed her petite but lush figure. Her arms were adorned with bracelets that tinkled musically when she moved. Long silver earrings with a purple stone dangled from her pierced ears. Her soulful, dark brown eyes had studied him with interest as if she saw through to his core and found him wanting.

He'd acted like a jerk. He didn't know what had made him accuse her of stealing the jewelry design from his family.

As he strolled away from her table, smoke from grills set up at one end of the park brought the succulent aroma of spicy pork. Memories shot through him. The arts festival crowd and tables wavered. Sweat broke out on his brow and he sagged against a tree trunk, fighting the onslaught of remembrances. *Not now*, he prayed. *Please not here with all these people.*

Despite his prayers, Stephen was transported back to Saigon, to an open-air market and the scent of wood fires. Vendors hawked fresh fruit, produce, cooked meat, and *bahn mi* sandwiches. Women with dark eyes looked him over as he strolled, some flirting, others eyeing him with suspicion.

His visions turned darker. He heard the whirring of Hueys flying over the dense jungles, the booms from the big guns, screams, saw the fires and blood. He began to shake.

"For God's sake, Stephen. Not another one. You've been home from Vietnam for eight months. We're all tired of the way you've been acting."

The hushed anger of the female voice and someone shaking his arm permeated his brain, diffusing the horrific images. He drew in shallow, too-fast breaths and fought his way back to the present.

He opened his eyes to Karen's ice-blue stare. His stomach clenched with dislike and he freed himself from her. He'd known Karen most of his life. At one time, he'd thought he'd marry her but they'd both changed. Or maybe she'd always been self-absorbed and he hadn't noticed. His parents apparently hadn't seen that side of Karen and still hoped they'd marry. He had to straighten them on that soon.

The war had changed everything, changed him. He no longer saw things the way he had before. He wasn't the same naïve guy who'd gone to war filled with patriotic fervor. Damaged, prone to shakes and bad dreams, he could never be that guy again.

Karen held up a sky-blue silk scarf. "See what I bought from some hippie." Her lips twisted in disdain at the word "hippie".

"Pretty," he said, scarcely looking at it.

She held it up to her chin. "Brings out the blue of my eyes, don't you think?"

"Uh-huh."

Something compelled him to look back at the exotic jeweler. Surprised to see her watching him with soft eyes, serenity stole over him as their gazes locked.

Karen shook his arm again, forcing him to look at her. "What's wrong with you, Stephen? You act like I'm not here. That's no way to treat your fiancée."

He tightened his jaw against his anger and annoyance. "We are not engaged."

"But we will be. It's what your parents want. It's what you wanted before you went to that awful war."

"Things changed."

She stamped her foot. "I hate that war."

He stepped away. "Lots of people hate it, especially the Vietnamese."

CHAPTER TWO

THE ARTS FESTIVAL OVER, ELENA carried her cases out to her VW Beetle parked under a tree. The setting sun danced off her car, brushing the deep orange with shades of gold. She opened the door and hefted the bags into the back seat. Although she'd left the windows open and parked in the shade, the early September sun had heated the car to an almost unbearable temperature.

Driving away with her windows open, she turned on the radio. Her favorite song, *We've Only Just Begun* by the Carpenters played. Cranking up the volume, she sang along as the warm air blew through the car, ruffling her hair. Unlike the song lyrics, Elena had never met a guy who made her dream of a future. That was okay. She liked her life, single and with the liberty to do as she pleased. Free of her family and their restrictive traditions. At the thought of her family, a knot of loneliness settled in her chest. She sang louder in a futile effort to loosen the stranglehold her memories had on her. She'd made her decision a long time ago and she didn't regret it.

Her thoughts went to Mr. Uptight and Gorgeous who'd come to her table earlier. She wondered if under that buttoned-up exterior lurked passion and fire. He had some sort of problem, though. She remembered one of her uncles sweating and shaking like that when she was a child. Her dad had explained her uncle was shell-shocked from fighting in the World War. She hoped the guy she saw today was okay.

Elena forced her mind to something more positive. Today had been good. She'd sold a lot of jewelry and may have found new customers interested in her custom work. Her parents, Old World traditionalists, had scoffed at her creativity. She longed to call them and share her successes, but they'd only nag her to come home and do what they expected. She'd fought hard for her freedom and didn't plan to lose it.

After several trips, she'd lugged her cases up the three flights to her apartment in Upper Darby. The overwhelming scent of patchouli made her sneeze. Sheila must have a client for her past-life regression readings. Her roommate said patchouli incense opened her clients' minds. Elena doubted that, but if Sheila thought so, she'd go along. She and Sheila had been friends since their days at art school in Philadelphia.

Elena entered the apartment and set her cases inside the door. The glass-beaded curtain to the small dining room where Sheila held her sessions was closed.

The sound of soft snores drew her attention to the red velvet sofa. Tim *No Last Name*, Sheila's latest stray, slept sprawled out, his lanky six-foot frame barely fitting on the sofa that also served as his bed. Elena loved her best friend, but wished she'd stop bringing strays of all persuasions home.

Keeping quiet so as not to disturb Sheila and her client, Elena tiptoed down the short hallway to the left of the living room where the bedrooms were located. The three cats Sheila had found as kittens a year ago, Amethyst, Onyx, and Quartz, slept on Elena's bed. She petted each cat, then changed into a tank top and shorts, turned on her small fan, and flopped on the bed. The calendar said September, but the temperature said August. She wished they had a bigger place with air conditioning, but this third-floor walkup was all she and Sheila could afford.

Elena's small bedroom barely accommodated her double bed, dresser, chest, and the long worktable where she created her designs. Maybe someday, she'd be successful enough to have a well-lit studio.

When she heard voices, then the door opening and closing, she knew Sheila's reading must be over. Elena went into the living room, where Tim sat on the sofa, stretching and yawning.

"Hey, Texas," he said, flipping his long brown hair over his shoulders.

"Not my name, Tim."

"But you're from there."

"I left when I was eighteen, eight years ago. I haven't looked back."

Tim formed the "V" for a peace sign with his fingers. "Be cool, man."

Elena shook her head and strode through the dining room to the kitchen. When she got there, she found Sheila standing in front of the open refrigerator. "Do we have anything for dinner?" Elena asked.

Sheila closed the refrigerator door and turned around. "Hi, sweetie. How'd it go today?"

"Good. I sold a lot of stuff, maybe picked up some new clients."

"Far out."

Dressed in one of her signature caftans, this one orange that matched her curly hair, Sheila reminded Elena of an Earth Mother. Sheila's curls shot out from her head like she'd stuck her finger in an electric socket. She always wore colorful, noisy bangles on her arms and beads around her neck. The aroma of patchouli trailed her. Despite their different temperaments, the women were close.

"I'm starving," Elena said.

"Let's go to the diner."

"We go there all the time."

"It's cheap and the food's good."

Elena held out her hands in surrender. "Okay."

Sheila moved closer, studying her. "You've got a new aura around you. You've met someone. Who is he?"

"I'm not one of your clients. I don't have an aura."

Sheila released an exasperated sigh. "You pretend you don't believe in my psychic abilities, but I know you do. Everyone has an aura. Yours is usually pink, signifying you're a loving person with a creative, sensual nature. Your aura is deep pink now, which means you've fallen in love."

"Stop it. How could I have fallen in love when I'm not with anyone?"

Sheila's mouth quirked in a smug smile. "But you have met your soulmate."

Elena's thoughts went to Mr. Uptight and Gorgeous. She whirled around and marched out of the room, afraid Sheila could read her mind. Chances were she'd never see him again. The guy might be good-looking but he had no personality. And he had problems.

CHAPTER THREE

A FTER DROPPING KAREN OFF AT her place, Stephen headed to Blackwood Farm. As he drove his car over the long, winding driveway to the large house, horses grazed in the white-fenced pasture to his left. Horseback riding over the fields and hills of the farm was one of the few things that helped dispel the demons that had plagued him since Vietnam.

The farmhouse came into view, stone flanked by wooden extensions added through the years and fronted by a wraparound porch with rocking chairs that invited a person to sit. Beyond the house, he could see the large barn. Around the barn and across a narrow land bridge stood the small cabin that had been his mother's home when she'd finally managed to make it home to the United States after escaping war-torn Europe. Stephen's heart filled with pride for this place that had been home to the Blackwood family since the 1700s.

Despite his love of Blackwood Farm, he wanted a different life than farming. He had to make his parents understand that. Vietnam had opened something in him. His time there, as a chopper pilot with a medical unit, had made him yearn to help others. He'd saved lives and he wanted his time over there to have some benefit here.

Stephen heard voices coming from the large, open kitchen as he walked in through the back door. He entered the kitchen to find his parents, Meri and Callum, having scones and tea at the scrubbed pine table that had been in the family for over one hundred years.

He set a small paper bag in front of his mother and bent to kiss her on the cheek. "Here's the honey you wanted." Stephen snatched a scone off the plate and sat at the table as he began chewing.

"How was the arts festival?" his mom asked. "See anything interesting?"

He swallowed and wiped crumbs from his chin. "It was okay. If you hadn't wanted the honey from that vendor, I wouldn't have gone."

His dad gave him a sly smile. "You spent time with Karen. Where is she? I thought you were bringing her home for dinner."

"She had other plans," Stephen said with a twinge of guilt. Karen had mentioned going out with friends tonight, but if he'd invited her for dinner, she would have gladly accepted. He didn't invite her.

The roar of a car engine broke through his thoughts.

"Beverly's going to get into trouble someday driving that fast," his dad said, shaking his head.

"You need to talk to her, Callum," Stephen's mom said, her voice accusing. "You're the one who bought her that yellow Mustang convertible over my wishes."

Beverly, Stephen's younger sister, had their dad wrapped around her dainty finger. Callum could deny her nothing. Beverly was spoiled, willful, and stubborn. They all loved her to death.

The back door slammed, then Beverly entered the kitchen like a whirlwind. Her long, curly brown hair framed her freckled face, and her bright green eyes shone.

"Peace, everyone." She bent to place kisses on her parents' cheeks. Swiping up a scone, she said to her mom, "Were there any phone calls for me?"

"Matt called about an hour ago."

"Matt!" she shrieked. "I need to call him back." She started out of the room.

"Stop right there, young lady," their mom said. "You don't take food to your room and ladies don't telephone men."

Beverly set the scone back onto the plate and wiped her hands down the sides of her hip-hugging bellbottoms. Her halter top came to just above her belly button, leaving an expanse of stomach showing. Their mom rolled her eyes, but didn't say anything. Fights over Beverly's clothing choices were common between mother and daughter.

"Mom, you are so square," Beverly said. "Girls call guys all the time now." She flounced out of the room.

When she'd gone, Meri shook her head. "Sometimes, she acts so young. I can't believe she'll be eighteen next month."

Stephen smiled and snatched another scone off the plate. "That's because we all spoil her."

"Do you think she knows about the surprise party we're having for her birthday?" his dad asked.

"Of course she does," Stephen said. "Nothing that happens here gets by Bev."

His mom glanced at the kitchen door, then leaned closer to Stephen to say in a low voice, "I've always told Beverly we'd buy her a nice strand of pearls from Bailey, Banks, and Biddle for her eighteenth birthday, but she informed me she doesn't want any 'old lady jewelry'. She wants something *hip*. I want you to go with me to Jewelers' Row in Philly tomorrow morning to help me pick out something for your sister. You probably know what's in style more than I do."

Stephen knew what his mom was doing. She'd asked him to get her the honey at the arts festival. Now, she wanted him to go into town with her. His parents tried to keep him too busy to dwell on his problems. They'd heard him cry out with bad dreams, had seen him shaking. They tried to get him to talk about his experiences, but he couldn't bring himself to burden them and put those images in their minds and their hearts.

"I'll be glad to go with you, Mom, but stop worrying about me. I'll be okay."

His dad cleared his throat. "We'll always worry about you, Son. When you get back from town tomorrow, we have to go over the farm's books. Even if you do this helicopter thing and don't take over for me, you should know where things stand."

The words *helicopter thing* made Stephen clench one hand on his thigh. "Dad, I know you want me to manage things here, but it's not what I want."

"Don't fight, you two," his mom said in a soothing voice. "Stephen, let's plan to leave early tomorrow for the city."

"We'll leave whenever you want." Jewelry shopping with his mom, not real exciting, but he liked to make her happy. A thought popped into his head. He hadn't stopped thinking about the exotic jewelry designer. He reached into his jeans pocket and drew out her card. *Unique Jewelry Designs by Elena Delgado.*

"We don't need to go to Jewelers' Row, Mom. I know where you can get something perfect for Bev. Leave it to me. I have a line on a jeweler."

CHAPTER FOUR

ELENA DRESSED IN HER FAVORITE jeans, the ones without tears or patches, for her meeting with her new client, the uptight guy from the arts festival two days ago. Her white, peasant top was new and fit just so across her chest. Dark brown leather platform sandals gave an additional four inches to her five-foot-one stature. Her long, beaded earrings, made from a Native American design, skimmed her collarbone. She decided to leave her hair loose, with no headband.

When she came into the living room, Tim slumped on the sofa watching TV while Sheila sat on the overstuffed, blue velvet chair reading a book. Sheila put down her book and gave Elena the once-over. "Lookin' bad, girl."

"Thanks."

Tim glanced up from the TV. "Cool, man. You got a date?"

"Just a client." But a client who excited her more than any man had in a long time.

The doorbell rang. "He's here. Wish me luck I sell something tonight." Elena ran down the stairs to the front door.

When she opened the door, her pulse ratcheted up a few notches. Mr. Uptight and Gorgeous wasn't so straight-laced tonight in a black T-shirt that stretched across his muscled chest and tight jeans that hugged legs that went on forever.

"Hey, Elena," he said.

"Hi, Stephen." She moved aside to let him in. "My place is on the third floor."

She led the way up the stairs. Her whole body tingled with awareness as Stephen followed closely. When they entered her apartment, Tim and Sheila stood, smiling.

"Hi, I'm Sheila. Welcome." She held out her hand.

"Stephen Blackwood."

As they shook hands, surprise flitted over Sheila's face. Elena shot her a questioning look that Sheila ignored.

"This is Tim," Elena said.

With hardened features, Tim studied Stephen. "You a narc?"

Stephen jerked his head up. "No. Why would you say that?"

"Only narcs and cops have hair that short."

"And military men," Stephen said.

Tim visibly relaxed. "You in the military?"

"Not anymore."

"Were you in country?"

Stephen nodded.

Elena widened her eyes. That could explain Stephen's actions at the arts festival, when he appeared to be sick. He'd served in Vietnam. He could be shell-shocked.

"I was infantry, stationed at Da Nang," Tim said. "You?"

"I was with a medical unit and flew choppers out of Saigon."

"I stayed in the field and only convoyed past Saigon."

Sensing, from the rigid set of his body, that Stephen didn't like talking about Vietnam, Elena said, "Let's get started. I'll show you some of my designs. Follow me."

Stephen and Elena sat in the dining room around the small table Sheila used for her readings. They'd pored through Elena's design books, and Elena made sketches of some of Stephen's favorites.

Elena rubbed her lower back and looked across the table to see Stephen studying her. His blue eyes darkened as they stared at each other. She shifted and broke eye contact.

Since the moment she'd seen him at her door tonight, her senses were on heightened alert, aware of his every movement, of his very presence. Going through her design books hadn't diminished the sparks that ignited between them. She wondered how his full lips would feel on her mouth, trailing down her body. Fighting the unwelcome erotic images, she rose.

"How about a drink?" she asked, her voice breathless.

"Sure," he said.

"Beer okay?"

Nodding, he pushed his chair back and stood. "I'll help you."

Shoot. A few minutes alone in the kitchen would have been a welcomed break to compose herself against his magnetic attraction.

She opened the refrigerator door and grabbed two longnecks.

"Opener?" Stephen asked.

"Second drawer on the left," she said, pointing. Elena scooted to the other side of the counter, putting distance between them, not trusting herself so close to him. His overt masculinity, mixed with the vulnerability she read in his eyes, were a lethal combination that made her want to gather him in comfort, then kiss him senseless.

Bottle opener in hand, he moved toward her. She set the bottles on the counter. He quickly opened each one.

Elena breathed in his fresh scent, soap with a hint of the outdoors. The heat of his body reached out to her. She gripped the counter edge.

He lifted one of the bottles and took a long swig, then set the bottle down. "I'm glad my mom gave me an excuse to see you again. But I would have come up with something if she hadn't."

His killer smile with that dimple made warmth pool in her stomach and lower.

"I hadn't expected to see you," she said. *But I hoped I would.*

"I've thought about you a lot the past few days." His voice had thickened and his gaze traveled to her mouth.

Elena ran her tongue over her suddenly dry lips. Stephen's eyes gleamed and he stepped closer until they were a whisper apart. She raised her head, her body on fire.

"What's crackin', guys?" Tim sauntered into the kitchen.

"Let's get back to work," Elena said.

They worked a while longer. Stephen had narrowed his selection to a sterling silver necklace and ring in a modern design. "I think Beverly will like these. Can we use something green for the stones?" He chuckled. "My little sister is very vain about her green eyes. I'm sure she'd want something to match them."

Elena laughed and gathered her papers into a neat pile. "I can do a peridot. That's a beautiful green stone." When she stood, he did, too.

"You're the artist. If you say peridot, then that's what we'll do. I guess we're finished here." He made no move to leave.

She shifted from one foot to the other. "I'll call you when the designs are done."

"Or I can call you."

"We'll be in touch." Nervousness made her brush strands of hair back from her face.

Stephen watched her, his eyes glazed with something that made her heart pound.

"I'll, um, see you out," she said.

"I can let myself out."

She chewed her lip. "I'll talk to you later."

With a smile, he headed out of the room.

Elena followed him to the door, then closed it behind him and leaned against it, listening to his steps as he walked down the stairs and out to the street.

She looked up to find Sheila staring at her, arms folded across her chest.

"What?" Elena asked.

"The red aura sizzling between you and Stephen almost set me on fire." Sympathy softened Sheila's features. "I felt a tingle when he and I touched. He's hurting inside. I couldn't see his aura well because your auras were intertwined."

Elena plopped down on the sofa next to Tim. "What the heck are you talking about?"

Sheila moved closer and leaned down until she and Elena were nose-to-nose. "I am talking about you meeting your soulmate."

"Stephen? Don't be ridiculous."

Wagging her finger, Sheila straightened. "You two have been together before, in another life. You've always had passion between you." She sighed. "I wish I could meet someone I had such strong feelings about."

"You know I don't believe any of that past life stuff or auras. I admit Stephen is great-looking but he's so uptight. Not my type."

"Sweetie, he is *so* your type."

CHAPTER FIVE

STEPHEN STEPPED FROM THE SHOWER and toweled off. It had felt good to be on a horse today. He and his dad had ridden over their property examining the fences and noting which ones needed repair.

Despite the busy morning, he'd found it hard to concentrate. His thoughts kept straying to last night and Elena. He'd wanted to kiss her, to feel her sweet lips against his. From the blush on her cheeks, he knew she'd wanted it, too.

His mind still on Elena, he dressed in a T-shirt and a pair of worn jeans. Elena was beautiful, exotic, and different from other women he'd known. Her striking beauty appealed to his baser instincts, but the kindness in her eyes and her soothing manner told him she'd understand the turmoil in his mind.

With some reluctance, he headed to the office to go over the accounts with his dad. The office door was partially opened. Stephen entered to find his father seated at the walnut desk, glasses perched on the end of his nose, studying the account books. His dad looked up and smiled.

"Have a seat," Callum said, indicating a chair next to him.

When Stephen sat down, his dad opened one of the books and pointed to a column. "We've had banner crops this summer. Our contracts with local supermarkets to sell our produce have brought a good income. I'm thinking of opening the two plots along the western edge and planting more lettuce and tomatoes next year."

"Good idea."

Callum removed his glasses and rubbed his eyes. "Glad you agree. If you take over, you can implement it."

Here it goes. "Dad, we've been over this. My mind is made up. I'm not taking over management. Mick has been here since he was a kid. He loves this place, and he's a good manager. You've said yourself you don't know how you could run this place without him."

"Mick Kellogg is a good man, but he's not family. That war changed you."

"But I made it back. Lots of men didn't," Stephen said softly.

"For that, we're grateful. But you didn't have to go. We needed you here. You could have gotten another deferment."

Fighting his frustration, Stephen stood and pushed his chair back. "I wanted to serve my country. It was my duty."

"You could have served your country here like I did, and saved your mother worry." Callum paused. "Help me understand why you'd rather do this medevac thing."

Stephen paced the small room, then whirled to face his dad. "I loved flying medical choppers in 'Nam. We saved lives. That's what I want to do here. There's a need for quick transport to medical care."

Stephen's mind went to the young medic, Johnny, a valuable member of their team in 'Nam. They'd saved others, but couldn't save him. Stephen swallowed against the remembered pain of that horrific day when Johnny had been killed.

"Did you hear me?" his dad asked.

Shaking away the memories, Stephen focused on the present. "Sorry. What were you saying?"

"What makes you think this medevac thing will be successful?" his dad asked in a gentle voice. "We hear you at night, we've seen the shaking. We know the transition back to civilian life has been hard. You know you can talk to us when you're ready. We've seen you stare into space, and know your mind goes back there. We worry being in a helicopter could split your attention and cause a crash. Don't rush into anything."

"I know you can't help worrying, Dad, but flying relaxes me. My partner and I know what we're doing. We've studied other medical transport companies here. There's been a successful one in Maryland the last two years. Next week, Nick and I are going down there to talk to the owners."

"What do you know about this Nick? Can you trust him? Where will you get the money you need?"

"Nick Bellini is from South Philly. He was a medical chopper pilot with me. He's a decent guy." Stephen held his father's gaze. "As for money, I've saved most of my Army pay and what you pay me here, plus Nick and I have found backers who are willing to invest in our company. If we don't have enough, we'll get a business loan."

Callum sighed and pushed one of the account books forward. "You've got no one to medevac now. Come look at these."

Guilt that he was abandoning the land his family had worked for over two centuries tied Stephen's stomach in knots.

"Later. I need to go out for a while." Before he could say anything he'd regret, Stephen strode to the door. With his hand on the doorknob, he twisted around to his dad. "Why don't you come to Maryland next week with Nick and me? You can meet Nick and learn about what we want to accomplish."

"I'll think about it."

Stephen took the steps two at a time to his room and snatched his car keys from his dresser. He'd take a long ride, sort out his thoughts. When he spotted the phone on the table next to the bed, he knew who he needed.

Taking a card from his pocket, he dialed. When Elena answered, he said, "This is Stephen Blackwood."

"Hi, Stephen."

Did he imagine the huskiness in her voice?

"Can we meet for coffee?" he asked. "I haven't been able to get you out of my mind. I'd like to see you,"

When she hesitated, disappointment filled his chest. "I have an idea for Beverly's jewelry," he blurted. He didn't know where that had come from, but he would say whatever he needed for Elena to agree to meet him.

"Uh-okay," she finally said.

He let out a relieved breath.

"How about the Westwood Diner down the street from my house? In an hour?" she said.

"See you then." He hung up the phone and hoped no one was listening on the extension.

Jingling his keys, he left his room.

CHAPTER SIX

L IGHT TRAFFIC AND HIS MUSTANG Mach One got Stephen to the diner in record time. Nervous as a fourteen-year-old kid on his first date, he nursed his second cup of coffee and tapped his fingers on the tabletop.

He spotted Elena crossing the street, and his heart somersaulted. Like a man craving a meal, he feasted his ravenous gaze on her as she walked gracefully toward the diner. Several men stared at her, unleashing unwelcome and surprising jealousy in Stephen.

She entered the diner and looked around. Seeing him, her full lips tilted in a sunny smile that made him want to take her in his arms and never let her go. He stood as she approached.

Tonight, she wore a tight-fitting yellow long-sleeved top that hugged her full breasts. Her bellbottom jeans skimmed long, slim legs, made longer by the platform boots she wore. He swallowed against the desire that flared in his stomach and spread lower.

"Hey, Stephen," she said when she reached him. "I was surprised to get your call."

I surprised myself making it.

They sat, and Elena signaled the waitress for some coffee.

"I hope you didn't mind meeting me on such short notice," he said.

"Of course not." She looked down at the table, then back to him. "I'm glad you called. I've been thinking about you, too."

He wanted to puff out his chest with pride.

She cleared her throat. "You wanted to discuss Beverly's jewelry design?"

Business first. Okay with him, so long as he could keep her with him. "I think my parents will love the ring and necklace you're designing for Bev. I'd like to surprise my sister with earrings to match." He'd come up with the idea for earrings on his drive here.

Elena thanked the waitress for her coffee, and stirred in cream and sugar. She took a sip before answering. "I think that's a wonderful idea. Since it's not as fashionable nowadays to wear too many pieces of matching jewelry, I can give the earrings a similar design, but not exact. What do you think?"

She could say she would make the earrings out of monkey ears and he'd love the idea. Anything to see her smile. "Great idea. Knowing Bev, she'll love anything you do."

Elena rewarded him with the smile he wanted.

"I'll draw up some designs right away and let you know when all the designs are ready."

"Sounds good. I'll stop by and pick them up to bring to my parents." Another chance to see Elena. "I'm hungry. How about some pie?" He'd use any excuse to keep her here.

She laughed. "I can't refuse pie. I love coconut custard, and this place makes the best."

"I'm partial to apple. We'll get a slice of each and share."

"Okay."

He ordered the pies and more coffee, then said to Elena, "Do I detect an accent? Where are you from?"

A shadow seemed to flicker over her face, and he wondered if he'd said the wrong thing.

She set her cup aside to rest her arms on the table. "I'm from Texas, but I've been in this area for eight years now, since art school."

"What part of Texas?"

"My family lives in San Antonio."

"I've always wanted to visit there to see the Alamo." He frowned. "Has your family always lived in San Antonio?"

She chuckled. "For over three hundred years."

"Really?" The longer he knew Elena, the more fascinating she became.

Nodding, she said, "The Delgados came to this country from Spain in 1603, before there was a United States. Or a Texas. We've got some Native American in us, too."

He moved back in his seat and let out a low whistle. "And I thought my family's been here a long time."

The waitress set the pies down on the table and refilled their coffee. He didn't touch his food, wanting to hear more of Elena's history.

"What made your family come here so long ago?"

"One of my ancestors was given 4,000 acres by the king of Spain."

"Impressive. My ancestor came over in 1716 as an indentured servant." He smiled. "Not quite the credentials of your family."

She shrugged and scooped pie onto her fork. "My family is heavy on tradition and act like they're still Spanish royalty."

He detected a note of bitterness in her voice and wondered if he was treading on dangerous ground.

She slid the forkful of pie into her mouth and moaned. "This is so good."

When she flicked her tongue out to skim her bottom lip, Stephen stabbed his pie with his fork, fighting the urge to lick the sweetness from her lips.

He shoved a piece of pie into his mouth instead, then pushed his plate toward her. "Have some."

They each shared a piece of the other's pie. Both were delicious, but not as scrumptious as the woman sitting across from him.

"Philly's a long way from Texas. What made you decide to settle here?" he asked.

"I fell in love with the city when I was here for art school. I've been in Philly longer than I'd planned." She lifted one shoulder in a shrug. "I should probably move on. I don't like feeling too comfortable in any one place."

He barely knew her, yet the thought of her leaving formed a knot of regret in his chest. "Will you go back to Texas?"

She finished off her pie and wiped her mouth on her napkin before answering. "There's nothing for me there."

"What about your family?"

"We're estranged."

Stunned at the casualness of her admission, he reached across the table and touched her hand. "I'm sorry, Elena."

Her big, dark eyes met his. "I'm not asking for pity."

"I'm not giving it. But I do want to know all about Elena Delgado."

She lifted her chin, stubbornness on her face. "Now you. Tell me about Stephen Blackwood. I know you were in 'Nam." Sympathy softened her eyes to velvet. "I saw you at the arts festival when you seemed sick. I had an uncle who was shell-shocked after World War Two. He had a hard time of it when he came home. Are you okay?"

Stephen inhaled deep breaths, fighting another attack and the memories that beleaguered him. "I'll be okay. Lots of guys are shell-shocked when they return from war. We get over it."

She watched him as if she didn't quite believe him. Frowning, she settled back in her seat. "At the arts festival, you were with a blonde woman. Girlfriend? Wife?"

He wondered if Elena were jealous, and decided he liked that she might be. "That was Karen. We're friends. We've known each other since kindergarten."

The relief that flitted over her face made him smile.

"Tell me about your family, Stephen."

"Not much to tell. We have deep roots in Chester County."

Elena's attention riveted on him, as if he were the most important person in the world. He suddenly wanted to share his frustrations with her. He signaled the waitress for more coffee. When she'd filled their cups, Stephen sipped his drink, his attention on Elena.

Setting aside his cup, he said, "We Blackwoods have lived on Blackwood Farm since the 1700s. My family wants me to take over the management, but it's not for me."

"What do you want?" she asked gently.

"I flew medical choppers in the war. We did a lot of good. I want to start my own medevac service here. An Army buddy and I have been saving to buy a helicopter. With help from investors, we're almost there."

Excitement settled over him as it always did when thinking about the company he and Nick planned to start.

Elena tilted her head and frowned. "What's a medevac service?"

"We'll fly critically ill people to hospitals for treatment. If an accident victim needs more treatment than a small, local hospital can provide, we fly the patient to a hospital that can treat him. Getting people to the proper medical care quickly can be the difference between life and death. I want to help people like I did in the war."

"That's a great idea. Your parents are against that?"

"I didn't think they understood how much the medevac company means to me, but my dad just admitted they're worried I'll have a flashback in a chopper. I won't. Flying was the best part of 'Nam for me."

Elena sipped her coffee and stared at him over the rim of her cup, studying him with serious eyes. Setting down her cup, she said, "You have to do what makes you happy, Stephen."

"I don't want to hurt my parents."

"I've never met your parents, but knowing how you feel about them, I'm sure they love you. They'll support you."

He lifted a brow. "I hope you're right. I hate fighting with my dad. What about your family. Don't you miss them?"

She glanced away, and he thought she wouldn't answer. When she faced him again, her features had tightened. "My friends, especially Sheila, are all the family I need."

"But you need your real family around you, too."

"I don't." She stood. "Thanks for the coffee and pie."

He'd scared her off. "I'll walk you home." He threw some bills on the table.

They were silent on the short walk to her place. Even wearing platforms, she barely reached his shoulders. Somehow, that made him feel protective. He suspected she might haul off and hit him if he suggested he'd like to protect her.

When they reached her building, she raised her gaze to him. "I'll have the designs to you shortly."

As she started to move away, he reached for her arm and gently turned her to face him. Cupping her shoulders, he bent toward her.

"I've wanted to do this all evening," he whispered before covering her lips with his.

She stiffened, then she relaxed against him and ran her hands up his arms to wind around his neck.

He deepened the kiss and was rewarded with a low moan from her. She tasted like coffee and coconut custard pie. He wanted to devour her.

After several passion-filled minutes, they pulled apart. In the dim light from the streetlamps, he saw longing and confusion in the depths of her eyes. Without a word, she hurried into her building.

He stood for minutes staring at the door she'd disappeared through. With reluctant steps, he strode away.

He wanted Elena Delgado. Like a beautiful and colorful bird, she wouldn't be easy to catch.

He was up to the challenge.

CHAPTER SEVEN

H ER MIND ON THAT KISS, that amazing kiss, Elena trudged upstairs to her apartment, and sighed with relief when she entered to quiet. Hopefully, Sheila and Tim had decided to go out. She knew Sheila would guess immediately that Elena had been kissed.

No such luck. Sheila came from the dining room, the beaded curtain tinkling with her movements. She stopped when she saw Elena. Hand on hip, Sheila moved closer.

"Hey, girl, your aura is going crazy." Narrowing her eyes, Sheila studied Elena. "You've got the *look*. You were with Stephen." She grinned. "And it went *very* well."

"It was a business meeting."

Sheila waved a hand. "Business? I don't think so. Your aura is flashing brilliant red. Stephen kissed you, didn't he? And you liked it."

"So what if we kissed? No big deal."

"It is a very big deal, especially when the kiss is from your soulmate."

"Okay. It was a great kiss, but he's not my soulmate."

"Oh, sweetie." Sheila enveloped Elena in a bear hug. She released her but held her at arm's length. "You're scared. I see it in your eyes and the dark brown that's edging your aura. Not all men are abusive like your ex-fiancé. You're stronger now."

Blinking back tears, Elena stepped away. "You're right. I am stronger. No man will ever hurt me again." She studied the floor before meeting Sheila's eyes again. "My parents, who should have been there for me, let me down."

"They didn't support you," Sheila said. "But you know they're sorry.

BRANDYWINE BRIDES ANTHOLOGY 319

You need to make peace with them and put the past behind you. Only then can you give Stephen a chance."

"I don't want to talk about it." Elena pivoted and stalked to her room. No one, not her parents, not Stephen Blackwood, would control her.

When she got to her room, she slammed the door shut and leaned against it. She ran a finger over her lips. She'd wanted to kiss Stephen almost from the first time she'd seen him. The vulnerability in his eyes reached out to her. He needed healing.

Sheila had often said that, at times, Elena's aura became forest green, indicating a natural healer. Elena refused to believe it.

It wasn't her job to heal Stephen Blackwood, or anyone. A part of her wanted to comfort him, to make his pain go away. He needed a friend. She didn't know if she could be that person.

☙

After a sleep-deprived night where he tossed and turned with erotic dreams about Elena Delgado, Stephen arose at dawn and saddled his favorite horse, Joey, a descendant of Buddy, the horse his ancestor brought back from the Civil War. A fast ride over the hills and valleys of Blackwood Farm would help vent his sexual frustrations.

A satisfying ninety minutes later, the horse cooled down and fed, Stephen went into the house where the tantalizing aroma of bacon, coffee, eggs, and toast led him to the kitchen. His mom sat at the table reading the paper. Her empty plate and a mug of coffee, steam spiraling out, rested in front of her. Their cook Hilda smiled at Stephen.

"Bacon and eggs, Stephen?" she asked.

"You spoil us, Hilda." He poured himself a mug of coffee from the pot on the stove and sat across from his mother.

Meri Blackwood lowered her paper and smiled at her son. "I knew you were out riding before I saw you."

"I need a shower, but I can't resist one of Hilda's breakfasts. I'm famished."

"Karen called last night," his mom said. "You'd left here in a hurry and we'd thought you went to see her, but I guess not. Is everything okay with you? You're not in any sort of trouble are you?"

He shook his head. "Mom, am I the kind of guy who gets into trouble?"

"You've never given us a moment's distress until now. Talk to me, Stephen."

Hilda set a steaming plate of scrambled eggs, bacon, and toast in front of him. The cook gave him a sympathetic smile before leaving the kitchen.

He dug into his breakfast, his hunger overriding the need for conversation. His hunger abated, he nodded at his mother. "How am I giving you problems now?"

"It's always been your father's dream you'd take over the farm someday. We're not getting any younger and we'd like to do some traveling." She smiled. "We've always thought, too, you and Karen would marry."

Stephen drank his coffee, giving himself time to gather his thoughts. Finished with his drink, he set down his mug. "Mom, I know you and Dad want what you think is best for me. I don't want to hurt you, but I've changed."

With a wry smile, she said, "We've noticed."

"Please try to understand. Before I went to 'Nam, I thought the world revolved around me. I realize now I was drifting, with no clear idea of what I wanted. You and Dad have given Bev and me everything a kid could want. I saw a whole other world over there. I appreciate what you've done for me, but I'm no longer a kid. It's time for me to take charge of my future."

His gaze met hers. "You should understand that. You had to fight for what you wanted, for your very life."

Her smile released some of the tension in the room. "I do understand, and of course we want to see you happy. We thought marrying Karen would make you so."

"Before I left for 'Nam, I expected I'd marry her. She's not what I want now."

"You've met someone, haven't you?"

"Why do you say that?"

"There's something different about you. You seem happier. Who is she?"

He could never fool his mother. It felt good to talk to her, to get things off his chest.

"Her name is Elena Delgado. She's a jewelry designer from Texas. And unlike any woman I've ever met. She's the one designing Bev's jewelry."

"You're smitten. She must be quite a woman to put that look on your face. How did you meet a jewelry designer from Texas?"

"I saw her at the West Chester Arts Festival and got her card. When you said you wanted something different for Bev, I thought of Elena."

Meri smiled like the Cheshire Cat. "I'll bet you did. I'd like to meet this Elena Delgado. Why don't you invite her to Beverly's party?"

CHAPTER EIGHT

STEPHEN SCANNED THE CROWDED DIVE bar on Philadelphia's South Street. The place reeked of beer, cigarette smoke, and marijuana. Long-haired young guys dressed in T-shirts and torn jeans, cigarettes dangling from their lips and beer bottles in hand, talked with young women with frizzy hair and dressed in skimpy tops and jeans or bright peasant-type skirts and tops. Some of the men wore Army jackets like the one Stephen had in the back of his closet, a jacket he never intended to wear again.

Through the open doors, he heard rock, classical, and jazz music from the many street musicians. Hippies crowded the sidewalks. Laughter and talk from outside mingled with the loud conversations inside the bar. Not much different from some of the bars in Saigon, he thought.

Shaking his head at his friend and business partner, Nick Bellini, seated across from him at the small table, Stephen said, "You know the nicest places."

"Cool out, man. You need to lighten up. You've been home for eight months now, and your hair is still a buzz cut. Let it grow. Get with the times."

Stephen laughed. "Like you?"

Nick ran a hand over his shoulder-length dark hair. "Damn straight."

Setting down his bottle of beer, Stephen said, "You're free to wear your hair any way you want, but we have to look professional when we talk to the hospitals about contracts for our medevac services."

"You and I are two of the best chopper pilots around. And we have medical transport experience. No one's going to care about the length of our hair when we're saving lives."

"I suppose, but we have to get the contracts first. What are the chances of us getting that helicopter? Your mechanic vouched it's in good shape?"

Nick nodded. "For a ten-year-old chopper, it's been well-maintained. I'm waiting for the owner to call me." He grinned. "We're on our way, man, to opening the first medevac company in these parts."

"To B&B Med-Flight Services," Stephen said, lifting his bottle.

The men toasted, then Nick's expression sobered. "What did your dad say after our trip to Maryland yesterday? He was quiet most of the way home. Do you think he changed his mind after talking to the guys who run that medevac?"

Stephen peeled the label off his bottle, thinking about their trip yesterday and all they'd learned. "Dad said he understands what we want to do. But he and my mom worry I'll be in over my head or have flashbacks to 'Nam and crash while flying. They figure the longer I'm home, the more I'll forget about the medevac and take over management of the farm. With or without their approval, I'm doing this."

"How are you feeling?" Concern tinged Nick's voice.

"Better," Stephen said, thinking of Elena. It had been five days since he'd met her at the diner, five days since that kiss. Working on the details of starting a business, plus the trip to Maryland, had consumed his time. He missed her. He'd call her tonight.

"Stay sharp, man," Nick said. "Some foxy hippie chick has been eye-balling you since she got here a few minutes ago. She's on her way to us now."

Stephen followed Nick's gaze and froze. Elena, dressed in a flowing multi-colored skirt and a tight blue T-shirt, a smile on her face, headed toward them.

Grinning with the joy that flowed through him, Stephen stood.

"Hey, Stephen," she said when she reached him.

"Elena. I'm surprised to see you here." He leaned closer. "But glad."

She blushed a pretty shade of pink. "I'm here with Sheila and Tim. We're giving Tim a sort of going-away party." She gave Nick, also standing, a curious glance.

"Elena Delgado, Nick Bellini," Stephen said. "Nick's my business partner."

Elena and Nick exchanged hellos.

Sheila and Tim threaded their way through the crowd. Stephen introduced everyone.

"I hear you're going away," he said to Tim.

"I'm heading out to California tomorrow with a couple of chicks. We hear Frisco's a happening place."

"Good luck."

"Drinks all around. My treat," Nick said, his attention on Sheila.

"Thanks, man," Tim said.

Elena reached for Stephen's hand. "Let's get out of here."

CHAPTER NINE

A S THEY WALKED HAND-IN-HAND ALONG South Street, dodg-
ing panhandlers and rowdy revelers, warmth flowed through Elena.
She looked up at Stephen, at his strong profile with his straight nose and
firm chin. Here was a man she could depend on.

Her fear of losing control, something that had dogged her since she
left Texas, reared its ugly head. She would dwell on that later. Being
with Stephen now acted as a balm for her soul.

"I'm glad we ran into each other," she said.

He stopped and stared down at her. "Are you?"

"Yes."

"I've been busy, but I can't stop thinking about you. I planned to call
you tonight."

Her pulse raced and she smiled. "This is better than a call."

The sound of a car backfiring popped through the noisy street. Stephen squeezed her hand so hard it hurt. Sweat broke out on his face.

"What's wrong?" she asked. When he began to shake, she guided him
into a small alleyway.

He staggered against the brick wall of a building, sweating and shaking.

"I'm here, Stephen." She held tightly to his hand. "I won't leave you.
You're safe. This is Philadelphia, not Saigon."

He swallowed but didn't respond. She cupped his face between her
hands. "Stephen, it's Elena. It's okay. Everything is all right. I'm here
for you."

He stared as if seeing her for the first time. "Elena."

She gathered him to her and laid her head on his chest. His fast-beating heart pounded through her. He rested his chin on the top of her head. She barely heard the street noises. They stood clinging to each other until she felt his breathing even out and his heartbeat slow.

Stepping away from her, he gripped her shoulders. "I'm sorry, Elena. I hadn't meant for you to see that."

She caressed his cheek. "You have nothing to be sorry for. I understand, and I'm here now, by your side. I won't leave you."

He closed his eyes for a few seconds, then gathered her tightly to him. Finally, he gently pushed her away and kissed her temple. "Let's go."

As he drove her home, she kept her hand over his on the console. They didn't speak, but she sensed he needed her with him, and she hoped she helped him.

❦

Elena had the designs for Beverly's jewelry ready two days later, and she called Stephen to tell him. He agreed to stop by her place and pick them up.

With Tim gone and Sheila having dinner with her tarot-reading friends, Elena had the place to herself. The weather had gotten cooler, and she wore jeans, a long-sleeved tie-dyed top, and Indian moccasins. Waiting for Stephen, she paced the living room and wiped her palms down the sides of her jeans, fighting nervousness. She hoped he wasn't embarrassed by what had happened the other night. She considered him a friend and wanted to help. Hopefully, he understood that.

As she paced, the flowery scent of her favorite cologne, Blue Grass, a ladylike fragrance that reminded her of her Catholic boarding school days, wafted around her. The Elizabeth Arden cologne had been a favorite of her mother's. In times of stress or excitement, Elena wore the fragrance for tranquility, remembering the long-ago days when she and her mom were close.

The doorbell rang. Butterflies partied in her stomach as she ran down the stairs and opened the door to Stephen. Dressed in faded jeans and a dark blue T-shirt, and with a light golden stubble on his chin, his rampant sex appeal made a lump form in her throat.

"Would you like a beer, or water, or iced tea?" she asked when they'd entered her apartment.

"Nothing, thanks," he said.

As she walked toward the dining room, his voice stopped her. "Elena?" Frowning, she whirled around.

"Thanks for your help the other night."

"That's what friends are for. How are you feeling?"

"Better, because of you."

She carried the image of his dimpled smile in her heart as went to the other room. They sat at the table, and she fanned pages with her designs out in front of Stephen. Leaning over, she pointed to her designs for the ring and necklace. "I know your family has a history with the luckenbooth," she said with a wry smile.

He chuckled. "You're never going to let me forget what I said at the arts festival, are you?"

"Not a chance." She pointed to her drawings. "I incorporated that design into the modern one you'd selected."

Stephen studied the drawings, then gave her a smile that set the butterflies in her stomach dancing like the kids on Bandstand.

"These are amazing. You're very talented. I think Bev and my parents will love them."

Warmed by his praise, she set another paper before him. "These are the earrings you commissioned. They complement the ring and necklace, but they're just different enough. What do you think?"

"I think you're wonderful."

His intense expression and the smoky sound of his voice sent waves of delicious tingles through her. She straightened in her chair. "If you like the earrings, I'll get started on them right away. I have the silver and the stones. Let me know as soon as you can about the others so I can be sure to have them done in time for your sister's birthday."

Stephen stood and took her hand to pull her gently up. Reaching out, he touched strands of her hair and twisted them around his finger. "Your designs are beautiful, like you."

His eyes drifted to her mouth and back up. With a low murmur, he cupped her shoulders and moved closer. She lifted her head, inviting his touch. He bent and covered her lips in a scorching kiss that electrified every cell in her body. On fire, she wound her arms around his neck and returned his kiss.

His tongue caressed the seam of her lips until she opened for him. Their tongues mated in an erotic dance as he skimmed his hands over her hips to her midriff and pulled her against him. Boneless, a puddle of need, she clung to him, afraid her legs wouldn't hold her.

With a groan, he took a step back and rested his forehead against hers. "I want you. Badly." His ragged breathing matched hers. "I've got too much going on in my life now, and, as you saw the other night, I'm sick. It wouldn't be fair to you to get involved."

She heaved a deep breath and slid away. Adjusting her top, she met his gaze as her good sense returned. "You're going through a rough patch, that's all. I've got some things I need to deal with. Let's stay friends and take things slowly."

She grabbed one of his hands in hers and squeezed. "Shell-shock is nothing to be ashamed of, and you're not sick. If you need anyone to talk to, I'm here. When things settle down for you, you'll find a woman who deserves you, someone stable. I'm not that person."

"Don't sell yourself short. You're a smart, sweet, and loving woman. Any man would be lucky to have you."

She grinned, faking a lightness she didn't feel. "We're both good people. Let's forget all this dark talk. How about a snack?"

They sat at the kitchen table, iced tea, chips, and dip in front of them. Elena ran a finger over the scarred Formica of the table Sheila and she had found in a trash heap. If her society matron mother could see the way she lived, she'd be appalled. But Elena was her own person and would live her own life.

She looked up to find Stephen intensely studying her. "What is it?" She ran a finger over her lips. "Do I have food on my face?"

"No, and if you did, you'd still be beautiful. You intrigue me. You're unlike any woman I've ever met. Tell me about your family, about your life in Texas."

Elena glanced away to stare at the clock on the far wall. The clock, the image of a grinning cow, its tail a pendulum, stared back.

A series of loud "meows" permeated the silence. Onyx, Amethyst, and Quartz bounded into the room, each staring at her with their "feed us" expressions. She jumped up, grateful for the distraction.

She felt Stephen's gaze on her as she scooped out dry food and added water to the cats' bowls. She'd only ever told Sheila about her family. She barely knew Stephen, but something deep inside told her he'd understand. Still…

Sitting again, she rubbed her fingers down the condensation on her glass of iced tea. "My family is very Old World. My dad makes all the decisions and my mom never fights him. Their marriage was arranged by their parents. They're happy enough, but I want more. They didn't understand, so I left. I don't like to talk about them."

"I know there's a story in there, but I won't press you. Someday, you'll trust me enough to tell me. Until then, we're friends, right?"

"Friends." Friends or not, she couldn't tell him the whole, humiliating story.

"My parents are giving Beverly a surprise birthday party," he said. "Would you be my date? No strings."

She chewed her lip. Part of her wanted to say no, to stay away from him, for his sake, and hers. Stephen Blackwood could make her fall in love with him.

He studied her, waiting.

"Yes, I'll go," she said.

CHAPTER TEN

OVER THE NEXT WEEK, STEPHEN and Nick firmed things up with their investors, got the price they wanted on the helicopter, and found a nearby airfield where they could keep the chopper. The hangar also included a small office which they planned to make their headquarters. Out of guilt and a sense of responsibility, Stephen had also spent whatever time he could with his dad, going over the books, scheduling repairs to the farm buildings and the house.

As he drove to the airfield now for another meeting with Nick, Stephen's thoughts went again to Elena, as they'd done the past week since he'd last seen her. The hot kisses they'd shared had dominated his waking hours and his dreams. He wanted her like he'd never wanted a woman before.

Physically, she was sexy as hell. Her vulnerability, her strength, and her independence drew him to her, too. He'd built a wall around his heart to deal with the horrors of war. Elena's warmth had begun to penetrate that wall. When he'd had his episode in front of her, instead of treating him as a pariah, she'd comforted him. His parents loved him, and he loved them too much to burden them. He wasn't sure talking to them would help him. Elena seemed to instinctively know what he needed, a soothing touch, a gentle voice in his ear.

𝕮

His long day over, Stephen tramped into the house. Soon B&B Med-

Flight Services would be up and running and able to help people get critical care quickly. Excitement put a spring into his step as he headed to his bedroom. He had time to freshen up and have that talk with his dad.

Showered and changed, Stephen hesitated outside his dad's office when he heard voices. Recognizing the voice of Mick Kellogg, he knocked.

At his dad's, "Come in," Stephen opened the door and stepped inside. Mick, seated in front of the desk, nodded to him, then stood.

"I hope you'll think about what I said, Callum," Mick said.

Callum shrugged. "A greenhouse? I don't know. I promise I'll give it thought."

"That's all I ask." With a nod toward Stephen, Mick left the room.

Stephen sat in the chair Mick had vacated and slid forward with his palms on his thighs. "We need to talk, Dad. Things are coming together for our medevac company. This is not only a dream of mine, but something I'm compelled to do."

Callum scrubbed a hand down his face. "I can't say I'm not disappointed you don't want to take your place here. It's was my dream to turn Blackwood Farm over to you."

"I love you, Dad, and I don't want to hurt you, but I have my own life to lead. I may not succeed but I have to try."

Releasing a resigned sigh, his dad said, "Visiting that medevac company in Maryland opened my mind to a lot of things." His features softened. "I saw how happy you were that day, more like the guy you were before you went to war. Your mother and I want what's best for you, and we worry about you."

Leaning back, Callum closed his eyes, as if in deep thought. The only sound in the quiet room was the ticking of the antique clock on the wall.

Stephen sank deeper into the plush leather chair and crossed his legs at the ankles. He gazed around the room with its dark green walls and Oriental carpets. Bookcases, filled with books of every genre, plus academic tomes, lined one wall. As a child, he'd loved to come in here and lose himself for hours in a book. The office always reminded him of his grandfather, especially the faint odor of tobacco from the pipe Pops occasionally smoked. Stephen glanced toward the window where the setting sun cast gold and pink streaks of light over the rolling hills. One of the horses, a chestnut, ran along the white fence. Peace stole over Stephen at the idyllic scene.

His dad cleared his throat, getting Stephen's attention. "Your mother and I are proud of you, Son, of how you served your country, keeping up the tradition of generations of Blackwood men. You've never talked about your war experiences. It might help if you did."

Stephen clenched his hands on his thighs. "I don't like to talk about it, and I don't want to upset you and Mom."

"We're your parents. You can talk to us about anything."

"I know, but some things are hard for me to…" He sucked in a harsh breath. "I saw death and devastation like I never hope to see again. I saw people at their worst, and at their best. The men I flew with in the medical unit were the best. We saved lives, lots of lives. We lost some good people who were part of our team." He could see Johnny's face. He had to do this for Johnny, for all the ones they'd lost.

Stephen flattened his palms on the desktop. "I want to save lives. I want to help others the way we helped in 'Nam. I'm going to do this with or without your blessing. I'd rather have your blessing."

"You've convinced your mother. She gave me hell for fighting you. You know how persuasive she can be." Callum stood and held out his hand. "You've convinced me, too. You have our blessing, Son. Go do what you feel you have to."

Stephen came around the desk and grabbed his dad in a bear hug. "Thanks, Dad."

His dad stepped away, his eyes moist with tears. "Get out of here before I change my mind."

Smiling, Stephen left the office.

His mom walked past, and Stephen hugged her, then swung her around. Laughing, she hit him on the arm. "Put me down. What's going on?"

"Thanks for your help, Mom. Dad gave me his blessing."

"Of course he did. He always listens to me," she added with a sly smile. "I was searching for you. I love your friend Elena's designs. She's very talented."

"She is."

"I know Beverly will be over the moon when she sees her gifts. Tell Elena we approve. I'll write out a check for the deposit and mail it right away."

"I'll take the check to her."

A smile played around his mom's mouth. "I thought you might say that."

"You'll meet Elena soon. She'll be at Bev's party."

CHAPTER ELEVEN

STEPHEN DELIVERED THE CHECK TO Elena and now they strolled hand-in-hand along an Upper Darby street. On this cool early autumn night, not many people were out. He looked down at Elena, feeling peace steal over him as it always did when they were together.

Tonight she wore a tight-fitting woven jacket in a geometrical design. The bright colors enhanced her dark beauty. Her flared jeans hugged her slim legs, and she wore boots with short heels. When he slipped his arm around her shoulders, she nestled against him.

"You seem happy," she said.

"I am. My parents have given their blessing on the medevac company."

She stopped walking and tugged on his hand, drawing him to the side. Her eyes gleamed in the dim light from the streetlamps. "Stephen, that's wonderful news. I know how much their approval means to you."

He smiled and skimmed his thumb down her cheek. "You have something to do with it."

"Me?"

"You're a hell of a woman—talented, creative, independent. I'm sorry you're estranged from your family, but I admire how you fought for yourself. You gave me the courage to fight for what I want."

Elena put her hand on his forearm. "You had the courage all along. You love your dad and didn't want to hurt him. That's commendable. Me, I left. I might have stayed, convinced them..." Her voice trailed off.

"My dad has always been intensely loyal to traditions," Stephen said. "Sometimes, I think the changes in the world bother him, and he worries about me."

Elena stepped away. "I've never thought of family resistance that way. I was young."

Sadness flitted across her exquisite face, a face he was coming to care deeply about.

"I understand about family loyalties and traditions," she said. "I found what makes me happy, and I fought for it, but lost my family. You're a great guy, you're strong, and you fought for our country. I'm glad your family understands and supports you."

"What about your family, Elena? Your parents must miss you. Have you thought of making amends with them?"

She stiffened. "We're talking about your family, not mine."

"I didn't mean to bring up bad memories for you. You said you're here for me. I'm here for you, too, whenever you need to talk."

Raising herself on tiptoe, she brushed a tender kiss on his lips. "You are a kind and wonderful man. And a good friend."

He wanted to be much more than friends with her. He recognized Elena's independent streak, her free spirit. He'd take it slow with her. He'd convinced his father. He'd convince Elena to take a chance on him. He wouldn't give up.

"Let's walk." With his arm around her waist again, he held her close as they strolled. The sweet woman at his side filled Stephen with the first real peace he'd known since before 'Nam.

He'd find a way to make Elena his.

CHAPTER TWELVE

NERVOUSNESS MADE ELENA TWIST THE fringe on her shawl around her fingers as she rode with Stephen to his sister's party. Having grown up with society parents, making small talk with strangers didn't frighten her. Meeting Stephen's parents scared her to death.

She hoped they liked her. She'd dressed in a short black silk dress, sleeveless, with a V-neck that showed her cleavage. To keep warm in the autumn chill, she wore a colorful shawl, hand dyed and sewn by a friend. Her ankle-strap platform sandals made her legs, clad in sheer stockings, seem longer. She'd wanted classy, yet sexy. The classy was for Stephen's parents; the sexy for him.

He glanced over at her. "It'll be okay. My parents will love you."

"I'm not nervous," she lied. "You look nice." His dark blue suit looked custom-made. His shirt was blindingly white, and his blue patterned tie complemented his look. Her fingers itched to run through his hair, noticing he'd started to let it grow. She liked the more casual, less uptight Stephen. Maybe liked him too much.

Anxiety churned an uneasy brew in her stomach. Since she'd cut ties with her parents, she'd been careful not to become emotionally involved with anyone. Whenever she felt herself drawing close to a man, she'd end the relationship. Stephen was different. She thought about him during the day and had erotic dreams about him at night. He made her feel happy and contented, yet curiously on edge, too.

"Nice car," she said in an effort to nudge away her thoughts.

"Thanks. It was the first thing I bought when I came home. One of these days, soon I hope, I'll drive you out to Coatesville to see our chopper and our office. We can stop for lunch at one of the nearby restaurants."

"That would be great." Relieved she sounded calm, his words provoked a new flash of panic. She couldn't get involved with him, couldn't be a couple, where she'd feel tied down and controlled.

They'd been driving through the rolling hills of Chester County for what seemed like an hour when Stephen turned down a long driveway, luminaries lining the way. When his house came into view, she gasped.

Stately, the stone and wood structure rose out of the dark like a magnificent castle dominating all around it. Inviting-looking white rockers were scattered on the wraparound porch. Lights blazed from the paned windows. She'd known about the Blackwoods, their history as one of the founding families of the county. The beauty, elegance, and warm charm of the house said more than words could about the family that lived here.

"Your house is beautiful," she said.

He chuckled. "It is something. We used to raise horses, but during World War Two, my dad grew crops for the troops. At first, it wasn't as profitable as raising horses, but we ended up making more money, so while we still keep horses, our main income is from farming."

He parked and helped her out of the car. With his hand on the small of her back, they headed up the flagstone walk. He opened the door and ushered her in.

People stood around in small groups, drinking and talking. A bar with a bartender was set up in a corner of the spacious living room. A roaring fire, its flames licking upward, burned in the fireplace, large enough for a person of her height to stand in.

A smiling, attractive middle-aged couple approached them. The woman, short and slight, wore an ankle-grazing black dress with lace trim at the scoop neck and at the cuffs of her long sleeves. Her pale blonde hair was styled in a graceful upsweep that showed her sculpted bone structure. The tall man with her resembled an older version of Stephen, with the same broad-shouldered build. He wore his graying dark hair very short.

"This must be Elena." The woman's blue-green eyes sparkled as she took both Elena's hands in hers. "I'm Meri Blackwood. Welcome to our home."

The warmth of her smile touched something deep in Elena's heart. She thought of her own mother. Fighting the homesickness that threat-

BRANDYWINE BRIDES ANTHOLOGY

ened to overwhelm her, she smiled. "Thank you for inviting me."

The older man stepped forward with a smile. "I'm Callum, Stephen's father. We've heard a lot about you. Friends of Stephen's are always welcome here."

Stephen slid his arm around Elena's waist, as if announcing to the world they belonged together. Heat and anxiety coiled into a knot in her stomach.

"You're a very talented artist," his mom said. "We love the jewelry you designed for Beverly. We know she will, too."

"Thank you," Elena said.

The doorbell rang. "We need to get that," his mom said. "Please, both of you, have something to drink."

As they walked toward the bar, Elena said to Stephen, "When do you expect Beverly?"

He looked at his watch. "In about thirty minutes."

Elena ordered a gin and tonic, and Stephen a beer.

"Let me introduce you to everyone," he said.

Before they could move, a tall blonde woman Elena recognized as the one with Stephen at the arts festival, approached them. Her ice-blue stare sent shivers up Elena's spine.

The woman turned toward Stephen, as if dismissing Elena as not worthy of her attention. "Stephen, darling, where have you been? I've been calling and leaving messages with your parents, but you haven't returned my calls."

Stephen stiffened. "I've been very busy, Karen."

Nostrils flaring, she glanced at Elena. "I see."

"Karen, this is Elena."

Lips tight, Elena nodded.

"Excuse us, Karen," Stephen said. "I want to introduce Elena around." He took Elena's free hand in his as they walked away.

"Seems like your friend Karen resents me," Elena said. "Is there something you forgot to tell me?"

"Nothing to tell." He stopped and faced her. "Our families have been friends for years. Karen believed I'd marry her someday. And maybe I would have, before the war. She's changed, or maybe I see her differently now. A marriage between us would end in disaster. I never made any promises to her." He bent toward Elena and his warm breath fanned her face. "You're the only woman I want."

The power of his words made a slow ache begin to build in her. Stephen Blackwood was easy to love. Too easy. She wanted him, but she needed to protect her heart.

She didn't know if she could have both.

CHAPTER THIRTEEN

TWIST AND SHOUT BY THE Beatles blasted though the house ninety minutes later, drowning out the talking and laughing. With the raucous party in full swing, Stephen drank his beer and looked around the living room. Clusters of his parents' friends ate, talked, and laughed, while Bev and most of her friends danced to the music played by a DJ his parents had hired.

Elena stood across the room chatting with one of Bev's male friends. The guy was obviously flirting with her. Stephen set his beer on the bar and threaded his way to Elena's side. When he reached her, he slid his arm around her waist, giving a clear signal to the other guy that she belonged to him. The thought surprised him. He'd never been a possessive guy, but he'd never met anyone like Elena.

The other guy nodded to Stephen and excused himself to wander off.

"Your parents know how to throw a party," Elena said. "Thanks for inviting me."

"You're having fun?"

"Of course." Chuckling, she turned her attention to where Bev danced with one of her friends. "Do you think your sister was surprised?"

"Did she look surprised?" he said, grinning.

"No. She'd never make it in Hollywood. But she was surprised by the jewelry you and your parents gave her."

Beverly had squealed with delight when she saw her jewelry. She'd given her parents and Stephen huge hugs, then hugged Elena and introduced her to the guests as the most talented jewelry designer ever. Stephen hoped Elena would find new clients from among the guests.

He whispered in Elena's ear. "My sister loves the jewelry. Someone very special made them."

"Thanks," Elena said, her voice thick.

He pulled her closer. She'd taken off her shawl, and her bared shoulders gleamed in the lamp light. Every time he saw her, he fell more under her spell. He couldn't tell her about his growing feelings for her yet. He didn't want to scare her away, and he didn't know how she felt about him. Building his business would take up most of his energy, but he'd make time for Elena.

"Let's get away from all these people." Holding her hand, he led her to the glass doors that opened to the enclosed patio, breathing a sigh of relief to see they were alone.

She slipped her hand from his and walked to the large windows that overlooked the extensive rose gardens. "It's beautiful here."

"Thanks. This was the original kitchen back in the 1800s."

He came up behind her and wrapped his arms around her waist, holding her against his chest. Her head tucked neatly under his chin and he inhaled the flowery scent of her hair. "You're beautiful."

She turned in his arms and gazed up at him, her eyes large, dark, and soft with need. Gliding her hands up his arms, she stood on tiptoe to kiss him tenderly on the lips.

He kissed her with all the pent-up frustration and longing that filled him. Her lush body molded perfectly to his, as if they were made for each other. Her breasts, soft and full, crushed against his chest. He slanted his lips over hers again and again. She opened to him, and their tongues sparred, sending waves of longing through him.

He cupped the back of her head, eliciting low moans from her. Leaving her luscious lips, he trailed kisses down her neck. Her soft skin smelled like spring flowers, transporting him to a magical place where only the two of them existed.

"I want to make love to you," he said against her throat.

"Why are we still here?" she said on a shaky breath.

They said quick good-byes to his parents and Beverly and made it back to Elena's place in record time. They entered her quiet apartment. Relieved they had the place to themselves, he let her lead him to her room.

The cats slept on the bed and Elena gently shooed them off. Her eyes, dark with desire, met his. Like two people possessed, they undressed quickly.

With a low murmur, he gathered her to him and held her close. "You're more gorgeous than I imagined," he said.

"So are you."

He brushed his lips over hers in a whisper-soft kiss. He wanted to go slow, to explore every inch of her delectable body. He kissed his way to her neck and behind her ear, provoking more groans from her. When she wrapped her arms around his waist and wiggled against him, he moaned loudly.

"If you keep doing that, I won't last long," he rasped.

"We have all night."

CHAPTER FOURTEEN

OW CRIES, LIKE A WOUNDED animal, dragged Elena from a dream
filled with Stephen. The thrashing of someone next to her woke her
fully. She sat up. Stephen, still sleeping, rolled his head back and forth,
reaching out his arms as if trying to stop someone. Through the sliver of
dawn stealing into the room, she could see the shine of sweat on his face.

"Stephen, wake up." She gently shook him.

He continued to toss and twist until he finally opened sleep-bleared
eyes and stilled.

"Elena?"

She leaned over him. "It's okay. You were having a bad dream."

Sighing, he rubbed his forehead. "I'm sorry."

"You have nothing to be sorry for." In his rolling around, his bedcovers had come off. She tugged his covers up and tucked them under his
chin. "Do you want to talk about it?"

"You don't want to hear my problems."

"I do. I'm a good listener."

When she kissed him lightly on the lips, he tightened his arms around
her and kissed her with urgency, as if she were a lifeline.

With a low moan, she ended the kiss and stroked his face. "Tell me
what's going on. Do you have bad dreams often? Are they about Vietnam?"

Stephen nodded. "You sure you want to hear this?"

"I am." She sat up and drew him with her. They arranged the bed-
clothes around their shoulders and leaned against the headboard.

"I saw horrific things there," he said softly. "I saw man's inhumanity to man alongside great courage."

He wrapped his arm around her shoulders holding her closer. "Something happened on my second tour there, something that almost broke me."

Stephen quieted. Elena wanted to touch his face, but she remained still, giving him the time he needed. Outside on the street, the sounds of the city waking up—car engines, the gentle roar of buses, people shouting—reached them. Inside, Elena felt cocooned in a world she and Stephen had created, a world of security she hadn't known for a long time.

He released an audible breath. "On my second tour, we had a young medic on our team, Johnny. He was twenty, a farm boy from Nebraska who'd never been out of his state before. He was the sweetest kid, anxious to help others. He didn't want to kill anyone, so he chose to train as a medic, knowing a medic's life expectancy in 'Nam was less than fourteen days. He'd been in country three months when he was killed helping a wounded soldier days before Christmas."

Stephen's voice broke. "Johnny's face was blown off. I can't get that image out of my mind. He didn't deserve to die like that. No one does."

Elena enfolded Stephen in her arms. Shaking, he clung to her.

"I'm here, Stephen. I understand."

He buried his face in her neck. She felt his tears against her skin. They stayed wrapped in each other for long minutes. Finally, he slid back and gave her a weak smile.

She kissed away the tears at the corners of his eyes.

"Thanks," he said. "I've needed to do that since I got home, but I felt bottled up inside, almost dead at times."

She rested her head on his bare chest, needing his closeness and his heat. "I'm glad I could be here for you. You were with Johnny at the end. That had to give him comfort."

"I hope so," he said softly. "When I got stateside, I went to Nebraska to see Johnny's parents and his girlfriend. I wanted them to know what a hero he'd been."

"You're a good man, Stephen Blackwood." Snuggled against him, she inhaled his scent of musk from their lovemaking. In a short time, she'd grown closer to Stephen than she ever had any man. A guy like him deserved a woman who would always be by his side, not someone ready to flee when anyone got too close.

Stephen touched her chin with his fingers until her eyes met his.

"I'm in love with you, Elena Delgado."

She stiffened as trepidation hit her like a Texas tornado. "Please don't say that." At the hurt in his eyes, she wanted to bite back her words. "Let's not talk anymore. Make love to me."

❦

They sat in the kitchen having a cheese and mushroom omelet Stephen had cooked. Sheila had left a note saying she had errands to run. Thankfully, he and Elena were alone. Cradling his mug of coffee, he looked over at her. Her face was flushed from their lovemaking, and her hair tangled around her face. He loved her with all his heart. He understood she was scared, but deep down he knew she loved him, too.

She finished her omelet and pushed the plate away. "That was delicious. I didn't know you could cook."

"I only cook for very special people."

Her face turned a darker shade of pink. "Thanks."

His gaze locked with hers. "I saw your eyes when I told you I love you. I'm a patient guy. I'll give you time. Help me understand what you're afraid of."

She looked away, then turned and met his gaze again. "You shared your family problems with me and you shared Johnny's story. You deserve to know about my family and why I'm afraid to love anyone, ever. You're a great guy. You need a woman who will always be here for you."

"You're the woman I want."

Tears glistened in her eyes.

He grasped her hand across the table. "Tell me, Elena." He kept his voice gentle.

She freed her hand and gripped her coffee mug until her knuckles whitened. "I'll tell you what you want to know. I've already mentioned my parents are traditionalists. They matched me with the son of friends, another family that has been in this country almost as long as ours."

"An arranged marriage?"

"Medieval, huh? I was only seventeen, and I'd been trained by the nuns at boarding school, and by my parents, to always do as I was told. My older sister still believes that, and is in a marriage with a very domineering man, although he treats her well. I convinced myself I was in love with the guy my parents had chosen, and I got engaged to him. I wanted to go to college before we married, specifically art school. My parents and fiancé were against it. They thought my jewelry designs were a cute hobby, but my real job was getting married and having babies."

Staring down at the table, she continued. "My fiancé and I fought a lot about my wanting to go to college. One night, he hit me. Almost broke my nose." She sobbed.

"Elena, honey." Stephen stood and gently pulled her up to gather her close. He stroked her hair and kissed her temple until she stopped sobbing.

She looked up at him, swiping at her tears. "When my parents saw what he'd done, I was sure they'd have him arrested. Instead, my dad said I had to marry my fiancé and do whatever he wanted, because that's what women did. My mom just stood there and didn't say a word."

Stephen rubbed his hand up and down her back. "What did you do?"

"I packed my bags, had a friend drive me to the train station. Got to Philly, found an apartment, and enrolled in art school. I had a scholarship from the school and a yearly income from a trust fund my Aunt Rosita had set up for me. I used that to survive until I could build up my jewelry business."

"Come with me." Taking her hand, Stephen led her into the living room. He sat and drew her down beside him.

She nestled against him, making him feel protective. He'd protect her with everything he had.

"That's why you're estranged from your family?" he asked.

Elena nodded against his shoulder. "My mom sent a long letter of apology to me at school. She begged me to come home, said she'd finally stood up to my dad. It's too late."

"Your family is always your family, Elena. Maybe you should try to reach out to them."

"You're close to your family. That's who you are."

He gently wiped away the single tear that ran down her face.

"I'll never let a man control my life," she said. "I like my freedom. I won't be tied to anyone. See why I can't get involved with you? We're too different."

"Maybe you should let me decide that."

She kissed him tenderly. "You're a nice guy."

"I'm not sure I want to be a 'nice guy'." He brushed hair back from her face. "We'll take it slow. I won't pressure you. Okay?"

She nodded, but the fright in her eyes said something else and fueled dread in his chest.

CHAPTER FIFTEEN

DESPITE THE LITTLE SLEEP HE'D gotten the night before and the exhausting day Stephen had put in trying to start a new business, his thoughts had strayed to Elena most of the day.

Her understanding and warmth had allowed him to finally release some of the pain he'd been in since he got back from the war. On his way to healing, he owed Elena.

It bothered him that she hadn't said she loved him, but he tried to understand her anxieties, and knew not to push her. Having her in his life was enough for now. He had plenty of time to convince her of his love.

Now, at seven in the evening, as he drove back to Blackwood Farm, feeling hopeful, he jacked up the volume on the radio. *Light My Fire* by the Doors played, and he tapped his fingers on the steering wheel in time to the music, thinking again of Elena. She sure lit his fire, and a whole lot more.

When he got home, the quiet of the house surrounded him in cocoon-like warmth. He loved this place, but the time had come to cut the ties and start his own life. He'd soon begin to look for a place closer to the offices of B&B Med-Flight Services.

Planning to call Elena, he ran up the steps to the second floor. When he reached his room, he shut the door behind him and strode to the telephone on the bedside table. He couldn't wait to hear Elena's voice. He dialed her number and waited for her to answer. When Sheila answered, disappointment settled over him.

"Hey, Sheila. It's Stephen. Is Elena in?"

"Oh, Stephen." Sheila began sobbing.

"What's going on?" he asked. "Is Elena okay? Are you okay?"

He could hear Sheila blowing her nose. "She's gone, Stephen. She's gone."

His breathing labored, he sank onto the bed. "Gone? Gone where?"

Sheila sniffed. "She wouldn't tell me. She left hours ago."

"Why did she leave?"

"Because she's in love with you."

A stab of joy cut through the rock of dread that stifled his breathing. "She's in love with me? And she left because of that?"

"She's scared. I know Elena well. She values her freedom. She's afraid if she gives her heart to someone, she'll be hurt, and caged."

"I would never hurt her. I'm not a guy who would control her in any way. I love how independent and strong-willed she is."

"I told her that. I tried to stop her. I'm so worried about her."

"If I knew where she's heading, I'd go after her."

"Even if you could find her, your chasing after her will scare her more. You need to let her go, let her realize she needs to stop running, to take a chance on you." Sheila hiccupped and blew her nose. "What's that saying that goes something like, if you love someone, let her go. If she loves you, she'll come back."

Feeling a heavy weight crashing onto his shoulders, he scrubbed a hand down his face. "Thanks, Sheila. If she calls, tell her I need to talk to her."

"I will."

They hung up, and he paced to the window to stare out at the sky, streaked purple in the dusk. If Elena loved him, she'd be back. He had to believe that.

CHAPTER SIXTEEN

ELENA HAD BEEN DRIVING FOR hours, heading for Maine. Dry-eyed now, she had no more tears left. She'd done the right thing. Stephen was great. She loved him, and that was the problem. Love meant loss of freedom. A little voice whispered that Stephen wouldn't try to control her, that he wouldn't hurt her. Her years on her own had helped build a shell around her heart. Stephen had cracked that shell. Confused and frightened, she'd run.

Her stomach rumbled. She hadn't eaten all day, and had stopped only once to use the bathroom at a rest stop. She'd survived the heavy traffic around New York City, and, despite the map she'd picked up at a gas station, she'd still managed to get lost in Connecticut. Now, heading to Keene, New Hampshire, hunger and thirst overrode her fierce desire to put as much distance as possible between herself and Stephen. And she needed to use the bathroom again. Spotting a sign for a restaurant, Elena exited the highway.

Thirty minutes later, bathroom duties settled, her stomach comfortably full with a hamburger, fries, and chocolate shake, Elena settled back in her seat at the wooden table in the homey family restaurant and nursed a cup of coffee.

She stared out the window at the dried leaves blowing through the parking lot. She felt like those leaves, uprooted, with no place to go. But she had a place, in Philadelphia, with Stephen. Before she could think further, she paid her bill and headed out to her VW.

She started the car and turned on the radio. *We've Only Just Begun* by the Carpenters played. As Elena listened to the lyrics about walking together and sharing horizons, just the two of them, about starting a life together, with room to grow, her tears flowed again.

Leaning her head on the steering wheel, she let the cleansing tears come, let the past unfold before her. She'd been running away for a long time. Afraid to stand up to her parents, she'd run. When her mother had reached out to her, she'd rejected her. So bound up in trying to be free, she'd created another kind of prison for herself, a prison of fear.

Now, she was running again, from the man she loved, a good man, a kind man. Life could be hard and overwhelming, but escaping didn't make it easier. When the song finished, Elena knew what she had to do.

She shut off the engine and exited the car, slamming the door closed. Hope propelled her forward as she strode into the restaurant. The few customers didn't give her a glance as she went to the pay phone hanging in a corner.

After dropping in the required coins, the operator connected her. As the phone rang, Elena shifted from one foot to the other as nervousness ate at her. Finally, the phone was answered by a voice she loved.

"Hello, Mom, it's Elena."

CHAPTER SEVENTEEN

STEPHEN HUNG UP THE PHONE with the hospital administrator in Philadelphia, confirming the appointment tomorrow to discuss signing a contract with B&B Med-Flight Services. Tired of sitting, Stephen pushed up from his chair in B&B's office and rolled his shoulders to relieve the tension that tightened his muscles.

He still had several calls to make, to the nurses and paramedics he and Nick had chosen to hire from the ones they'd interviewed. Hopefully, their company would take off and they could afford another chopper and pilot, along with more medical personnel. In some flights, a doctor would accompany them, depending on the severity of the patient's condition.

Despair tempered his happiness that things were progressing well with their fledging company. Elena had been gone almost two days. He massaged his temples where the beginnings of a headache pulsed. For the hundredth time he wondered how he could have done things differently with her. He shouldn't have blurted that he loved her. He'd scared her off. He'd known to go slow, yet his need for her and the overwhelming love he felt had compelled him to throw aside caution.

The office door opened and Nick stuck his head in. "Hey, buddy, someone's here to see you."

Stephen frowned. "I've got a few more calls to make. Can't you take care of it?"

"You're on your own with this one." Nick left but kept the door partially opened.

Stephen's heart pounded against a hope he was afraid to name.

Elena came in and closed the door quietly behind her. "Hi, Stephen." Words failed him, and he could only stare. His hungry gaze devoured her. Tendrils of her long, black hair had loosened from her ponytail and framed her expressive face. The dark circles under her exotic brown eyes made him want to hold her close. Dressed in an old leather jacket, and wearing jeans, T-shirt, and boots, her casual beauty wrapped his heart in love.

He went to her and gathered her into his arms. Her head rested on his chest as he stroked her hair. "You came back."

"I'm sorry I ran away. I was scared and I took the coward's way out."

He touched a finger to her lips. "That's not important. All that matters is you've come back to me."

She cupped his face and kissed him sweetly, tenderly. "I love you, Stephen Blackwood. I have from the minute I saw you. I didn't mean to hurt you. I'm frightened of losing control, but I'm more afraid of not having you in my life."

He held her in the circle of his arms. "All I want and need is your love. I can't promise you an easy life, but I will promise to never hurt you in any way. I don't know if B&B Med-Flight Services will be successful. I need you by my side, Elena. With you next to me, I can accomplish anything."

Tears streamed down her cheeks. "I promise to always be here for you, Stephen."

"Elena." He kissed her hungrily, pouring out his love, his hope, his need.

From the hangar, he heard the radio playing *We've Only Just Begun*.

He and Elena had begun their life together, a life filled with hardships and trials, but love, mostly love.

EPILOGUE

Seven months later

A FLOWER-SCENTED MAY BREEZE WAFTED THROUGH the open windows in the small room off the vestibule of the historic church in Philadelphia. Through the closed door, Elena could hear guests arriving for her wedding to Stephen. She held her bouquet with shaking fingers.

"Relax," Sheila, her maid of honor, said. "You are the most beautiful bride I've ever seen. Stephen won't be able to take his eyes off you."

Elena's mother, smiling, tears glistening in her brown eyes, kissed Elena on the cheek. "You are beautiful. I'm very proud of you."

Blinking back tears, Elena said, "Thanks, Mom. I'm glad you, Dad, Eva, and her family could be here." Elena's parents, sister, and her sister's husband and two children had come from Texas for the wedding.

A few months before, Elena and Stephen had flown to San Antonio so he could meet her family. The first meeting had been awkward, with lingering vestiges of hard feelings. But her family had loved Stephen and embraced him.

B&B Med-Flight Services was more successful than they'd dare dream. They were taking on new clients every day. They'd bought a second chopper and hired another pilot and more medical personnel. Best of all, they'd saved lives.

Smiling, Elena swirled around to face the full-length mirror. She liked her gown, a slim-fitting ivory silk that flowed smoothly down her body. Rather than a veil, she wore a garland of fresh flowers, miniature white roses, around her head. She rubbed a finger over the smooth silver of the antique luckenbooth brooch with the purple stone she'd pinned to her bodice. The jewelry had been in Stephen's family for over two hundred years.

She glanced over at Sheila, for once not wearing one of her caftans. Sheila's silk gown in a pale green enhanced her full figure. She wore a garland of miniature yellow roses around her head, and her wild curls were tamed.

A knock on the door made Elena start. One of the church volunteers opened the door and peeked inside. "It's time for the mother of the bride."

Elena pressed her bouquet to her chest. Her mother placed her hand on Elena's shoulder. "It will be okay, darling. When you walk down that aisle and see your groom, you won't notice anything else." She kissed Elena on the cheek, then left.

Sheila and Elena exchanged grins. The strains of Pachelbel's *Canon in D*, performed by a harpist, started, signaling to the women their time had come to walk down the aisle. They hugged, then went into the church vestibule, where Elena's father waited.

As Sheila began her walk along the white carpet, Elena put her arm through her father's. He squeezed her hand.

"You look beautiful, my Elena," he said.

"Thank you, Dad."

"I'm glad I could be here for you."

"So am I."

The harpist began playing *We've Only Just Begun*.

Arm-in-arm, Elena and her father started to the altar.

Elena's attention went toward the front of the church where Stephen waited with his best man, Nick, and the priest. Wearing a tuxedo, with his collar-length blond hair brushed back from his face, Stephen's beauty made her heart stutter. Their gazes locked as she walked toward him. Her mom was right. Elena saw only Stephen.

When they reached the altar, her father smiled and placed her hand in Stephen's, then sat next to his wife.

Tears shone in Stephen's eyes as he leaned forward to whisper, "You are so beautiful and I love you so much."

"I love you, too. I always will."

They turned to face the priest and the start of their life as husband and wife.

CARA MARSI

A N AWARD-WINNING AND ECLECTIC AUTHOR, Cara Marsi is published in romantic suspense, paranormal romance, and contemporary romance. She loves a good love story, and believes everyone deserves a second chance at love. Sexy, sweet, thrilling, or magical, Cara's stories are first and foremost about the love. Treat yourself today, with a taste of romance.

When not traveling or dreaming of traveling, Cara and her husband live on the East Coast of the United States in a house ruled by two spoiled cats who compete for attention.

Visit Cara at *www.caramarsi.com* to read about all her books .

BOOKS BY CARA MARSI:

A Catered Romance
A Cat's Tale & Other Love Stories
A Cinderella Christmas
A Groom for Christmas
Accidental Love
Capri Nights
Cursed Mates
Her Forever Husband
Her Snow White Christmas (Snow Globe Magic Book 1)
Her Frog Prince Holiday (Snow Globe Magic Book 2)
Her Red Riding Hood Valentine (Snow Globe Magic Book 3)
Snow Globe Magic Holiday Boxed Set
Logan's Redemption (Redemption Book 1)
Franco's Fortune (Redemption Book 2)
Luke's Temptation (Redemption Book 3)
The Redemption Series Boxed Set
Love Potion
Loving Or Nothing
Murder, Mi Amore
Storm of Desire
Sweet Temptations
Sweet Temptations Boxed Set
The One Who Got Away
The Ring
Wedding Dreams Boxed Set

MULTI-AUTHOR BOXED SETS

Entice Me: Luscious Love Stories
Holiday Magic

Letterbox Love Stories Boxed Set, Volume 1
Season of Magic Holiday Boxed Set
Season of Surprises Holiday Boxed Set
Season of Promises Holiday Boxed Set
Sizzling Summer Boxed Set
The Marriage Coin Boxed Set

FINN'S LEGACY

By

MARIAH STEWART

2017

WHEN ABBY MONTGOMERY ARRIVED AT Blackwood Farms to interview artist Meri Johannson Blackwood about her life, her art, and her legendary love of Callum Blackwood, the last thing she expected to find was a legend-worthy love of her own.

DEDICATION

For Saint Loretta the Divine, who is missed
and remembered with much love and gratitude

CHAPTER ONE

T HE NARROW TWO-LANE ROAD SWEPT over and around gentle hills, the trees on either side casting shadows so deep that the driver of the small sports car was forced to push her sunglasses to the top of her head in order to see. Abigail Montgomery, lifelong city-dweller, was unprepared for the sudden blocking of sunlight and all the dips and twists she'd encountered on her way through the Chester County countryside. Why didn't her GPS have warnings such as *Hairpin turn ahead! And Heavy shade! Remove sunglasses now!*

She saw the sign announcing her destination seconds after she passed it. Blackwood Farm. Est. 1721.

It had been several years since she'd been here, and she'd forgotten the farm was just around that last bend in the road.

There was no room to make a U-turn, so she drove a hundred yards to an intersection and made a sweeping turn there. Downshifting as she drew closer to the farm, she eased into the driveway and paused at the end to take in the property that lay before her. Fenced pastures ran to the edge of the road on either side of the drive that wound its way to the farmhouse. The horses grazing in the field to her left raised their heads for a moment to study her, then apparently finding her of no import, resumed their munching.

Nothing new to see here. Even the horses looked familiar.

The drive curved to the left, much as the road had, just as she remembered from long-ago visits. As she rounded the turn, the farm came into full view. Abby downshifted once more, sliding into first gear, then rolled to a stop next to an ancient pickup truck. She got out of the car and leaned against the front fender for a good look at the farmhouse. So little had changed since her last visit. The architectural styles spoke of sections added on through the years as the family expanded and their fortunes grew. Despite its many faces, or perhaps because of them, the house looked less like a mansion and more like a true Chester County farmhouse that had served as a comfortable, welcoming family home for almost three centuries.

Once upon a time, it had welcomed her.

Abby walked along a shaded, slightly uneven, brick path lined with azalea well past their bloom, her heart pounding with the nerves that had kept her awake last night. *Maybe he won't be here. Maybe he's no more looking forward to seeing me than I am seeing him. Which is not at all. Maybe I should have said no when the call first came.*

Right. As if I could have passed up this chance to score the interview of a lifetime. Fat chance.

Around the front porch grew a variety of shade-loving plants that promised color and texture throughout the summer: hosta, astilbe and foxglove. Abby climbed the steps and lifted the large, brass, lion's head knocker and struck the door. She stepped back and waited, listening for footsteps from within the house, her anxiety increasing. Moments later, still waiting, she knocked again. She peered through the glass panels which stood on either side of the door. A long hallway led from the foyer straight through to the back of the house, but no one appeared. The only face she saw in the glass was her own reflection: oval-shaped, anchored by a long, straight nose spattered with freckles, wide-set green eyes, sunburned cheeks framed by dark auburn hair that had come loose from its moorings to curl around her forehead.

Pushing her dark glasses to the top of her head, Abby walked around the porch to a side door and rapped on it. Still there was no sound from within. From the end of the porch, she could see three cars parked in front of the garage. Obviously someone was home.

Perhaps around back...

She'd barely gotten halfway around the house when she heard voices. The sound led her to a sort of secret garden where roses twisted around an arbor – new since her last visit - beneath which had been placed a cushioned wicker sofa and several chairs. A dark-haired woman sat upon one chair, and an elderly couple graced the sofa. Between the two stood a tall dark-haired man, his thumbs through his belt loops, an annoyed expression on his face. Finn Blackwood. She'd have known him anywhere just from his stance. Damn. She was hoping he'd have had the good sense to excuse himself, if not from the farm, at least from this meeting.

She tried to ignore the fact that he'd filled out since she'd last seen him, grown some stubble that wouldn't have been acceptable at the small, private school they'd attended as children. Muscled up, too, in the years since he broke her heart.

As she came closer, Abby heard scraps of conversation.

"I still think it's a bad idea," Finn was saying.

"No one asked you, Finn," the dark-haired woman – his sister, Sophie – told him.

"Maybe someone should have. Maybe..."

"Excuse me," Abby stepped beneath the arbor.

Sophie turned and her face lit when she saw Abby. She opened her arms for a hug and said, "We were just talking about you."

"Somehow, I think I knew that." Abby returned the hug.

Sophie held Abby at arm's length for a moment. "You look wonderful, Abby. It's so good to see you."

"Wonderful to see you again and, for the record, you look fabulous. My sister, Lucy, is going to want to know what you're doing to stop the clock. I swear, you don't look any older than you did the last time I saw you."

"I saw Lucy three weeks ago and she said no such thing, but I appreciate the compliment." She took Abby by the elbow and turned in the direction of the couple on the sofa. "You remember my grandparents, Meri and Callum Blackwood. Nana, Pop, this is Abigail Montgomery. We spoke with her on the phone last week. She's Lucy Anderson's sister." Sophie paused, no doubt trying to diplomatically phrase what came next, and apparently settled upon that which would not require further explanation. "Abby went to school with Finn at Carver Prep."

Oh, if only that had been the extent of it.

"Yes, of course I remember. You used to visit the farm quite a bit, I recall. And, of course, I remember Sophie's friend, Lucy." The elderly woman smiled. "Thank you for agreeing to come out to chat with me."

"I'm honored that you asked for me, Mrs. Blackwood. I'm looking forward to interviewing you." Abby deliberately turned her back on Finn and leaned over to take the hand the woman offered.

"Call me Meri." The older woman's eyes sparkled. "Makes me feel young. Well, younger."

Abby addressed the white-haired gentleman. "Mr. Blackwood, thank you for agreeing to share your wife with me for a few hours."

Callum Blackwood nodded his head. "I've been saying for years that all of Meri's story should be told. All the books written about her focused only on her activities during the war. Not to say that her escapades weren't intriguing, but there's so much more to her. When she finally decided to talk about her art, I said, there's no time like the present. Let's get it done."

"My champion," Meri murmured as she reached to touch Callum's face.

Callum's devotion and pride in Meri could not have been more obvious. It was clear that the man was totally in love with his wife. It was evident in his voice, his words, and in the way he looked at her. That forever love – the kind that lasted a lifetime, come what may – didn't exist in Abby's world.

What would it be like, she wondered, to love and be loved that deeply?

There was a time she thought she knew, a time when such a happily-ever-after had seemed possible. She pushed the thought aside.

Now, with Finn just a few feet away, wasn't the time to think of what might have been.

"Finn, aren't you going to say hello to Abby?" Sophie frowned at him.

"I was just about to." Abby knew it was a lie, and he knew that she knew. "How are you, Abby?"

She looked past him to the arbor. The last thing she wanted was to look into his eyes which, dark and alert, seemed to be studying her. He reminded Abby of a wolf watching its prey, waiting for any excuse to spring.

The chill drifted from him to Abby in a frosty glare. *How dare he,* Abby thought. *One would think he'd been the injured party.*

"I'm well, thank you, Finn." She forced a civil tone and turned from him to Meri lest he or anyone else realize what it had taken for her to speak his name aloud. "Especially since I'm going to be spending some time with your remarkable grandmother."

Sophie touched Abby's arm and gestured for her to sit in the chair closest to Meri.

"I've been an admirer of your work since I was in college," Abby told Meri as she took the proffered seat.

"Sophie mentioned you were an art history major," Meri said. "The University of Delaware, was it?"

Abby nodded, painfully aware that Finn was still standing in the same defensive pose.

"Yes, I graduated Delaware. Their art history and art conservation departments were highly recommended."

"Ah, yes, they have an excellent faculty and, of course, there's that connection to Winterthur." Meri nodded, referencing the estate, once home of the du Pont family in Delaware, which now housed one of the world's most important collections of Americana. "Lovely place. It's been years since I've been." She smiled wanly. "I don't get around as well as I once did."

"I'd love to see your newly-returned paintings when you feel like sharing them with me."

"Of course. That was the purpose of my call." Meri nodded. "It's a miracle they were found. It's been such a circuitous journey, it's still hard to believe they're really here. But once I saw them again, I wanted to tell the whole story of my journey as an artist."

The tale of how the young American art student, Meri Johansson, had been stranded in Italy just as the Second World War broke out had been well publicized. Her perilous journey to escape through Europe had captured the imagination of millions when her story came to light first via a best-selling book, then an acclaimed film. But while the story of the young war heroine was well known, it was Meri's journey as an artist that she now wanted told. When a large cache of forgotten art stolen by the German army was uncovered in recent months – eight of the works being Meri's – Meri decided that it was time to tell that part of her story as well. While many well-known journalists had contacted Meri wanting to meet with her to talk about the news, it was important that she find the right person, one who would appreciate her work and respect her as an artist and who could understand that only part of her story had been told. It was Sophie who had suggested Abby, who had made a name for herself as a sensitive biographer when her book on a terminally ill, former Oscar winning actress was published the year before.

"I'm looking forward to showing those paintings to you," Meri said as she stood, somewhat unsteadily. In the blink of an eye, Finn was at her elbow.

"Easy, Nana." He gently took her arm and turned to Abby, no trace of gentleness in his hard gaze. "I think my grandmother has had enough for today."

"Ah..." Abby was taken off guard. She'd expected to conduct her interview over the course of several days, and had expected that one of those days would be today.

"We've set you up in the guest house," Sophie told her. "I'll walk you over."

Before Abby could respond, Meri held out a hand to her.

"I'm glad you've come," she told Abby. "I apologize for my overly protective family. They hover over me like...what do they call those women who are always hanging over their children? Helicopter mothers? Yes. Like that. I have helicopter grandchildren. They insist that Callum and I nap for an hour every day at the same time, like toddlers. Perhaps you and I can lock ourselves in the cabin tomorrow and Finn and Sophie will leave us alone."

"Fat chance," Finn muttered.

Callum rose to take Meri's hand, and he winked at Abby. "We're both at the mercy of these two," he said as he tilted his head in the direction of Finn and Sophie. "They think we're weak and frail just because we're old."

"You are old, Pops, and deaf as a stone without your hearing aids." Finn smiled fondly at his grandfather even as he steered them in the direction of the house without another glance in Abby's direction.

"Please join us for dinner, Abby," Meri said over her shoulder as she was escorted from the room. "I'd love to chat a bit after."

Abby smiled but didn't respond either way.

"I should apologize for my brother's zeal in protecting the two of them, but they're both in their nineties now and Finn's been gone these past few years. Oh, I guess you know that." Sophie held the door for Abby and they both stepped outside.

Abby knew all too well about Finn's absence.

"He's only been home for a few months," Sophie continued, Abby following her down the steps. "He's still getting used to the fact that our grandparents aren't as hardy as they once were. They've both gone downhill considerably during the time he was away. I've been with them on a daily basis and watched their gradual decline, but it came to a shock to Finn."

They rounded the side of the house.

"How 'bout we get you settled into the cabin? Did you park out front? Let's get your things..."

Abby fell in step with Sophie along the narrow path that led back to her car.

"Oh, is this yours?" Sophie pointed to the sporty two seater, its top down, where Abby had parked under a tall maple tree.

"All mine." Abby grinned. The car was her one indulgence. She'd bought it with the money she'd saved for her wedding. Once she realized that wasn't going to happen, she decided to put the money into something that would cheer her up. Something for her and her alone to enjoy.

"I always wanted a sporty little convertible, just big enough for me and two bags of groceries." Sophie's fingers trailed along one side of the car.

Abby laughed. "That's about all she holds, but she's fast and slick and I loved her the minute I saw her."

"I have serious car envy, I don't mind saying." Sophie gazed admiringly.

"We'll take her out while I'm here." Abby opened the tiny trunk and took out the bag she'd packed. "You can be the two bags of groceries in the passenger seat."

"Works for me." Sophie took one last lingering look at the car, then pointed in the direction of a two-story stone barn. "The guest house – we call it the cabin - is this way. Maybe you remember? There's mostly farm equipment in the big barn now but Finn's been talking about getting a few cows." She pointed to the barn under discussion as they approached it. "There's another barn on the other side of the house where they used to raise horses, but we're down to just a few now. You might have seen them in the front pasture as you drove in." She paused. "You probably know most of this, right?"

Abby nodded without comment.

In an awkward silence, Sophie led Abby around the barn and across a narrow land bridge that separated a pond from the meadow where summer wildflowers were just coming into bloom. At the far side of the bridge stood a small log cabin.

"This is one of the early buildings on the property," Sophie was saying as they approached the cabin. "Over the years, it's served many purposes. Mostly, it's been used as a guest house by whomever needed a place to stay. One of my great-grandmothers lived here for a time, and before that, a spinster great-aunt." She hesitated. "You can stop me anytime if this is old news."

Abby merely smiled. She knew the history of the Blackwood Farm as well – maybe better – than she knew her own family history. No reason to point that out, especially since the lump in her throat was growing as they passed the pond where she'd spent many a happy afternoon sitting on the grassy bank, Finn's head on her lap. Abby had believed that with him loving her, she owned the world.

"It does have heat, hot water, and air conditioning now," Sophie explained, "because my grandfather insisted we could never have guests here without modern amenities. There's also a small kitchen and a modern bath."

A porch ran across the front of the cabin. It was just wide enough for the rocking chairs that lined up like soldiers standing at attention. If Abby allowed, right about now she'd be remembering a long ago summer night when she and Finn sat in those chairs and watched the fireflies flit across the meadow. She was determined not to allow the past interfere with the present, and so she put one foot in front of the other and followed Sophie up the one step to the front door. Sophie opened it without a key.

"The local historical society has been after us for years to remove the porch to return it to its original façade so the cabin could be added to the register of historic places, but my grandparents won't hear of it. They've watched the sunset from that porch for years and, when they can, they still come down here to sit in their rocking chairs, hold hands, and watch the ducks and geese on the pond. There's a heron that visits most days in the late afternoon. My grandmother named it JoJo."

Tentatively, Abby followed Sophie into the dark room and waited while a lamp was turned on. The room was every bit as small as Abby remembered, and looked exactly as it had the last time she'd crossed the threshold. There was the loveseat covered in a cheery floral chintz, the chair in a coordinating plaid, the wicker rocker. A few side tables were new, but the drop-leaf table with its blue enameled top still sat near the front window. The wicker chairs that surrounded it were painted white. Paintings of landscapes adorned all the walls.

Sophie began to raise the window shades.

"This was where my grandmother stayed when she first arrived in this country. Over the years, she put her stamp on it, including the covered patio out back. She swears it's her favorite place on the property, the place where she feels most content. My grandfather courted her here and, for many years, this was her studio. There's still paint on the floor here and there." Sophie turned to Abby. "I can't remember if you stayed here back when...when you visited."

"I never stayed here," Abby replied without volunteering anything else.

Sunlight flooded the room and it was easy to see why Meri chose this place in which to paint. The light was perfect.

"The bedroom is the door on the left. The bath is next to it." Sophie stood in the center of the room, her hands on her hips. "Any questions about your accommodations?"

"Not really." Abby walked around the room, looking out each window before going into the kitchen. There was a sink overlooking a stone patio, a small refrigerator about the same age as the vintage stove, and an island with a dark green marble top. Two stools stood next to the island and three wooden cabinets hung from the wall, two on the right side of the window, one on the left. White dishes were stacked on the bottom shelf in one, a few mismatched wine glasses stood in another.

Abby opened the back door and stepped down to the patio, beyond which the meadow encroached so wildflowers grew right up to the low-walled border of stacked stone. Birdsong filled the air and butterflies drifted lazily from one flower to another. A hummingbird feeder hung from a shepherd's hook and a finch feeder from a nearby tree branch.

"What do you think?" Sophie stood in the doorway.

"It's totally charming." Abby turned to Sophie. "No mystery as to why your grandmother loves this place."

"I'm glad you're okay with it. Some of our guests over the years have been less than enchanted. I have several cousins who swear the cabin's haunted and, a few years ago, a visitor claimed he saw three men dressed like Revolutionary War soldiers walking through the field." Sophie grinned and pointed off toward a meadow to their right. "I'm sure they were reenactors headed for the Brandywine Battlefield who somehow got lost, but I didn't tell my cousins that. The battlefield is quite a walk from here, though I guess they thought they were taking a shortcut." Sophie paused. "Maybe I shouldn't have told you that."

"I don't believe in ghosts. I understand why your grandmother found inspiration here."

"You'll be interviewing her here, for the most part. Her request." Sophie turned in the doorway as if about to leave. "After you get settled, come up to the farmhouse. We'd love for you to take your meals with us unless, of course, you prefer not to. You're certainly welcome to go out to eat or to use the kitchen here, but I should mention that I am an excellent cook. No pressure, but I know my grandmother is eager to talk to you."

"I appreciate that, but I'm not here to infringe on your family time. I really just want to complete the interview and get out of your hair."

"About that." Sophie stuck her hands into the pockets of her jeans. "You do understand Meri is well into her nineties and she's had some health issues this past year, right? She'll sit with you for an hour at a time – two at the very most if she's having a good day – but no more than that."

Abby frowned. "That wasn't mentioned in any of our correspondence or conversations." Nor had anyone mentioned that Finn was living there.

"I'm sorry. I thought she'd made that clear." Sophie paused, then laughed. "Of course, she would not have. Meri thinks she's made of iron. I don't think she realizes how quickly she tires. Is this going to be a problem for you?"

"Well, no. I suppose not. I just assumed I'd be here a day or two." Which, considering Finn's presence, might be about all she could take.

"A day or two if a few hours will give you what you need, but given the complexity of her life, that's doubtful. But I'll leave that up to you. I'm sure you'll know when you have enough material."

Abby nodded and followed Sophie back into the cabin and to the front door.

"I'm glad you're here," Sophie told her. "Meri is looking forward to finally having an opportunity to talk about her art. She's often said that she wished the focus could be on her paintings, on what she's created, rather than on everything that happened so long ago. She hasn't wanted to dwell on those years, and yet having the paintings show up has brought back a lot of things she's tried to forget."

"I promise not to go anywhere she doesn't want to go. I will follow her lead, but I imagine any mention of the war years will be in the context of the paintings that were just returned."

Sophie stepped off the porch, then turned back to Abby.

"Dinner is usually at six. Again, please feel free to come up to the house and join us." Sophie stared at Abby for a long moment. "Abby, I know it's a little awkward for you. I don't know what happened between you and Finn a few years ago, but I'm hoping you won't let that ruin your stay here. Meri's delighted that you are here and so am I. I'm sorry that you and my brother..."

Abby held up a hand as if to stop the flow of words.

"It's okay, Sophie. That was then and this is now. We're all adults. I've moved past it." A little voice inside her head taunted her. *Liar, liar, pants on fire.*

"I'm happy to hear that," Sophie said, though she looked unconvinced.

"Thanks for the dinner invitation," Abby said without committing herself. How could she eat while in the crosshairs of Finn's death glare? And what was up with that? She tried to think of reasons why he might feel like the injured party, but couldn't. He was the one who walked out on her and joined the army to see the world. She was the one left behind feeling as if she'd been hit by a Mack truck. It had been several years but, in her heart, Abby still felt the pain of his desertion.

Abby opened the bedroom door and stepped into the room which, like the front room, was darkened by shades that blocked the light. She dropped her bags onto an upholstered chair and lifted the shades, then opened two windows. Light spilled across the double bed covered with a white chenille spread. A blue blanket was folded across the footboard and a green pottery vase on the dresser held a handful of wild flowers: Queen Anne's lace, cornflowers, and black-eyed Susans. Small paintings hung here and there throughout the room. An old-fashioned alarm clock stood on the table next to the bed. The room was small, but charming, and someone – she suspected Sophie – had made an effort to make her feel welcome.

She was suddenly grateful she'd be sleeping here instead of the farmhouse.

A door opened directly into the bathroom, which had been outfitted with a pedestal sink, a toilet, and a small tub with an overhead shower. Another door opened from the bathroom into the living room. All in all, the accommodations were more than adequate, if not gracious. Still, she had no intentions of joining the family at mealtimes.

Abby took a notebook, pen, and her glasses to the patio and rested on one of the comfy lounges, all new since her last visit. She banished all thought of Finn from her mind and decided to focus on the questions she'd ask Meri. She studied the photos of the recently recovered paintings. Using her phone, Abby pulled up pictures of Meri's later paintings and compared the later works to the earlier, newly found ones.

She wasn't surprised to find that the landscapes Meri painted while she was in Italy as the rumors of war were just beginning to swirl around them were darker with a definite hint of something ominous about to manifest itself. Vineyards were depicted with grapes on the ground, as if they'd been plucked and trampled. Churchyards were painted as if by night, with a murky sky overhead. The far end of a bridge disappeared as it crossed over raging waters. Pastures stood empty and a garden was in the last stages of bloom, the flowers on broken stems or rotting on the ground.

In contrast, the works Meri created after the war and while still a student at the Brandywine School presented a distinctly different phase in the artist's growth. While many of the subjects reflected those her earlier work – landscapes, a vineyard, gardens – the colors were brighter, the shadows not as deep, the light clearer.

Abby noted the earlier paintings, despite the preponderance of grays and blacks and browns, had small flowers painted in their natural hues and tucked in unexpected places. Here a tall stalk of bright blue flowers grew against a brown stone wall amidst dark gray shadows. There, small yellow flowers grew in the shade of a cypress tree.

"Excuse me."

The voice from behind the lounge startled her and she jumped from her seat to find Finn standing at the edge of the patio.

"You scared the crap out of me." Abby glared at him.

"Sorry." He stared back.

They stared at each other for several beats longer than Abby would have liked. Finally, she asked, "Did you want something?"

"My grandmother was afraid you'd miss dinner. She sent me to get you and bring you back to the house."

"Please thank your grandmother for me. I appreciate the invitation, but I wasn't planning on dining with your family tonight." *Or any other night, if I can avoid it.* "I'll see your grandmother in the morning."

"She's counting on seeing you now. I think she wanted to show you something."

That got Abby's attention.

"Oh? What?"

He shrugged.

"I didn't ask. But she's set on having you join us and, for as long as we have her, one of my goals is to make her happy. So if you wouldn't mind." He blew out a long breath, then said as if it pained him, "Please come up to the house and make an old woman happy."

"Nice to know my presence will make someone happy." She couldn't help herself. The words just came out of her mouth as if on their own. She locked eyes with him so there was no question who she referred to.

"You're not here to make me happy. But Meri…"

"Right. Meri has summoned me." She busied herself with putting her things back into her bag so that she had an excuse not to look at him.

"She doesn't summon. She asks."

"So the 'or else' vibe I'm picking up is strictly yours?"

Finn crossed his arms over his chest. "You coming or not?"

She was tempted to say *thanks, but no thanks.* But there was something Meri wanted her to see, and it was important enough to her that she sent her grandson for Abby.

"All right. Give me a minute." She started toward the kitchen door, then turned back to Finn. "I can find my way to the house. You don't have to wait for me."

"I was warned not to come back without you."

Was that really a smile that played at the corners of his mouth?

"Have it your way. I'll need about five minutes." Abby went into the cabin and closed the door behind her.

She actually needed ten to brush her hair and change into clothes that weren't road-weary. She hadn't brought a lot with her, but she had packed a navy blue dress that looked like a long t-shirt and a good pair of sandals. At the last minute, she added a striped belt and a swipe of mascara, some color to her cheeks, pretty earrings, though she wasn't sure why she bothered.

Oh, who was she kidding? She wanted to look good so that he'd burn with regret at having dumped her. Because that was what their breakup had been. He'd dumped her with the dumbest of excuses. She was dying to ask him why, but she wasn't about to give him reason to think it still bothered her, or – God forbid - that after four years, she still cared.

Just for fun, she tacked on another five minutes to make him wait.

When Abby stepped out onto the front porch, she'd expected to find Finn waiting for her. She hadn't expected his slow and steady once over from her head to her toes and back again that gave her goose bumps. She was almost tempted to ask if he liked what he saw, but wouldn't give him the satisfaction of thinking that she'd noticed.

She paused on the step and pointed at the door. "There's no way to lock up."

"You could have the crown jewels of England in there and they'd be safe. As far as I know, there isn't even a key." He rose from the chair. "But I guess we could find a padlock if it would make you feel better."

"I'm just not used to leaving things unsecured," she explained, not wanting to look wimpish. "I've lived in the city for so long, locking the door behind me comes as naturally as brushing my teeth."

"This isn't the city. We've never had a break in out here." He set out on long legs across the grassy natural bridge that led around the pond. As they passed, frogs which had been hiding amongst the cattails dove for safety into the water and ducks took off for the opposite bank. Abby struggled a bit to keep up, but was determined not to fall behind. When they reached the house, Finn stopped to hold the door for her.

"Thank you." She met his eyes as if daring him to continue to ignore her.

His eyes held hers for a very long moment. She would not allow herself to be the first to look away.

"You're welcome." He stepped aside allowing her to enter the house before him.

The spacious foyer where portraits hung side by side with paintings of the farm – horses in the pasture, the barn, the farmhouse, an old mill that once stood somewhere near the pond – opened onto a huge living room that was, despite its size, remarkably cozy. A large brick fireplace took up almost one wall, and a sofa with deep cushions stood opposite. Two wing chairs, separated by a round table, flanked the fireplace. Meri Blackwood sat in one chair, her husband in the other.

"Ah, there you are." Meri smiled. "Thank you, Finn, for fetching our guest for me." To Abby, Meri said, "I hope you don't mind that I took it upon myself to insist that you join us. I'm so eager to speak with you, I was finding it hard to wait until tomorrow. Besides, Sophie is a wonderful cook. I think you'll be glad you came."

"I'm happy to spend time with you, anytime." Meri's gentleness and gracious manner dissolved any resentment Abby harbored at having been summoned and, despite Finn's denial, a summons it had been.

Meri grasped the arm of her chair and began to rise. Once again, in less than a blink of an eye, Finn was at her side, cradling her elbow in one of his big hands to steady her.

"I'm quite capable..." Meri protested.

"Of course you are, Nana. But this way I get to hold your hand for a minute." He took her hand in his and walked slowly with her into the dining room. "Pops, how 'bout you escort Abby into dinner?"

Abby watched in fascination as the tall, strapping man and the tiny elderly woman made their way into the next room. The gentleness he showed Meri through his voice and his actions spoke volumes about his love for her. Abby hadn't needed the sudden ache in her heart to remind her that he'd once loved her, too.

"I guess it's you and me, missy." Callum stood unsteadily.

Taking her cue from Finn, Abby closed the distance between them and took the older man's arm.

"It's my pleasure." Abby smiled. She slowed her pace and matched Callum's measured steps.

Once in the dining room, where Finn was seating Meri at one end of the table, Callum gestured to the chair – apparently "his" chair – opposite from his wife, who was being served by Sophie. Abby pulled the chair away from the table and patiently waited for Callum to be seated.

"Thank you, dear." Callum nodded his head. "What did you say your name was again?"

"Abby," she reminded him.

"You have to speak louder," Sophie told her. "He's too proud to wear his hearing aids."

"I'm Abby Montgomery," Abby repeated, louder this time.

"Montgomery, you say?" Callum's eyebrows raised. "You from Chester County?"

"No, I grew up in Philadelphia," she told him as she seated herself in the chair Finn – unexpectedly – held for her. "But relatives of ours owned some property out here in the county generations ago. My great-great-great..." Abby shrugged. "I don't even know how many *greats* ago."

"Hmmm." Callum sat back as Sophie served him portions of salmon, potatoes and summer squash before passing the serving platters to Abby. "You know, the first Blackwood who came to this country was aided by a man named Montgomery. I'll tell you the story sometime if you're interested."

"I'd love to hear it," Abby assured him, though she'd heard the story many times before.

Throughout dinner, Callum proceeded to treat Abby – and the others - to a recitation of his family's lineage. At one point, Meri tried to protest, but her husband had waved her off.

"We've a proud legacy here in the county, Meri. It wouldn't hurt for Abby to hear it." Callum chatted through dessert, finally concluding. "You should ask your father if there's a Richard Montgomery, a good and solid Quaker gentleman, in your lineage."

"Montgomery's not an unusual name, Pops," Sophie noted from

across the table.

"I'm sure it would be an honor to be descended from a man connected to your family. We did have Quaker relatives in Chester County." They'd had this conversation a few years ago, but clearly Callum had forgotten. "My sister, Lucy, talked about putting together a family tree a few years ago, but I don't know if she ever followed through. I can ask her."

"Knowing Lucy, it's probably already done." Sophie began to clear the table as everyone had finished eating.

Abby rose to assist Sophie. She took her plate and reached for Finn's.

"I'll get that." He turned to look her squarely in the face. The depth of his dark eyes, for a moment no longer hostile, startled her.

"I don't mind." Abby finished gathering dishes and took them into the kitchen.

"Thanks, Abby. I wasn't trying to rush you through dessert." Sophie went to the sink and began to rinse the plates. "I know you must be antsy to see what my grandmother wanted to show you, but I know she won't leave the table until it's been cleared. She's so enthused about getting the story of her paintings out there she couldn't wait until tomorrow." Sophie stacked the plates in the dishwasher. "Let's get everyone into the living room so she can begin her show and tell."

Five minutes later, Abby sat with Meri on the sofa, awaiting Finn's retrieval of something from his grandparents' bedroom. Meri's fingers found the brooch she'd fastened near the neck of her blouse.

The luckenbooth.

Abby recalled a previous visit long ago when the significance of the piece had been explained by Elena, Finn's mother. Abby had noticed it appeared on several of the paintings that were hanging in the front hall. She'd always admired it, and had been just about to say so when Meri spoke up.

"Thank you, Finn." Meri beamed when he returned carrying a package wrapped in plain brown paper. "Here, on the table, if you would..."

Finn placed the package on the table in front of the sofa and Meri began to carefully remove the wrappings.

"I painted this shortly before I left Florence. I knew I was being watched and I feared not so much for my own life, but for the lives of the kind people I stayed with. I'm assuming you know the story."

"I'd love to hear it." Though Abby had heard the story before, Meri had a faraway look on her face of memories that needed to be spoken aloud.

"German soldiers had been looking for me and, on more than one occasion, had searched the villa where I stayed, but my friend, Lola, knew of a very secure hiding place. I'd given her the painting and requested she find a way to send it to my grandfather in America along with a letter I'd written asking him to show the painting to an old friend, Daniella Sachs." She paused and cleared her throat, prompting Finn to go into the kitchen for a glass of water. He handed her the glass and she took a small sip.

"Why did you want your friend to have the painting?" Abby asked.

"Because the painting contained a message and I knew she would have understood it." Meri paused to take another sip of water. "Her father worked for the defense department. He was very close to President Roosevelt. I felt certain she'd pass the painting on to her father."

The last bit of paper slipped away and Meri turned the painting over. Abby recognized it as one of the works that had been in the articles she'd read that afternoon. The colors were even more striking in person, the contrast between the gloomy grays and blacks and browns with the blues of the flowers and the greens of the cypress tree.

"It's a striking work," Abby said, "but I'm not sure I see a message there."

"Tell me what you do see." Meri sat back and allowed Abby to study the canvas. Finn appeared behind the sofa to lean over Abby's shoulder, not touching her, but close enough that she could sense him there. She tried unsuccessfully to ignore him and the zing that went up her back and flooded through her.

"Abby?" Meri's soft voice refocused her attention. Abby cleared her throat.

"I see a church surrounded by dark shadows. It's dark as midnight, but the flowers blooming in the churchyard are as bright as if they were in sunlight." Abby paused. "What am I not seeing?"

"I'm sure you are aware that the Victorians used flowers to send messages. If a man gave a woman a bouquet of roses, for example, it would mean he was in love with her – particularly if the roses were red, and in full bloom. There's a long history of flowers being used to convey certain sentiments going back to the early Chinese dynasties."

Abby nodded. None of this was new to her.

"Things were getting very dark throughout Europe very quickly, and I knew it was coming to Italy rapidly. It was like watching a tsunami form out at sea, then wondering when and where it would strike land. I desperately wanted out, but there was no sure path back to America. It was too dangerous to travel openly. Poland had fallen, France had already been invaded, the UK was under attack. The signs were all around that Italy would be next. I couldn't send a letter telling my family what I was seeing because I didn't know whose hands it would fall into. So I did what, in my mind, was the next best thing."

"The flowers in the paintings are the message?" Abby still didn't understand.

Meri smiled and nodded, leaning closer to the canvas. She had the rapt attention of everyone in the room, all of whom had gathered around the sofa.

"The blue flowers near the foundation of the church are monkshood. Aconitum. In the language of flowers they say, *beware*. It's a warning that something evil is coming, you see, because every part of this plant is poison. The cypress trees in the background stand for death. Several people from the village had disappeared and were later found shot. The yellow marigolds hint of the grief yet to come. And here..." Meri repositioned the painting so everyone could see more clearly. "Here we have the national flowers of Poland, France, the United Kingdom, Italy – the iris, red poppy, the rose, the lily, respectively."

The room fell silent for a very long moment. Finally, Finn said, "So by including Italy with the others, you were telling her you suspected Italy would be the next target?"

"Yes."

"Nan, that was really clever of you," Finn said softly.

"Thank you, dear, but unfortunately, the painting never made it out of Europe, so all my cleverness was for naught, I'm afraid. In retrospect, I'm sure our government didn't need me to tell them what was going on. Surely they knew. It was quite cheeky of me to imagine that I would be telling them something they didn't already know, but when you're young..." Meri shrugged.

"How did you know your friend would understand the message?" Sophie asked.

"We'd read Hamlet in English class one year, and as part of the lesson, our teacher talked about how flowers had meanings. You recall, I'm sure, *rosemary for remembrance, pansies for thoughts*. Daniella and I started using flowers in our notes, like before a test, we'd send each other a note with a sketch of bells of Ireland. They mean good luck," Meri explained.

"So you were hoping she'd realize you were telling her war was coming to Italy and you needed out," Abby murmured. "So she'd tell her father and maybe somehow they could figure a way to bring you home."

"I was hopeful, yes. My own activities had come to the attention of the wrong people, but there were other Americans in Florence at the time as well. I was hoping, perhaps, there'd be a way to get all of us ex-Pats out safely. Frankly, in retrospect, I don't know what I was expecting the government to do, but when you're young and frightened, you don't think of logistics, or that perhaps the president was busy doing other things for other people who were far more important than you." Meri smiled. "Strange how things play out, isn't it? Eventually I was reunited with my family, and now I've been reunited with works I never thought I'd see again."

Meri's voice was increasingly softer, the words coming more slowly.

"That was a wonderful story, Nan, but I think you've had enough for tonight." Finn walked around the sofa and took the painting from her hands and rewrapped it. "I'll carry this for you if you like."

Meri turned to Abby. "That's my boy's way of telling me the show is over." She patted Abby's arm. "We'll talk more in the morning. We rise early here, so breakfast is usually around seven-thirty. If you don't make it, I'll be down sometime around nine if that's all right?"

"That's fine." Abby didn't commit to breakfast though she'd miss coffee if there wasn't a means to make it in the cabin. She should have checked that out.

Finn helped his grandmother up, then tapped Callum on the shoulder to awaken him.

"What's that?" Callum blinked and sat up.

"Time for bed, Pops." Finn motioned to Sophie to give Callum a hand.

"Wait, Abby, and I'll walk you back to the cabin." Finn told her.

"I can find my way to..." Abby began but he cut her off.

"I said, I'll walk you." The look he sent her clearly said *wait*.

Was there a flower, Abby mused, that could have delivered *that* message any clearer?

Finn waited until his sister arrived to help their grandmother prepare for bed before he went downstairs. His mind was a total muddle, had been since it had been decided that Abby would be interviewing Meri for what the family suspected might be their matriarch's last interview. He'd tried to convince himself that he'd be fine with seeing Abby again, that it wouldn't bother him to have her here, but he'd only been fooling himself. All it took was the sound of her voice to wreck him, before he even saw her face. He'd even thought about inventing an excuse to leave the farm for the time she was there, but he couldn't come up with anything that didn't sound like what it was: a means of avoiding the one person in this world who could shatter the façade he'd adopted since the day he walked out of her life.

Like our paths were never going to cross again, he taunted himself.

Somehow he'd known it was just a matter of time before he'd have to look on the face he'd once lived for. But there was no way he was going to let her or anyone else know what it meant to him to have her there at the farm, where they'd spent so many happy times. He knew in his heart she must hate him for what he'd done but, at the time, it had seemed like the best thing – if not the right thing – to do for her.

There'd been a time when he'd been so sure of how he felt, of how she felt, that words hadn't been necessary. They always knew they'd marry, have a family, live happily ever after. They belonged together and that was a fact. He'd looked forward to making her his wife as much as she'd looked forward to making him her husband.

And then Finn had a terrible choice to make and, once the reality of what he'd be asking her to do set in, well, there was nothing for him to do but sever those ties. He knew that volunteering for the most dangerous assignments in the Middle East could result in him not coming home, and he knew, too, that there was no way he could make her live with the daily uncertainty. If he didn't survive his tour of duty, what would that do to Abby? No, better to let her go, let her find someone who was not going to be playing Russian roulette with fate. She could meet someone who could give her the stability and security he would be depriving her of. Surely, in the long run, Abby would be better off without him. A clean cut would be best.

And so he'd picked her up one night and had driven her to one of their favorite restaurants. They'd had a great dinner and she'd talked excitedly about a wedding venue she'd visited that day. If she'd noticed his silence, she hadn't commented on it.

He'd driven her home and parked in front of her building, the car engine running while he dropped the bombshell. Without having told her of his plans – because he knew she'd have tried to talk him out of it – he'd joined the military and would be leaving soon for training. It was better for everyone, he'd told her, if they cut off their relationship right then and there. He loved her, but he couldn't guarantee her the kind of future they'd dreamed about. Find someone else, he'd told her through his own tears, someone who can give you the life you deserve.

Once his words had settled in, she'd slapped him as hard as she could, gotten out of the car, and ran into her apartment building. He hadn't seen her since that day until this, and the pain in his heart was spreading throughout his body.

He hadn't forgotten how beautiful she was. He just wasn't prepared for how much more so she'd grown over the past few years.

What does a man say to the woman he loves after he's broken her heart – and his?

He leaves it in the past and picks up on today. And today, she was here as a guest of his family. The anger he felt inside – mostly directed at himself but some reserved for the fates that brought her back – had caused him to behave in the exact opposite manner he felt. He'd wanted to tell her how much he'd missed her every day, that he'd never gotten past the pain of not having her in his life but, instead, he'd been snarky and rude. Just as well, though. There was no way she could ever forgive him for what he'd done – no way he'd ever have the nerve to even ask her to – and so it was probably for the best that they ignore what was and what might have been. Surely Abby had moved on. Now that he was back, he would have to work twice as hard to move on as well.

He just hadn't counted on it being so hard.

He took a deep breath and walked into the living room where Abby stood gazing out the window, her back to him. He wished he could freeze the moment before she looked at him with contempt on her face and disdain in her eyes.

"Ready?" he asked. Without waiting for her answer, he walked to the door and opened it.

CHAPTER TWO

"I REALLY COULD HAVE FOUND MY way back by myself, you know." Abby followed the path back to the cabin. "It isn't dark yet, and it's just over there." She gestured in its direction. "I doubt too many people have gotten lost making the trip."

"I wasn't worried about you losing your way," Finn replied. "I just wanted to talk to you about my grandparents. Particularly Meri. She isn't as strong as she thinks she is. She tires easily."

"Could have fooled me."

"That's exactly my point. She has fooled you. You think I'm overly protective of her, but you don't know what she's gone through over the past year or so."

"Well, she seems to think she's fine and she feels great." Abby stopped in the middle of the path. "If she wants to talk – and apparently tonight, she did – as far as I'm concerned, she can talk as long as she wants. She's a fascinating woman. So if she tells me to sit and listen to her, I'm going to sit and listen."

"She'll be ninety-six on her next birthday, Abby." He said it as if age alone were enough of a reason.

"And a remarkable almost ninety-six she is."

"She had pneumonia last year. We could have lost her."

"Has her doctor recommended restricting her activities or suggested she might be susceptible to a relapse?"

"Not that I know of, but still..."

"Anyone can see she loves talking about her work. Her eyes absolutely lit up tonight when she was describing how she tried to work messages into her paintings. She's so obviously proud of her efforts, and so happy to have those works in her hands again. It's clear she wants to get that part of her story out."

Abby'd tried to keep her voice calm when she felt like yelling at him, tried to be rational when what she really wanted to do was smack him. Why couldn't he see how happy Meri was when she was talking about her work?

If the truth were to be told, there were other reasons Abby wanted to smack him. For one thing, he was standing too close. For another, he still hadn't apologized – or explained – how he'd gone from "I love you and I want to marry you," to "I think it's best for both of us if we go our separate ways."

Finn brought her back to the conversation by volleying the one thing she couldn't dispute.

"She and my grandfather aren't your responsibility. If you can't respect that maybe I know better for her than you, I'm going to have to blow the whistle on this project."

"And what would you tell Meri? That you ran me off because I was giving her more credit than you do?"

"I'll think of something."

Abby took a deep breath. "Finn, I would never – *never* – do anything that would put Meri in harm's way. Please give me a little credit." When he said nothing, she added, "You know me better than that."

"I did."

"I haven't changed," she told him softly. "I'm the same girl you used to know." *The same girl you used to love*, threatened to roll off her tongue.

For a moment, she thought he was about to say something that might have reminded her of the old Finn. Instead, he backed off a step or two, and said, "Thanks for listening to Meri tonight."

"That's what I'm here for, remember?"

"Yeah, I remember."

"I have tremendous respect for her. She's an amazing woman. She's led an astonishing life and survived crazy odds because of her bravery and her wit. I admire her more than I can say. I always liked her, but now..." Abby attempted a smile. "She's my hero."

"She's mine, too. I guess if anyone would do right by her, it would be you."

"Well, thank you for that." Abby softened just enough to add, "Look, I understand why you feel so protective of her and your granddad, but..."

"What is it you think you understand?" he asked.

"That while you were away, they'd both gone a little downhill..."

Unexpectedly, Finn laughed. "Downhill? Well, I guess that's one way of putting it."

"How would you put it?"

"What exactly did Sophie tell you? I'm assuming that's where any information you might have came from."

Abby's sandal rolled on a stone in the path and she stumbled. Finn reached out for her before she fell, his hand strong and warm on her arm. They'd passed the pond before he'd let go. The sun had set behind the trees, and the only light to guide them came from the rising moon that bathed the cabin and the meadow in a pale light.

"Just that when you came back, you found your grandparents had aged, that their health had declined."

"I found my grandfather had had a heart attack and my grandmother had been in the hospital with pneumonia and the doctor said she'd barely made it. I found the farm in total disarray and my grandfather's heart was breaking because he figured the time had come to sell the place. All of it. After almost three hundred years of Blackwoods living here, farming here, he was going to have to see it pass into someone else's hands. The thought of losing this land was killing him, and I don't mean that figuratively. I couldn't let that happen."

"I thought they'd hired someone to run the farm."

"They had. Nice guy but he was overwhelmed. I think he tried his best, but he just couldn't keep up with everything that had to be done. Besides, no one takes care of yours the way you would."

They'd reached the cabin, and both paused at the step.

"So you thought it was up to you to somehow save the family farm?"

"Who else was there? My father hated farming. He just didn't have that gene. He's built a good solid business flying choppers. Why would he give up something he loved to do something he hated?"

"You have cousins..."

"The only ones who cared about the farm were Connor and Danny. Connor had just started to work with a big law firm and his wife was about to have their second child." Finn fell silent for a moment. "And Danny was dead, as you know."

Finn thought for a moment before continuing. "So now you know. I will take care of them because I love them and I will take care of the farm because it matters, and because there's no one else to do it."

He turned to her and asked, "Any other questions?"

Yes, she'd wanted to say. *Why didn't I matter as much? Why didn't you love me as much? I needed you, too.* But her pride wouldn't permit her to speak her heart, and she merely said, "No other questions."

"Then I'll see you in the morning."

It wasn't until he'd rounded the corner of the barn and disappeared that she went inside and closed the door behind her.

Abby went directly to the kitchen where she poured a glass of water. She walked out to the patio and sat on one of the lounges and thought about the half-hour she'd spent with Finn. Her emotions were so conflicted she could barely sort them out. On the one hand, she was still angry with him, still wanted an explanation of what had happened between them. On the other hand, looking at him, hearing his voice, just the awareness of him was probably going to make her snap before too much longer.

Had she really thought she could be here and not feel the way she was feeling? Had she wanted to prove she was over him, so much so that she could be under the same roof with him, sit at the same table, breathe the same air, and be all right with it?

Or somewhere in her heart, had she secretly hoped that, maybe, being here would remind him of how good things had been between them, how much they'd loved each other, of the life they'd planned together?

Why, she asked herself again, had she thought this would be a good idea?

She watched a flock of birds land in the trees behind the cabin, chirping to each other. Bullfrogs in the pond began to call to each other and a gentle breeze rustled the cattails as an owl made a swoop across the meadow. It was a perfect summer evening and Abby wanted to enjoy it, but her heart ached all over again. She sat suspended somewhere between anger, compassion, and misery until the mosquitoes discovered her.

Abby smacked at two spots on her bare leg where the flying little monsters had begun to feast. "I am outta here."

Abby fled to the safety of the cabin, hoping she'd left all the blood suckers outside.

There was no TV, but there was Wi-Fi, so she set up her tablet on the kitchen table and read several chapters of each of the books previously written about Meri Johansson Blackwood. Before too long, her eyes were closing and she was having difficulty focusing her attention. She turned off her iPad and went to lock the front door, then remembered there was no lock. Abby stood in front of the door for a moment, wondering what to do. She'd never slept in an unsecured place before and it made her uncomfortable.

The Blackwoods apparently had more faith in their fellow man than Abby did.

"Well, if anyone comes in and kills me in my sleep, I hope Finn is the one who finds me," she muttered. "It would serve him right."

She stared at the door. She couldn't lock it but she could barricade it. She pulled over a table to block it. At least if anyone tried to come in, she'd hear them and wake up.

Abby had no clue what she would do should that actually happen, but she wasn't going to stare at the ceiling all night worrying about it. She'd forgotten how dark it got out here in farm country. Dense clouds had moved in to cover the face of the moon, blocking its earlier glow, and the nearest street lamp was at least a half-mile away.

She pushed away the thought of midnight marauders and climbed into bed. She fell asleep thinking not of all the questions she should ask Meri tomorrow, but of the ones she wished she could ask Finn.

*

The sun coming through the window opposite the bed woke Abby at dawn. It took her a moment to remember where she was and why she was there.

She stretched, got out of bed, and wandered into the kitchen in search of coffee that wasn't there. With a sigh, she took a quick shower, dressed, and headed in the direction of the farmhouse. It was almost eight-thirty, so there was no question of joining the early-rising Blackwoods for breakfast. She got into her car and set off for the nearest convenience store where she knew the coffee was plentiful and delicious and awaited her pleasure. While there, she grabbed a donut, a banana, a few containers of yogurt, a loaf of raisin bread, a jar of peanut butter and a pound of butter. Before leaving, she went back to the coffee counter and bought a second cup, just in case she needed a pick-me-up later.

It was another gorgeous morning and she was glad she'd taken the drive, even if it was only ten minutes from the farm. It was cooler than it had been all week and she eased up on the gas to make the drive last a little longer. She parked closer to the barn this time to shorten her walk to the cabin since she had two coffees in a drink carrier and a bag of groceries. The bullfrogs in the pond were already chatting and the ducks were busy leading their babes across the pond, so Abby stopped for a moment to watch before heading back to the cabin. She was almost there when she realized someone was rocking on the chairs on the porch.

"Nan was starting to worry that you'd left us, but I told her you weren't a quitter." Finn sat in the chair closest to the door, his feet up on the porch railing.

"Where is your grandmother?"

"She's inside with Sophie. She hoped you wouldn't mind – her going in when you weren't here."

"It's her cabin. I'm just a visitor." Abby set the drink carrier down on the step and juggled the bag that had begun to slip. "You don't have to hang around, you know. I'll take good care of her."

"A little reminder never hurts." Finn lowered his legs to the porch deck. "Besides which, Meri's already spent part of her hour waiting for you."

And with that, he managed to tap into that last nerve. Where was the sensitive, friendly, likable guy she used to know? The one she fell in love with in seventh grade and never looked back? The one from last night who almost seemed to remember things she'd thought for sure he'd forgotten?

"Well, I'm here now, so you can just go on back to whatever it is that you do."

He gave no indication he'd be moving anytime soon, annoying her even further. "By the way," he said, "I put the table back in its place."

"What table?" Abby frowned.

"The one you used to block the front door. It's on wheels, as you probably noticed, so it was easy to move away from the door." He paused. "From outside."

"Thanks for pointing that out."

"If you plan on barricading yourself in again tonight, you might want to use something a little less mobile."

"I'll keep that in mind."

"Finn! Knock it off!" Sophie called from inside.

"Just trying to be helpful," he called back.

With the bag in one arm, Abby picked up the coffee and opened the door.

"Good morning, dear." Meri sat at the table near the window. "I apologize for coming in..."

"Please don't apologize. I should have been here to greet you. It's my fault for not watching the time."

"It's hardly after nine. Actually, we were early." Sophie rose from the chair she'd been sitting in.

"Let me just put these things in the kitchen..." Abby tossed the yogurt into the small refrigerator and left everything else in the bag on the counter. Looking longingly at the donut, which would have to wait for later, she opened one of the containers of coffee and took a long satisfying sip. "Yes," she whispered before returning to the front room.

"How'd you sleep last night?" Sophie had one hand on the door knob, obviously ready to depart.

"Like the dead, thank you." Abby gathered up her notebook and a pen from her bag.

"Glad to hear you were comfortable. Have a good chat, ladies. I'm off to run some errands." Sophie opened the door. "Finn's around if you need anything."

"Finn is keeping watch right outside the door," Abby said.

"Get used to it," Sophie said apologetically as she left the cabin. She obviously stopped to have words with her brother, but Abby couldn't hear exactly what was being said.

"I'm embarrassed I wasn't here when you arrived." Abby took the chair across the table from Meri. "I thought I'd have time to run out and run back before you got here."

"You could have joined us for breakfast, but I understand why you'd want to be on your own," Meri said.

"You do?"

Meri nodded. "Of course."

"Oh. Well." Abby was lost for words. She couldn't tell Meri what she really thought of the woman's grandson right at that moment.

Meri stared at her for a moment, then laughed. "You're so gracious, Abby. Far too gracious to say what you're really thinking."

"What am I really thinking?"

"That you would rather stick a fork in your eye than have to deal with Finn this early in the day."

Abby felt the color rise to her cheeks. "I'm afraid I've already dealt with Finn. On my way in a few minutes ago."

"He means well," Meri said softly. "He's had a lot to deal with over the past few months."

"So I heard."

"Just know that he's doing what he thinks is best, and he's new to the task."

"I understand." Best to let it ride. "But since the project is important to both of us, let's talk about your paintings. I was delighted to see the canvas you showed me last night, but I know there are others."

"Yes, several others. I thought we'd talk for a while each morning. After dinner each night, I'd show you another of my newly returned paintings and tell you its story. But I'd also like to show you some other canvases that have never been displayed before."

Abby tried to hide her disappointment. She'd thought she'd get to see all of the paintings at once. Did Meri really intend to dole them out, one at a time? That would keep Abby here for much longer than she'd intended.

But still...Meri was offering to show her not only the stolen works that had just come back into her possession, but other works that...

Wait, did Meri say they've *never been seen before?*

"Do I understand you to mean you have paintings that have never been exhibited?"

Meri nodded. "No one outside of my family has seen any of them."

Abby was tempted to pinch herself. "Meri, that's very generous of you to offer to share them with me. But why now? Why me?"

"Now, because, let's face it, at my age, every day is a gift. Who knows how many more I might have? I never expected to make it to ninety and, yet, here I am, closer to one hundred than I ever expected to be." Meri smiled and shook her head slowly. "I want all of my work made public, but on my terms. The only way I can guarantee that is to make them public myself."

"Why didn't you do that years ago?" Abby asked. "The works you're talking about releasing..."

"Are paintings I worked on right here, in this cabin, when I first came back after the war. As time went on and I became stronger, more sure of myself, I painted more boldly, and most of *those* works have been sold and now hang in museums and private collections. But the works I painted when I first came here to Blackwood Farm – I think of those as my interim paintings because they fell between my time in Italy and my later works. I want the work from the different stages of my life to be seen side by side. Taken as a whole, they tell the story of my life. What better time to tell the entire tale than when it's almost at the end?"

Abby tried to come up with a reply, but was unable to. What does one say in response to such a declaration?

Meri reached across the table to pat Abby's hand. "No need to try to be reassuring, my dear. If you're lucky enough to live to my old age, you'll understand perfectly what I'm saying." One last pat and Meri withdrew her hand. "But now we have much to discuss. I want to talk about my journey as an artist. Not all of the work I did in Italy had disappeared, you understand. Everything I did when I first arrived at the villa, when we still could travel through the countryside at will – all those were sent to my grandfather before the war threatened. Those all hang in the Greenville Museum in Delaware along with selections of my work of the past sixty years."

"And now that your missing paintings have been returned, your story is now complete." Abby's *why* now was clear. But still...why *her*?

"With one very important omission: the paintings I worked on here, in the cabin, when I first came back. These were my attempts to deal with what had happened to me. At the time, I didn't think they were particularly good, landscapes in soft, muted colors. I saw them as more amateurish than anything I'd done in a long time. I thought I'd lost whatever ability I may have had but, even still, I couldn't stop painting. Now I recognize those works for what they are – my soul trying to heal after all the horrors I'd seen. Soft colors and gentle scenes were easy on my mind." Meri fell silent, and Abby sat quietly, respecting the silence, waiting for the older woman to resume.

"So now I'd like those interim paintings, those healing works of art, to be displayed with the others, in order of date, to tell the story. I think it will speak accurately to what war can do to the human spirit, and how the human spirit recovers." Meri took a sip of water then placed the glass carefully on the table. "I'm looking forward to seeing how you interpret the story."

"But why me?" Abby pressed. "Surely there were others – more accomplished and experienced - who wanted to interview you once the news of the lost paintings got out."

"Oh my, yes." Meri laughed. "There were dozens of calls from so many publications and television shows. I lost track of them all. When Sophie mentioned your works of the past few years, I thought, why not talk to you?" Her blue-green eyes met Abby's questioning gaze.

"On the phone, that first time we spoke, you asked me how it felt to see my paintings again. You were the only one who wanted to discuss my work. The only one who didn't want to talk about the war. The only one who understood the emotional connection I had to those 'lost children' of mine. Your approach to the story appealed to me. Besides, it felt right. Of course, I knew Lucy, and I had a vague memory of you as both a child and as a young adult."

"I appreciate your giving me the opportunity, Meri. I will try to do justice to your story."

"I've no doubt you will, dear."

"But I have to ask, where are the paintings you've kept hidden all these years? The ones you referred to as your healing paintings."

Meri gestured to the four walls in the room in which they sat. "They're all around you."

Abby glanced around the room, as if seeing the canvases for the first time.

"All these paintings are yours?" Abby could barely contain her surprise. "You left them here, in this unlocked cabin? Where anyone could walk in and walk out with what would surely be a fortune..."

"Surely you glanced at them. Did you suspect?"

"No, it never occurred to me that any of the paintings would be your originals. I'd assumed all of your work would be under lock and key."

"What good is a work of art if it's hidden from view?" Meri frowned, and for the first time since Abby arrived, appeared annoyed. "Just as you assumed the work was of no value, so did everyone else who stayed here."

"I can't decide whether that makes you the cleverest woman I ever met, or the most trusting."

Meri laughed out loud. "I painted each of these here during the first year of my arrival. These were the Italy I remembered from before the war, like the marketplace in the painting there." Meri pointed to the far wall. "I needed to remember the loveliness, the gentleness of Florence and sheer natural beauty of the farms of Tuscany. I had to blot out the ugliness that followed. So I poured my heart into remembering the good times, the beautiful times, so that I could go on with my life."

"And it helped, obviously..."

"Oh, yes. It was cathartic. Once I'd purged myself of the horrors, I could begin to live again."

"But you studied at the Brandywine School, and I've seen some of the beautiful work you did there."

Meri nodded. "Yes, yes, I did. I used what I learned there to paint the hills and farms and vistas of this place that was now my home, the beautiful, serene Brandywine Valley. So much of it was still unspoiled. Those are my best known works."

"Those paintings are what made you a household name."

"That's true."

Meri glanced around the room from one canvas to the next. "These were a look back into the past, my way of honoring an Italy that was no more. The others – the ones that hang in galleries all over the world – were painted by a woman who had regained confidence in herself and her talent, and who was looking toward a future with a man she adored. They reflected the hope I had for our life together. There are no dark places, no shadows, no threats in any of the work I did once I began my studies here. I'd rid myself of the darkness in those very first works I'd painted after I arrived. Once I'd exorcised those devils, I was free to remember the good times, before the war, free to look ahead without fear, free to believe in a life where there would be love and laughter and life."

Abby nodded. She understood exactly what Meri was saying.

"With the return of the stolen paintings, my journey is now complete," Meri said quietly.

"You are a remarkable talent, Meri. To have been able to have painted such darkness, then later with such poignancy, and finally with such a sense of hope and joy." Abby shook her head. "You're..."

"One in a million." The deep voice seemed to come from the cabin itself. It wasn't until Abby turned that she realized Finn had come in through the kitchen. She'd been so engrossed in Meri's story that she hadn't heard the door open or close. "See, Nana? I'm not the only one who recognizes how very unique and special you are. But you know what I'm going to say next, right?"

Meri sighed. "Time to go back to the farmhouse."

"Time to have some lunch with Pop, and then a little siesta. But Abby is more than welcome to join us."

"Thanks, but I have some work I'd like to do here," Abby replied.

"Then dinner." Finn turned to Abby, his dark eyes fixed on her face. "Really, we'd love to have you with us again tonight."

When Abby didn't respond – mostly because she was so surprised by the invitation and what appeared to be sincerity – Finn lowered his voice. "Please."

Abby nodded noncommittedly and helped Meri from her seat.

"Thank you so much for sitting with me, for sharing so much of yourself with me, Meri," Abby said.

"You're a good listener, Abby." Meri gave her arm to her grandson and they started out the front door. Meri turned back and said, "I noticed you didn't take any notes for your article."

"No need to," Abby assured her. "I remember every word."

CHAPTER THREE

THE FOLLOWING WEEK SEEMED TO fly by. Abby met with Meri every morning to discuss whichever painting was on her mind that day and every night, after dinner at the farmhouse, everyone gathered in the living room where another of Meri's returned works would be analyzed. Abby grew closer to Meri with each passing day, her admiration for the older woman increasing as well.

Her annoyance with Finn grew at the same rate.

There were times she'd catch him looking at her with an unreadable expression on his face. He'd kept his distance except for an occasional reminder that Meri needed to rest. At least once a day, Abby questioned the wisdom of having taken the assignment, though she knew she wouldn't have missed this opportunity for anything. She was loving the work and excited about the possibilities of what she might do with the information she was gathering but, at the same time, her heart hurt every time she looked at Finn, every time he spoke her name. She refused to examine what that might mean. She didn't want to know.

On Saturday morning, Abby packed up her things and headed to her car. She came around the corner of the barn to find Finn on his way to the cabin.

"Sophie said you're leaving."

Abby nodded. "That's right."

"Does Meri know?" he asked.

"Of course she knows." She walked past him and opened the trunk of her car. She dropped in her bag and slammed the lid. "Meri and I decided we'd take the weekend off."

"Why am I the last to know?" The frown reached all the way to his hairline.

"Why do you need to know?" she shot back.

He hesitated for a moment. "Because...I could have made other plans if I'd known I wouldn't be needed to walk Meri to the cabin."

"Well, you can just go ahead and make those plans." Abby got into the car without looking at him. It felt too much like the last time they'd said goodbye. She slammed the door, turned the key in the ignition, then rolled down the window. "And for the record, Sophie is perfectly capable of walking your grandmother from the farmhouse to the cabin and back."

Another pause before he said, "If Meri fell, Sophie couldn't carry her."

Abby stared at him through the open window, then said, "Have a nice weekend, Finn."

She turned the car around and headed for the driveway. When she eased onto the road at the end of the drive, she felt a hitch in her heart, a little prickly pain that stayed with her all the way to Lucy's house on the other side of West Chester.

The drive took thirty minutes, but it passed in a blink because Abby was reliving the past week as she drove. When she pulled into Lucy's driveway, she was more confused than she had been in a long time.

"How's the new project going?" Lucy met her on the front lawn with a big hug. "Isn't Meri fascinating? If I could write as well as you do, believe me, I'd have taken on that interview myself."

"Meri is wonderful. I'm loving every minute I spend with her."

Abby could feel her sister watching as she retrieved her bag from the trunk.

"How's everything at Blackwood Farm?" Lucy asked as they walked from the driveway to the house.

"Everything's fine. Why wouldn't it be?"

Lucy shrugged and pushed open the front door to her twin house. "Just asking. Sophie said you're staying in the old cabin."

"I am. It's very cool. I thought it would be weird at first – did you know there are no locks on the cabin doors?" Abby dropped her bag at the foot of the stairs. "I thought it was strange at first and it made me feel uncomfortable. You know how we're taught to lock everything up so tightly, and out there, nothing? But when I found out about all of Meri's paintings that are in the cabin, I near died thinking about how the old place is so vulnerable."

"What are you talking about? What paintings...?"

Abby explained as they went into the kitchen where Lucy poured them cool drinks of iced water infused with lemons and limes. They sat at the small wooden table made of old barn wood that Lucy had picked up in Lancaster County the summer before.

"But you can't tell anyone," Abby said. "About the paintings in the cabin and there not being a lock on the door and..."

"Abigail, you're babbling."

Abby stared at her sister from across the table. "What?"

"I said you're babbling." Lucy calmly took a sip from her glass and asked, "So what are you going to do about him?"

"Crap." Abby rested her fingers along the side of her glass but did not lift it. "Is it that obvious?"

"Sadly so. I was wondering how this was going to play out. This thing with you and Finn." Lucy sighed. "From what Sophie tells me, Finn isn't faring much better than you."

"Finn couldn't care less whether I'm there or not. It's as if the past barely exists for him. Like that song? I'm just somebody that he used to know." Her shoulders slumped.

"That may be the impression he's trying to give you, but that isn't how Sophie sees it."

"What's she telling you?"

"That Finn hasn't been himself since you arrived at the farm."

"That's probably the guilt he feels about having dumped me."

"She doesn't think that's what it is." Lucy took another sip. "Have you thought about talking to him?"

"To what end?"

Lucy laughed out loud. "Please. It's obvious that you've never gotten over him and from what Sophie tells me, he's still carrying the torch for you."

"She's wrong, she..."

"...is his sister and she knows him inside and out. Just the way I know you. You've never moved past it, Ab. In four years, you haven't given any other guy a second look."

"That's not true," Abby protested. "I've gone out with lots of guys since Finn and I broke up."

"And how'd that work for you?"

Silence.

"Okay, I admit it's been hard, seeing him every day. I still don't know why he did what he did, so maybe you're right. Maybe I should just ask. Maybe if we talk about it, we could both move past it."

"Or maybe find your way back. Either way," Lucy said, "you need to air things out. Ignoring it isn't doing either of you any good, apparently."

That much was true, Abby reflected as she drove back to the farm on Sunday morning. The day away had helped clear her mind. As much as she wished it weren't true, she had to admit that her sister was right. She'd have to pick the right time, but Abby was resolved not to leave Blackwood Farm until she had confronted Finn and gotten to the truth about their breakup. She might not like what he had to say, but at least she'd know.

☾

Finn wandered into the barn for the third – or was it the fourth time that day. He'd spend most of the day in his office, working on the plans he was making to turn Blackwood Farm into a force of organic produce for the following growing season. It was too late in the season to do much of what he wanted to do on the scale on which he planned but, in the time he'd been home, he'd planted a few rows of this and a few rows of that to experiment with different varieties of vegetables to see which did best in this climate and this soil. He'd read up on modern farming techniques and had already decided which pastures to plow up and where to plant what.

He'd been watching his maturing plants to evaluate their production and had lists made of what seeds he'd be purchasing and which organic growers to buy from. He'd placed an order for what the local farmers called a high top, a greenhouse that could be easily and quickly constructed over rounded metal poles and covered with plastic. The sides could roll up to permit warm air in on those early spring days to come. He'd plant up trays of seeds so he could set out small plants once the soil warmed. He'd already contacted a neighboring Amish farmer about hiring a few of the man's sons part-time in the spring to help set the plants out.

Finn had his future pretty much set. He was going to save his family farm and set his grandfather's heart and mind at rest. If there was a huge empty hole in that future, well, he had no one to blame but himself.

He looked down at the pad of paper on the desk in front of him where he'd started making a list of things to do, and realized he'd covered the page with squiggles and looping lines that meant nothing. He smiled in spite of himself. No one would ever suggest he'd inherited any of his grandmother's talent. His eyes narrowed as he realized that in the midst of all those random designs, he'd printed the letters AEM.

Abigail Emerson Montgomery.

Finn covered the letters with circles of black ink to blot them out, and sighed heavily. Even his subconscious was beginning to pick on him. Bad enough he'd had to listen to Sophie's lecture an hour ago on how he needed to deal with his past. Meaning Abby. He'd denied it and tried to brush her off, but he knew she was right. The fact that his heart burned every time he looked at Abby, that every day, more and more, he had barely a thought that didn't have her at its core, should tell him all he needed to know. The fact remained that what he'd done was unforgivable, but he couldn't deny that he still loved her. He hadn't wanted to, but there it was. He was going to have to come clean with her. The only questions now were how and when to tell her. Maybe it would clear the air, maybe it would anger her all over again. But right now it was an open wound, and it was time to close it.

He spent the rest of Saturday trying to figure out how best to do that.

(6

On Monday afternoon, Abby sat at the table near the front window writing notes on that morning's interview. She'd taken photos of each of the paintings in the cabin, analyzing them with a more critical eye this time around. They'd all been painted on smaller canvases than her later work, and Abby wondered if that had been deliberate.

"Something to ask Meri about," she murmured as she jotted down the thought.

Abby'd arrived at Blackwood Farm with a specific outline in mind of how she would write her article and where she might like it to be published, but she'd come to realize it would be Meri's vision of the story, not hers, that would be presented to the rest of the world. This was Meri's journey and, that, Abby mused, could be the title of the work she produced, in whatever form it might take.

The idea forming in Abby's head began to take shape less like an article and more like a book. There were so many paintings, each with its own tale. Many of Meri's works were well known and those would not be included in the telling unless Meri requested their inclusion. For Abby, the real story lay in the newly returned paintings and the secret paintings that hung in the cabin. That was the story no one knew.

She was still trying to decide how best to tell the story when she heard a soft rap at the door. She glanced out the window and was surprised to see Finn at the door.

Abby opened the door and stood in the doorway, her hands on her hips. "What's up, Finn?"

"I was wondering if you could spare a few minutes."

"For what purpose?"

"Just to talk. I..." He swallowed. "I want to apologize. I haven't exactly been Mr. Congeniality since you got here. I'm sorry I wasn't nicer." He paused before adding, "It was - " He cleared his throat. "Hard to see you again."

"That's it? That's what you want to apologize for? For being rude to me? Because it was hard for you to see me after you walked out of my life?"

Lucy was right. Time to blow the whistle on this farce. She stepped out onto the porch.

"Okay, let's shine the light on the elephant in the room." She tried to keep her emotions in check, wanted desperately to keep the quiver from her voice and, God forbid, avoid tears that would betray how she really felt.

"You're behaving as if you were the injured party, Finn. As if I were the one who dumped you." She stared into his eyes and willed herself not to blink. "And that is not what happened. One minute we were discussing wedding plans and the next minute, it was, 'I think we need to take a break'. No explanation. Not even a freaking phone call before you left for the army. I had to learn that from my sister. So, if anyone has the right to be obnoxious and surly and, yes, rude - that would be me."

"You want to hash over old news?" Oddly, he didn't look surprised.

"It may be old news to you, bucko, but it's news I still haven't heard." She took a deep breath. "So yes. I want to hear it. Usually, when one party in a close relationship falls out of love with the other, he - or she - mans up."

"I never fell out of love with you," he snapped. The words came so quickly, Abby wasn't sure she'd heard them. "I didn't stop loving you,

Ab."

"Then *what?*" She sank onto the one porch step and waited, her heart in her mouth. "Why did you dump me?"

"I wish you'd stop saying that. I didn't dump you. Dumping is when you break up with someone suddenly and just sort of walk away."

"And that would be different from what you did...how?"

Finn sighed and sat next to her on the step, his long legs stretched out onto the grass. For a long time, they sat in silence that was only broken by birdsong or the chatter of the frogs.

Finally, Finn said, "You remember my cousin, Danny."

"Of course. He was killed in Iraq."

"Do you remember that he was married?"

"Sure. We were at his wedding." *Planning how we would do ours, what we would do differently.* "He married a pretty blonde girl. Erica, right?"

Finn was staring at the ground, so she couldn't see his eyes.

"When Dan died, Erica lost it. She couldn't accept that he was gone, went into total denial and started using heroin to numb herself from reality. About two weeks after Danny died, they found her on a sidewalk in Kensington, dead of an overdose, the needle still in her arm."

"God, that's horrible." Abby covered her face with her hands. "I heard that she died, but I hadn't heard the details."

"Dan's parents, my aunt, Celia, and my uncle, Pat, took it real hard. I don't think they'll ever recover from his death."

The silence returned.

"I'm sorry your family had to endure such tragedy. I remember Dan and Connor were your best friends growing up. They were both so fun-loving and vibrant," Abby said softly. "And Erica..." Abby shook her head. "What a terrible thing. Maybe if she'd gotten counseling..."

"She'd been on edge since the day he left. A few years of that kind of worry doesn't go away." Finn turned to her, his eyes narrow and dark. "I was so angry when he died, I had to do something. I couldn't let them get away with killing him."

"So that's why you joined the army? Revenge?"

"It made sense to me at the time. When I saw how everyone in his family had been destroyed by his death, I felt like I had to do something. I didn't tell you but I signed up the day after his funeral."

"And you couldn't have told me this?" The anger was beginning to rise within her all over again. "We weren't casual friends, Finn. We'd been together for years. You'd asked me to marry you."

"And after I heard about Dan, I was sorry I had."

"Oh, well, thank you very much. That's just what I've waited to hear all this time." Abby got up, her hands on her hips, her eyes flashing fire.

"It's not what you think," he said hastily. "It wasn't that I'd changed my mind. But I knew there was as much a chance that I'd come back alive as not. I couldn't put you through that. What Erica did..."

"I am not Erica, and you are a bigger fool than I thought you were." She stared at his face – the face she'd loved for so long. "But if you didn't know me better than that, after all the years we'd known each other, then you were right to walk away."

She walked past him onto the porch, opened the door, and closed it quietly behind her.

☙

Well, that went well.

Finn tried to talk his body into a standing position, but it was as if he were made of stone. He wanted to go somewhere to take shelter from the look in Abby's eyes right before she turned her back and walked into the cabin. It was so like the look she'd had that night when he'd told her they should go their separate ways. Shock first. Then disbelief. Then that flood of pain on her face and in her eyes that he could still see if he permitted himself to call up that dark memory.

Why hadn't he said what he'd wanted to say? That by trying to protect her from one kind of pain, he'd inflicted another? That he could see that now and he was sorry to his soul?

Why couldn't he just tell her how wrong he'd been? Why couldn't he have told her the truth? That he still loved her.

In his heart he knew the answer: odds were she'd just say something like, "Thanks for admitting you were wrong. You're still a dumbass."

Sort of like what she just did.

He sighed deeply. She was right to be offended by his assumption she wouldn't have been strong if the worst had happened. That she wouldn't have been able to take it. He should have known better. This was Abby. She would have survived, she would have lived with the pain for longer than he could guess. Her strength of character, her faith, her family, would have helped pull her through. As he recalled, Erica had had none of those things to support her.

So what now, genius?

Now I have to decide if I am going to put it all on the line and tell her everything, or if I'm going to write her off as just someone I used to love.

He almost laughed out loud. There was no used to. He should have realized that the first time Sophie mentioned Abby's name as someone Meri might want to talk with about her newly returned paintings. That stab of pain in his chest should have been his first clue that his love for Abby Montgomery was still alive and well. Okay, so maybe not so *well* right now, but definitely alive.

From time to time he'd tried seeing other women, but none of them had measured up. No one he'd met had been as smart or as funny, as quick-witted or as thoughtful. No one walked the way she did with that purposeful stride, or smelled the way she did, like the peonies from his grandmother's garden, or did that sweet thing she did when she kissed him, her fingers so slowly caressing the side of his face.

He could have argued more vigorously against even considering her for this project. But he hadn't uttered one word of protest. Because, deep inside, he wanted her here. Wanted to see her and just be close to her, and maybe...just maybe...

The door opened and he turned at the sound.

"What are you doing, Finn?" Abby stood in the doorway. "Why are you still here?"

"Because I can't seem to make myself leave until I've said what I need to say." He stood and faced her.

"And what's that?" Her jaw was set, an expression he knew meant she was displeased.

"That I'm sorry I didn't trust you to be strong. That I underestimated you. I thought I was doing what was right for you. I thought I'd be sparing you from pain and a future that might have turned out to be a nightmare for you. If I hadn't come back..."

"You think I'm the only woman who would have married a soldier knowing he might not come back? Every military wife understands that possibility. You don't not love someone because you're afraid of what the future might bring. You love because you can't not love." Tears welled in her eyes and, for a moment, he could not move. "I loved you with everything I had. If the worst had happened, yes, it would have blown a hole in my heart the size of Blackwood Farm. But understand this: married or not, together or not, if something had happened to you, the hole in my heart would have been just as big. I didn't stop loving you because you broke up with me. I didn't stop worrying about you or praying for your safety because we weren't...we weren't..."

The tears spilled onto her cheeks and ran down her face. She half-turned back toward the inside of the cabin, but Finn was at the door before she could disappear again.

"Abby, I'm sorry. I am so, so sorry." His arms slid around her and he pulled her close, rocking her gently from side to side. "If I could go back to that day, I'd never have broken it off. I was so afraid for you, I thought maybe you'd be better off finding someone else. Someone who wasn't going to leave you and maybe never come back." He swallowed hard. "I really didn't think I'd be coming back, Abs. I really thought I was going to die there, like Danny did." He stroked her back. "Actually, I was almost surprised when I didn't."

"I'm glad you didn't die," she said softly.

"Me, too." He tilted her chin and looked into her eyes. "I tried really hard to ignore it, did my best to pretend there was nothing left between us, but I was wrong. Abby, I still love you. I never stopped loving you. I don't expect you to feel the same after what I did, but I want you to know there's never been anyone else in my life. I don't expect there ever will be. You're my heart, Abby. Always have been. Always will be."

She let him hold her, took comfort in the gentle sway of their bodies. "So what exactly are you saying?"

"I'm saying I love you and I want another chance to make it work for us. I need you in my life." He leaned back and looked into her eyes. "When I first asked you to marry me, I was headed to law school and planning on a big ticket job with a city firm. Now I'm a farmer. No big ticket here. I'm not going to pretend life here would be as cushy as it would have been when we were making plans back then. But it's what I've got these days."

Abby nodded slowly. "Are you asking me to marry you, Finn? Because if you are, you're going to have to spell it out for me."

"Make me work for it, will you?" Finn smiled and dropped to one knee. "Abby, I am desperately in love with you. I've never stopped loving you. If you can forgive me, I will try my best to never be as stupid as I was four years ago. No guarantees, but I promise to try."

She smiled at the admission. She'd never been one to want to see anyone ever grovel, but she had to admit, he was adorable doing it.

"Can you forgive me? Do you still love me? Will you marry me, Abby?"

"That was three questions." She sat on his knee. "Can I forgive you? I wish you'd told me everything before, but better late than never, so yes, I forgive you. I understand where you were coming from after Dan's death and his family's reaction. But you should have told me." She watched her words sink in before continuing. "I've loved you since seventh grade, so I'm pretty sure I always will. There's no one else for me. There never has been, so obviously, yes, I still love you." She smiled and touched the side of his face. "Yes, I will marry you." She watched that, too, sink in.

"Really?" Finn looked fearfully hopeful. "After all this, after I've been such a knucklehead, you'll marry me?"

"You're a knucklehead, but you're my knucklehead." She pretended to sigh deeply. "But it has to be soon. I've waited long enough to be your wife."

"We can do soon. We can do...next week." His eyes brightened.

"Next week might be a little too soon." She laughed. "For one thing, I have to find a dress..."

"Unless things have changed a lot, I'm betting you have a whole closet or two of dresses."

"I want a special dress." It could be doable, though. She had seen something she'd loved in a window at the King of Prussia Mall two weeks ago. It was lacy and white and flowy and in passing, it had made her think of an informal country wedding. Just the thing. Maybe it was still there. "We need to find a venue."

He gestured around them. "We can get married right here at the farm. Next?"

"Someone to marry us."

"My sister, Cristina, married a minister," he reminded her. "We can have a great party here. Sophie has been thinking about going into organic catering and this would be a great opportunity to show what she can do."

"Flowers. I want lots and lots of flowers."

"Hello, wildflowers? You always used to love Queen Anne's lace. It's all around us." Before she could reply, he added, "Sophie has a friend over near Oxford who is a flower farmer. Next?"

She held up her left hand. "Ring?"

"I'm working on that. In the meantime, will this do?" He reached into his pocket and pulled out the silver brooch set with purple and green stones.

"The luckenbooth," Abby sighed. "The last time I saw that, Meri was wearing it." She touched the pretty purple stone, then narrowed her eyes, teasing, "Does your grandmother know you have this?"

"She gave it to me, to give to you. I never could put anything past that woman." He pinned it to the front of her t-shirt. "So what else you got? Or have we covered everything?"

"I'm thinking."

She'd let him know he'd worn her down, and he grinned. "Three weeks, then. We can pull this together in three weeks. It doesn't have to be so complicated."

Abby smiled. How could she argue against such logic? "Okay. I'll call my parents tonight. Maybe we could do just family. And a few friends." She frowned suddenly. "We'll need invitations."

"We'll send emails."

"Tacky."

"Too bad."

She laughed, then kissed him. All the scattered pieces of her life seemed to come back together in that sweet moment. This was right. This was good. This was her destiny. She'd always known it.

"You sure you want to do this?" he whispered. "You're sure you want to live out here, be a farmer's wife? I'm always going to be a farmer, Ab. I'm going to keep this land in my family, save it for our kids."

"I'm positive. The only thing I ever really wanted was to be your wife." She ran her fingers through his hair. "And, of course, you'll keep the farm for our children. It's their legacy..."

MARIAH STEWART

A NEW YORK TIMES, USA TODAY and Publishers Weekly best-selling author, Mariah Stewart has published 40-plus novels, short stories, and novellas in women's fiction, contemporary romance, and romantic suspense. Her latest works include THE LAST CHANCE MATINEE (the first in her women's fiction Hudson Sisters series) and THE CHESA-PEAKE BRIDE, book #11 in the NYT best-selling Chesapeake Diaries series (summer 2017).

She makes her home amidst the rolling hills of Chester County, PA, with her husband and their two rambunctious rescue dogs. She is currently working in her next novel, The Sugarhouse Blues, book #2 in the Hudson Sisters series. Friend her at *www.Facebook.com/AuthorMariah-Stewart* and follow her on Instagram *@mariah_stewart_books.*

BOOKS BY MARIAH STEWART:

The Last Chance Matinee - 3/21/2017 - Gallery Books
Driftwood Point - The Chesapeake Diaries #11 -
July 2016 - Pocket Books
That Chesapeake Summer - The Chesapeake Diaries #10 -
July 2015 - Pocket Books
Coming August 2017 - The Chesapeake Bride - The Chesapeake
Diaries #12 - Pocket Books

Check her website for others: *www.mariahstewart.com* !

Made in the USA
Middletown, DE
16 May 2017